Elizabeth George's first novel, *A Great Deliverance*, was honoured with the Anthony and Agatha Best First Novel awards in America and received the Grand Prix de Littérature Policière in France. The critically acclaimed *Payment in Blood* followed, and *Well-Schooled in Murder*, which was awarded the prestigious German prize for international mystery fiction, the MIMI, in 1990. *A Suitable Vengeance, For the Sake of Elena, Missing Joseph, Playing for the Ashes, In the Presence of the Enemy, Deception on his Mind* and most recently, *In Pursuit of the Proper Sinner* were also highly acclaimed by critics:

'Elizabeth George reigns as queen of the mystery genre. The Lynley books constitute the smartest, most gratifyingly complex and impassioned mystery series now being published.'
Entertainment Weekly

'[A] rich, multi-layered novel ... All the important contemporary themes are covered and handled with a skill and sureness of touch that only years of practice can achieve ... it all feels so right and real'
Guardian

'She can compete with the best ... a book worthy of her immense talent'
The Times

'George is excellent at slowly unfolding plot and atmosphere ... fine writing and sensitive handling of relationships'
Independent

Elizabeth George divides her time between Huntington Beach, California, and London. She is currently working on her eleventh novel.

Also by Elizabeth George

The Evidence
Exposed

Elizabeth George

NEW ENGLISH LIBRARY
Hodder & Stoughton

This work first published in Great Britain in 1999
by Hodder and Stoughton
First published in paperback in 1999
by Hodder and Stoughton
A division of Hodder Headline

A NEL Paperback

A CIP catalogue record for this book is available
from the British Library

ISBN 0 340 75062 6

Typeset by Palimpsest Book Production Limited,
Polmont, Stirlingshire
Printed and bound in Great Britain by
Clays Ltd, St Ives plc

Hodder and Stoughton
A division of Hodder Headline
338 Euston Road
London NW1 3BH

For Rob and Glenda,
with love

Contents

The Evidence Exposed

The Evidence Exposed

Adele Manners gave her room one last look. The bed was made. The clothes were picked up. Nothing betrayed her.

Satisfied, she shut the door and descended the stairs to join her fellow students for breakfast. The dining hall rang with the clatter of their dishes and the clamour of their talk. As always, one voice managed to soar above the rest, shrill and determined to fix attention upon the speaker.

'Hypoglycaemia. Hy-po-gly-cae-mia. You know what that is, don't you?'

Adele wondered that anyone could avoid knowing since, in their two weeks at St Stephen's College, Noreen Tucker hadn't missed an opportunity to expatiate upon hypoglycaemia or anything else. Seeing that she was doing so once again, Adele decided to take her plate of scrambled eggs and sausage to another location, but as she turned, Howard Breen came to her side, smiled, said, 'Coming?' and carried his own plate to where Noreen Tucker reigned, outfitted by Laura Ashley in an ensemble more suited to a teenager than a romance writer at the distant end of her fifth decade.

Adele felt trapped. She liked Howard Breen. From the first moment they had bumped into each other and discovered they were neighbours on the second floor of L staircase, he had been very kind to her, preternaturally capable of reading past her facade of calm yet at the same time willing to allow her to keep her personal miseries to herself. That was a rare quality in a friend. Adele valued it. So she followed Howard.

'I'm just a martyr to hypoglycaemia,' Noreen was asserting vigorously. 'It renders me useless. If I'm not careful . . .'

Adele blocked out the woman's babbling by scanning the room and engaging in a mental recitation of the details she had learned in her two weeks as a student in the Great Houses of Britain class. *Gilded capitals on the pilasters*, she thought, *a segmented pediment above them*. She smiled wryly at the fact that she'd become a virtual encyclopedia of architectural trivia while at Cambridge University. Cram the mind full of facts that one would never use and perhaps they might crowd out the big fact that one could never face.

No, she thought. *No, I won't. Not now.* But the thought of him came to her anyway. Even though it was finished between them, even though it had been her choice, not Bob's, she couldn't be rid of him. Nor could she bury him.

She had made the decision to end their affair, putting a period to five years of anguish by coming to this summer session at St Stephen's College in the hope that an exposure to fine minds would allow her to forget the humiliation of having lived for half a decade in the fruitless expectation that a married man would leave his wife for her. Yet nothing was working to eradicate Bob from memory, and Noreen Tucker was certainly not the incarnation of razor intellect that Adele had hoped to find at Cambridge.

She gritted her teeth as Noreen went on. 'I don't know what would have happened to me if Ralph here hadn't insisted that I go to the doctor. Always weak at the knees. Always feeling faint. Blacking out on the freeway that time. On the freeway! If Ralph here hadn't grabbed the wheel . . .' When Noreen shuddered, the ribbon on her straw hat quivered in sympathy. 'So I keep my nuts and chews with me all the time. Well, Ralph here keeps them for me. Ten, three, and eight p.m. If I don't eat them right on the dot, I go positively limp. Don't I, Ralph?'

It was no surprise to Adele when Ralph Tucker said nothing. She couldn't remember a time when he had managed to make a satisfactory response to some remark of his wife's. At the moment his head was lowered; his eyes were fixed on his bowl of cornflakes.

'You *do* have my trail mix, don't you, Ralph?' Noreen Tucker asked. 'We've got the trip to Abinger Manor this morning, and from what I could tell from looking at that brochure, it's going to be lots of walking. I'll need my nuts and chews. You haven't forgotten?'

Ralph shook his head.

'Because you did forget last week, sweetie, and the bus driver wasn't very pleased with us, was he, when we had to stop to get me a bite to eat at three o'clock?'

Ralph shook his head.

'So you *will* remember this time?'

'It's up in the room, hon. But I won't forget it.'

'That's good. Because . . .'

It was hard to believe that Noreen actually intended to go on, harder to believe that she could not see how tiresome she was. But she nattered happily for several more minutes until the arrival of Dolly Ragusa created a diversion.

Silently, Adele blessed the girl for having mercy upon them. She wouldn't have blamed Dolly for taking a place at another table. More than anyone, Dolly had a right to avoid the Tuckers, for she lived across the hall from them on the first floor of M staircase, so there could be no doubt that Dolly was well versed in the vicissitudes of Noreen Tucker's health. The words *my poor blood* were still ringing in the air when Dolly joined them, a black fedora pulled over her long blonde hair. She wrinkled her nose, rolled her eyes, then grinned.

Adele smiled. It was impossible not to like Dolly. She was the youngest student in the Great Houses class – a twenty-three-year-old art history graduate from the University of Chicago – but she moved among the older students with an easy confidence that Adele admired and a spirit she envied.

Dolly reached for the pitcher of orange juice as Howard Breen said to Adele, 'The Cleareys had a real blow-out this morning. Six-thirty. I thought Frances was going to put Sam through the window. Did you hear them?'

The question was spoken in an undertone, but Noreen looked up from straightening the sailor collar on her dress. 'A fight?'

The two words were spoken casually enough, but Adele saw how the information had piqued Noreen's interest. She had made no secret of her fascination with Sam Clearey, a U.C. Berkeley botanist.

'I was talking to Adele,' Howard said, not unkindly. 'You might have misheard.'

'I don't think that's the case,' Noreen replied. 'Six-thirty in the morning? A fight? About what?'

'Maybe he was out after curfew,' Adele said to deflect her. She felt Howard's foot hit hers beneath the table. Her sardonic remark – it seemed – had struck the truth.

'What a delicious thought!' Noreen rejoined. 'Was he out on the town or in on the bed? And whose?' She laughed and cast her eyes round the table. They settled on Dolly speculatively.

'I love these Cambridge intrigues,' Dolly said, 'Just like high school all over again.'

'The walls are thin, Dolly dear,' Noreen pointed out.

Dolly laughed, unaffected. 'You have got to be kidding. He's sixty years old, Noreen. Come on.' She twirled a lock of hair around her finger and looked reflective. 'But he is pretty great for an older guy, isn't he? All that grey hair. And the way he dresses. I wonder who snagged him?'

'I saw him in the bar last night with that blonde

from the Austen class,' Howard Breen offered.

Noreen Tucker's lips pursed. 'I hardly think that Sam Clearey would be taken in by a forty-nine-year-old divorcée with three teenagers and dyed hair. He's a college professor, Howard. He has taste. And intelligence. And breeding.'

'Thanks. You *were* talking about me, I assume?' Cleve Houghton slid into place next to Dolly Ragusa, carrying a plate heaped with eggs and sausages, grilled tomatoes and mushrooms.

Adele felt a quick release of tension at Cleve's arrival. Through mentioning the fact that Sam Clearey had shown interest in another woman, Howard Breen had innocently raised Noreen's ire. And Noreen was not the type of woman to let such a slight go by unanswered. Cleve's presence prevented her from doing so for the moment.

'Ran eight miles this morning,' he was saying. 'Along the backs to Granchester. The rest of you should try it. Hell, it's the best exercise known to man.' He tossed back his hair and contemplated Adele with a lazy smile. 'The *second* best exercise, that is.'

Heat took Adele's face. She crumpled her napkin in her fist.

'Goodness. In mixed company, Cleve.' Noreen Tucker's gaze was hungrily taking in the most salient aspect of Cleve Houghton's figure: jeans sculpted to muscular thighs. He was fifty but looked at least a decade younger.

'Damn right in mixed company,' Cleve Houghton replied. 'Wouldn't consider it in any other kind.'

'I certainly hope not,' Noreen declared. 'There's nothing worse than a man wasting himself on another man, is there? In one of my novels, I deal with just that topic. A woman falls in love with a homo and saves him. And when he realizes what it's like to have a woman and be normal, he melts. Just melts. I called it *Wild Seed of Passion. Seed* seemed appropriate. There's something in the Bible about spilling seed, isn't there? And that's exactly what those homos are up to. If you ask me, all they need is a real womanly woman and that would take care of that. Don't you agree, Howard?'

'I'd no idea you'd done research in this area,' he said.

'I . . . research?' Noreen pressed a hand to her chest. 'Don't be silly. It's only reasonable to assume that when a man and a woman . . . Heavens, surely I don't have to point out the obvious to *you*? Besides, a creative artist sometimes has to take licence with—'

'Reality? The truth? What?' Howard spoke pleasantly enough, but Adele saw the tightening muscles of his hand and she knew very well that Noreen saw the same.

Noreen reached across the table and patted his arm. 'Now confess to us, Howard. Are you one of those San Francisco liberals with half a dozen homosexual friends? Have I offended you? I'm just an old-fashioned girl who loves romance. And romance is all about true love, which as we all know can only exist between a man and a woman. You know that, don't you?' She smiled at him coolly. 'If you don't, you can ask our little Dolly. Or Cleve here. Or even Adele.'

Howard Breen stood. 'I'll forgo that pleasure for now,' he said, and left them.

'Whoa. What's the matter with him?' Dolly Ragusa asked, her fork poised in midair.

Cleve Houghton lifted a hand, dropped it to dangle limply from his wrist. 'Howard's a hell of a lot more likely to chase after me than you.' he said.

'Oh, Cleve!' Noreen Tucker chuckled, but Adele did not miss the glint of malicious triumph in her eyes. She excused herself and went in search of Howard.

She didn't find him until 8:45, when she went to join the rest of the Great Houses class at their appointed meeting place: the Queen's Gate of St Stephen's College. He was leaning against the arch of the gateway, stuffing a lunch bag into his tattered rucksack.

'You all right?' Adele took her own lunch from the box in which the kitchen staff had deposited it.

'I took a walk along the river to cool off.'

Howard didn't look that composed, no matter his words. A tautness in his features hadn't been there earlier. Even though she knew it was a lie, Adele said, 'I don't think she really knew what she was saying. Obviously, she *doesn't* know about you or she wouldn't have brought the subject up at all.'

He gave a sharp, unamused laugh. 'Don't kid yourself. She's a viper. She knows what she's doing.'

'Hey, you two. Smile!' Some ten yards away, Dolly Ragusa held a camera poised. She was making adjustments to an enormous telephoto lens.

'What are you shooting with that thing, our nostrils?' Howard asked.

Dolly laughed. 'It's a macro-zoom. Wide angles. Close-ups. It does everything but wash the dishes.'

Nearby, Cleve Houghton was pulling on a sweater. 'Why are you carting that thing around anyway? It looks like a pain.'

Dolly snapped his picture before she answered. 'Art historians always have cameras smashed up to their faces. Like extra appendages. That's how you recognize us.'

'I thought that's how you recognize Japanese tourists.' Sam Clearey spoke as he rounded the yew hedge that separated the main court from the interior of the college. As had been his habit for all their excursions, he was nattily dressed in tweeds, and his grey hair gleamed. His wife, a few steps behind him, however, looked terrible. Her eyes were bloodshot and her nose was puffy.

Seeing Frances Clearey, Adele felt a perfect crescent of pain in her chest. It came from recognizing a fellow sufferer. *Men are such shits*, she thought, and was about to join Frances and offer her the distraction of conversation when Victoria Wilder-Scott steamed down from Q staircase and rushed to join them, clipboard in hand.

'Right,' she said, breezily. 'You've read your brochures, I trust? And the section in *Great Houses of the Isles*? So you know we've dozens of things to see at Abinger Manor. That marvellous collection of rococo silver you saw in your text-book. The paintings by Gainsborough, Le Brun, Lorrain, Reynolds. That lovely piece by Whistler. The Holbein. Some remarkable furniture. The gardens are exquisite, and the park . . . You have your notebooks? Your cameras?'

'Dolly seems to be taking pictures for all of us,' Howard Breen said as Dolly snapped one of their instructor.

Victoria Wilder-Scott blinked at the girl, then

beamed. She made no secret of the fact that Dolly was her favourite student. They shared a similar education in art history and a mutual passion for *objets d'art*.

'Right. Then, shall we be off?' Victoria said. 'We're all here? No. Where are the Tuckers?'

The Tuckers arrived as she asked the question, Ralph shoving a plastic bag of trail mix into the front of his safari jacket while Noreen stooped to pick up their lunches, opened hers, and grimaced at its contents.

Her students assembled, Victoria Wilder-Scott lifted an umbrella to point the way and led them out of the college, over the bridge, and down Garret Hostel Lane toward the minibus.

Adele thought that Noreen Tucker intended to use their walk to the minibus as an opportunity to mend her fences with Howard, for the romance writer joined them with an alacrity that suggested some positive underlying intent. In a moment, however, her purpose became clear as she gave her attention to Sam Clearey, who apparently had decided that a walk with Howard and Adele was preferable to his wife's hostile silence. Noreen slipped her hand into the crook of his arm. She smiled at Howard and Adele, an invitation to become her fellow conspirators in whatever was to follow.

Adele shrank from the idea, feeling torn between walking more quickly in an attempt to leave Noreen behind and remaining where she was in the hope that somehow she might protect Sam, as she had been unable to protect Howard earlier. The nobler motive was ascendant. She remained with the little group, hating herself for being such a sop but unable to abandon Sam to Noreen, no matter how much he might deserve five minutes of her barbed conversation. She was, Adele noted, even now winding up the watch of her wit.

'I understand you were a naughty little boy last night,' Noreen said. 'The walls have ears, you know.'

Sam seemed to be in no mood to be teased. 'They don't need to have ears. Frances makes sure of that.'

'Are we to know the lady who was favoured with your charms? No, don't tell us. Let me guess.' Noreen played her fingers along the length of her hair. It was cut in a shoulder-length pageboy with a fringe of bangs, its colour several shades too dark for her skin.

'Have you read the brochure on Abinger Manor?' Adele asked.

The attempt to thwart Noreen was a poor one, and she countered without a glance in Adele's direction. 'I doubt our Sam's had much time to read. Affairs of the heart always take precedence, don't they?' She gave a soft, studied laugh. 'Just ask our Dolly.'

Ahead of them, Dolly's laughter rang out. She was walking with Cleve Houghton, gesturing to the spires of Trinity College to their right and bobbing her head emphatically to underscore a comment she was making.

With Sam within her grasp, Noreen's suddenly dropping the subject of his assignation on the previous night and moving on to target Dolly seemed out of character. It was not quite in keeping with Noreen's penchant for public humiliation, especially since there was no chance that Dolly could hear her words.

'Just look at them,' Noreen said, 'Dolly's digging for gold and she's found the mother lode, apparently.'

'Cleve Houghton?' Howard said. 'He's probably older than her father.'

'What does age matter? He's a doctor. Divorced. Piles of money. I've heard Dolly sighing over those slides Victoria shows us. You know the ones. Antiques, jewellery, paintings. Cleve's just the one to give her that sort of thing. And he'd be happy to do so, make no mistake of that.'

Sam Clearey said, 'She doesn't seem the type—'

Noreen squeezed his arm. 'What a gentleman you are, Sam. But you didn't see them in the bar last night. With Cleve holding forth about seducing women by getting to know their souls and appealing to their minds, and all the time his eyes were just boring into Dolly. Ask Adele. She was sitting right next to him, weren't you, dear? Lapping up every word like a thirsty cat.'

Noreen's teeth glittered in a feral smile, and for the first time Adele felt the bite of the woman's words directed against herself. A chill swept over her at the realization that nothing escaped Noreen's observation. For she *had* listened to Cleve. She had heard it all.

'Little Dolly may like to play virgin in the bush,' Noreen concluded placidly, 'but if Cleve Houghton's doing eight miles in the morning, I'd bet they're right between Dolly's legs. She's across the hall from me, Sam. And as I told you, the walls have ears.'

Sam disengaged Noreen's hand from his arm. 'Yes. Well. If you'll excuse me, I'd better see to Frances.'

Once he had gone, Noreen Tucker seemed to feel little need to remain with Howard and Adele. She left them to themselves and went to join her husband.

'Still think she doesn't mean any harm?' Howard asked. When Adele didn't reply, he looked her way.

She tried to smile, tried to shrug, failed at both, and hated herself for losing her composure in front of him. As she knew he would, Howard saw past the surface.

'She got to you,' he said.

Adele looked from Dolly Ragusa to Cleve Houghton

to Sam Clearey. She had received Noreen's message without any difficulty. Nasty though it was, it was loud. It was clear. As had been her message to Howard at breakfast. As, no doubt, had been her message to Sam Clearey.

'She's a viper,' Adele agreed.

The worst part of those brief moments with Noreen was the fact that her cruelty brought everything back in a rush. No matter that there was no direct correlation between Noreen's comment and the past; her veiled declaration of knowledge did more than merely make perilous inroads into Adele's need for privacy. It forced her to remember.

The minibus trundled along the narrow road. Signposts flashed by intermittently: Little Abington, Linton, Horseheath, Haverhill. Around Adele, the noise of conversation broke into Victoria Wilder-Scott's amplified monologue, which was droning endlessly from the front of the bus. Adele stared out the window.

She had been thirty-one and three years divorced when she'd met Bob. He'd been thirty-eight and eleven years married. He had three children and a wife who sewed and swept and ironed and packed lunches. She was loyal, devoted, and supportive. But she didn't have passion, Bob declared. She didn't speak to his soul. Only Adele spoke to his soul.

Adele believed it. Belief gave dignity to what otherwise would have been just a squalid affair. Elevated to a spiritual plane, their relationship was justified. More, it was sanctified. Having found her soul mate, she grew adept at rationalizing why she couldn't live without him. And how quickly five years had passed in this manner. How easily they decimated her meagre self-esteem.

It was two months now since Bob had been gone from her life. She felt like an open wound. 'You'll be back,' he'd said. 'You'll never have with another man what you have with me.' It was true. Circumstances had proven him correct.

'You can't get anything inside the bus. There's not enough light.'

Adele roused herself to see that Cleve Houghton was chuckling at Dolly Ragusa. She was kneeling on the seat in front of him, focusing her camera on his swarthy face.

'Sure I can.' *Click*.

'Then let me take one of you.'

'No way.'

'Come on.' He reached out.

She dodged him by slipping into the aisle. She moved among the seats, photographing one student after another: Ralph Tucker dozing with his head against the window, Howard Breen reading the brochure on Abinger Manor, Sam Clearey turning from the scenery outside as she called his name.

From the front of the minibus, Victoria Wilder-Scott continued her monologue about the Manor. '. . . family remained staunchly Royalist to the end. In the north tower, you'll see a priest's hole where Charles II was hidden prior to escaping to the Continent. And in the long gallery, you'll be challenged to find a Gibb door that's completely concealed. It was through this door that King Charles—'

'Doesn't she think we can read the brochure? We know all about the paintings and the furniture and the silver gee-gaws, for God's sake.' Noreen Tucker examined her teeth in the mirror of a compact. She rubbed at a spot of lipstick and got to her feet – intent, it seemed, upon Sam Clearey, who sat apart from his wife.

Restlessly, Adele turned in her seat. Her eyes met Cleve Houghton's. His gaze was frank and direct, the sort of appraisal that peeled off clothing and judged the flesh beneath.

He smiled. 'Things on your mind?' he asked.

Dolly provided Adele with an excuse not to answer. She was perched on the arm of Ralph Tucker's seat, talking cheerfully to Frances Clearey.

'I think it's great that you and Sam do things like this together,' Dolly said. 'This Cambridge course. I tried to get my boyfriend to come with me, but he wouldn't even consider it.'

Frances Clearey made an effort to smile, but it was evident that her concentration was on Noreen Tucker, who had dropped into the vacant seat next to Frances's husband.

'D'you two do this sort of thing every summer?' Dolly asked.

'This is our first time.' Frances's eyes flicked to

the side as Noreen Tucker laughed and inclined her head in Sam Clearey's direction.

Adele saw Dolly move so that her body blocked Frances's view of Sam and Noreen. 'I'm going to tell David – that's my boyfriend – all about you two. If a marriage is going to work, it seems to me that the husband and wife need to share mutual interests. And still give each other space at the same time. Like you and Sam. David and I . . . he can really be possessive.'

'I'm surprised he didn't come with you, then.'

'Oh, this is educational. David doesn't worry if I'm involved in art history. It's like him and his monkeys. He's a physical anthropologist. Howlers.'

'Howlers?'

Dolly lifted her camera and snapped Frances's picture. 'Howler monkeys. That's what he studies. Their poop, if you can believe it. I ask him what he's going to learn from putting monkey poop under a microscope. He says looking at it's not so bad. Collecting it is hell.'

Frances Clearey smiled. Dolly laughed.

Adele marvelled at how easily the girl had managed to bring Frances out of herself, even for a moment. How wise she was to point out subtly to Frances the strengths of her marriage instead of allowing her to sit in solitude, brooding upon its most evident weakness. Noreen Tucker was nothing, Dolly was saying. Other women are nothing. Sam belongs to you.

Dolly's was a decidedly insouciant attitude toward life. But why should she offer any other perspective? Her future stretched before her, uncomplicated and carefree. She had no past to haunt her. She was, at the heart of it, so wonderfully young.

'Why so solemn this morning?' Cleve Houghton asked Adele from across the aisle. 'Don't take yourself so seriously. Start enjoying yourself. Life's to be lived.'

Adele's throat tightened. She'd had quite enough of living.

Click.

'Adele!' Dolly was back with her camera.

When they arrived at their destination, the sight of

Abinger Manor roused Adele from her blackness of mood. Across a moat that was studded with lily pads, two crenellated towers stood at the sides of the building's front entry. On either side of them, crow-stepped gables were surmounted by impossibly tall, impossibly decorated chimneys. Bay windows, a later addition to the house, extended over the moat and gave visual access to an extensive garden. This was edged on one side with a tall yew hedge and on the other with a brick wall against which grew an herbaceous border of lavender, aster, and dianthus. The Great Houses of Britain class wandered toward this garden with a quarter of an hour to explore it prior to the Manor's first tour.

Adele saw that they were not to be the only visitors to the Manor that morning. A large group of Germans debouched from a tour coach and joined Dolly Ragusa in extensively photographing the garden and the exterior of the house. Two family groups entered the maze and began shouting at one another as they immediately lost their way. A handsome couple pulled into the car park in a silver Bentley and stood in conversation next to the moat. For

a moment, Adele thought that these last visitors
were actually the owners of the Manor – they were
extremely well dressed and the Bentley suggested
a wealth unassociated with taking tours of great
houses. But they joined the others in the garden,
and as they strolled past Adele, she overheard a
snatch of conversation pass between them.

'Really, Tommy, darling, I can't recall agreeing to
come here at all. Is this one of your tricks?'

'Salmon sandwiches,' was the man's unaccountable reply.

'Salmon sandwiches?'

'I bribed you, Helen. Early last week. A picnic.
Salmon sandwiches. Stilton cheese. Strawberry tarts.
White wine.'

'Ah. *Those* salmon sandwiches.'

They laughed together quietly. The man dropped
his arm around the woman's shoulders. He was tall,
very blond, clear-featured, and handsome. She was
slender, dark-haired, with an oval face. They walked
in perfect rhythm with each other. Lovers, Adele
thought bleakly, and forced herself to turn away.

When a bell rang to call them for the tour,

Adele went gratefully, hoping for distraction, never realizing how thorough that distraction would be.

Their guide was a determined-looking girl in her mid-twenties with pimples on her chin and too much eye make-up. She spoke in staccato. They were in the original screens passage, she told them. The wall to their left was the original screen. They would be able to admire its carving when they got to the other side of it. If they would please stay together and not stray behind the corded-off areas . . . Photographs were permissible without a flash.

As the group moved forward, Adele found herself wedged between two German matrons who needed to bathe. She breathed shallowly and was thankful when the size of the Great Hall allowed the crowd to spread out.

It was a magnificent room, everything that Victoria Wilder-Scott, their textbook, and the Abinger Manor brochure had promised it would be. While the guide catalogued its features for them, Adele dutifully took note of the towering coved ceiling, of the minstrel gallery and its intricate fretwork, of the tapestries, the portraits, the fireplace, the marble floor. Near her, cameras focused and shutters clicked. And then at her ear: 'Just what I was looking for. *Just*.'

Adele's heart sank. She had successfully avoided Noreen Tucker in the garden, after having almost stumbled upon her and Ralph in the middle of a Noreenian rhapsody over a stone bench upon which she had determined the lovers in her new romance novel would have their climactic assignation.

'The ball. Right in here!' Noreen went on. 'Oh, I *knew* we were clever to take this class, Ralph!'

Adele looked Noreen's way. She was dipping her hand into the plastic bag that protruded from her husband's safari jacket. Ten o'clock, Adele thought, trail-mix time. Noreen munched away, murmuring, 'Charles and Delfinia clasped each other as the music from the gallery floated to caress them. "This is madness, darling. We must not. We cannot." He refused to listen. "We *must*. Tonight." So they—'

Adele walked away, grateful for the moment when the guide began ushering them out of the Great Hall.

They went up a flight of stairs and into a narrow, lengthy gallery.

'This long gallery is one of the most famous in England,' their guide informed them as they assembled behind a cord that ran the length of the room. 'It contains not only one of the finest collections of rococo silver, which you see arranged to the left of the fireplace on a demilune table – that's a Sheraton piece, by the way – but also a Le Brun, two Gainsboroughs, a Reynolds, a Holbein, a charming Whistler, and several lesser-known artists. In the case at the end of the room you'll find a hat, gloves, and stockings that belonged to Queen Elizabeth I. And here's one of the most remarkable features of the room.'

She walked to the left of the Sheraton table and pushed lightly on a section of the panelling. A door swung open, previously hidden by the structure of the wall.

'It's a Gibb door. Clever, isn't it? Servants could come and go through it and never be seen in the public rooms of the house.'

Cameras clicked. Necks craned. Voices murmured.

The Evidence Exposed

'And if you'll especially take note of—'

'Ralph!' Noreen Tucker gasped. '*Ralph!*'

Adele was among those who turned at the interruption. Noreen was standing just outside the cord, next to a satinwood table on which sat a china bowl of potpourri. She was quite pale, her eyes wide, her extended hand trembling. Hypoglycaemia seemed to be getting the better of her.

'Nor? *Hon*? Oh, damn, her blood—' Ralph Tucker had no chance to finish. With an inarticulate cry, Noreen fell across the table, splintering the bowl and scattering potpourri across the Persian carpet. Down the length of the room, the satin cord ripped from the posts that held it in place as Noreen Tucker crashed through it on her way to the floor.

Adele found herself immobilized, although around her, everyone else seemed to move at once. She felt caught up in a swell as some people pressed forward toward the fallen woman and others backed away. Someone screamed. Someone else called upon the Lord. Three Germans dropped in shock onto the couches that were made available to them now that the cord of demarcation was gone. There was a cry for water, a shout for air.

Ralph Tucker shrieked, 'Noreen!' and dropped to his knees amid the potpourri and china. He pulled at his wife's shoulder. She had fallen on her face, her straw hat rolling across the carpet.

Adele called wildly, 'Cleve. *Cleve*,' and then he was pushing through the crowd. He turned Noreen over, took one look at her face, and began administering CPR. 'Get an ambulance!' he ordered.

Adele swung around to do so. Their tour guide was rooted to her spot next to the fireplace, her attention fixed upon the woman on the floor as if she herself had had a part in putting her there.

'An ambulance!' Adele cried.

Voices came from everywhere.

'Is she . . .'

'God, she *can't* be . . .'

'Noreen! Nor! Hon!'

'Sie ist gerade ohnmächtig geworden, nicht wahr . . .'

'Get an ambulance, goddamn it!' Cleve Houghton raised his head. 'Move!' he yelled at the guide.

She flew through the Gibb door and pounded up the stairs.

Cleve paused, took Noreen's pulse. He forced her mouth open and attempted to resuscitate her.

'Noreen!' Ralph wailed.

'Kann er nicht etwas unternehmen?'

'Doesn't anyone . . .'

'Schauen Sie sich die Gesichtsfarbe an.'

'She's gone.'

'It's no use.'

'Diese dummen Amerikaner!'

Over the swarm, Adele saw the blond man from the Bentley remove his jacket and hand it to his companion. He eased through the crowd, straddled Noreen, and took over CPR as Cleve Houghton continued his efforts to get her to breathe.

'Noreen! Hon!'

'Get him out of the way!'

Adele took Ralph's arm, attempting to ease him to his feet. 'Ralph, if you'll let them—'

'She needed to eat!'

Victoria Wilder-Scott joined them. 'Please, Mr Tucker. If you'll give them a chance . . .'

The tour guide crashed back into the room.

'I've phoned . . .' She faltered, then stopped altogether.

Adele looked from the guide to Cleve. He had raised his head. His expression said it all.

Events converged. People reacted. Curiosity, sympathy, panic, aversion. Leadership was called for, and the blond man assumed it, wresting it from the guide with the simple words, 'I'm Thomas Lynley. Scotland Yard CID.' He showed her a piece of identification she seemed only too happy to acknowledge.

Thomas Lynley organized them quickly, in a manner that encouraged neither protest nor question. They would continue with the tour, he informed them, in order to clear the room for the arrival of the ambulance.

He remained behind with his companion, Ralph Tucker, Cleve Houghton, and the dead woman. Adele saw him bend, saw him open Noreen's clenched hand. Cleve said, 'Heart failure. I've seen them go like this before,' but although Lynley nodded, he looked not at Cleve but raised his head from examining Noreen's hand and focused on the group, his brown eyes speculating upon each one of them as they left the room. Ralph Tucker sank onto a delicate chair. Thomas Lynley's companion went to him, murmured a few words, put her hand on his shoulder.

Then the door closed behind them and the group was in the drawing room, being asked to examine the pendant plasterwork of its remarkable ceiling. It was called the King Edward Drawing Room, their much-subdued guide told them, its name taken from the statue of Edward IV that stood over the mantelpiece. It was a three-quarter-size statue, she explained, not life-size, for unlike most men of his time, Edward IV was well over six feet tall. In fact, when he rode into London on 26 February 1460 . . .

Adele did not see how the young woman could go on. There was something indecent about being asked to admire chandeliers, flocked wallpaper, eighteenth-century furniture, Chinese vases, and a French chimneypiece in the face of Noreen Tucker's death. Adele had certainly disliked Noreen, but death was death and it seemed that, out of respect to her passing, they might well have abandoned the rest of the tour and returned to Cambridge. She couldn't understand why Thomas Lynley had not instructed them to do so. Surely it would have been far more humane than to expect them to traipse round the rest of the house as if nothing had happened.

But even Ralph had wanted them to continue. 'You go on', he had said to Victoria when she had attempted to remain with him in the long gallery. 'People are depending on you.' He made it sound as if a tour of Abinger Manor were akin to a battle upon whose outcome the fate of a nation depended. It was just the sort of comment that would appeal to Victoria. So the tour continued.

Everyone was restless. The air was close. Composure seemed brittle. Adele had no doubt that she was not the only person longing to escape from Abinger Manor.

There was a murmur when Cleve Houghton rejoined them in the winter dining room.

'They've taken her,' he said in a low voice to Adele.

'And that man? The policeman?'

'Still in the gallery when I left. He's put out a call for the local police.'

'Why?' Adele asked. 'I saw him looking at . . . Cleve, you don't . . . She seemed healthy, didn't she?'

Cleve's eyes narrowed. 'I know a heart attack when I see one. Jesus, what are you thinking?'

Adele didn't know what she was thinking. She only knew that she had recognized something on Lynley's face when he had looked up from examining Noreen Tucker's trail mix. Consternation, suspicion, anger, outrage. Something had been there. If that were the case, then it could only mean one thing. Adele felt her stomach churn. She began to evaluate her fellow students in an entirely new way: as potential killers.

Frances Clearey seemed to have been shaken from her morning's fury at her husband. She was close at Sam's side, pressed to his arm. Perhaps Noreen's death had allowed her to see how fleeting life was, how insignificant its quarrels and concerns were once one came to terms with its finitude. Or perhaps she simply had nothing further to worry about now that Noreen was eliminated.

She hadn't been at breakfast, Adele recalled, so she could have slipped into Noreen's room and put something into her trail mix. Especially if she knew that Sam had spent the night with Noreen in town somewhere. Removing a rival to a man's love seemed an adequate motive for murder.

But Sam himself had also not been at breakfast. So he, too, had access to Noreen's supply of food. If Noreen had known with whom he had spent the night – and perhaps that's what she had been hinting at this morning – perhaps Sam had seen the need to be rid of her. Especially if she had been the woman herself.

It was hard to believe. Yet at the same time, looking at Sam, Adele could see how Noreen's death had affected him. Beneath his tan, his face was worn, his mouth set. His eyes seemed cloudy. In each room, they alighted first upon Dolly, as if her beauty were an anodyne for him.

Dolly herself had come into breakfast late, so she also had access to Noreen's supply of nuts.

But Noreen had not given Dolly an overt reason to harm her, and surely Noreen's gossip about the girl – even if Dolly had heard it, which was doubtful – would only have amused her.

As it would have amused Cleve Houghton. And pleased him. And swelled his ego substantially. Indeed, Cleve had every reason to keep Noreen alive. She had been doing wonders to build repute of his sexual prowess. On the other hand, Cleve had come into breakfast late, so he, too, had access to the Tuckers' room.

Howard Breen seemed to be the only one who hadn't had time to get to Noreen's trail mix. Except, Adele remembered, he had left breakfast early and she hadn't been able to find him.

Everyone, then, had the opportunity to mix something in with the nuts, raisins, and dried fruit. But what had that something been? And how on earth had someone managed to get hold of it? Surely one didn't walk into a Cambridge chemist's shop and ask for a quick-acting poison. So whoever tampered with the mix had to have experience with poisons, had to know what to expect.

They were in the library when Thomas Lynley and his lady rejoined them. He ran his eyes over everyone in the room. His companion did the same. He said something to her quietly, and the two of them separated, taking positions in different parts of the crowd. Neither of them paid the slightest attention to anything other than to the people. But they gave their full attention to them.

From the library they went into the chapel, accompanied only by the sounds of their own footsteps, the echoing voice of the guide, the snapping of cameras. Lynley moved through the group, saying nothing to anyone save to his companion, with whom he spoke a few words at the door. Again they separated.

From the chapel they went into the armoury. From there into the billiard room. From there to the music room. From there down two flights of stairs and into the kitchen. The buttery beyond it had been turned into a gift shop. The Germans made for this. The Americans began to do likewise. That was when Lynley spoke.

'If I might see everyone, please,' he said as they

began to scatter. 'If you'll just stay here in the kitchen for a moment.'

Protests rose from the German group. The Americans said nothing.

'We've a problem to consider,' Lynley told them, 'regarding Noreen Tucker's death.'

'Problem?' Behind Adele, Cleve Houghton spoke. Others chimed in.

'What do you want with us anyway?'

'What's going on?'

'It was heart failure,' Cleve asserted. 'I've seen enough of that to tell you—'

'As have I,' a heavily accented voice said. The speaker was a member of the German party, and he looked none too pleased that their tour was once again being disrupted. 'I am a doctor. I, too, have seen heart failure. I know what I see.'

Lynley extended his hand. In his palm lay a half dozen seeds. 'It looked like heart failure. That's what an alkaloid does. It paralyses the heart in a matter of minutes. These are yew, by the way.'

'Yew?'

'What was yew—'

'But she wouldn't—'

Adele kept her eyes on Lynley's palm. Seeds. Plants. The connection was horrible. She avoided looking at the one person in the kitchen who would know beyond a doubt the potential for harm contained in a bit of yew.

'Surely those came from the potpourri,' Victoria Wilder-Scott said. 'It spilled all over the carpet when Mrs Tucker fell.'

Lynley shook his head. 'They were mixed in with the nuts in her hand. And the bag her husband carried was thick with them. She was murdered.'

The Germans protested heartily at this. The doctor led them. 'You have no business with us. This woman was a stranger. I insist that we be allowed to leave.'

'Of course,' Lynley answered. 'As soon as we solve the problem of the silver.'

'What on earth are you talking about?'

'It appears that one of you took the opportunity of the chaos in the long gallery to remove two pieces of rococo silver from the table by the fireplace. They're salt cellars. Very small. And definitely missing. This isn't my jurisdiction, of course, but until the local police arrive to start their inquiries into Mrs Tucker's death, I'd like to take care of this small detail of the silver myself.'

'What are you going to do?' Frances Clearey asked.

'Do you plan to keep us here until one of us admits to something?' the German doctor scoffed. 'You cannot search us without some authority.'

'That's correct,' Lynley said. 'I can't search you. Unless you agree to be searched.'

Feet shuffled. A throat cleared. Urgent conversation was conducted in German. Someone rustled papers in a notebook.

Cleve Houghton was the first to speak. He looked over the group. 'Hell, I have no objection.'

'But the women . . .' Victoria pointed out.

Lynley nodded to his companion, who was standing by a display of copper kettles at the edge of the group. 'This is Lady Helen Clyde,' he told them. 'She'll search the women.'

As one body, they turned to Lynley's companion. Resting upon them, her dark eyes were friendly.

Her expression was gentle. What an absurdity it would be to resist cooperating with such a lovely creature.

The search was carried out in two rooms: the women in the scullery and the men in a warming room across the hall. In the scullery, Lady Helen made a thorough job of it. She watched each woman undress, redress. She emptied pockets, handbags, canvas totes. She checked the lining of raincoats. She opened umbrellas. All the time she chatted in a manner designed to put them at ease. She asked the Americans about their class, about Cambridge, about great houses they had seen and where they were from. She confided in the Germans about spending two weeks in the Black Forest one summer and confessed to an embarrassed dislike of the out-of-doors. She never mentioned the word *murder*. Aside from the operation in which they were engaged, they might have been new acquaintances talking over tea. Yet Adele saw for herself that Lady Helen was quite efficient at her job, for all her friendliness and good breeding. If she didn't work for the police herself – and her relationship

with Lynley certainly did not suggest that she was
employed by Scotland Yard – she certainly had
knowledge of their procedures.

Nonetheless, she found nothing. Nor, apparently,
did Lynley. When the two groups were gathered once
again in the kitchen, Adele saw him shake his head at
Lady Helen. If the silver had been taken, it was not
being carried by anyone. Even Victoria Wilder-Scott
and the tour guide had been searched.

Lynley told them to wait in the tearoom. He
turned back to the stairway at the far end of the
kitchen.

'Where's he going now?' Frances Clearey asked.

'He'll have to look for the silver in the rest of the
house,' Adele said.

'But that could take forever!' Dolly protested.

'It doesn't matter, does it? We're going to have to
wait to talk to the local police anyway.'

'It was heart failure,' Cleve said. 'There's no silver
missing. It's probably being cleaned somewhere.'

Adele fell to the back of the crowd as they walked
across the pebbled courtyard. A sense of unease
plucked at her mind. It had been with her much

of the morning, hidden like a secondary message between the lines of Noreen Tucker's words, trying to fight its way to the surface of her consciousness in the minibus, lying just beyond the range of her vision ever since they had arrived at the Manor. Like the children's game of What's Wrong With This Picture, there was a distortion somewhere. She could feel it distinctly. She simply couldn't see it.

Her thoughts tumbled upon one another without connection or reason, like images produced by a kaleidoscope. There were yew hedges in the courtyard of St Stephen's College. Sam and Frances Clearey had had a fight. The walls have ears. The silver was available. It was pictured in their text. It was in the brochures. They'd seen both in advance. Dolly wanted Cleve. She loved antiques. Sam Clearey liked women, liked the blonde from the Dickens class, liked . . .

Once again Adele saw Lady Helen go through their belongings. She saw her empty, probe, touch, leave nothing unexamined. She saw her shake her head at Lynley. She saw Lynley frown.

The two groups entered the tearoom and segregated themselves from each other. The Americans took positions at a refectory table at the far end. The Germans lined up for coffee and cakes.

'Victoria, can we go back to Cambridge?' Frances asked. 'I mean, when this is over? We've another house to see today, but we can drop it, can't we?'

Victoria was hesitant. 'Ralph did specifically want us to—'

'Screw Ralph Tucker!' Sam said. 'Come on, Victoria, we've had it.'

'There's the minibus to consider, the driver's salary . . .'

'Couldn't we just chip in some money and tip him or something?' Dolly set her camera on the table in front of her.

And there it was in an instant. Right before her. Adele saw it at last. She knew what Noreen Tucker had been saying during their walk to the bus. She knew the source of her own disquiet on the journey to Abinger Manor. She acknowledged what she had seen without seeing from the moment they had arrived at the Manor. Thirty-six was the key, but it had been exceeded long ago. The knowledge brought to Adele an attendant rush of wrenching illness. Thomas Lynley had made an assumption from the facts at hand.

But Lynley was wrong.

She pushed herself to her feet and left the group. Someone called after her, but she continued on her way. She found Lynley in the drawing room, directing three workmen who were crawling across the floor.

How can I do this? she asked herself. And then, *Why? With the future a blank slate upon which nothing but hope and success were written. Why?*

Lynley looked up. Lady Helen Clyde did likewise. Adele did not even have to speak to them. They joined her at once and followed her to the tearoom.

'What's going on?' Cleve asked.

Adele didn't look at him. 'Dolly, give the inspector your camera.'

Dolly's blue eyes widened. 'I don't understand.'

'Give him the camera, Dolly. Let him look at the lens.'

'But you—'

Lynley lifted the camera from the girl's shoulder. Lined along its strap were containers for film. All of them were empty. Adele had seen that earlier, had seen it and had thought no more about it than she had thought about the fact that there had been no film in Dolly's shoulder bag. Nor had there been any in her pockets. She'd been shooting pictures all morning with no film in her camera at all, in order to conceal her real reason for carrying the camera with her to the Manor in the first place.

Lynley twisted off the macro-zoom lens. It was useless, hollowed. Two pieces of rococo silver tumbled out.

Howard dropped into the seat next to Adele. 'You okay?'

'Okay.' She didn't want to talk about it. She felt like a Judas. She wanted to go home. She tried to keep from thinking about Dolly being led off by the police.

'How did you figure Dolly?'

'She took too many pictures. She would have had

to change film, but she never did that. Because there was no film.'

'But Noreen. Why did Dolly . . .'

Adele's limbs felt numb. 'I don't think she cared one way or the other about Noreen. Probably intended the seeds to make Noreen good and sick, not kill her. She just needed a diversion to get to the silver.'

'But could she possibly have known what yew seeds do?'

'Sam. He probably didn't know what he was telling her or why she was asking. He probably didn't think of anything except what it felt like to be his age and to be in bed with someone like Dolly.' Even that was hard to bear. Knowing that Dolly's solicitous conversation with Frances Clearey about her marriage had been nothing more than part of the game. Just another diversion, just another lie.

'*Sam* and Dolly?' Howard looked across the aisle to where Cleve Houghton lounged in his seat, eyes half closed. 'I thought Cleve . . . when Noreen was telling us that Cleve was talking last night about seducing women . . .'

'She was talking to me. About me. Cleve wasn't with Dolly last night, Howard.' Adele looked out the window, said nothing more. After a moment, she felt Howard leave the seat and move away.

I will bury you, Bob, she had thought with Cleve Houghton. *I will end it between us this way.* So she had drunk in the college bar with him, she had walked on the backs and listened to him talk, she had pretended to find him intriguing and delightful, a man of passion, a soul mate, a replacement for Bob. And when he wanted her, she had obliged. Hurried grappling, urgent coupling, a body in her bed. To feel alive, to feel wanted, to feel a creature of worth. But not to bury Bob. It hadn't worked that way.

'Hey.' Adele pretended not to hear him, but Cleve crossed the aisle and dropped into the seat. He carried a flask in his hand. 'You look like you need a drink. Hell, I need one.' He drank, spoke again in a lower voice. 'Tonight?'

Adele raised her eyes to his face, trying and failing to force his features into the shape of another man's.

'Well?' he said.

Of course, she thought. Why not? What difference did it make when life was so fleeting and youth without meaning?

'Sure,' she said. 'Tonight.'

I, Richard

I, Richard

Malcolm Cousins groaned in spite of himself. Considering his circumstances, this was the last sound he wanted to make. A sigh of pleasure or a moan of satisfaction would have been more appropriate. But the truth was simple and he had to face it: No longer was he the performance artist he once had been in the sexual arena. Time was when he could bonk with the best of them. But that time had gone the way of his hair and at forty-nine years old, he considered himself lucky to be able to get the appliance up and running twice a week.

He rolled off Betsy Perryman and thudded onto his back. His lower vertebrae were throbbing like drummers in a marching band, and the always-dubious pleasure he'd just taken from Betsy's corpulent, perfume-drenched charms was quickly transformed to a faint memory. Jesus God, he thought with a gasp. Forget justification altogether. Was the end even *worth* the bloody means?

Luckily, Betsy took the groan and the gasp the way Betsy took most everything. She heaved herself onto her side, propped her head upon the palm of her hand and observed him with an expression that was meant to be coy. The last thing Betsy wanted him to know was how desperate she was for him to be her lifeboat out of her current marriage – number four this one was – and Malcolm was only too happy to accommodate her in the fantasy. Sometimes it got a bit complicated, remembering what he was supposed to know and what he was supposed to be ignorant of, but he always found that if Betsy's suspicions about his sincerity became aroused, there was a simple and expedient, albeit back-troubling, way to assuage her doubts about him.

She reached for the tangled sheet, pulled it up, and extended a plump hand. She caressed his hairless pate and smiled at him lazily. 'Never did it with a baldy before. Have I told you that, Malc?'

Every single time the two of them – as she so poetically stated – did it, he recalled. He thought of Cora, the springer spaniel bitch he'd adored in childhood, and the memory of the dog brought suitable fondness to his face. He eased Betsy's fingers down his cheek and kissed each one of them.

'Can't get enough, naughty boy,' she said. 'I've never had a man like you, Malc Cousins.'

She scooted over to his side of the bed, closer and closer until her huge bosoms were less than an inch from his face. At this proximity, her cleavage resembled Cheddar Gorge and was just about as appealing a sexual object. God, another go round? he thought. He'd be dead before he was fifty if they went on like this. And not a step nearer to his objective.

He nuzzled within the suffocating depths of her mammaries, making the kinds of yearning noises that she wanted to hear. He did a bit of sucking and then made much of catching sight of his wrist-watch on the bedside table.

'Christ!' He grabbed the watch for a feigned better look. 'Jesus, Betsy, it's eleven o'clock. I told those Aussie Ricardians I'd meet them at Bosworth Field at noon. I've got to get rolling.'

Which is what he did, right out of bed before she could protest. As he shrugged into his dressing gown, she struggled to transform his announcement into something comprehensible. Her face screwed up and she said, 'Those Ozzirecordians? What the hell's that?' She sat up, her blonde hair matted and snarled and most of her make-up smeared from her face.

'Not Ozzirecordians,' Malcolm said. 'Aussie. Australian. Australian Ricardians. I told you about them last week, Betsy.'

'Oh, that.' She pouted. 'I thought we could have a picnic lunch today.'

'In this weather?' He headed for the bathroom. It wouldn't do to arrive for the tour reeking of sex and Shalimar. 'Where did you fancy having a picnic in January? Can't you hear that wind? It must be ten below outside.'

'A bed picnic,' she said. 'With honey and cream.

You *said* that was your fantasy. Or don't you remember?'

He paused in the bedroom doorway. He didn't much like the tone of her question. It made a demand that reminded him of everything he hated about women. Of *course* he didn't remember what he'd claimed to be his fantasy about honey and cream. He'd said lots of things over the past two years of their liaison. But he'd forgotten most of them once it had become apparent that she was seeing him as he wished to be seen. Still, the only course was to play along. 'Honey and cream,' he sighed. 'You brought honey and cream? Oh Christ, Bets . . .' A quick dash back to the bed. A tonguely examination of her dental work. A frantic clutching between her legs. 'God, you're going to drive me mad, woman. I'll be walking round Bosworth with my prong like a poker all day.'

'Serves you right,' she said pertly and reached for his groin. He caught her hand in his.

'You love it,' he said.

'No more'n you.'

He sucked her fingers again. 'Later,' he said. 'I'll

trot those wretched Aussies round the battlefield and if you're still here then . . . You know what happens next.'

'It'll be too late then. Bernie thinks I've only gone to the butcher.'

Malcolm favoured her with a pained look, the better to show that the thought of her hapless and ignorant husband – his old best friend Bernie – scored his soul. 'Then there'll be another time. There'll be hundreds of times. With honey and cream. With caviar. With oysters. Did I ever tell you what I'll do with the oysters?'

'What?' she asked.

He smiled. 'Just you wait.'

He retreated to the bathroom, where he turned on the shower. As usual, an inadequate spray of lukewarm water fizzled out of the pipe. Malcolm shed his dressing gown, shivered, and cursed his circumstances. Twenty-five years in the classroom, teaching history to spotty-faced hooligans who had no interest in anything beyond the immediate gratification of their sweaty-palmed needs, and what did he have to show for it? Two up and two down in an ancient terraced house down the street from Gloucester Grammar. An ageing Vauxhall with no spare tyre. A mistress with an agenda for marriage and a taste for kinky sex. And a passion for a long dead King that – he was determined – would be the wellspring from which would flow his future. The means were so close, just tantalizing centimetres from his eager grasp. And once his reputation was secured, the book contracts, the speaking engagements, and the offers of gainful employment would follow.

'Shit!' he bellowed as the shower water went from warm to scalding without a warning. 'Damn!' He fumbled for the taps.

'Serves you right,' Betsy said from the doorway. 'You're a naughty boy and naughty boys need punishing.'

He blinked water from his eyes and squinted at her. She'd put on his best flannel shirt – the very one he'd intended to wear on the tour of Bosworth Field, blast the woman – and she lounged against the doorjamb in her best attempt at a seductive pose. He ignored her and went about his showering. He could tell she was determined to have her way, and her way was another bonk before he left. Forget it, Bets, he said to her silently. Don't push your luck.

'I don't understand you, Malc Cousins,' she said. 'You're the only man in civilization who'd rather tramp round a soggy pasture with a bunch of tourists than cozy up in bed with the woman he says he loves.'

'Not says, does,' Malcolm said automatically. There was a dreary sameness to their post-coital conversations that was beginning to get him decidedly down.

'That so? I wouldn't've known. I'd've said you fancy whatsisname the King a far sight more'n you fancy me.'

Well, Richard was definitely more interesting a character, Malcolm thought. But he said, 'Don't be daft. It's money for our nest egg anyway.'

'We don't need a nest egg,' she said. 'I've told you that about a hundred times. We've got the—'

'Besides,' he cut in hastily. There couldn't be too little said between them on the subject of Betsy's expectations. 'It's good experience. Once the book is finished, there'll be interviews, personal appearances, lectures. I need the practice. I need' – this with a winning smile in her direction – 'more than an audience of one, my darling. Just think what it'll be like, Bets. Cambridge, Oxford, Harvard, the Sorbonne. Will you like Massachusetts? What about France?'

'Bernie's heart's giving him trouble again, Malc,' Betsy said, running her finger up the doorjamb.

'Is it, now?' Malcolm said happily. 'Poor old Bernie. Poor bloke, Bets.'

The problem of Bernie had to be handled, of course. But Malcolm was confident that Betsy Perryman was up for the challenge. In the afterglow of sex and inexpensive champagne, she'd told him once that each one of her four marriages had been a step forward and upward from the marriage that had preceded it, and it didn't take a hell of a lot of brains to know that moving out of a marriage to a dedicated inebriate – no matter how affable – into a relationship with a school teacher on his way to unveiling a piece of mediaeval history that would set the country on its ear was a step in the right direction. So Betsy would definitely handle Bernie. It was only a matter of time.

Divorce was out of the question, of course. Malcolm had made certain that Betsy understood that while he was desperate mad hungry and all the etceteras for a life with her, he would no more ask her to come to him in his current impoverished circumstances than would he expect the next Princess of Wales to take up life in a bed-sit on the south bank of the Thames. Not only would he not ask that of her, he wouldn't allow it. Betsy – his beloved – deserved so much more than he would be able to give her, such as he was. But when his ship came in, darling Bets . . . Or if, God forbid, anything should ever happen to Bernie . . . This, he hoped, was enough to light a fire inside the spongy grey mass that went for her brain.

Malcolm felt no guilt at the thought of Bernie Perryman's demise. True, they'd known each other in childhood as sons of mothers who'd been girl-hood friends. But they'd parted ways at the end of adolescence, when poor Bernie's failure to pass more than one A-level had doomed him to life on the family farm while Malcolm had gone on to University. And after that . . . well, differing levels of education *did* take a toll on one's ability to communicate with one's erstwhile – and less educated – mates, didn't it? Besides, when Malcolm returned from University, he could see that his old friend had sold his soul to the Black Bush devil, and what would it profit him to renew a friendship with the district's most prominent drunk? Still, Malcolm liked to think he'd taken a modicum of pity on Bernie Perryman. Once a month for years, he'd gone to the farmhouse – under cover of darkness, of course – to play chess with his former friend and to listen to his inebriated musings about their childhood and the what-might-have-beens.

Which was how he first found out about The Legacy, as Bernie had called it. Which was what he'd spent the last two years bonking Bernie's wife in order to get his hands on. Betsy and Bernie had no children. Bernie was the last of his line. The Legacy was going to come to Betsy. And Betsy was going to give it to Malcolm.

She didn't know that yet. But she would soon enough.

Malcolm smiled, thinking of what Bernie's legacy would do to further his career. For nearly ten years, he'd been writing furiously on what he'd nicknamed *Dickon Delivered* – his untarnishing of the reputation of Richard III – and once The Legacy was in his hands, his future was going to be assured. As he rolled towards Bosworth Field and the Australian Ricardians awaiting him there, he recited the first line of the penultimate chapter of his magnum opus. 'It is with the alleged disappearance of Edward the Lord Bastard, Earl of Pembroke and March, and Richard, Duke of York, that historians have traditionally begun to rely upon sources contaminated by their own self-interest.'

God, it was beautiful writing, he thought. And better than that, it was the truth as well.

The tour coach was already there when Malcolm roared into the car park at Bosworth Field. Its occupants had foolishly disembarked. All apparently female and of depressingly advanced years, they were huddled into a shivering pack, looking sheep-like and abandoned in the gale-force winds that were blowing. When Malcolm heaved himself out of his car, one of their number disengaged herself from their midst and strode towards him. She was sturdily built and much younger than the rest, which gave Malcolm hope of being able to grease his way through the moment with some generous dollops of charm. But then he noted her short clipped hair, elephantine ankles, and massive calves . . . not to mention the clipboard that she was smacking into her hand as she walked. An unhappy lesbian tour guide out for blood, he thought. God, what a deadly combination.

Nonetheless, he beamed a glittering smile in her direction. 'Sorry,' he sang out. 'Blasted car trouble.'

'See here, mate,' she said in the unmistakable discordant twang – all long a's becoming long i's – of a denizen of Deepest Down Under, 'when Romance of Great Britain pays for a tour at noon, Romance of Great Britain expects the bleeding tour to begin at noon. So why're you late? Christ, it's like Siberia out here. We could die of exposure. Jaysus, let's just get on with it.' She turned on her heel and waved her charges over towards the edge of the car park where the footpath carved a trail round the circumference of the battlefield.

Malcolm dashed to catch up. His tips hanging in the balance, he would have to make up for his tardiness with a dazzling show of expertise.

'Yes, yes,' he said with insincere joviality as he reached her side. 'It's incredible that you should mention Siberia, Miss . . . ?'

'Sludgecur,' she said, and her expression dared him to react to the name.

'Ah. Yes. Miss Sludgecur. Of course. As I was saying, it's incredible that you should mention Siberia because this bit of England has the highest elevation west of the Urals. Which is why we have these rather Muscovian temperatures. You can imagine what it might have been like in the fifteenth century when—'

'We're not here for meteorology,' she barked. 'Get on with it before my ladies freeze their arses off.'

Her ladies tittered and clung to one another in

the wind. They had the dried apple faces of octo-genarians, and they watched Sludgecur with the devotion of children who'd seen their parent take on all comers and deck them unceremoniously.

'Yes, well,' Malcolm said. 'The weather's the principal reason that the battlefield's closed in the winter. We made an exception for your group because they're fellow Ricardians. And when fellow Ricardians come calling at Bosworth, we like to accommodate them. It's the best way to see that the truth gets carried forward, as I'm sure you'll agree.'

'What the bloody hell are you yammering about?' Sludgecur asked. 'Fellow who? Fellow what?'

Which should have told Malcolm that the tour wasn't going to proceed as smoothly as he had hoped. 'Ricardians,' he said and beamed at the elderly women surrounding Sludgecur. 'Believers in the innocence of Richard III.'

Sludgecur looked at him as if he'd sprouted wings. 'What? This is the Romance of Great Britain you're looking at, mate. Jane Bloody Eyre, Mr Flaming Rochester, Heathcliff and Cathy, Maxim de Winter. Gabriel Oak. This is Love on the Battlefield Day, and we mean to have our money's worth. All right?'

Their money was what it was all about. The fact that they were paying was why Malcolm was here in the first place. But, Jesus, he thought, did these Seekers of Romance even know where they were? Did they know – much less care – that the last King to be killed in armed combat met his fate less than a mile from where they were standing? *And* that he'd met that same fate because of sedition, treachery, and betrayal? Obviously not. They weren't here in support of Richard. They were here because it was part of a package. Love Brooding, Love Hopeless, and Love Devoted had already been checked off the list. And now he was somehow supposed to cook up for them a version of Love Deadly that would make them part with a few quid apiece at the end of the afternoon. Well, all right. He could do that much.

Malcolm didn't think about Betsy until he'd paused at the first marker along the route, which showed King Richard's initial battle position. While his charges took snapshots of the White Boar standard that was whipping in the icy wind from the flagpole marking the King's encampment, Malcolm glanced beyond them to the tumbledown buildings of Windsong Farm, visible at the top of the next hill. He could see the house and he could see Betsy's car in the farmyard. He could imagine – and hope about – the rest.

Bernie wouldn't have noticed that it had taken his wife three and a half hours to purchase a package of minced beef in Market Bosworth. It was nearly half past noon, after all, and doubtless he'd be at the kitchen table where he usually was, attempting to work on yet another of his Formula One models. The pieces would be spread out in front of him and he might have managed to glue one onto the car before the shakes came upon him and he had to have a dose of Black Bush to still them. One dose of whiskey would have led to another until he was too soused to handle a tube of glue.

Chances were good that he'd already passed out onto the model car. It was Saturday and he was supposed to work at St James Church, preparing it for Sunday's service. But poor old Bernie'd have no idea of the day until Betsy returned, slammed the minced beef onto the table next to his ear, and frightened him out of his sodden slumber.

When his head flew up, Betsy would see the imprint of the car's name on his flesh, and she'd be suitably disgusted. Malcolm fresh in her mind, she'd feel the injustice of her position.

'You been to the church yet?' she'd ask Bernie. It was his only job, as no Perryman had farmed the family's land in at least eight generations. 'Father Naughton's not like the others, Bernie. He's not about to put up with you just because you're a Perryman, you know. You got the church *and* the graveyard to see to today. And it's time you were about it.'

Bernie had never been a belligerent drunk, and he wouldn't be one now. He'd say, 'I'm going, sweet Mama. But I got the most godawful thirst. Throat feels like a sandpit, Mama girl.'

He'd smile the same affable smile that had won Betsy's heart in Blackpool where they'd met. And the smile would remind his wife of her duty, despite

Malcolm's ministrations to her earlier. But that was fine, because the last thing that Malcolm Cousins wanted was Betsy Perryman forgetting her duty.

So she'd ask him if he'd taken his medicine, and since Bernie Perryman never did anything – save pour himself a Black Bush – without having been reminded a dozen times, the answer would be no. So Betsy would seek out the pills and shake the dosage into her palm. And Bernie would take it obediently and then stagger out of the house – sans jacket as usual – and head to St James Church to do his duty.

Betsy would call after him to take his jacket, but Bernie would wave off the suggestion. His wife would shout, 'Bernie! You'll catch your death—' and then stop herself at the sudden thought that entered her mind. Bernie's death, after all, was what she needed in order to be with her Beloved.

So her glance would drop to the bottle of pills in her hand and she would read the label: *Digitoxin. Do not exceed one tablet per day without consulting physician.*

Perhaps at that point, she would also hear the doctor's explanation to her: 'It's like digitalis. You've heard of that. An overdose would kill him, Mrs Perryman, so you must be vigilant and see to it that he never takes more than one tablet.'

More than one tablet would ring in her ears. Her morning bonk with Malcolm would live in her memory. She'd shake a pill from the bottle and examine it. She'd finally start to think of a way that the future could be massaged into place.

Happily, Malcolm turned from the farmhouse to his budding Ricardians. All was going according to plan.

'From this location,' Malcolm told his audience of eager but elderly seekers of Love on the Battlefield, 'we can see the village of Sutton Cheney to our northeast.' All heads swivelled in that direction. They may have been freezing their antique pudenda, but at least they were a cooperative group. Save for Sludgecur who, if she had a pudendum, it was no doubt swathed in long underwear. Her expression challenged him to concoct a Romance out of the Battle of Bosworth. Very well, he thought, and picked up the gauntlet. He'd give them Romance. He'd also give them a piece of history that would change their lives. Perhaps this group of Aussie oldies hadn't been Ricardians when they'd arrived at Bosworth Field, but they'd damn well be neophyte Ricardians when they left. *And* they'd return Down Under and tell their grandchildren that it was Malcolm Cousins – *the* Malcolm Cousins, they would say – who had first made them aware of the gross injustice that had been perpetrated upon the memory of a decent King.

'It was there in the village of Sutton Cheney, in St James Church, that King Richard prayed on the night before the battle,' Malcolm told them. 'Picture what the night must have been like.'

From there, he went onto automatic pilot. He'd told the story hundreds of times over the years that he'd served as Special Guide for Groups at Bosworth Field. All he had to do was to milk it for its Romantic Qualities, which wasn't a problem.

The King's forces – 12,000 strong – were encamped on the summit of Ambion Hill where Malcolm Cousins and his band of shivering Neo-Ricardians were standing. The King knew that the morrow would decide his fate: whether he would continue to reign as Richard III or whether his crown would be taken by conquest and worn by an upstart who'd lived most of his life on the Continent, safely tucked away and coddled by those whose ambitions had long been to destroy the York dynasty. The King would have been well aware that his fate rested in the hands of the Stanley brothers: Sir William and Thomas, Lord Stanley. They had arrived at Bosworth with a large army and were encamped to the north, not far from the King, but also – and ominously – not far from the King's pernicious adversary, Henry Tudor, Earl of Richmond, who also happened to be Lord Stanley's stepson. To secure the father's loyalty, King Richard had taken one of Lord Stanley's blood sons as a hostage, the young man's life being the forfeit if his father betrayed England's anointed King by joining Tudor's forces in the upcoming battle. The Stanleys, however, were a wily lot and had shown themselves dedicated to nothing but their own self-interest, so – holding George Stanley hostage or not – the King must have known how great was the risk of entrusting the security of his throne to the whimsies of men whose devotion to self was their most notable quality.

The night before the battle, Richard would have seen the Stanleys camped to the north, in the direction of Market Bosworth. He would have sent a messenger to remind them that, as George Stanley was still being held hostage and as he was being held hostage right there in the King's encampment, the wise course would be to throw their lot in with the King on the morrow.

He would have been restless, Richard. He would have been torn. Having lost first his son and heir and then his wife during his brief reign, having been faced with the treachery of once-close friends, can there be any doubt that he would have wondered – if only fleetingly – how much longer he was meant to go on? And, schooled in the religion of his time, can there be any doubt that he knew how great a sin was despair? And, having established this fact, can there be any question about what the King would have chosen to do on the night before the battle?

Malcolm glanced over his group. Yes, there was a satisfactorily misty eye or two among them. They

saw the inherent Romance in a widowed King who'd
lost not only his wife but his heir and was hours away
from losing his life as well.

Malcolm directed a victorious glance at Sludgecur.
Her expression said, Don't press your luck.

It wasn't luck at all, Malcolm wanted to tell her.
It was the Great Romance of Hearing the Truth. The
wind had picked up velocity and lost another three
or four degrees of temperature, but his little band
of Antique Aussies were caught in the thrall of that
August night in 1485.

The night before the battle, Malcolm told them,
knowing that if he lost, he would die, Richard
would have sought to be shriven. History tells us
that there were no priests or chaplains available
among Richard's forces, so what better place to find
a confessor than in St James Church. The church
would have been quiet as Richard entered. A votive
candle or rushlight would have burned in the nave,
but nothing more. The only sound inside the building
would have come from Richard himself as he moved
from the doorway to kneel before the altar: the
rustle of his fustian doublet (satin-lined, Malcolm

informed his scholars, knowing the importance of detail to the Romantic Minded), the creak of leather from his heavy soled battle shoes and from his scabbard, the clank of his sword and dagger as he—

'Oh my goodness,' a Romantic Neo-Ricardian chirruped. 'What sort of man would take swords and daggers into a church?'

Malcolm smiled winsomely. He thought, A man who had a bloody good use for them, just the very things needed for a bloke who wanted to prise loose a stone. But what he said was, 'Unusual, of course. One doesn't think of someone carrying weapons into a church, does one? But this was the night before the battle. Richard's enemies were everywhere. He wouldn't have walked into the darkness unprotected.'

Whether the King wore his crown that night into the church, no one can say, Malcolm continued. But if there was a priest in the church to hear his confession, that same priest left Richard to his prayers soon after giving him absolution. And there in the darkness, lit only by the small rushlight in the nave, Richard made peace with his Lord God and prepared to meet the fate that the next day's battle promised him.

Malcolm eyed his audience, gauging their reactions and their attentiveness. They were entirely with him. They were, he hoped, thinking about how much they should tip him for giving a bravura performance in the deadly wind.

His prayers finished, Malcolm informed them, the King unsheathed his sword and dagger, set them on the rough wooden bench, and sat next to them. And there in the church, King Richard laid his plans to ruin Henry Tudor should the upstart be the victor in the morrow's battle. Because Richard knew that he held – and had always held – the whip hand over Henry Tudor. He held it in life as a proven and victorious battle commander. He would hold it in death as the single force who could destroy the usurper.

'Goodness me,' someone murmured appreciatively. Yes, Malcolm's listeners were fully attuned to the Romance of the Moment. Thank God.

Richard, he told them, wasn't oblivious of the scheming that had been going on between Henry

Tudor and Elizabeth Woodville – widow of his brother Edward IV and mother of the two young Princes whom he had earlier placed in the Tower of London.

'The Princes in the Tower,' another voice remarked. 'That's the two little boys who—'

'The very ones,' Malcolm said solemnly. 'Richard's own nephews.'

The King would have known that, holding true to her propensity for buttering her bread not only on both sides but along the crust as well, Elizabeth Woodville had promised the hand of her eldest daughter to Tudor should he obtain the crown of England. But should Tudor obtain the crown of England on the morrow, Richard also knew that every man, woman, and child with a drop of York blood in his body stood in grave danger of being eliminated – permanently – as a claimant to the throne. And this included Elizabeth Woodville's children.

He himself ruled by right of succession and by law. Descended directly – and more important legitimately from Edward III – he had come to the throne after the death of his brother Edward IV, upon the revelation of the licentious Edward's secret pledge of marriage to another woman long before his marriage to Elizabeth Woodville. This pledged contract of marriage had been made before a bishop of the church. As such, it was as good as a marriage performed with pomp and circumstance before a thousand onlookers, and it effectively made Edward's later marriage to Elizabeth Woodville bigamous at the same time as it bastardized all of their children.

Henry Tudor would have known that the children had been declared illegitimate by an Act of Parliament. He would also have known that, should he be victorious in his confrontation with Richard III, his tenuous claim to the throne of England would not be shored up by marriage to the bastard daughter of a dead King. So he would have to do something about her illegitimacy.

King Richard would have concluded this once he heard the news that Tudor had pledged to marry the girl. He would also have known that to legitimatize Elizabeth of York was also to legitimatize all her sisters . . . and her brothers. One could not declare the eldest child of a dead King legitimate while simultaneously claiming her siblings were not.

Malcolm paused meaningfully in his narrative. He waited to see if the eager Romantics gathered round him would twig the implication. They smiled and nodded and looked at him fondly, but no one said anything. So Malcolm did their twigging for them.

'Her brothers,' he said patiently, and slowly to make sure they absorbed each Romantic detail. 'If Henry Tudor legitimatized Elizabeth of York prior to marrying her, he would have been legitimatising her brothers as well. And if he did that, the elder of the boys—'

'Gracious me,' one of the group sang out. '*He* would've been the true King once Richard died.'

Bless you, my child, Malcolm thought. 'That,' he cried, 'is exactly spot on.'

'See here, mate,' Sludgecur interrupted, some sort of light dawning in the cobwebbed reaches of her brain. 'I've heard this story, and Richard killed those little blighters himself while they were in the Tower.'

Another fish biting the Tudor bait, Malcolm realized. Five hundred years later and that scheming

Welsh upstart was still successfully reeling them in. He could hardly wait until the day when his book came out, when his history of Richard was heralded as the triumph of truth over Tudor casuistry.

He was Patience itself as he explained. The Princes in the Tower – Edward IV's two sons – had indeed been long reputed by tradition to have been murdered by their uncle Richard III to shore up his position as King. But there were no witnesses to any murder and as Richard was King through an Act of Parliament, he had no motive to kill them. And since he had no direct heir to the throne – his own son having died, as you heard moments ago – what better way to ensure the Yorks' continued possession of the throne of England than to designate the two Princes legitimate . . . after his own death? Such designation could only be made by Papal decree at this point, but Richard had sent two emissaries to Rome and why send them such a distance unless it was to arrange for the legitimatizing of the very boys whose rights had been wrested from them by their father's lascivious conduct?

'The boys were indeed rumoured to be dead,'

Malcolm aimed for kindness in his tone. 'But that rumour, interestingly enough, never saw the light of day until just before Henry Tudor's invasion of England. He wanted to be King, but he had no rights to kingship. So he had to discredit the reigning monarch. Could there possibly be a more efficacious way to do it than by spreading the word that the Princes – who were gone from the Tower – were actually dead? But this is the question I pose to you, ladies: What if they weren't?'

An appreciative murmur went through the group. Malcolm heard one of the ancients commenting, 'Lovely eyes, he has', and he turned them towards the sound of her voice. She looked like his grandmother. She also looked rich. He increased the wattage of his charm.

'What if the two boys had been removed from the Tower by Richard's own hand, sent into safe-keeping against a possible uprising? Should Henry Tudor prevail at Bosworth Field, those two boys would be in grave danger and King Richard knew it. Tudor was pledged to their sister. To marry her, he had to declare her legitimate. Declaring her legitimate made them legitimate. Making them legitimate made one of them – young Edward – the true and rightful King of England. The only way for Tudor to prevent this was to get rid of them. Permanently.'

Malcolm waited a moment to let this sink in. He noted the collection of grey heads turning towards Sutton Cheney. Then towards the north valley where a flagpole flew the seditious Stanleys' standard. Then over towards the peak of Ambion Hill where the unforgiving wind whipped Richard's White Boar briskly. Then down the slope in the direction of the railway tracks where the Tudor mercenaries had once formed their meagre front line. Vastly outnumbered, outgunned, and outarmed, they would have been waiting for the Stanleys to make their move: for King Richard or against him. Without the Stanleys' throwing their lot in with Tudor's, the day would be lost.

The Grey Ones were clearly with him, Malcolm noted. But Sludgecur was not so easily drawn in. 'How was Tudor supposed to kill them if they were gone from the Tower?' She'd taken to beating her hands against her arms, doubtless wishing she were pummelling his face.

'He didn't kill them,' Malcolm said pleasantly, 'although his Machiavellian fingerprints are all over the crime. No. Tudor wasn't directly involved. I'm afraid the situation's a little nastier than that. Shall we walk on and discuss it, ladies?'

'Lovely little bum as well,' one of the group murmured. 'Quite a crumpet, that bloke.'

Ah, they were in his palm. Malcolm felt himself warm to his own seductive talents.

He knew that Betsy was watching from the farmhouse, from the first floor bedroom from which she could see the battlefield. How could she possibly keep herself from doing so after their morning together? She'd see Malcolm shepherding his little band from site to site, she'd note that they were hanging onto his every word, and she'd think about how she herself had hung upon him less than two hours earlier. And the contrast between her drunken sot of a husband and her virile lover would be painfully and mightily on her mind.

This would make her realize how wasted she was on Bernie Perryman. She was, she would think, forty years old and at the prime of her life. She deserved better than Bernie. She deserved, in fact, a man who understood God's plan when He'd created the first man and woman. He'd used the man's rib, hadn't He? In doing that, He'd illustrated for all time that women and men were bound together, women taking their form and substance from their men, living their lives in the service of their men for which their reward was to be sheltered and protected by their men's superior strength. But Bernie Perryman only ever saw one half of the man-woman equation. She – Betsy – was to work in his service, care for him, feed him, see to his wellbeing. He – Bernie – was to do nothing. Oh, he'd make a feeble attempt to give her a length now and again if the mood was upon him and he could keep it up long enough. But whiskey had long since robbed him of whatever ability he'd once had to be pleasing to a woman. And as for understanding her subtler needs and his responsibility in meeting them . . . forget that area of life altogether.

Malcolm liked to think of Betsy in these terms: up in her barren bedroom in the farmhouse, nursing a righteous grievance against her husband. She would proceed from that grievance to the realisation that he, Malcolm Cousins, was the man she'd been intended for, and she would see how every other relationship in her life had been but a prologue to the connection she now had with him. She and Malcolm, she would conclude, were suited for each other in every way.

Watching him on the battlefield, she would recall their initial meeting and the fire that had existed between them from the first day when Betsy had begun to work at Gloucester Grammar as the Headmaster's Secretary. She'd recall the spark she'd felt when Malcolm had said, 'Bernie Perryman's wife?' and admired her openly. 'Old Bernie's been holding back on me, and I thought we shared every secret of our souls.' She would remember how she'd asked, 'You know Bernie?' still in the blush of her newlywed bliss and not yet aware of how Bernie's drinking was going to impair his ability to care for her. And she'd well remember Malcolm's response: 'Have done for years. We grew up together, went to school together, spent holidays roaming the countryside. We even shared our first woman—' and she'd remember his smile – 'so we're practically blood brothers if it comes to that. But I can see there might be a decided impediment to our future relationship, Betsy.' And his eyes had held hers just long enough for her to realize that her newlywed bliss wasn't nearly as hot as the look he was giving her.

From that upstairs bedroom, she'd see that the group Malcolm was squiring round the field comprised women, and she'd begin to worry. The distance from the farmhouse to the field would prevent her from seeing that Malcolm's antiquated audience had one collective foot in the collective grave, so her thoughts would turn ineluctably to the possibilities implied by his current circumstances. What was to prevent one of those women from becoming captivated by the enchantment he offered?

These thoughts would lead to her desperation, which was what Malcolm had been assiduously massaging for months, whispering at the most tender of moments, 'Oh God, if I'd only known what it was going to be like to have you, finally. And now to want you completely . . .' And then the tears, wept into her hair, and the revelation of the agonies of guilt and despair he experienced each time he rolled deliciously within the arms of his old friend's wife. 'I can't bear to hurt him, darling Bets. If you and he were to divorce . . . How could I ever live with myself if he ever knew how I've betrayed our friendship?'

She'd remember this, in the farmhouse bedroom with her hot forehead pressed to the cold window-pane. They'd been together for three hours that morning, but she'd realize that it was not enough. It would never be enough to sneak round as they were doing, to pretend indifference to each other when they met at Gloucester Grammar. Until they were a couple – legally, as much as they were already a couple spiritually, mentally, emotionally, and physically – she could never have peace.

But Bernie stood between her and happiness, she would think. Bernie Perryman, driven to alcohol by the demon of fear that the congenital abnormality that had taken his grandfather, his father, and both of his brothers before their forty-fifth birthdays would claim him as well. 'Weak heart,' Bernie had doubtless told her, since he'd used it as an excuse for everything he'd done – and not done – for the last thirty years. 'It don't ever pump like it ought. Just a little flutter when it oughter be a thud. Got to be careful. Got to take m' pills.'

But if Betsy didn't remind her husband to take his pills daily, he was likely to forget there were pills altogether, let alone a reason for taking them. It was almost as if he had a death wish, Bernie Perryman. It was almost as if he was only waiting for the appropriate moment to set her free.

And once she was free, Betsy would think, The Legacy would be hers. And The Legacy was the key to her future with Malcolm. Because with The Legacy in hand at last, she and Malcolm could marry and Malcolm could leave his ill-paying job at Gloucester Grammar. Content with his research, his writing, and his lecturing, he would be filled with gratitude for her having made his new lifestyle possible. Grateful, he would be eager to meet her needs.

Which is, she would think, certainly how it was meant to be.

*　　*　　*

In the Plantagenet pub in Sutton Cheney, Malcolm counted the tip money from his morning's labour. He'd given his all, but the Aussie Oldies had proved to be a niggardly lot. He'd ended up with forty pounds for the tour and lecture – which was an awesomely cheap price considering the depth of information he imparted – and twenty-five pounds in tips. Thank God for the pound coin, he concluded morosely. Without it, the tightfisted old sluts would probably have parted with nothing more than fifty pence apiece.

He pocketed the money as the pub door opened and a gust of icy air whooshed into the room. The flames of the fire next to him bobbled. Ash from the fireplace blew onto the hearth. Malcolm looked up. Bernie Perryman – clad only in cowboy boots, blue jeans, and a T-shirt with the words *Team Ferrari* printed on it – staggered drunkenly into the pub. Malcolm tried to shrink out of view, but it was impossible. After the prolonged exposure to the wind on Bosworth Field, his need for warmth had taken him to the blazing beechwood fire. This put him directly in Bernie's sightline.

'Malkie!' Bernie cried out joyfully, and went on as he always did whenever they met. 'Malkie ol' mate! How 'bout a chess game? I miss our matches, I surely do.' He shivered and beat his hands against his arms. His lips were practically blue. 'Shit on toast. It's blowing a cold one out there. Pour me a Blackie,' he called out to the publican. 'Make it a double and make it double quick.' He grinned and dropped onto the stool at Malcolm's table. 'So. How's the book comin', Malkie? Gotcher name in lights? Found a publisher yet?' He giggled.

Malcolm put aside whatever guilt he may have felt at the fact that he was industriously stuffing this inebriate's wife whenever his middle-aged body was up to the challenge. Bernie Perryman deserved to be a cuckold, his punishment for the torment he'd been dishing out to Malcolm for the last ten years.

'Never got over that last game, did you?' Bernie grinned again. He was served his Black Bush which he tossed back in a single gulp. He blubbered air out between his lips. He said, 'Did me right, that,' and called for another. 'Now what was the full-on tale again, Malkie? You get to the good part of the story yet? 'Course, it'll be a tough one to prove, won't it, mate?'

Malcolm counted to ten. Bernie was presented with his second double whiskey. It went the way of the first.

'But I'm givin' you a bad time for nothing,' Bernie said, suddenly repentant in the way of all drunks. 'You never did me a bad turn – 'cept that time with the A levels, 'course – and I shouldn't do you one. I wish you the best. Truly, I do. It's just that things never work out the way they're s'posed to, do they?'

Which, Malcolm thought, was the whole bloody point. Things – as Bernie liked to call them – hadn't worked out for Richard either, that fatal morning on Bosworth Field. The Earl of Northumberland had let him down, the Stanleys had out-and-out betrayed him, and an untried upstart who had neither the skill nor the courage to face the King personally in decisive combat had won the day.

'So tell Bern your theory another time. I love the story, I do, I do. I just wished there was a way for you to prove it. It'd be the making of you, that book would. How long you been working on the manuscript?' Bernie swiped the interior of his whiskey glass with a dirty finger and licked off the residue. He wiped his mouth on the back of his hand. He hadn't shaved that morning. He hadn't bathed in days. For a moment, Malcolm almost felt sorry for Betsy, having to live in the same house with the odious man.

'I've come to Elizabeth of York,' Malcolm said as pleasantly as he could manage, considering the antipathy he was feeling for Bernie. 'Edward IV's daughter. Future wife to the King of England.'

Bernie smiled, showing teeth in serious need of cleaning. 'Cor, I always forget that bird, Malkie. Why's that, d'you think?'

Because everyone always forgot Elizabeth, Malcolm said silently. The eldest daughter of Edward IV, she was generally consigned to a footnote in history as the oldest sister of the Princes in the Tower, the dutiful daughter of Elizabeth Woodville, a pawn in the political power game, the later wife of that Tudor usurper Henry VII. Her job was to carry the seed of the dynasty, to deliver the heirs, and to fade into obscurity.

But here was a woman who was one-half Woodville, with the thick blood of that scheming and ambitious clan coursing through her veins. That she wanted to be Queen of England like her mother before her had been established in the seventeenth century when Sir George Buck had written – in his *History of the Life and Reigne of Richard III* – of young Elizabeth's letter asking the Duke of Norfolk to be the mediator between herself and King Richard on the subject of their marriage, telling him that she was the King's in heart and in thought. That she was as ruthless as her two parents was made evident in the fact that her letter to Norfolk was written prior to the death of Richard's wife, Queen Anne.

Young Elizabeth had been bundled out of London and up to Yorkshire, ostensibly for safety's sake, prior to Henry Tudor's invasion. There she resided at Sheriff Hutton, a stronghold deep in the country-side where loyalty to King Richard was a constant of life. Elizabeth would be well-protected – not to mention well-guarded – in Yorkshire. As would be her siblings.

'You still hot for Lizzie?' Bernie asked with

a chuckle. 'Cor, how you used to go on about that girl.'

Malcolm suppressed his rage but did not forbid himself from silently cursing the other man into eternal torment. Bernie had a deep aversion for anyone who tried to make something of his life. That sort of person served to remind him of what a waste he'd made of his own.

Bernie must have read something on Malcolm's face because as he called for his third double whiskey, he said, 'No, no, get on with you. I 'as only kidding. What's you doing out here today anyway? Was that you in the battlefield when I drove by?'

Bernie knew it was he, Malcolm realized. But mentioning the fact served to remind them both of Malcolm's passion and the hold that Bernie Perryman had upon it. God, how he wanted to stand on the table and shout, 'I'm bonking this idiot's wife twice a week, three or four times if I can manage it. They'd been married two months when I bonked her the first time, six days after we were introduced.'

But losing control like that was exactly what Bernie Perryman wanted of his old friend Malcolm Cousins: payback time for having once refused to help Bernie cheat his way through his A-levels. The man had an elephantine memory and a grudge-bearing spirit. But so did Malcolm.

'I don't know, Malkie,' Bernie said, shaking his head as he was presented with his whiskey. He reached unsteadily for it, his bloodless tongue wetting his lower lip. 'Don't seem natural that Lizzie'd hand those lads over to be given the chop. Not her own brothers. Not even to be Queen of England. Sides, they weren't even anywheres near her, were they? All speculation, 'f you ask me. All speculation and not a speck of proof.'

Never, Malcolm thought for the thousandth time, never tell a drunkard your secrets or your dreams.

'It was Elizabeth of York,' he said again. 'She was ultimately responsible.'

Sheriff Hutton was not an insurmountable distance from Rievaulx, Jervaulx, and Fountains Abbeys. And tucking individuals away in abbeys, convents, monasteries, and priories was a great tradition at that time. Women were the usual recipients of a one-way ticket to the ascetic life. But two young boys – disguised as youthful entrants into a novitiate – would have been safe there from the arm of Henry Tudor should he take the throne of England by means of conquest.

'Tudor would have known the boys were alive,' Malcolm said. 'When he pledged himself to marry Elizabeth, he would have known the boys were alive.'

Bernie nodded. 'Poor little tykes,' he said with factitious sorrow. 'And poor old Richard who took the blame. How'd she get her mitts on them, Malkie? What d'you think? Think she cooked up a deal with Tudor?'

'She wanted to be a Queen more than she wanted to be merely the sister to a King. There was only one way to make that happen. And Henry had been looking elsewhere for a wife at the same time that he was bargaining with Elizabeth Woodville. The girl would have known that. And what it meant.'

Bernie nodded solemnly, as if he cared a half fig for what had happened more than five hundred years ago on an August night not two hundred yards from the pub in which they sat. He shot back his third double whiskey and slapped his stomach like a man at the end of a hearty meal.

'Got the church all prettied up for tomorrow,' he informed Malcolm. ''Mazing when you think of it, Malkie. Perrymans been tinkering round St James Church for two hundred years. Like a family pedigree, that. Don't you think? Remarkable, I'd say.'

Malcolm regarded him evenly. 'Utterly remarkable, Bernie,' he said.

'Ever think how different life might've been if your dad and granddad and his granddad before him were the ones who tinkered round St James Church? P'rhaps I'd be you and you'd be me. What d'you think of that?'

What Malcolm thought of that couldn't be spoken to the man sitting opposite him at the table. Die, he thought. Die before I kill you myself.

'Do you want to be together, darling?' Betsy breathed the question wetly into his ear. Another Saturday. Another three hours of bonking Betsy. Malcolm wondered how much longer he'd have to continue with the charade.

He wanted to ask her to move over – the woman was capable of inducing claustrophobia with more efficacy than a plastic bag – but at this point in their relationship he knew that a demonstration of post-coital togetherness was as important to his ultimate objective as was a top-notch performance between the sheets. And since his age, his inclinations, and his energy were all combining to take his performances down a notch each time he sank between Betsy's well-padded thighs, he realized the wisdom of allowing her to cling, coo, and cuddle for as long as he could endure it without screaming once the primal act was completed between them.

'We *are* together,' he said, stroking her hair. It was wire-like to the touch, the result of too much bleaching and even more hair spray. 'Unless you mean that you want another go. And I'll need some recovery time for that.' He turned his head and pressed his lips to her forehead. 'You take it out of me and that's the truth of it, darling Bets. You're woman enough for a dozen men.'

She giggled. 'You love it.'

'Not it. You. Love, want, and can't be without.'
He sometimes pondered where he came up with the
nonsense he told her. It was as if a primitive part of
his brain reserved for female seduction went onto
autopilot whenever Betsy climbed into his bed.

She buried her fingers in his ample chest hair. 'I
mean really be together, darling. Do you want it?
The two of us? Like this? Forever? Do you want it
more than anything on earth?'

The thought alone was like being imprisoned in
concrete. But he said, 'Darling Bets,' by way of
answer and he trembled his voice appropriately.
'Don't. Please. We can't go through this again.'
And he pulled her roughly to him because he
knew that was the move she desired. He sank
his face into the curve of her shoulder and neck.
He breathed through his mouth to avoid inhaling
the day's litre of Shalimar that she'd doused herself
with. He made the whimpering noises of a man
in extremis. God, what he wouldn't do for King
Richard.

'I was on the Internet,' she whispered, fingers

caressing the back of his neck. 'In the school library. All Thursday and Friday lunch, darling.'

He stopped his whimpering, sifting through this declaration for deeper meaning. 'Were you?' He temporised by nibbling at her ear lobe, waiting for more information. It came obliquely.

'You *do* love me, don't you, Malcolm dearest?'

'What do you think?'

'And you do want me, don't you?'

'That's obvious, isn't it?'

'Forever and ever?'

Whatever it takes, he thought. And he did his best to prove it to her, although his body wasn't up to a full performance.

Afterwards, while she was dressing, she said, 'I was so surprised to see all the topics. You c'n look up anything on the Internet. Fancy that, Malcolm. Anything at all. Bernie's playing in chess night at the Plantagenet, dearest. Tonight, that is.'

Malcolm furrowed his brow, automatically seeking the connection between these apparently unrelated topics. She went on.

'He misses your games, Bernie does. He always

wishes you'd come by on chess night and give it another go with him, darling.' She padded to the chest of drawers where she began repairing her make-up. ''Course, he doesn't play well. Just uses chess as an extra excuse to go to the pub.'

Malcolm watched her, eyes narrowed, waiting for a sign.

She gave it to him. 'I worry about him, Malcolm dear. His poor heart's going to give out someday. I'm going with him tonight. Perhaps we'll see you there? Malcolm, dearest, do you love me? Do you want to be together more than anything on earth?'

He saw that she was watching him closely in the mirror even as she repaired the damage he'd done to her make-up. She was painting her lips into bee-stung bows. She was brushing her cheeks with blusher. But all the time she was observing him.

'More than life itself,' he said.

And when she smiled, he knew he'd given her the correct answer.

That night at the Plantagenet pub, Malcolm joined

the Sutton Cheney Chessmen, of whose society he'd once been a regular member. Bernie Perryman was delighted to see him. He deserted his regular opponent – seventy-year-old Angus Ferguson who used the excuse of playing chess at the Plantagenet to get as sloshed as Bernie – and pressed Malcolm into a game at a table in the smoky corner of the pub. Betsy was right, naturally: Bernie drank far more than he played, and the Black Bush served to oil the mechanism of his conversation. So he also talked incessantly.

He talked to Betsy, who was playing the role of serving-wench for her husband that evening. From half past seven until half past ten, she trotted back and forth from the bar, bringing Bernie one double Black Bush after another, saying, 'You're drinking too much,' and 'This is the last one, Bernie,' in a monitory fashion. But he always managed to talk her into 'just one more wet one, Mama girl', and he patted her bum, winked at Malcolm and whispered loudly what he intended to do to her once he got her home. Malcolm was at the point of thinking he'd utterly misunderstood Betsy's implied message to him in bed that morning when she finally made her move.

It came at half past ten, one hour before George the Publican called for last orders. The pub was packed, and Malcolm might have missed her manoeuvre altogether had he not anticipated that something was going to happen that night. As Bernie nodded over the chessboard, contemplating his next move eternally, Betsy went to the bar for yet another 'double Blackie'. To do this, she had to shoulder her way through the Sutton Cheney Dartsmen, the Wardens of the Church, a women's support group from Dadlington, and a group of teenagers intent upon success with a fruit machine. She paused in conversation with a balding woman who seemed to be admiring Betsy's hair with that sort of artificial enthusiasm women reserve for other women whom they particularly hate, and it was while she and the other chatted that Malcolm saw her empty the vial into Bernie's tumbler.

He was awestruck at the ease with which she did it. She must have been practising the move for days, he realized. She was so adept that she did it with one hand as she chatted: slipping the vial out of her sweater sleeve, uncapping it, dumping it, returning it to her sweater. She finished her conversation, and she continued on her way. And no one save Malcolm was wise to the fact that she'd done something more than merely fetch another whiskey for her husband. Malcolm eyed her with new respect when she set the glass in front of Bernie. He was glad he had no intention of hooking himself up with the murderous bitch.

He knew what was in the glass: the results of Betsy's few hours surfing the Internet. She'd crushed at least ten tablets of Digitoxin into a lethal powder. An hour after Bernie ingested the mixture, he'd be a dead man.

Ingest it Bernie did. He drank it down the way he drank down every double Black Bush he encountered: he poured it directly down his throat and wiped his mouth on the back of his hand. Malcolm had lost count of the number of whiskeys Bernie had imbibed that evening, but it seemed to him that if the drug didn't kill him, the alcohol certainly would.

'Bernie,' Betsy said mournfully, 'let's go home.'

'Can't just yet,' Bernie said. 'Got to finish my bit with Malkie boy here. We haven't had us a chess-up in years. Not since . . .' He smiled at Malcolm blearily. 'Why, I 'member that night up the farm, doanchew, Malkie? Ten years back? Longer was it? When we played that last game, you and me?'

Malcolm didn't want to get onto that subject. He said, 'Your move, Bernie. Or do you want to call it a draw?'

'No way, Joe-zay.' Bernie swayed on his stool and studied the board.

'Bernie . . .' Betsy said coaxingly.

He patted her hand, which she'd laid on his shoulder. 'You g'wan, Bets. I c'n find my way home. Malkie'll drive me, woanchew, Malkie?' He dug his car keys out of his pocket and pressed them into his wife's palm. 'But doanchew fall asleep, sweet Mama. We got business together when I get home.'

Betsy made a show of reluctance and a secondary show of her concern that Malcolm might have had too much to drink himself and thereby be an unsafe driver for her precious Bernie to ride along with. Bernie said, ''F he can't do a straight line in the car park, I'll walk. Promise, Mama. Cross m' heart.'

Betsy levelled a meaningful look at Malcolm. She said, 'See that you keep him safe, then.'

Malcolm nodded. Betsy departed. and all that was left was the waiting.

For someone who was supposed to be suffering from congenital heart failure, Bernie Perryman seemed to have the constitution of a mule. An hour later, Malcolm had him in the car and was driving him home, and Bernie was still talking like a man with a new lease on life. He was just itching to get up those farmhouse stairs and rip off his wife's knickers, to hear him tell it. Nothing but the Day of Judgement was going to stop Bernie from showing his Sweet Mama the time of her life.

By the time Malcolm had taken the longest route possible to get to the farm without raising Bernie's suspicions, he'd begun to believe that his paramour hadn't slipped her husband an overdose of his medication at all. It was only when Bernie got out of the car at the edge of the drive that Malcolm had his hopes renewed. Bernie said, 'Feel peaked a bit, Malkie. Whew. Nice lie down. Tha's just the ticket', and staggered in the direction of the distant house. Malcolm watched him until he toppled into the hedgerow at the side of the drive. When he didn't move after the fall, Malcolm knew that the deed had finally been done.

He drove off happily. If Bernie hadn't been dead when he hit the ground, Malcolm knew that he'd be dead by the morning.

Wonderful, he thought. It may have been ages in the execution, but his well laid plan was going to pay off.

Malcolm had worried a bit that Betsy might muff her role in the ensuing drama. But during the next few days, she proved herself to be an actress of formidable talents. Having awakened in the morning to discover herself alone in the bed, she'd done what any sensible wife-of-a-drunk would do: she went looking for her husband. She didn't find him anywhere in the house or in the other farm buildings, so she placed a few phone calls. She checked the pub;

she checked the church; she checked with Malcolm. Had Malcolm not seen her poison her husband with his own eyes, he would have been convinced that on the other end of the line was a woman anxious for the welfare of her man. But then, she *was* anxious, wasn't she? She needed a corpse to prove Bernie was dead.

'I dropped him at the end of the drive,' Malcolm told her, help and concern personified. 'He was heading up to the house the last I saw him, Bets.'

So out she went and found Bernie exactly where he'd fallen on the previous night. And her discovery of his body set the necessary events in motion.

An inquest was called, of course. But it proved to be a mere formality. Bernie's history of heart problems and his 'difficulty with the drink', as the authorities put it, combined with the fiercely inclement weather they'd been having to provide the coroner's jury with a most reasonable conclusion. Bernie Perryman was declared dead of exposure, having passed out on the coldest night of the year, teetering up the lengthy drive to the farmhouse after a full night of drink at the Plantagenet pub, where sixteen witnesses called to testify had seen him down at least eleven double whiskeys in less than three hours.

There was no reason to check for toxicity in his blood. Especially once his doctor said that it was a miracle the man had lived to forty-nine, considering the medical history of his family, not to mention his 'problem with the drink'.

So Bernie was buried at the side of his forebears, in the graveyard of St James Church, where his father and all the fathers before him for at least the past two hundred years had toiled in the cause of a neat and tidy house of worship.

Malcolm soothed what few pangs of guilt he had over Bernie's passing by ignoring them. Bernie'd had a history of heart disease. Bernie had been a notorious drunk. If Bernie, in his cups, had passed out on the driveway a mere fifty yards from his house and died from exposure as a result . . . well, who could possibly hold himself responsible?

And while it was sad that Bernie Perryman had had to give his life for the cause of Malcolm's search for the truth, it was also the truth that he'd brought his premature death upon himself.

After the funeral, Malcolm knew that all he needed to employ was patience. He hadn't spent the last two years industriously ploughing Betsy's field, only to be thwarted by a display of unseemly haste at the moment of harvest. Besides, Betsy was doing enough bit chomping for both of them, so he knew it was only a matter of days – perhaps hours – before she took herself off to the Perrymans' longtime solicitor for an accounting of the inheritance that was coming her way.

Malcolm had pictured the moment enough times during his liaison with Betsy. Sometimes picturing the moment when Betsy learned the truth was the only fantasy that got him through his interminable lovemaking sessions with the woman.

Howard Smythe-Thomas would open his Nuneaton office to her and break the news in a suitably funereal fashion, no doubt. And perhaps at first, Betsy would think his sombre demeanour was an air adopted for the occasion. He'd begin by calling her 'My dear Mrs

Perryman', which should give her an idea that bad news was in the offing, but she wouldn't have an inkling of how bad the news was until he spelled out the bitter reality for her.

Bernie had no money. The farm had been mortgaged three times; there were no savings worth speaking of and no investments. The contents of the house and the outbuildings were hers, of course, but only by selling off every possession – and the farm itself – would Betsy be able to avoid bankruptcy. And even then, it would be touch and go. The only reason the bank hadn't foreclosed on the property before now was that the Perrymans had been doing business with that same financial institution for more than two hundred years. 'Loyalty,' Mr Smythe-Thomas would no doubt intone. 'Bernard may have had his difficulties, Mrs Perryman, but the bank had respect for his lineage. When one's father and one's father's father and his father before him have done business with a banking establishment, there is a certain leeway given that might not be given to a personage less well known to that bank.'

Which would be legal doublespeak for the fact that since there were no other Perrymans at Windsong Farm – and Mr Smythe-Thomas would be good about gently explaining that a short-term wife of a long-term alcoholic Perryman didn't count – the bank would probably be calling in Bernie's debts. She would be wise to prepare herself for that eventuality.

But what about The Legacy? Betsy would ask. 'Bernie always nattered on about a legacy.' And she would be stunned to think of the depth of her husband's deception.

Mr Smythe-Thomas, naturally, would know nothing about a legacy. And considering the Perryman history of ne'er-do-wells earning their keep by doing nothing more than working round the church in Sutton Cheney . . . He would kindly point out that it wasn't very likely that anyone had managed to amass a fortune doing handywork, was it?

It would take some hours – perhaps even days – for the news to sink into Betsy's skull. She'd think at first that there had to be some sort of mistake. Surely there were jewels hidden somewhere, cash tucked away, silver or gold or deeds to property heretofore unknown packed in the attic. And thinking this, she would begin her search. Which was exactly what Malcolm intended her to do: search first and come weeping to Malcolm second. And Malcolm himself would take it from there.

In the meantime, he happily worked on his magnum opus. The pages to the left of his typewriter piled up satisfactorily as he redeemed the reputation of England's most maligned King.

Many of the righteous fell that morning of 22 August 1485, and among them was the Duke of Norfolk, who commanded the vanguard at the front of Richard's army. When the Earl of Northumberland refused to engage his forces to come to the aid of Norfolk's leaderless men, the psychological tide of the battle shifted.

Those were the days of mass desertions, of switching loyalties, of outright betrayals on the field of battle. And both the King and his Tudor foe would have known that. Which went far to explain why both men simultaneously needed and doubted the Stanleys. Which also went far to explain why – in the midst of the battle – Henry Tudor made a run for the Stanleys, who had so far refused to enter the fray. Outnumbered as he was, Henry Tudor's cause would be lost without the Stanleys' intervention. And he wasn't above begging for it, which is why he made that desperate ride across the plain towards the Stanley forces.

King Richard intercepted him, thundering down Ambion Hill with his Knights and Esquires of the Body. The two small forces engaged each other a bare half mile from the Stanleys' men. Tudor's knights began falling quickly under the King's attack: William Brandon and the banner of Cadwallader plummeted to the ground; the enormous Sir John Cheyney fell beneath the King's own axe. It was only a matter of moments before Richard might fight his way to Henry Tudor himself, which was what the Stanleys realized when they made their decision to attack the King's small force.

In the ensuing battle, King Richard was unhorsed and could have fled the field. But declaring that he would 'die King of England', he continued to fight even when grievously wounded. It took more than one man to bring him down. And he died like the Royal Prince that he was.

The King's army fled, pursued hotly by the Earl of Oxford whose intent it would have been to kill as many of them as possible. They shot off towards the village of Stoke Golding, in the opposite direction from Sutton Cheney.

This fact was the crux of the events that followed. When one's life is hanging in the balance, when one is a blood relative of the defeated King of England, one's thoughts turn inexorably towards self-preservation. John de la Pole, Earl of Lincoln and nephew to King Richard, was among the fleeing forces. To ride towards Sutton Cheney would have put him directly into the clutches of the Earl of Northumberland who had refused to come to the King's aid and would have been only too happy to cement his position in Henry Tudor's affections – such as they were – by handing over the dead King's nephew. So he rode to the south instead of to the north. And in doing so, he condemned his uncle to five hundred years of Tudor propaganda.

Because history is written by the winners, Malcolm
thought.

Only sometimes history gets to be rewritten.

And as he rewrote it, in the back of his mind was
the picture of Betsy and her growing desperation.
In the two weeks following Bernie's death, she
hadn't returned to work. Gloucester Grammar's
Headmaster – the snivelling Samuel, as Malcolm
liked to call him – reported that Betsy was prostrate
over her husband's sudden death. She needed time
to deal with and to heal from her grief, he told the
staff sorrowfully.

Malcolm knew that what she had to deal with
was finding something that she could pass off as
The Legacy so as to bind him to her despite the
fact that her expectations of inheritance had come
to nothing. Tearing through the old farmhouse like a
wild thing, she would probably go through Bernie's
wardrobe one thread at a time in an attempt to
unearth some item of value. She'd shake open
books, seeking everything from treasure maps to
deeds. She'd sift through the contents of the half

dozen trunks in the attic. She'd knock about the outbuildings with her lips turning blue from the cold. And if she was assiduous, she would find the key.

And the key would take her to the safe deposit box at that very same bank in which the Perrymans had transacted business for two hundred years. Widow of Bernard Perryman with his will in one hand and his death certificate in the other, she would be given access. And there, she'd come to the end of her hopes.

Malcolm wondered what she would think when she saw the single grubby piece of paper that was the long heralded Legacy of the Perrymans. Filled with handwriting so cramped as to be virtually illegible, it looked like nothing to the untrained eye. And that's what Betsy would think she had in her possession when she finally threw herself upon Malcolm's mercy.

Bernie Perryman had known otherwise, however, on that long ago night when he'd shown Malcolm the letter.

'Have a lookit this here, Malkie,' Bernie had said. 'Tell ol' Bern whatchoo think of this.'

He was in his cups, as usual, but he wasn't yet entirely blotto. And Malcolm, having just obliterated him at chess, was feeling expansive and willing to put up with his childhood friend's inebriated ramblings.

At first he thought that Bernie was taking a page from out of a large old Bible, but he quickly saw that the Bible was really an antique leather album of some sort and the page was a document, a letter in fact. Although it had no salutation, it was signed at the bottom and next to the signature was the remains of a wax imprint from a signet ring.

Bernie was watching him in that sly way drunks have: gauging his reaction. So Malcolm knew that Bernie knew what it was that he had in his possession. Which made him curious, but wary as well.

The wary part of him glanced at the document, saying, 'I don't know, Bernie. I can't make much of it.' While the curious part of him added, 'Where'd it come from?'

Bernie played coy. 'That ol' floor always gave

them trouble, di'n't it, Malkie? Too low it was, stones too rough, never a decent job of building. But what else c'n you expect when a structure's donkey's ears old?'

Malcolm mined through this non sequitur for meaning. The old buildings in the area were Gloucester Grammar School, the Plantagenet pub, Market Bosworth Hall, the timbered cottages in Rectory Lane, St James Church in—

His gaze sharpened, first on Bernie and then on his document. St James Church in Sutton Cheney, he thought. And he gave the document a closer look.

Which is when he deciphered the first line of it – *I, Richard, by the Grace of God Kyng of England and France and Lord of Ireland* – which is when his glance dropped to the hastily scrawled signature, which he also deciphered. *Richard R.*

Holy Jesus God, he thought. What had Bernie got his drunken little hands on?

He knew the importance of staying cool. One indication of his interest and he'd be Bernie's break-fast. So he said, 'Can't tell much in this light, Bernie. Mind if I have a closer look at home?'

But Bernie wasn't about to buy that proposal. He said, 'Can't let it out of m' sight, Malkie. Family legacy, that. Been our goods for donkey's ears, that has, and every one of us swore to keep it safe.'

'How did you . . . ?' But Malcolm knew better than to ask how Bernie had come to have a letter written by Richard III among his family belongings. Bernie would tell him only what Bernie deemed necessary for Malcolm to know. So he said, 'Let's have a look in the kitchen, then. That all right with you?'

That was just fine with Bernie Perryman. He, after all, wanted his old mate to see what the document was. So they went into the kitchen and sat at the table and Malcolm pored over the thick piece of paper.

The writing was terrible, not the neat hand of the professional scribe who would have attended the King and written his correspondence for him, but the hand of a man in agitated spirits. Malcolm had spent nearly twenty years consuming every scrap of information on Richard Plantagenet, Duke of Gloucester, later Richard III, called the Usurper, called England's Black Legend, called the Bunch-Backed Toad and virtually every other obloquy imaginable. So he knew how possible it actually was that here in this farmhouse, not two hundred yards from Bosworth Field and little over a mile from St James Church, he was looking at the genuine article. Richard had lived his last night in this vicinity. Richard had fought here. Richard had died here. How unimaginable a circumstance was it that Richard had also written a letter somewhere nearby, in a building where it lay hidden until . . .

Malcolm thought about everything he knew of the area's history. He came up with the fact he needed. 'The floor of St James Church,' he said. 'It was raised two hundred years ago, wasn't it?' And one of the countless ne'er-do-well Perrymans had been there, had probably helped with the work, and had found this letter.

Bernie was watching him, a sly smile tweaking the corners of his mouth. 'Whatcho think it says, Malkie?' he asked. 'Think it might be worth a bob or two?'

Malcolm wanted to strangle him, but instead he studied the priceless document. It wasn't long, just a few lines that, he saw, could have altered the course of history and that would – when finally made public through the historical discourse he instantaneously decided to write – finally redeem the King who for five hundred years had been maligned by an accusation of butchery for which there had never been a shred of proof.

I, Richard, by the Grace of God Kyng of England and France and Lord of Ireland, on thys daye of 21 August 1485 do with thys document hereby enstruct the good fadres of Jervaulx to gyve unto the protection of the beerrer Edward hytherto called Lord Bastarde and hys brother Richard, called Duke of Yrk. Possession of thys document wyll suffyce to identyfie the beerrer as John de la Pole, Earl of Lyncoln, beloved nephew of the Kyng. Wrytten in hast at Suton Chene. Richard R.

Two sentences and a phrase only, but enough to redeem a man's reputation. When the King had died on the field of battle that 22 August 1485, his two young nephews had been alive.

Malcolm looked at Bernie steadily. 'You know what this is, don't you, Bernie?' he asked his old friend.

'Numbskull like me?' Bernie asked. 'Him what couldn't even pass his A levels? How'd I know what that bit of trash is? But what d'you think? Worth something if I flog it?'

'You can't sell this, Bernie.' Malcolm spoke before he thought and much too hastily. Doing so, he inadvertently revealed himself.

Bernie scooped the paper up and manhandled it to his chest. Malcolm winced. God only knew the damage the fool was capable of doing when he was drunk.

'Go easy with that,' Malcolm said. 'It's fragile, Bernie.'

'Like friendship, isn't it?' Bernie said. He tottered from the kitchen.

It would have been shortly after that that Bernie

had moved the document to another location, for Malcolm had never seen it again. But the knowledge of its existence had festered inside him for years. And only with the advent of Betsy had he finally seen a way to make that precious piece of paper his.

And it would be, soon. Just as soon as Betsy got up her nerve to phone him with the terrible news that what she'd thought was a legacy was only – to her utterly unschooled eyes – a bit of old paper suitable for lining the bottom of a parakeet cage.

While awaiting her call, Malcolm put the finishing touches on his *The Truth About Richard and Bosworth Field*, ten years in the writing and wanting only a single, final, and previously unseen historical document to serve as witness to the veracity of his theory about what happened to the two young Princes. The hours that he spent at his typewriter flew by like leaves blown off the trees in Ambion Forest, where once a marsh had protected Richard's south flank from attack by Henry Tudor's mercenary army.

The letter gave credence to Malcolm's surmise

that Richard would have told someone of the boys' whereabouts. Should the battle favour Henry Tudor, the Princes would be in deadly danger, so the night before the battle Richard would finally have had to tell someone his most closely guarded secret: where the two boys were. In that way, if the day went to Tudor, the boys could be fetched from the monastery and spirited out of the country and out of the reach of harm.

John de la Pole, Earl of Lincoln, and beloved nephew to Richard III, would have been the likeliest candidate. He would have been instructed to ride to Yorkshire if the King fell, to safeguard the lives of the boys who would be made legitimate – and hence the biggest threat to the usurper – the moment Henry Tudor married their sister.

John de la Pole would have known the gravity of the boys' danger. But despite the fact that his uncle would have told him where the Princes were hidden, he would never have been given access to them, much less had them handed over to him, without express direction to the monks from the King himself.

The letter would have given him that access. But he'd had to flee to the south instead of to the north. So he couldn't pull it from the stones in St James Church where his uncle had hidden it the night before the battle.

And yet the boys disappeared, never to be heard of again. So who took them?

There could be only one answer to that question: Elizabeth of York, sister to the Princes but also affianced wife of the newly crowned-right-there-on-the-battlefield King.

Hearing the news that her uncle had been defeated, Elizabeth would have seen her options clearly: Queen of England should Henry Tudor retain his throne or sister to a mere youthful King should her brother Edward claim his own legitimacy the moment Henry legitimatized her or suppressed the Act by which she'd been made illegitimate in the first place. Thus, she could be the matriarch of a royal dynasty or a political pawn to be given in marriage to anyone with whom her brother wished to form an alliance.

Sheriff Hutton, her temporary residence, was no great distance from any of the abbeys. Ever her uncle's favourite niece and knowing his bent for things religious, she would have guessed – if Richard hadn't told her directly – where he'd hidden her brothers. And the boys would have gone with her willingly. She was their sister, after all.

'I am Elizabeth of York,' she would have told the abbot in that imperious voice she'd heard used so often by her cunning mother. 'I shall see my brothers alive and well. And instantly.'

How easily it would have been accomplished. The two young Princes seeing their older sister for the first time in who knew how long, running to her, embracing her, eagerly turning to the abbot when she informed them that she'd come for them at last . . . And who was the abbot to deny a Royal Princess – clearly recognized by the boys themselves – her own brothers? Especially in the current situation, with King Richard dead and sitting on the throne a man who'd illustrated his bloodthirstiness by making one of his first acts as King a declaration of treason against all who had fought on the side of Richard at Bosworth Field? Tudor wouldn't look kindly on the abbey that was found to be sheltering the two boys. God only knew what his revenge would be should he find them.

Thus it made sense for the abbot to deliver Edward the Lord Bastard and his brother Richard the Duke of York into the hands of their sister. And Elizabeth, with her brothers in her possession, handed them over to someone. One of the Stanleys? The duplicitous Earl of Northumberland who went on to serve Henry Tudor in the North? Sir James Tyrell, one-time follower of Richard, who was the recipient of two general pardons from Tudor not a year after he took the throne?

Whoever it was, once the Princes were in his hands, their fates were sealed. And no one wishing to preserve his life afterwards would have thought about levelling an accusation against the wife of a reigning monarch who had already shown his inclination for attainting subjects and confiscating their land.

It was, Malcolm thought, such a brilliant plan on Elizabeth's part. She was her mother's own daughter, after all. She knew the value of placing self-interest above everything else. Besides, she would have told herself that keeping the boys alive would only prolong a struggle for the throne that had been going on for thirty years. She could put an end to the bloodshed by shedding just a little more blood. What woman in her position would have done otherwise?

The fact that it took Betsy more than three months to develop the courage to break the sorrowful news to Malcolm did cause him a twinge of concern now and then. In the time-line he'd long ago written in his mind, she'd have come to him in hysterics not twenty-four hours after discovering that her Legacy was a scribbled-up scrap of dirty paper. She'd have thrown herself into his arms and wept and waited for rescue. To emphasize the dire straits she was in, she'd have brought the paper with her to show him how ill Bernie Perryman had used his loving wife. And he – Malcolm – would have taken the paper from her shaking fingers, would have given it a glance, would have tossed it to the floor and joined in her weeping, mourning the death of their dearly held dreams. For she was ruined financially and he, on a mere paltry salary from Gloucester Grammar, could not offer her the life she deserved. Then, after a vigorous and memorable round of mattress poker, she would leave, the scorned bit of paper still lying on the floor. And the letter would be his. And when his tome was published and the lectures, television interviews, chat shows, and book tours began cluttering up his calendar, he would have no time for a bumpkin housewife who'd been too dim to know what she'd had in her fingers.

That was the plan. Malcolm felt the occasional pinch of worry when it didn't come off quickly and without a hitch. But he told himself that Betsy's reluctance to reveal the truth to him was all part of God's Great Plan. This gave him time to complete his manuscript. And he used the time well.

Since he and Betsy had decided that discretion was in order following Bernie's death, they saw each other only in the corridors of Gloucester Grammar when she returned to work. During this time, Malcolm phoned her nightly for telesex once he realized that he could keep her oiled and proofread the earlier chapters of his opus simultaneously.

Then finally, three months and four days after Bernie's unfortunate demise, Betsy whispered a request to him in the corridor just outside the Headmaster's office. Could he come to the farm for dinner that night? She didn't look as solemn-faced as Malcolm would have liked, considering her impoverished circumstances and the death of her dreams, but he didn't worry much about this. Betsy had already proved herself a stunning actress. She wouldn't want to break down at the school.

Prior to leaving that afternoon, swollen with the recognition that his fantasy was about to be realized, Malcolm handed in his notice to the Headmaster. Samuel Montgomery accepted it with a rather disturbing alacrity which Malcolm didn't much like, and although the Headmaster covered his surprise and delight with a spurious show of regret at losing 'a veritable institution here at GG', Malcolm could see him savouring the triumph of being rid of someone he'd decided was an educational dinosaur. So it gave him more satisfaction than he would have thought possible, knowing how great his own triumph was going to be when he made his mark upon the face of English history.

Malcolm couldn't have been happier as he drove to Windsong Farm that evening. The long winter of his discontent had segued into a beautiful spring, and he was minutes away from being able to right a five-hundred-year-old wrong at the same time as he carved a place for himself in the pantheon of the Historical Greats. God is good, he thought as he made the turn into the farm's long driveway. It was unfortunate that Bernie Perryman had had to die, but as his death was in the interests of historical redemption, it would have to be said that the end richly justified the means.

As he got out of the car, Betsy opened the farmhouse door. Malcolm blinked at her, puzzled at her manner of dress. It took him a moment to digest the fact that she was wearing a full-length fur coat. Silver mink by the look of it, or possibly ermine. It wasn't the wisest get-up to don in these days of animal rights activists, but Betsy had never been a woman to think very far beyond her own desires.

Before Malcolm had a moment to wonder how Betsy had managed to finance the purchase of a fur coat, she had thrown it open and was standing in the doorway, naked to her toes.

'Darling!' she cried. 'We're rich, rich, rich. And you'll never guess what I sold to make us so!'

The Surprise of His Life

The Surprise of His Life

When Douglas Armstrong had his first consultation with Thistle McCloud, he had no intention of murdering his wife. His mind, in fact, didn't turn to murder until two weeks after consultation number four.

Douglas watched closely as Thistle prepared herself for a revelation from another dimension. She held his wedding band in the palm of her left hand. She closed her fingers around it. She hovered her right hand over the fist she'd made. She hummed five notes that sounded suspiciously like the beginning of 'I Love You Truly'. Gradually, her eyes rolled back, up, and out of view beneath her yellow-shaded lids, leaving him with the disconcerting sight of a thirty-something female in a straw boater, white shirt and polka-dotted tie, looking as if she were one quarter of a barber-shop quartet in desperate hope of finding her partners.

When he'd first seen Thistle, Douglas had appraised her attire – which in subsequent visits had not altered in any appreciable fashion – as the insidious get-up of a charlatan who wished to focus her clients' attention on her personal appearance rather than on whatever machinations she would be going through to delve into their pasts, their presents, their futures, and – most importantly – their wallets. But he'd come to realize that Thistle's odd get-up had nothing to do with distracting anyone. The first time she held his old Rolex watch and began speaking in a low, intense voice about the prodigal son, about his endless departures and equally endless returns, about his ageing parents who welcomed him always with open arms and open hearts, and about his brother who watched all this with a false fixed smile and a silent shout of, What about me? Do I mean nothing?, he had a feeling that Thistle was exactly what she purported to be: a psychic.

He'd first come to her store-front operation because he'd had forty minutes to kill prior to his yearly prostate exam. He dreaded the exam and the teeth-grating embarrassment of having to answer his doctor's jovial, rib-poking, 'Everything up and about as it should be?' with the truth, which was that Newton's law of gravity had begun asserting itself lately into his dearest appendage. And since he was six weeks short of his fifty-fifth birthday, and since every disaster in his life had occurred in a year that was a multiple of five, if there was a chance of knowing what the gods had in store for him and his prostate, he wanted to be able to do something to head off the chaos.

These things had all been in his mind as he spun along Pacific Coast Highway in the dim gold light of a late December afternoon. On a drearily commercialized section of the road – given largely to pizza parlours and boogie-board shops – he had seen the small blue building that he'd passed a thousand times before and read *Psychic Consultations* on its hand-painted sign. He'd glanced at his gas gauge for an excuse to stop and while he pumped super unleaded into the tank of his Mercedes across the street from that small blue building, he made his decision. What the hell, he'd thought. There were worse ways to kill forty minutes.

So he'd had his first session with Thistle McCloud, who was anything but what he'd expected of a psychic since she used no crystal ball, no Tarot cards, nothing at all but a piece of his jewellery. In his first three visits, it had always been the Rolex watch from which she'd received her psychic emanations. But today she'd placed the watch to one side, declared it diluted of power, and set her fog-coloured eyes on his wedding ring. She'd touched her finger to it, and said, 'I'll use that, I think, if you want something further from your history and closer to your heart.'

He'd given her the ring precisely because of those last two phrases: *further from your history and closer to your heart*. They told him how very well she knew that the prodigal son business rose from his past while his deepest concerns were about his future.

With the ring now in her closed fist and with her eyes rolled upward, Thistle stopped the five-note humming, breathed deeply six times, and opened her eyes. She observed him with a melancholia that made his stomach feel hollow.

'What?' Douglas asked.

'You need to prepare yourself for a shock,' she said. 'It's something unexpected. It comes out of nowhere and because of it, the essence of your life will be changed forever. And soon. I feel it coming very soon.'

Jesus, he thought. It was just what he needed to hear three weeks after having had an indifferent index finger shoved up his ass to see what was the cause of his limp dick syndrome. The doctor had said it wasn't cancer, but he hadn't ruled out half a dozen other possibilities. Douglas wondered which one of them Thistle had tuned her psychic antennae into.

Thistle opened her hand, and they both looked at his wedding ring, faintly sheened by her sweat. 'It's an external shock,' she clarified. 'The source of upheaval in your life isn't from within. The shock comes from outside and rattles you to your core.'

'Are you sure about that?' Douglas asked her.

'As sure as I can be, considering the armour you

wear.' Thistle returned his ring to him, her cool fingers grazing his wrist. She said, 'Your name isn't David, is it? It never was David. It never will be David. But the *D*, I feel, is correct. Am I right?'

He reached into his back pocket and brought out his wallet. Careful to shield his driver's licence from her, he clipped a fifty dollar bill between his thumb and index finger. He folded it once and handed it over.

'Donald,' she said. 'No. That isn't it either. Darrell perhaps. Dennis. I sense two syllables.'

'Names aren't important in your line of work, are they?' Douglas asked.

'No. But the truth is always important. Someday, Not-David, you're going to have to learn to trust people with the truth. Trust is the key. Trust is essential.'

'Trust', he told her, 'is what gets people screwed.'

Outside, he walked across the coast highway to the cramped side street that paralleled the ocean. Here he always parked his car when he visited Thistle. With its vanity licence plate DRIL4IT virtually announcing who owned the Mercedes, Douglas had early on decided that it wouldn't encourage new investors if anyone put out the word that the president of South Coast Oil had begun seeing a psychic regularly. Risky investments were one thing. Placing money with a man who could be accused of using parapsychology rather than geology to find oil deposits was another. He wasn't doing that, of course. Business never came up in his sessions with Thistle. But try telling that to the Board of Directors. Try telling that to anyone.

He unarmed the car and slid inside. He headed south, in the direction of his office. As far as anyone at South Coast Oil knew, he'd spent his lunch hour with his wife having a romantic winter's picnic on the bluffs in Corona del Mar. The cellular phone will be turned off for an hour, he'd informed his secretary. Don't try to phone and don't bother us, please. This is time for Donna and me. She deserves it. I need it. Are we clear on the subject?

Any mention of Donna always did the trick when it came to keeping South Coast Oil off his back for a few hours. She was warmly liked by everyone in the company. She was warmly liked by everyone period. Sometimes, he reflected, she was too warmly liked. Especially by men.

You need to prepare for a shock.

Did he? Douglas considered the question in relation to his wife.

When he pointed out men's affinity for her, Donna always acted surprised. She told him that men merely recognized in her a woman who'd grown up in a household of brothers. But what Douglas saw in men's eyes when they looked at his wife had nothing to do with fraternal affection. It had to do with getting her naked, getting down and dirty, and getting laid.

Getting laid was behind every man-woman interaction on the planet. Douglas knew this well. So while his recent failures to get it up and get it on with Donna frustrated him, his real fear was that her patience with him was trickling away. Once it was gone, she'd start looking around. That was natural. And once she started looking, she was going to find or be found herself.

The shock comes from outside and rattles you to your core.

Shit, Douglas thought. If chaos was about to steamroller into his life as he approached his fifty-fifth birthday – that rotten bad luck integer – Douglas had to admit that his wife Donna would probably be sitting at the wheel. She was thirty-five, four years in place as wife number three, and while she acted content, he'd been around women long enough to know that still waters did more than simply run deep. They hid rocks that could sink a boat in seconds if a sailor didn't keep his wits about him. And love made people lose their wits, didn't it? Didn't love make people go a little bit nuts?

Of course, *he* wasn't nuts. He had his wits about him. But being in love with a woman twenty years his junior, a woman whose scent caught the nose of every male within sixty yards of her, a woman whose physical appetites he was failing to satisfy on a nightly basis . . . and had been failing to satisfy for weeks . . . a woman like that . . .

'Get a grip,' Douglas told himself brusquely. 'This psychic stuff is bullshit, right? Right.' But still he thought of the coming shock, the upset to his life, and its source: external. Not his prostate, not his dick, not an organ in his body. But another human being. 'Shit,' he said.

He guided the car up the incline that led to Jamboree Boulevard, six lanes of concrete that rolled between stunted liquidambar trees through some of the most expensive real estate in Orange County. It took him to the bronzed glass tower that housed his pride: South Coast Oil.

Once inside the building, he navigated his way through an unexpected encounter with two of SCO's engineers, through a brief conversation with a geologist who simultaneously waved an ordnance survey map and a report from the EPA, and through a hallway conference with the head of the accounting department. His secretary handed him a fistful of messages when he finally managed to reach his office. She said, 'Nice picnic? The weather's unbelievable, isn't it?' followed by 'Everything all right, Mr Armstrong?' when he didn't reply.

He said, 'Yes. What? Fine,' and looked through the messages. He found that the names meant nothing to him. Absolutely nothing.

He walked to the window behind his desk and looked at the view through its enormous pane of tinted glass. Below him, Orange County's airport sent jet after jet hurtling into the air at an angle so acute that it defied both reason and aerodynamics, although it did protect the delicate auditory sensibilities of the millionaires who lived in the flight path below. Douglas watched these planes without really seeing them. He knew he had to answer his telephone messages, but all he could think about were Thistle's words: *an external shock.*

What could be more external than Donna?

She wore Obsession. She put it behind her ears and beneath her breasts. Whenever she passed through a room, she left the scent of herself behind.

Her dark hair gleamed when the sunlight hit it. She wore it short and simply cut, parted on the left and smoothly falling just to her ears.

Her legs were long. When she walked, her stride was full and sure. And when she walked with him – at his side, with her hand through his arm and her head held back – he knew that she caught the attention of everyone. He knew that together they were the envy of all of their friends and of strangers as well.

He could see this reflected in the faces of people they passed when he and Donna were together. At the ballet, at the theatre, at concerts, in restaurants, glances gravitated to Douglas Armstrong and his wife. In women's expressions, he could read the wish to be young like Donna, to be smooth-skinned again, to be vibrant once more, to be fecund and ready. In men's expression, he could read desire.

It had always been a pleasure to see how others reacted to the sight of his wife. But now he saw how dangerous her allure really was and how it threatened to destroy his peace.

A shock, Thistle had said. *Prepare for a shock. Prepare for a shock that will change your world.*

That evening, Douglas heard the water running as soon as he entered the house: fifty-two hundred square feet of limestone floors, vaulted ceilings, and picture windows on a hillside that offered an ocean view to the west and the lights of Orange County to the east. The house had cost him a fortune, but that had been all right with him. Money meant nothing. He'd bought the place for Donna. But if he'd had doubts about his wife before – born of his own performance anxiety, growing to adulthood through his consultation with Thistle – when Douglas heard that water running, he began to see the truth. Because Donna was in the shower.

He watched her silhouette behind the blocks of translucent glass that defined the shower's wall. She was washing her hair. She hadn't noticed him yet, and he watched her for a moment, his gaze travelling over her uplifted breasts, her hips, her long legs. She usually bathed – languorous bubble baths in the raised oval tub that looked out on the lights of the city of Irvine. Taking a shower suggested a more energetic and earnest effort to cleanse herself. And washing her hair suggested . . . Well, it was perfectly clear what that suggested. Scents got caught up in the hair: cigarette smoke, sautéing garlic, fish from a fishing boat, or semen and sex. Those last two were the betraying scents. Obviously, she would have to wash her hair.

Her discarded clothes lay on the floor. With a hasty

glance at the shower, Douglas fingered through them and found her lacy underwear. He knew women. He knew his wife. If she'd actually been with a man that afternoon, her body's leaking juices would have made the panties' crotch stiff when they dried, and he would be able to smell the afterscent of intercourse on them. They would give him proof. He lifted them to his face.

'Doug! What on earth are you doing?'

Douglas dropped the panties, cheeks hot and neck sweating. Donna was peering at him from the shower's opening, her hair lathered with soap that streaked down her left cheek. She brushed it away.

'What are *you* doing?' he asked her. Three marriages and two divorces had taught him that a fast offensive manoeuvre threw the opponent off balance. It worked.

She popped back into the water – clever of her, so he couldn't see her face – and said, 'It's pretty obvious. I'm taking a shower. God, what a day.'

He moved to watch her through the shower's opening. There was no door, just a partition in the glass-blocked wall. He could study her body and

look for the telltale signs of the kind of rough lovemaking he knew that she liked. And she wouldn't
know that he was even looking since her head was
beneath the shower as she rinsed off her hair.

'Steve phoned in sick today,' she said, 'so I had
to do everything at the kennels myself.' She raised
chocolate labradors. He had met her that way, seeking a dog for his youngest son. Through a reference
from a veterinarian, he had discovered her kennels
in Midway City – less than one square mile of
feed-stores, other kennels, and dilapidated post-war
stucco and shake roofs posing as suburban housing.
It was an odd place for a girl from the pricey side of
Corona del Mar to end up professionally, but that
was what he liked about Donna. She wasn't true to
type, she wasn't a beach bunny, she wasn't a typical
southern California girl. Or at least that's what he
had thought.

'The worst was cleaning the dog runs,' she said.
'I didn't mind the grooming – I never mind that –
but I hate doing the runs. I completely reeked of dog
poop when I got home.' She shut off the shower and
reached for her towels, wrapping her head in one

and her body in the other. She stepped out of the stall with a smile and said, 'Isn't it weird how some smells cling to your body and your hair while others don't?'

She kissed him hello and scooped up her clothes. She tossed them down the laundry chute. No doubt she was thinking, Out of sight, out of mind. She was clever that way.

'That's the third time Steve's phoned in sick in two weeks.' She headed for the bedroom, drying off as she went. She dropped the towel with her usual absence of self-consciousness and began dressing, pulling on wispy underwear, black leggings, a silver tunic. 'If this keeps up, I'm going to let him go. I need someone consistent, someone reliable. If he's not going to be able to hold up his end . . .' She frowned at Douglas, her face perplexed. 'What's wrong, Doug? You're looking at me so funny. Is something wrong?'

'Wrong? No.' But he thought, That looks like a love bite on her neck. And he crossed to her for a better look. He cupped her face for a kiss and tilted her head. The shadow of the towel that was wrapped round her head dissipated, leaving her skin unmarred. Well, what of it? He thought. She wouldn't be so stupid as to let some heavy breather suck bruises into her flesh, no matter how turned on he had her. She wasn't that dumb. Not his Donna.

But she also wasn't as smart as her husband.

At 5:45, he went to the personnel department. It was a better choice than the Yellow Pages because at least he knew that whoever had been doing the background checks on incoming employees at South Coast Oil was simultaneously competent and discreet. No one had ever complained about some two-bit gumshoe nosing into his background.

The department was deserted, as he'd hoped. The computer screens at every desk were set to shifting images that preserved them: a field of swimming fish, bouncing balls, and popping bubbles. The director's office at the far side of the department was unlit and locked, but a master key in the hand of the company president solved that problem. Douglas went inside and flipped on the lights.

He found the name he was looking for among

the dog-eared cards of the director's Rolodex, a curious anachronism in an otherwise computer-age office. *Cowley and Son, Inquiries*, he read in faded typescript. This was accompanied by a telephone number and by an address on Balboa Peninsula.

Douglas studied both for the space of two minutes. Was it better to know or to live in ignorant bliss? But he wasn't living in bliss, was he? And he hadn't been living in bliss from the moment he'd failed to perform as a man was meant to. So it was better to know. Some things in life one had to know, whatever the consequences.

He picked up the phone.

Douglas always went out for lunch – unless a conference was scheduled with his geologists or the engineers – so no one raised a hair of an eyebrow when he left South Coast Oil before noon the following day. He used Jamboree once again to get to the coast highway, but this time instead of heading north toward Newport where Thistle made her prognostications, he drove directly across the highway and down the incline where a modestly arched bridge spanned an oily stretch of Newport Harbour that divided the mainland from an amoeba-shaped portion of land that was Balboa Island.

In summer the island was infested with tourists, who bottled up the streets with their cars and rode their bicycles in races on the sidewalk around the island's perimeter. No local in his right mind ventured onto Balboa Island during the summer without good reason, unless he lived there. But in winter, the place was virtually deserted. It took less than five minutes to snake through the narrow streets to the island's north end where the ferry waited to take cars and pedestrians on the eye-blink voyage across to the peninsula.

There, a stripe-topped carousel and a Ferris wheel spun like two opposing gears of an enormous clock, defining an area called the Fun Zone, which had long been the summertime bane of the local police. Today, however, no bands of juveniles roved with cans of spray paint at the ready. The only inhabitants of the Fun Zone were a paraplegic in a wheelchair and his bike-riding companion.

Douglas passed them as he drove off the ferry.

They were intent upon their conversation. The Ferris wheel and carousel did not exist for them. Nor did Douglas and his blue Mercedes, which was just as well. He didn't particularly want to be seen.

He parked just off the beach, in a lot where fifteen minutes cost a quarter. He pumped in four. He armed the car and headed west toward Main Street, a tree-shaded lane some sixty yards long that began at a *faux* New England restaurant overlooking Newport Harbour and ended at Balboa Pier, which stretched out into the Pacific Ocean, grey-green today and unsettled by roiling waves from a winter Alaskan storm.

Number 107-B Main was what he was looking for, and he found it easily. Just east of an alley, 107 was a two-storey structure whose bottom floor was taken up by a time-warped hair salon called JJ's – heavily devoted to macramé, potted plants, and posters of Janis Joplin – and whose upper floor was divided into offices that were reached by a structurally questionable stairway at the north end of the building. 107-B was the first door upstairs – JJ's Natural Haircutting appeared to be 107-A

– but when Douglas turned the discoloured brass knob below the equally discoloured brass nameplate announcing the business as *Cowley and Son, Inquiries,* he found the door locked.

He frowned and looked at his Rolex. His appointment was for 12:15. It was currently 12:10. So where was Cowley? Where was his son?

He returned to the stairway, ready to head to his car and his cellular phone, ready to track down Cowley and give him hell for setting up an appointment and failing to be there to keep it. But he was three steps down when he saw a khaki clad man coming his way, sucking up an Orange Julius with the enthusiasm of a twelve-year-old. His thinning grey hair and sun-lined face marked him at least five decades older than twelve, however. And his limping gait – in combination with his clothes – suggested old war wounds.

'You Cowley?' Douglas called from the stairs.

The man waved his Orange Julius in reply. 'You Armstrong?' he asked.

'Right,' Douglas said. 'Listen, I don't have a lot of time.'

'None of us do, son,' Cowley said, and he hoisted himself up the stairway. He nodded in a friendly fashion, pulled hard at the Orange Julius straw, and passed Douglas in a gust of aftershave that he hadn't smelled for a good twenty years. Canoe. Jesus. Did they still sell that?

Cowley swung the door open and cocked his head to indicate that Douglas was to enter. The office comprised two rooms: one was a sparsely furnished waiting area through which they passed; the other was obviously Cowley's demesne. Its centrepiece was an olive green steel desk. Filing cabinets and bookshelves of the same issue matched it.

The investigator went to an old oak office chair behind the desk, but he didn't sit. Instead, he opened one of the side drawers and, just when Douglas was expecting him to pull out a fifth of bourbon, he dug out a bottle of yellow pills instead. He shook six of them into his palm and knocked them back with a long swig of Orange Julius. He sank into his chair and gripped its arms.

'Arthritis,' he said. 'I'm killing it with evening

primrose oil. Give me a minute, okay? You want a couple?'

'No.' Douglas glanced at his watch to make certain Cowley knew that his time was precious. Then he strolled to the steel bookshelves.

He was expecting to see munitions manuals, penal codes, and surveillance texts, something to assure the prospective clients that they'd come to the right place with their troubles. But what he found was poetry, volume after volume neatly arranged in alphabetical order by author, from Matthew Arnold to William Butler Yeats. He wasn't sure what to think.

The occasional space left at the end of a bookshelf was taken up by photographs. They were clumsily framed, snapshots mostly. They depicted grinning small children, a grey-haired grandma type, several young adults. Among them, encased in Plexiglass, was a military Purple Heart. Douglas picked this up. He'd never seen one, but he was pleased to know that his guess about the source of Cowley's limp had been correct.

'You saw action,' he said.

'My butt saw action,' Cowley replied. Douglas

looked his way, so the investigator continued. 'I took it in the ass. Shit happens, right?' He moved his hands from their grip on the arms of his chair. He folded them over his stomach. Like Douglas's own, it could have been flatter. Indeed, the two men shared a similar build: stocky, quickly given to weight if they didn't exercise, too tall to be called short and too short to be called tall. 'What can I do for you, Mr Armstrong?'

'My wife,' Douglas said.

'Your wife?'

'She may be . . .' Now that it was time to articulate the problem, Douglas wasn't sure that he could. So he said, 'Who's the son?'

'What?'

'It says Cowley and Son, but there's only one desk. Who's the son?'

Cowley reached for his Orange Julius and took a pull on its straw. 'He died,' he said. 'Drunk driver got him on Ortega Highway.'

'Sorry.'

'Like I said. Shit happens. What shit's happened to you?'

Douglas returned the Purple Heart to its place. He caught sight of the greying grandma in one of the pictures and said, 'This your wife?'

'Forty years my wife. Name's Maureen.'

'I'm on my third. How'd you manage forty years with one woman?'

'She has a sense of humour.' Cowley slid open the middle drawer of his desk and took out a legal pad and the stub of a pencil. He wrote *Armstrong* at the top in block letters and underlined it. He said, 'About your wife . . .'

'I think she's having an affair. I want to know if I'm right. I want to know who it is.'

Cowley carefully set down his pencil. He observed Douglas for a moment. Outside, a gull gave a raucous cry from one of the rooftops. 'What makes you think she's seeing someone?'

'Am I supposed to give you proof before you'll take the case. I thought that's why I was hiring you. To give *me* proof.'

'You wouldn't be here if you didn't have suspicions. What are they?'

Douglas raked through his memory. He wasn't

about to tell Cowley about trying to smell up Donna's underwear, so he took a moment to examine her behaviour over the last few weeks. And when he did so, the additional evidence was there. Jesus, how the hell had he missed it? She'd changed her hair; she'd bought new underwear – that black lacy Victoria's Secret stuff; she'd been on the phone twice when he'd come home and as soon as he walked into the room, she'd hung up hastily; there were at least two long absences with insufficient excuse for them; there were six or seven engagements that she'd said were with friends.

Cowley nodded thoughtfully when Douglas listed his suspicions. Then he said, 'Have you given her a reason to cheat on you?'

'A reason? What is this? I'm the guilty party?'

'Women don't usually stray without there being a man behind them, giving them a reason.' Cowley examined him from beneath unclipped eyebrows. One of his eyes, Douglas saw, was beginning to form a cataract. Jeez, the guy was ancient. A real antique.

'No reason,' Douglas said. 'I don't cheat on her. I don't even want to.'

'She's young, though. And a man your age . . .' Cowley shrugged. 'Shit happens to us old guys. Young things don't always have the patience to understand.'

Douglas wanted to point out that Cowley was at least ten years his senior, if not more. He also wanted to take himself from membership in the club of *us old guys*. But the detective was watching him compassionately, so instead of arguing, Douglas told the truth.

Cowley reached for his Orange Julius and drained the cup. He tossed it in the trash. 'Women have needs,' he said, and he moved his hand from his crotch to his chest, adding, 'A wise man doesn't confuse what goes on here –' the crotch – 'with what goes on here' – the chest.

'So maybe I'm not wise. Are you going to help me out or not?'

'You sure you want help?'

'I want to know the truth. I can live with that. What I can't live with is not knowing. I just need to know what I'm dealing with here.'

Cowley looked as if he was taking a reading of Douglas's level of veracity. He finally appeared to make a decision, but one he apparently didn't like because he shook his head, picked up his pencil, and said, 'Give me some background, then. If she's got someone on the side, who're our possibilities?'

Douglas had already thought about this. There was Mike, the pool-man who visited once a week. There was Steve, who worked with Donna at her kennels in Midway City. There was Jeff, her personal trainer. There were also the postman, the Fed Ex man, the UPS driver, and Donna's too-youthful gynaecologist.

'I take it you're accepting the case?' Douglas said to Cowley. He pulled out his wallet from which he extracted a wad of bills. 'You'll be wanting a retainer.'

'I don't need cash, Mr Armstrong.'

'All the same . . .' All the same, Douglas had no intention of leaving a paper trail via a cheque. 'How much time do you need?' he asked.

'Give it a few days. If she's seeing someone, he'll surface eventually. They always do.' Cowley sounded despondent.

'Your wife cheat on you?' Douglas asked shrewdly.

'If she did, I probably deserved it.'

That was Cowley's attitude, but it was one that Douglas didn't share. He didn't deserve to be cheated on. Nobody did. And when he found out who was doing the job on his wife . . . Well, they would see a kind of justice that Attila the Hun had been incapable of extracting.

His resolve was strengthened in the bedroom that evening when his hello kiss to his wife was interrupted by the telephone. Donna pulled away from him quickly and went to answer it. She gave Douglas a smile – as if recognizing what her haste revealed – and shook back her hair as sexily as possible, running slim fingers through her hair as she picked up the receiver.

Douglas listened to her side of the conversation while he changed his clothes. He heard her voice brighten as she said, 'Yes, yes. Hello . . . No . . . Doug just got home and we were talking about the day . . .'

So her caller knew he was in the room. Douglas could imagine what the bastard was saying, whoever he was: '*So you can't talk?*'

To which Donna, on cue, answered, 'Nope. Not at all.'

'*Shall I call later?*'

'Gosh, that would be nice.'

'*Today was what was nice, baby. I love to fuck you.*'

'Really? Outrageous. I'll have to check it out.'

'*I want to check you out, babe. Are you wet for me?*'

'I sure am. Listen, we'll connect later on, okay? I need to get dinner started.'

'*Just as long as you remember today. It was the best. You're the best.*'

'Right. Bye.' She hung up and came to him. She put her arms round his waist. She said, 'Got rid of her. Nancy Talbert. God. Nothing's more important in her life than a shoe sale at Neiman-Marcus. Spare me. Please.' She snuggled up to him. He couldn't see her face, just the back of her head where it reflected in the mirror.

'Nancy Talbert?' he said. 'I don't think I know her.'

'Sure you do, honey.' She pressed her hips against him. He felt the hopeful but useless heat in his groin. 'She's in Soroptimists with me. You met her last month after the ballet. Hmm. You feel nice. Gosh, I like it when you hold me, Doug. Should I start dinner or d'you want to mess around?'

Another clever move on her part: he wouldn't think she was cheating if she still wanted it from him. No matter that he couldn't give it to her. She was hanging in there with him and this moment proved it. Or so she thought.

'Love to,' he said and smacked her on the butt. 'But let's eat first. And after, right there on the dining room table . . .' He managed what he hoped was a lewd enough wink. 'Just you wait, kiddo.'

She laughed and released him and went off to the kitchen. He walked to the bed where he sat disconsolately. The charade was torture. He had to know the truth.

He didn't hear from Cowley and Son, Inquiries,

for two agonizing weeks during which he suffered through three more coy telephone conversations between Donna and her lover, four more phoney excuses to cover unscheduled absences from home, and two more midday showers sloughed off to Steve's absence from the kennels again. By the time he finally made contact with Cowley, Douglas's nerves were shot.

Cowley had news to report. He said he'd hand it over as soon as they could meet. 'How's lunch?' Cowley asked. 'We could do Tail of the Whale over here.'

No lunch, Douglas told him. He wouldn't be able to eat anyway. He would meet Cowley at his office at 12:45.

'Make it the pier, then,' Cowley said. 'I'll catch a burger at Ruby's and we can talk after. You know Ruby's? The end of the pier?'

Who didn't know Ruby's? A fifties' coffee shop, it sat at the end of Balboa Pier, and he found Cowley there as promised at 12:45, polishing off a bacon cheeseburger and fries, with a manila envelope sitting next to his strawberry milk-shake.

Cowley wore the same khakis he'd had on the day they'd met. He'd added a panama hat to his ensemble. He touched his index finger to the hat's brim as Douglas approached him. His cheeks were bulging with burger and fries.

Douglas slid into the booth opposite Cowley and reached for the envelope. Cowley's hand slapped down on it. 'Not yet,' he said.

'I've got to know.'

Cowley slid the envelope off the table and onto the vinyl seat next to himself. He twirled the straw in his milk-shake and observed Douglas through opaque eyes that seemed to reflect the sunlight outside. 'Pictures,' he said. 'That's all I've got for you. Pictures aren't the truth. You got that?'

'Okay. Pictures.'

'I don't know what I'm shooting. I just tail the woman and I shoot what I see. What I see may not mean shit. You understand?'

'Just show me the pictures.'

'Outside.'

Cowley tossed a five and three ones onto the table, called, 'Catch you later, Susie', to the waitress and led the way. He walked to the railing where he looked out over the water. A whale-watching boat was bobbing some quarter mile off shore. It was too early in the year to catch sight of a pod migrating to Alaska, but the tourists on board probably wouldn't know that. Their binoculars winked in the light.

When Douglas joined the investigator, Cowley said, 'You got to know that she doesn't act like a woman guilty of anything. She just seems to be doing her thing. She met a few men – I won't mislead you – but I couldn't catch her doing anything cheesy.'

'Give me the pictures.'

Cowley gave him a sharp look instead. Douglas knew his voice was betraying him. 'I say we tail her for another two-three weeks,' Cowley said. 'What I've got here isn't much to go on.' He opened the envelope. He stood so that Douglas only saw the back of the pictures. He chose to hand them over in sets.

The first set was taken in Midway City not far from the kennels, at the feed and grain store where Donna bought food for the dogs. In these, she was loading fifty pound food sacks into the back of her

Toyota pick-up. She was being assisted by a Calvin Klein type in tight jeans and a T-shirt. They were laughing together, and in one of the pictures Donna had perched her sunglasses on top of her head, the better to look at her companion directly.

She appeared to be flirting, but she was a young, pretty woman and flirting was normal. This seemed okay. She could have looked less happy to be chatting with the stud, but she was a business woman and she was conducting business. Douglas could deal with that.

The second set was of Donna in the Newport gym where she worked with a personal trainer twice a week. Her trainer was one of those sculpted bodies with a head of hair on which every strand looked as if it had been seen to professionally on a daily basis. In the pictures, Donna was dressed to work out – nothing Douglas had not seen before – but for the first time he noted how carefully she assembled her work-out clothes. From the leggings to the leotard to the headband she wore, everything enhanced her. The trainer appeared to recognize this because he squatted before her as she did her vertical butterflies.

Her legs were spread and there was no doubt what he was concentrating on. This looked more serious.

He was about to ask Cowley to start tailing the trainer, when the investigator said, 'No body contact between them other than what you'd expect,' and handed him the last set of pictures, saying, 'These're the only ones that look a little shaky to me, but they may mean nothing. You know this guy?'

Douglas stared, with *know this guy, know this guy* ringing in his skull. Unlike the other pictures in which Donna and her companion-of-the-moment were in one location, these showed Donna at a view table in an ocean-front restaurant, Donna on the Balboa ferry, Donna walking along a dock in Newport. In each of these pictures, she was with a man, the same man. In each of these pictures there was body contact. It was nothing extreme because they were out in public. But it was the kind of body contact that betrayed: an arm around her shoulders, a kiss on her cheek, a full body hug that said, Feel me up, baby, cause I ain't limp like him.

Douglas felt that his world was spinning, but he

managed a wry grin. He said, 'Oh hell. Now I feel like a class-A fool.'

'Why's that?' Cowley asked.

'This guy?' Douglas indicated the athletic-looking man in the picture with Donna. 'Jesus. This is her brother.'

'You're kidding.'

'Nope. He's a walk-on coach at Newport Harbour High. His name is Mike. He's a free spirit type.' Douglas gripped the railing with one hand and shook his head with what he hoped looked like chagrin. 'Is this all you've got?'

'That's it. I can tail her for a while longer and see—'

'Nah. Forget it. Jesus. I sure feel dumb.' Douglas ripped the photographs into confetti. He tossed this into the water where it formed a mantle that was quickly shredded by the waves that arced against the pier's pilings. 'What do I owe you, Mr Cowley?' he asked. 'What's this dumb ass got to pay for not trusting the finest woman on earth?'

He took Cowley to Dillman's on the corner of Main

and Balboa Boulevard, and they sat at the snake-like bar with the locals, where they knocked back a couple of brews apiece. Douglas worked on his affability act, playing the abashed husband who suddenly realizes what a dickhead he's been. He took all of Donna's actions over the past weeks and reinterpreted them for Cowley. The unexplained absences became the foundation for a treat she was planning for him: the purchase of a new car, perhaps; a trip to Europe; the refurbishing of his boat. The secretive telephone calls became messages from his children who were in the know. The new underwear metamorphosed into a display of her wish to make herself desirable for him, to work him out of his temporary impotence by giving him a renewed interest in her body. He felt like a total idiot, he told Cowley. Could they burn the damn negatives together?

They made a ceremony of it, torching the negatives of the damning pictures in the alley behind JJ's Natural Haircutting. Afterwards, Douglas drove in a daze to Newport Harbour High School. He sat numbly across the street from it. He waited two hours. Finally, he saw his youngest brother arrive for the afternoon's coaching session, a basketball tucked under his arm and an athletic bag in his hand.

Michael, he thought. Returned from Greece this time, but always the prodigal son. Before Greece, it was a year with Greenpeace on the *Rainbow Warrior*. Before that, it was an expedition up the Amazon. And before that, it was marching against apartheid in South Africa. He had a resumé that would be the envy of any pre-pubescent kid out for a good time. He was Mr Adventure, Mr Irresponsibility, and Mr Charm. He was Mr Good Intentions without any follow-through. When a promise was due to be kept, he was out of sight, out of mind, and out of the country. But everyone loved the son of a bitch. He was forty years old, the baby of the Armstrong brothers, and he always got precisely what he wanted.

He wanted Donna now, the miserable bastard. No matter that she was his brother's wife. That made having her just so much more fun.

Douglas felt ill. His guts rolled around like marbles in a bucket. Sweat broke out in patches on his body. He couldn't go back to work like this. He reached for the phone and called his office.

He was sick, he told his secretary. Must have been something he ate for lunch. He was heading home. She could catch him there if anything came up.

In the house, he wandered from room to room. Donna wasn't home – wouldn't be home for hours – so he had plenty of time to consider what to do. His mind reproduced for him the pictures that Cowley had taken of Michael and Donna. His intellect deduced where they had been and what they'd been doing prior to those pictures being taken.

He went to his study. There, in a glass curio cabinet, his collection of ivory erotica mocked him. Miniature Asians posed in a variety of sexual postures, having themselves a roaring good time. He could see Michael and Donna's features superimposed on the creamy faces of the figurines. They took their pleasure at his expense. They justified their pleasure by using his failure. No limp dick here, Michael's voice taunted. What's the matter, big brother? Can't hang onto your wife?

Douglas felt shattered. He told himself that he

could have handled her doing anything else, he could have handled seeing her with anyone else. But not Michael, who had trailed him through life, making his mark in every area where Douglas himself had previously failed. In high school it had been in athletics and student government. In college it had been in the world of fraternities. As an adult it had been in embracing adventure rather than in tackling the grind of business. And now, it was in proving to Donna what real manhood was all about.

Douglas could see them together as easily as he could see his pieces of erotica intertwined. Their bodies joined, their heads thrown back, their hands clasped, their hips grinding and grinding against each other. God, he thought. The pictures in his mind would drive him mad. He felt like killing.

The telephone company gave him the proof he required. He asked for a print-out of the calls that had been made from his home. And when he received it, there was Michael's number. Not once or twice, but repeatedly. All of the calls had been made when he – Douglas – wasn't at home.

It was clever of Donna to use the nights when she knew Douglas would be doing his volunteer stint at the Newport suicide hotline. She knew he never missed his Wednesday evening shift, so important was it to him to have the hotline among his community commitments. She knew he was building a political profile to get himself elected to the city council, and the hotline was part of the picture of himself that he wished to paint: Douglas Armstrong, husband, father, oilman, and compassionate listener to the emotionally distressed. He needed something to put into the balance of his environmental lapses. The hotline allowed him to say that while he may have spilled oil on a few lousy pelicans – not to mention some miserable otters – he would never let a human life hang there in jeopardy.

Donna had known he'd never skip even a part of his evening shift, so she'd waited till then to make her calls to Michael. There they were on the print-out, every one of them made between 6:00 and 9:00 on a Wednesday night.

Okay, the bitch liked Wednesday night so well. Wednesday night would be the night that he killed her.

*   *   *

He could hardly bear to be around her once he had the proof of her betrayal. She knew something was wrong between them because he didn't want to touch her any longer. Their thrice-weekly attempted couplings – as disastrous as they'd been – fast became a thing of the past. Still, she carried on as if nothing and no one had come between them, sashaying through the bedroom in her Victoria's Secret selection-of-the-night, trying to entice him into making a fool of himself so she could share the laughter with his brother Michael.

No way, baby, Douglas thought. You'll be sorry you made a fool out of me.

When she finally cuddled next to him in bed and murmured, 'Doug, is something wrong? You want to talk? You okay?' it was all he could do not to shove her from him. He wasn't okay. He would never be okay again. But at least he'd be able to salvage a measure of his self-respect by giving the little bitch her due.

It was easy enough to plan once he decided on the very next Wednesday.

A trip to Radio Shack was all that was necessary. He chose the busiest one he could find, deep in the barrio in Santa Ana, and he deliberately took his time browsing until the youngest clerk with the most acne and the least amount of brainpower was available to wait on him. Then he made his purchase with cash: a call diverter, just the thing for those on-the-go SoCal folks who didn't want to miss an incoming phone call. No answering machine for those types. This would divert a phone call from one number to another by means of a simple computer chip. Once Douglas programmed the diverter with the number he wanted incoming calls diverted to, he would have an alibi for the night of his wife's murder. It was all so easy.

Donna had been a real numbskull to try to cheat on him. She had been a bigger numbskull to do her cheating on Wednesday nights because the fact of her doing it on Wednesday nights was what gave him the idea of how to snuff her. The volunteers on the hotline worked it in shifts. Generally there were two people present, each manning one of the telephone lines. But Newport Beach types actually didn't feel suicidal very often, and if they did, they were more likely to go to Neiman-Marcus and buy their way out of their depression. Midweek especially was a slow time for the pill-poppers and wrist-slashers, so the hotline was manned on Wednesdays by only one person a shift.

Douglas used the days prior to Wednesday to get his timing down to a military precision. He chose 8:30 as Donna's death hour, which would give him time to sneak out of the hotline office, drive home, put out her lights, and get back to the hotline before the next shift arrived at 9:00. He was carving it out fairly thin and allowing only a five minute margin of error, but he needed to do that in order to have a believable alibi once her body was found.

There could be neither noise nor blood, obviously. Noise would arouse the neighbours. Blood would damn him if he got so much as a drop on his clothes, DNA typing being what it is these days. So he chose his weapon carefully, aware of the irony of his choice. He would use the satin belt of one of her Victoria's Secret slay-him-where-he-stands dressing gowns. She had half a dozen, so he would remove one of them in advance of the murder, separate it from its belt, dispose of it in a dumpster behind the nearest Von's in advance of the killing – he liked that touch, getting rid of evidence *before* the crime, what killer ever thought of that? – and then use the belt to strangle his cheating wife on Wednesday night.

The call diverter would establish his alibi. He would take it to the suicide hotline, plug the phone into it, program the diverter with his cellular phone number, and thus appear to be in one location while his wife was being murdered in another. He made sure Donna was going to be at home by doing what he always did on Wednesdays: by phoning her from work before he left for the hotline.

'I feel like dogshit,' he told her at 5:40.

'Oh, Doug, no!' she replied. 'Are you ill or just feeling depressed about—'

'I'm feeling punk,' he interrupted her. The last thing he wanted was to listen to her phoney sympathy. 'It may have been lunch.'

'What did you have?'

Nothing. He hadn't eaten in two days. But he came up with, 'Shrimp', because he'd gotten food poisoning from shrimp a few years back and he thought she'd remember that, if she remembered anything at all about him at this point. He went on, 'I'm going to try to get home early from the hotline. I may not be able to if I can't pull in a substitute to take my shift. I'm heading over there now. If I can get a sub, I'll be home pretty early.'

He could hear her attempt to hide her dismay when she replied, 'But Doug . . . I mean, what time do you think you'll make it?'

'I don't know. By 8:00 at the latest, I hope. Why? What difference does it make?'

'No. None at all. But I thought you might like dinner . . .'

What she really thought was how she was going to have to cancel her hot romp with his baby brother. Douglas smiled at the realization of how nicely he'd just cooked her little caboose.

'Hell, I'm not hungry, Donna. I just want to go to bed if I can. You be there to rub my back? You going anywhere?'

'Of course not. Where would I be going? Doug, you sound strange. Is something wrong?'

Nothing was wrong, he told her. What he didn't tell her was how right everything was, felt, and was going to be. He had her where he wanted her now: she'd be home, and she'd be alone. She might phone Michael and tell him that his brother was coming home early so their tryst was off, but even if she did that, Michael's statement after her death would conflict with Douglas's uninterrupted presence at the suicide hotline that evening.

Douglas just had to make sure that he was back at the hotline with time to disassemble the call diverter. He'd get rid of it on the way home – nothing could be easier than flipping it into the trash behind the huge movie theatre complex that was on his route from the hotline to Harbour Heights where he lived – and then he'd arrive at his usual time of 9:20 to 'discover' the murder of his beloved.

It was all so easy. And so much cleaner and cheaper than divorcing the little whore.

He felt remarkably at peace, considering everything. He'd seen Thistle again and she'd held his Rolex, his wedding band, and his cuff links to take her reading. She'd greeted him by telling him that his aura was strong and that she could feel the power pulsing from him. And when she closed her eyes over his possessions, she'd said, 'I feel a major change coming into your life, Not-David. A change of location, perhaps, a change of climate. Are you taking a trip?'

He might be, he told her. He hadn't had a vacation in months. Did she have any suggested destinations?

'I see lights,' she responded, going her own way. 'I see cameras. I see many faces. You're surrounded by those you love.'

They would be at Donna's funeral, of course. And the press would cover it. He was somebody, after all. They wouldn't ignore the murder of Douglas Armstrong's wife. As for Thistle, she'd find out who he really was if she read the paper or watched the local news. But that made no difference since he'd never mentioned Donna and since he'd have an alibi for the time of her death.

He arrived at the suicide hotline at 5:56. He was relieving a UCI psych student named Debbie who was eager enough to be gone. She said, 'Only two calls, Mr Armstrong. If your shift is like mine, I hope you brought something to read.'

He waved his copy of *Money* magazine and took her place at the desk. He waited ten minutes after she'd left before he went out to his car to get the call diverter.

The hotline was located in the dock area of Newport, a maze of narrow one-way streets that traversed the top of Balboa Peninsula. By day, the streets' antique stores, marine chandleries, and second-hand clothing boutiques attracted both locals and tourists. By night, the place was a ghost town, uninhabited expect for the New Wave beatniks who visited a dive called the Omega Café three streets away, where anorexic girls dressed in black read poetry and strummed guitars. So no one was on the street to see Douglas fetch the call diverter from his Mercedes. And no one was on the street to see him leave the suicide hotline's small cubbyhole behind the real estate office at 8:15. And should any desperate individual call the hotline during his drive home, that call would be diverted onto his cellular phone and he could deal with it. God, the plan was perfect.

As he drove up the curving road that led to his house, Douglas thanked his stars that he'd chosen to live in an environment in which privacy was everything to the homeowners. Every estate sat, like Douglas's, behind walls and gates, shielded by trees. On one day in ten, he might actually see another resident. Most of the time – like tonight – there was no one around.

Even if someone had seen his Mercedes sliding up the hill, however, it was January dark and his was just another luxury vehicle in a community of Rolls-Royces, Bentleys, BMWs, Lexuses, Range Rovers, and other Mercedes. Besides, he'd already decided that if he saw someone or something suspicious, he would just turn around, go back to the hotline, and wait for another Wednesday.

But he didn't see anything out of the ordinary. He didn't see anyone. Perhaps a few more cars were parked on the street, but these were empty. He had the night to himself.

At the top of his drive, he shut off the engine and coasted to the house. It was dark inside, which told him that Donna was in the back, in their bedroom.

He needed her outside. The house was equipped
with a security system that would do a bank vault
proud, so he needed the killing to take place outside
where a Peeping Tom gone bazooka or a burglar or
a serial killer might have lured her. He thought of
Ted Bundy and how he'd snagged his victims by
appealing to their maternal need to come to his aid.
He'd go the Bundy route, he decided. Donna was
nothing if not eager to help.

He got out of the car silently and paced over to the
door. He rang the bell with the back of his hand, the
better to leave no trace on the button. In less than ten
seconds, Donna's voice came over the intercom.

'Hi, babe,' he said. 'My hands are full. Can you
let me in?'

'Be a sec,' she told him.

He took the satin belt from his pocket as he
waited. He pictured her route from the back of
the house. He twisted the satin round his hands
and snapped it tight. Once she opened the door,
he'd have to move like lightning. He'd have only
one chance to fling the cord round her neck. The
advantage he already possessed was surprise.

He heard her footsteps on the limestone. He gripped the satin and prepared. He thought of Michael. He thought of her together with Michael. He thought of his Asian erotica. He thought of betrayal, failure, and trust. She deserved this. They both deserved it. He was only sorry he couldn't kill Michael right now too.

When the door swung open, he heard her say, 'Doug! I thought you said—'

And then he was on her. He leapt. He yanked the belt round her neck. He dragged her swiftly out of the house. He tightened it and tightened it and tightened it and tightened it. She was too startled to fight back. In the five seconds it took her to get her hands to the belt in a reflex attempt to pull it away from her throat, he had it digging into her skin so deeply that her scrabbling fingers could find no slip of material to grab onto.

He felt her go limp. He said, 'Jesus. Yes. *Yes.*'

And then it happened.

The lights went on in the house. A Mariachi band started playing. People shouted 'Surprise! Surprise! Sur—'

Douglas looked up, panting, from the body of his wife, into popping flashes and a video camcorder. The joyous shouting from within his house was cut off by a single female shriek. He dropped Donna to the ground and stared without comprehension into the entry and, beyond that, the living room. There, at least three dozen people were gathered beneath a banner that said, 'Surprise, Dougie! Happy Five-Five!'

He saw the horrified faces of his brothers and their wives and children, of his own children, of his parents, of one of his former wives. And among them, his colleagues and his secretary. The chief of police. And the mayor.

He thought, What is this, Donna? Some kind of joke?

And then he saw Michael coming from the direction of the kitchen, Michael with a birthday cake in his hands, Michael calling out, 'Did we surprise him, Donna? Poor Doug. I hope his heart—' And then saying nothing at all when he saw his brother and his brother's wife.

Shit, Douglas thought. What have I done?

Which was, indeed, the question he'd be answering for the rest of his life.

Whet your appetite for murder with this taste of Elizabeth George's new bestseller, *In Pursuit of the Proper Sinner*, available now from Hodder & Stoughton.

It was just after seven the next morning when Julian returned to Maiden Hall. If he hadn't explored every possible site from Consall Wood to Alport Height, he certainly felt as if he had. Torch in one hand, loud hailer in the other, he'd gone through the motions: He'd trudged the leafy woodland path from Wettonmill up the steep grade to Thor's Cave. He'd scoured along the River Manifold. He'd shone his torchlight up the slope of Thorpe Cloud. He'd followed the River Dove as far south as the old medieval manor at Norbury. At the village of Alton, he'd hiked a distance along the Staffordshire Way. He'd driven as many as he could manage of the single lane roads that Nicola favoured. And he'd paused periodically to use the loud hailer in calling her name. Deliberately marking his presence in every location, he'd awakened sheep, farmers, and campers during his eight hours' search for her. At heart, he'd known there was no chance that he would find her, but at least he'd been *doing* something instead of waiting at home by the phone. At the end of it all, he felt anxious and empty. And completely fagged out, with throbbing eyeballs, bruised calves, and a back that ached from the night's exertion.

He was hungry as well. He could have eaten a leg of lamb had one been offered. It was odd, he thought. Just the previous night – wrought up with anticipation and nerves – he'd barely been able to touch his dinner. Indeed, Samantha had been a bit put out at the manner in which

201

he merely picked at her fine sole amandine. She'd taken his lack of appetite personally, and while his father had leered about a man having other appetites to take care of, Sam, and wasn't their Julie about to do just that with we-all-know-who this very night, Samantha had pressed her lips together and cleared the table.

He'd have been able to do justice to one of her table-groaning breakfasts now, Julian thought. But as it was . . . Well, it didn't seem right to think about food – let alone to ask for it – despite the fact that the paying guests in Maiden Hall would be tucking into everything from corn flakes to kippers within the half hour.

He needn't have worried about the propriety in hoping for food under the circumstances, however. When he walked into the kitchen of Maiden Hall, a plate of scrambled eggs, mushrooms, and sausage sat untouched before Nan Maiden. She offered it to him the moment she saw him, saying, 'They want me to eat, but I can't. Please take it. I expect you could do with a meal.'

They were the early kitchen staff: two women from the nearby village of Grindleford who cooked in the mornings when the sophisticated culinary efforts of Christian-Louis were as unnecessary as they would be unwanted.

'Bring it with you, Julian.' Nan put a cafetiere on a tray with coffee mugs, milk, and sugar. She led the way into the dining room.

Only one table was occupied. Nan nodded at the couple who'd placed themselves in the bay window overlooking the garden and after politely inquiring about their night's sleep and their day's plans, she joined Julian at the table he'd chosen some distance away by the kitchen door.

The fact that she never wore make-up put Nan at a

disadvantage this morning. Her eyes were troughed by blue-grey flesh. Her skin, which was lightly freckled from time spent on her mountain bicycle when she had a free hour in which to exercise, was otherwise completely pallid. Her lips – having long ago lost the natural blush of youth – bore fine lines that began beneath her nose and were ghostly white. She hadn't slept; that much was clear.

She had, however, changed her clothes from the night before, apparently knowing that it would hardly do for the proprietress of Maiden Hall to greet her guests in the morning wearing what she'd worn as their hostess at dinner on the previous night. So her cocktail dress had been replaced by stirrup trousers and a tailored blouse.

She poured them each a cup of coffee and watched as Julian tucked into the eggs and mushrooms. She said, 'Tell me about the engagement. I need something to keep from thinking the worst.' When she spoke, tears caused her eyes to look glazed and unfocused, but she didn't weep.

Julian made himself mirror her control. 'Where's Andy?'

'Not back yet.' She circled her hands round her mug. Her grip was so tight that her fingers – their nails habitually bitten to the quick – were bleached of colour. 'Tell me about the two of you, Julian. Please. Tell me.'

'It's going to be all right,' Julian said. The last thing he wanted to force upon himself was having to concoct a scenario in which he and Nicola fell in love like ordinary human beings, realised that love, and founded upon it a life together. He couldn't face that at the moment. 'She's an experienced hiker. And she didn't go out there unprepared.'

'I know that. But I don't want to think about what it means that she hasn't come home. So tell me about the engagement. Where were you when you asked her? What did you say? What kind of wedding will it be? And when?'

Julian felt a chill at the double direction Nan's thoughts were taking. In either case, they brought up subjects he didn't want to consider. One led him to dwell upon the unthinkable. The other did nothing but encourage more lies.

He went for a truth that both of them knew. 'Nicola's been hiking in the Peaks since you moved from London. Even if she's hurt herself, she knows what to do till help arrives.' He forked up a portion of egg and mushrooms. 'It's lucky that she and I had a date. If we hadn't, God knows when we might've set out to find her.'

Nan looked away, but her eyes were still liquid. She lowered her head.

'We should be hopeful,' Julian went on. 'She's well-equipped. And she doesn't panic when things get dicey. We all know that.'

'But if she's fallen . . . or got lost in one of the caves . . . Julian, it happens. You know that. No matter how well prepared someone is, the worst still happens sometimes.'

'There's nothing that says anything's happened. I only looked in the south part of the White Peak. There're more square miles out there than can be covered by one man in total darkness in an evening. She could be anywhere. She could even have gone to the Dark Peak without our knowing.' He didn't mention the nightmare Mountain Rescue faced whenever someone *did* disappear in the Dark Peak. There was, after all, no mercy in fracturing Nan's tenuous hold on her calm. She knew the reality about the Dark Peak, anyway, and she didn't need him to point out to her that while roads made most of the White Peak accessible, its sister to the north could only be traversed by horseback, on foot, or by helicopter. If a hiker got lost or hurt up there, it generally took bloodhounds to find him.

'She said she'd marry you, though,' Nan declared, more to herself than to Julian, it seemed. 'She *did* say that she'd marry you, Julian?'

The poor woman seemed so eager to be lied to that Julian found himself just as eager to oblige her. 'We hadn't quite *got* to yes or no yet. That's what last night was supposed to be about.'

Nan lifted her coffee with both hands and drank. 'Was she . . . Did she seem pleased? I only ask because she'd seemed to have . . . Well, she'd seemed to have some sort of plans, and I'm not quite sure . . .'

Carefully Julian speared a mushroom. 'Plans?'

'I'd thought . . . Yes, it seemed so.'

He looked at Nan. Nan looked at him. He was the one to blink. He said steadily, 'Nicola had no plans that I know of, Nan.'

The kitchen door swung open a few inches. The face of one of the Grindleford women appeared in the aperture. She said, 'Mrs Maiden, Mr Britton,' in a low, hushed voice. And she used her head to indicate the direction of the kitchen. *You're wanted*, the motion implied.

Andy was leaning against one of the work tops, facing it, his weight on his hands and his head bowed. When his wife said his name, he looked up.

His face was drawn with exhaustion, and his growth of peppery whiskers fanned out from his moustache and shadowed his cheeks. His grey hair was uncombed, looking windblown although there wasn't any wind to speak of this morning. His eyes went to Nan, then slid away. Julian prepared himself to hear the worst.

'Her car's on the edge of Calder Moor,' Andy told them.

His wife drew her hands into a fist at her breast. 'Thank *God*,' she said.

Still, Andy didn't look at her. His expression indicated that thanks were premature. He knew what Julian knew and what Nan herself might well have acknowledged had she paused to probe for the possibilities that were indicated by the location of Nicola's Saab. Calder Moor was vast. It began just west of the road stretching between Blackwell and Brough, and it comprised endless expanses of heather and gorse, four caverns, numerous cairns and forts and barrows spanning time from Paleolithic through Iron Age, gritstone outcroppings and limestone caves and fissures through which more than one foolish tripper had crawled for adventure and become hopelessly stuck. Julian knew that Andy was thinking of this as he stood in the kitchen at the end of his long night's search for Nicola. But Andy was thinking something else as well. Andy was *knowing* something else, in fact. That much was evident from the manner in which he straightened and began slapping the knuckles of one hand against the heel of the other.

Julian said, 'Andy, for God's sake, *tell* us.'

Andy's gaze fixed on his wife. 'The car's not on the verge, like you'd think it should be.'

'Then where . . . ?'

'It's out of sight behind a wall, on the road out of Sparrowpit.'

'But that's good, isn't it?' Nan said eagerly. 'If she went

camping, she wouldn't want to leave the Saab on the road. Not where it could be seen by someone who might break into it.'

'True,' he said. 'But the car's not alone.' And with a glance towards Julian as if he wished to apologise for something, 'There's a motorcycle with it.'

'Someone out for a hike,' Julian said.

'At this hour?' Andy shook his head. 'It was wet from the night. As wet as her car. It's been there just as long.'

Nan eagerly said, 'Then she didn't go onto the moor alone? She met someone there?'

'Or she was followed,' Julian added quietly.

'I'm calling the police,' Andy said. 'They'll want to bring in Mountain Rescue now.'

When a patient died, it was Phoebe Neill's habit to turn to the land for comfort. She generally did this alone. She'd lived alone for most of her life, and she wasn't afraid of solitude. And in the combination of solitude and a return to the land, she received consolation. When she was out in nature, nothing manmade stood between her and the Great Creator. Thus on the land, she was able to align herself with the end of a life and the will of God, knowing that the body we inhabit is but a shell that binds us for a period of temporal experience prior to our entering the world of the spirit for the next phase of our development.

This Thursday morning things were different, though. Yes, a patient had died on the previous evening. Yes, Phoebe Neill turned to the land for solace. But on this occasion, she hadn't come alone. She'd brought with her a mixed breed dog of uncertain lineage, the now-orphaned pet of the young man whose life had just ended.

She'd been the one to talk Stephen Fairbrook into getting a dog as a companion during the last year of his illness. So when it had become clear that the end of Stephen's life was fast approaching, she knew that she'd make his passing easier if she reassured him about the dog's fate. 'Stevie, when the time comes, I'm happy to take Benbow,' she'd told him one morning as she bathed his skeletal body and massaged lotion into his shrunken limbs. 'You're not to worry about him. All right?'

You can die now was what went unspoken. Not because words like *die* or *death* were unmentionable round Stephen Fairbrook, but because once he'd been told his disease, been through countless treatments and drugs in an effort to stay alive long enough for a cure to be found, watched his weight decline and his hair fall out and his skin bloom with bruises that turned into sores, *die* and *death* were old companions to him. He didn't need a formal introduction to guests who were already dwelling within his house.

On the last afternoon of his master's life Benbow had known Stephen was passing. And hour after hour, the animal lay quietly next to him, moving only if Stephen moved, his muzzle resting in Stephen's hand until Stephen had left them. Benbow, in fact, had known before Phoebe that Stephen was gone. He'd risen, whimpered, howled once, and was silent. He'd then sought out the comfort of his basket, where he'd stayed until Phoebe had collected him.

Now he raised himself on his hind legs, his plumed tail wagging hopefully as Phoebe parked her car in a lay-by near a drystone wall and reached for his lead. He barked once. Phoebe smiled. 'Yes. A walk shall make us right as rain, old chap.'

She clambered out. Benbow followed, leaping agilely from the Vauxhall and sniffing eagerly, nose pressed to the sandy ground like a canine Hoover. He led Phoebe directly to the wall and snuffled along it until he came to the stile that would allow him access to the moor beyond. This he leapt over easily, and once on the other side he paused to shake himself off. His ears pricked up and he cocked his head. He gave a sharp bark to tell Phoebe that a solo run, not a walk on a lead, was what he had in mind.

'Can't do it, old boy,' Phoebe told him. 'Not till we see what's what and who's who on the moor, all right?' She was cautious and overprotective that way, which made for excellent skills when it came to nursing the house-bound dying through their final days, particularly those whose conditions required hyper-vigilance on the part of their care giver. But when it came to children or to dog ownership, Phoebe knew intuitively that the natural hovering born of a cautious nature would have produced a fearful animal or a rebellious child. So she'd had no child – although she'd had her opportunities – and she'd had no dog till now. 'I hope to do right by you, Benbow,' she told the mongrel. He lifted his head to look at her, past the scraggly kelp-coloured mop of fur that flopped into his eyes. He swung back round towards the open moor, mile after mile of heather creating a purple shawl that covered the shoulders of the land.

Had the moor consisted of heather alone, Phoebe would not have given a second thought to letting Benbow have his romp unrestrained. But the seemingly endless flow of the heather was deceptive to the uninitiated. Ancient limestone quarries produced unexpected lacunae in the landscape, into which the dog could tumble, and the caverns, lead mines, and caves into which he could scamper – and where she could not follow – served as a siren enticement for any animal, an enticement with which Phoebe Neill didn't care to compete. But she was willing to let Benbow snuffle freely through one of the many birch copses that grew in irregular clumps on the moor, rising like feathers against the sky, and she grasped his lead firmly and began heading northwest where the largest of the copses grew.

It was a fine morning, but there were no other walkers about yet. The sun was low in the eastern sky, and Phoebe's shadow stretched far to her left as if it wished to pursue a cobalt horizon that was heaped with clouds so white they might have been giant sleeping swans. There was little wind, just enough of a breeze to slap Phoebe's windcheater against her sides and flip Benbow's tangled fur from his eyes. There was no scent on this breeze that Phoebe could discern. And the only noise came from an unkindness of ravens somewhere on the moor and a flock of sheep bleating in the distance.

Benbow snuffled along, investigating nasally every inch of the path as well as the mounds of heather that edged it. He was a cooperative walker, as Phoebe had discovered from the thrice-daily strolls she and he had taken once Stephen had been completely confined to bed. And because she didn't have to tug him along or pull him back or encourage the little dog in any way, their jaunt on the moor gave her time to pray.

She didn't pray for Stephen Fairbrook. She knew that Stephen was now at peace, quite beyond the necessity of an intervention – Divine or otherwise – in the process of the inevitable. What she prayed for was greater understanding. She wanted to know why a scourge had come to dwell among them, felling the best, the brightest, and frequently those with the most to offer. She wanted to know what conclusion she was meant to draw from the deaths of young men who were guilty of nothing, of the deaths of children whose crime was to be born of infected mothers, and of the deaths of those unfortunate mothers as well.

When Benbow wanted to pick up the pace, she was willing to do so. In this manner, they strode into the heart of the moor, ambling along one path, forking off onto another. Phoebe wasn't worried about becoming lost. She knew that they'd begun their walk southeast of a limestone outcrop that was called Agricola's Throne. It was the remains of a great Roman fort, a windswept outlook shaped not unlike an enormous chair that marked the edge of the moor. It towered above a valley of pastures, villages, and derelict mills, and anyone sighting off the throne during a hike was unlikely to get lost.

They'd been trekking for an hour when Benbow's ears pricked up and his stance altered. From shuffling along happily, he came to a sudden halt. His body elongated, back legs stretching out. His feathery tail stiffened into an immobile quill. A low whine issued from his throat.

Phoebe studied what lay before them: the copse of birches she'd intended to allow Benbow to gambol in. 'Gracious me,' she murmured. 'Aren't you the clever one, Bennie?' She was deeply surprised and just as deeply touched

by the mongrel's ability to read her intentions. She'd
silently promised him freedom when they reached the
copse. And here the copse was. He read her mind and
was eager to be off the lead. 'Can't blame you a bit,'
Phoebe said as she knelt to unhook the lead from his
collar. She wound the rope of braided leather round her
hand and rose with a grunt as the dog shot ahead of her
into the trees.

Phoebe walked after him, smiling at the sight of his
compact body bouncing along the path. He used his
feet like springs as he ran, bounding off the ground
with all four legs at once as if it were his intention to
fly. He skirted a large column of roughly hewn limestone on the edge of the copse and vanished among the
birches.

This was the entrance to Nine Sisters' Henge, a Neolithic
earth-banked enclosure that encircled nine standing stones
of varying heights. Assembled some thirty-five hundred
years before the time of Christ, the henge and the stones
marked a spot for rituals engaged in by prehistoric man. At
the time of its use, the henge had been standing in open land
that had been cleared of its natural oak and alder forest.
Now, however, it was hidden from view, buried within a
thick growth of birches, a modern encroachment on the
resulting moorland.

Phoebe paused and surveyed her surroundings. The
eastern sky – without the clouds of the west – allowed
the sun to pierce unimpeded through the trees. Their
bark was the white of a seagull's wing, but patterned
with diamond-shaped cracks the colour of coffee. Leaves
formed a shimmering green screen in the morning breeze,
which served to shield the ancient stone circle within the

copse from an inexperienced hiker who didn't know it was there. Standing before the birches, the sentry stone was hit by the light at an oblique angle. This deepened its natural pocking, and from a distance the shadows combined to effect a face, an austere custodian of secrets too ancient to be imagined.

As Phoebe observed the stone, an unaccountable chill passed through her. Despite the breeze, it was silent here. No noise from the dog, no bleating of a sheep lost among the stones, no call of hikers as they crossed the moor. It was altogether too silent, Phoebe thought. And she found herself glancing round uneasily, overcome by the feeling that she was being watched.

Phoebe thought herself a practical woman, one not given to casual fancies or an imagination run riot with ghosties and ghoulies and things that go bump in the night. Nonetheless, she felt the sudden need to be away from this place, and she called for the dog. There was no response.

'Benbow!' she called a second time. 'Here, boy. *Come.*'
Nothing. The silence intensified. The breeze stilled. And Phoebe felt the hair stirring on the back of her neck.

She didn't wish to approach the copse, but she didn't know why. She'd walked among the Nine Sisters before. She'd even had a quiet picnic lunch there one fine spring day. But there was something about the place this morning . . .

A sharp bark from Benbow and suddenly what seemed like hundreds of ravens took to the air in an ebony swarm. For a moment they entirely blocked out the sun. The shadow they cast seemed like a monstrous fist sweeping over Phoebe. She shuddered at the distinct sensation of having been marked somehow, like Cain before being sent to the east.

She swallowed and turned back to the copse. There was no further sound from Benbow, no response to her calling. Concerned, Phoebe hurried along the path, passed the limestone guardian of that sacred place, and entered the trees.

They grew thickly, but visitors to the site had trod a path through them over the years. On this, the natural grass of the moor had been flattened and worn through to the earth in spots. To the sides, however, bilberry bushes formed part of the undergrowth, and the last of the wild purple orchids gave off their characteristic scent of cats in the tough moor grass. It was here beneath the trees that Phoebe looked for Benbow, drawing nearer to the ancient stones. The silence round her was so profound that the very fact of it seemed like an augur, mute but eloquent all at once.

Then, as Phoebe drew near the circle's boundary, she finally heard the dog again. He yelped from somewhere, then emitted something between a whine and a growl. It was decidedly fearful. Worried that he'd encountered a hiker who was less than welcoming of his canine advances, Phoebe hastened towards the sound, through the remaining trees and into the circle.

At once, she saw a mound of bright blue at the inner base of one of the standing stones. It was at this mound that Benbow barked, backing off from it now with his hackles up and his ears flattened back against his skull.

'What is it?' Phoebe asked, over his noise. 'What've you found, old boy?' Uneasily, she wiped her palms on her skirt and glanced about. She saw the answer to her question lying round her. What the dog had found was a scene of chaos. The centre of the stone circle was strewn with white feathers, and the detritus of some thoughtless campers lay scattered about: everything from a tent to a cooking pot to an opened rucksack spilling its contents onto the ground.

Phoebe approached the dog through this clutter. She wanted to get Benbow back on the lead and get both of them out of the circle at once.

She said, 'Benbow, come here,' and he yelped more loudly. It was the sort of sound she'd never heard from him before.

She saw that he was clearly upset by the mound of blue, the source of the white feathers that dusted the clearing like the wings of slaughtered moths.

It was a sleeping bag, she realised. And it was from this bag that the feathers had come, because a slash in the nylon that served as its cover spat more white feathers when Phoebe touched the bag with her toe. Indeed, nearly all the feathers that constituted its stuffing were gone. What remained was like a tarpaulin. It had been completely unzipped and it was shrouding something, something that terrified the little dog.

Phoebe felt weak-kneed, but she made herself do it. She lifted the cover. Benbow backed off, giving her a clear look at the nightmare vignette that the sleeping bag had covered.

Blood. There was more in front of her than she'd ever seen before. It wasn't bright red because it had obviously been exposed to air for a good number of hours. But Phoebe didn't require that colour to know what she was looking at.

'Oh my Lord.' She went light-headed.

She'd seen death before in many guises, but none had been as grisly as this. At her feet, a young man lay curled like a foetus, dressed head-to-toe in nothing but black, with that same colour puckering burnt flesh from eye to jaw on one side of his face. His cropped hair was black as well, as was the pony tail that sprang from his skull. His goatee was black. His fingernails were black. He wore an onyx ring and an earring of black. The only colour that offered relief from the black – aside from the sleeping bag of blue – was the magenta of blood, and that was everywhere: on the ground beneath him, saturating his clothes, pooling from scores of wounds on his torso.

Phoebe dropped the sleeping bag and backed away from the body. She felt hot. She felt cold. She knew that she was about to faint. She chided herself for her lack of backbone. She said, 'Benbow?' and over her voice, she heard the dog barking. She realised that he'd never stopped. But four of her senses had deadened with shock, heightening and honing her fifth sense: sight.

She scooped up the dog and stumbled from the horror.

DIAMOND wasn't always a s████████ ██ ██ ███niless
parents who longed fo██████ ████ ███thy son,
she was a dainty █████ ████ ████nter – and a
bit███ ███ ████ment.

Discovering an extraordinary gift for acrobatics, Diamond
tries to use her talent to earn a few pennies, but brings
shame on her family. Then a cruel-eyed stranger spots
her performing, and makes a deal with her father.
Diamond is sold for five guineas, and is taken, alone
and frightened, to become an acrobat at
Tanglefield's Travelling Circus.

The crowds adore Diamond, but life behind
the red velvet curtains is far from glamorous.
Her master is wicked and greedy, forcing Diamond
to attempt ever more daring and dangerous tricks.
But there are friends to be found at the circus, too:
gentle Mister Marvel; kindly Madame Adeline;
and Emerald Star, Tanglefield's brand-new
ringmaster, and Diamond's heroine.

When life at the circus becomes too dangerous
to bear any longer, what will the future
hold for Diamond? And will her beloved
Emerald be a part of it?

www.**randomhousechildrens**.co.uk

Jacqueline Wilson

From the world of Hetty Feather

DIAMOND

A new star, a new story

ILLUSTRATED BY NICK SHARRATT

CORGI YEARLING

DIAMOND
A CORGI YEARLING BOOK 978 0 440 86986 3

First published in Great Britain by Doubleday,
an imprint of Random House Children's Publishers UK
A Random House Group Company

Doubleday edition published 2013
This edition published 2014

3 5 7 9 10 8 6 4 2

The Random House Group Limited supports the Forest Stewardship Council®
(FSC®), the leading international forest-certification organisation. Our books
carrying the FSC label are printed on FSC®-certified paper. FSC is the
only forest-certification scheme supported by the leading environmental
organisations, including Greenpeace. Our paper procurement policy
can be found at www.randomhouse.co.uk/environment.

MIX
Paper from
responsible sources
FSC® C016897

Set in New Century Schoolbook

Random House Children's Publishers UK,
61–63 Uxbridge Road, London W5 5SA

www.randomhousechildrens.co.uk
www.totallyrandombooks.co.uk
www.randomhouse.co.uk

Addresses for companies within The Random House Group Limited
can be found at: www.randomhouse.co.uk/offices.htm

THE RANDOM HOUSE GROUP Limited Reg. No. 954009

A CIP catalogue record for this book is available from the British Library.

Printed and bound in Great Britain by CPI Group (UK) Ltd, Croydon CR0 4YY

In memory of Joan Beswick,
who was like a second mother to me

My name is Diamond. I used to be called Ellen-Jane Potts, but my dear friend Hetty says it doesn't matter a jot if you change your name. *She* has changed her name three times. She calls herself Emerald Star for all the shows – and now she has fashioned herself an emerald-green riding jacket and has shiny swashbuckling boots to stride about in. Oh, she looks such a picture! No wonder she has 'Star' for a name: she is the true star of the show. She is the cleverest girl in all the world.

1

She is smiling now as I say this, going as red as her hair. She is writing down my story for me. I am a fool when it comes to printing and spelling because I have never been to school. Hetty has laboured hard teaching me, but without any real success. I can only write about a c-a-t sitting on a m-a-t, and so my life-story would be very limited without Hetty's help.

There *was* a cat that lived in Willoughby Buildings, along with us and all the other families – a big black creature of the night called Mouser. I don't know about mice, but he certainly dined well on rats, of which there were plenty. Mouser was the only creature in Willoughby who went to sleep with a full stomach. Sometimes we were so hungry we almost considered dining on rats ourselves.

But that was in the bad old days. Shall I get started on them? No, Hetty says I should simply tell it straight. She forgets that I am a bendy girl, so I can walk bent over like a crab and turn a back flic-flac on command! But I shall try to do my best to please her, because she is my dearest friend in all the world – and she is holding the pen.

I was born in 1883, the fifth child of my mother, Lizzie Potts, and my father, Samuel. I was the second girl, and I'm afraid I was a bitter disappointment to my parents. I have a feeling my mother had been brought up to be a bad girl. Whenever we complained about our own lot, she would not speak of her child-hood but shook her head at us and said, 'You don't know you're born.' This always struck me as a little odd, because of course I knew I'd been born, and my mother – and doubtless several of my siblings – had been a witness to the fact. Not my pa though. He always made himself scarce at such times.

He stayed out all night while Ma was labouring, and sometimes the next night as well. He'd be down at the King's Arms, celebrating the new baby – or drowning his sorrows, whichever way you want to look at it. Not that he needed an excuse to go to those estab-lishments, or any other public house, for that matter. He was famous for his love of the drink – which is strange considering he was a patterer by profession and specialized in selling religious tracts and homilies against the demon drink.

You don't know what a patterer is, Hetty? There! You don't know everything, for all your wonderful edu-cation. A patterer is like a pedlar, but he doesn't sell toys and gimcracks, he sells cards and pamphlets and papers. He wanders from village to village, setting up in the middle of the street on market days and crying out his wares. I reckon you'd be good at that job, Hetty, seeing as you can come out with all the spiel and sweet-talk whenever you fancy.

My pa specialized in little gelatine cards with gilt

edges – ever so pretty, decorated with bluebirds and rosebuds and little angels. He bought them penny plain, and Ma coloured in the drawings: blue for the birds, red for the roses, pink for the cheeks and gold for the hair – dab dab dab, and there was another one done. It's easy enough. Mary-Martha and I learned to do thirty an hour or thereabouts – you could say we were dab hands at it!

As a single man, Pa had travelled up and down England calling out his wares. *'Take the Lord Jesus into your heart and lead your life accordingly,'* he'd bellow. *'Don't forget the Sabbath. Bow your head in worship'* – though Pa himself spent Sunday lying in his lodging house till dinner time before crawling out of bed with a sore head, because even in those days, before all the troubles, he haunted all the alehouses and gin palaces his tracts warned against.

One Sunday he met up with my mother. She'd been staying overnight in the same lodging house and I don't doubt she had a sore head too. I always thought of Ma as old because she had such a careworn face and her tiny body was all skin and bone, but Pa said she was a beautiful, fresh young girl when he met her, with cheeks as rosy as the cherubs on his tracts, and long fair hair curling to her waist.

Perhaps Pa would never have had the nerve to approach her if she'd been dressed up in all her finery, because he was a plain man with a great red nose like Punch, and he was a good fifteen years older than Ma to boot. But she was sitting hunched in a corner in her nightgown and shawl, weeping bitterly because some young man had treated her badly.

Pa took pity on her, and it wasn't long before she'd buried that fine head of hair in his shoulder. He patted her back with awkward tenderness. 'There now, my girl. Old Sam will look after you and see you're all right,' he said, or something to that effect – and he was as good as his word at first.

They made an odd couple, but Pa said they were as happy as two little lambs frisking in the meadow. That was his pet name for Ma. 'Where's my little lamb?' he called when he came back from his pattering travels, and Ma would go flying into his arms.

They rented their own little home: just two rooms in a big converted house, but Ma kept them spotlessly clean and stuck Pa's tracts on one wall like a mosaic picture, making it look ever so pretty. She read the tracts each day too, pointing along with one finger and muttering aloud because she struggled with her reading like me.

'Repent and praise the Lord,' she said – and she did just that. Every Sunday she went along to the church at the end of the road and stood self-consciously at the back, not sure where to go or what to do, worried that the good churchgoers would point at her and the vicar cast her out – but instead they welcomed her eagerly. They gave her a hymn book, and as she had a good ear and a light, tuneful voice, she could soon praise the Lord for all she was worth.

She begged Pa to go with her to church, but he always shook his head.

'It's not for me, little lamb. I don't take the old tracts too serious, I just sells them to put food in our bellies. Beats me why you should want to run out on a Sunday morning, my one free day, when you could stay warm and cosy in bed with me – but if that's what you want to do, I'll not stop you. I just want you to be happy.'

That's what he said to her, and that's what she told us, over and over.

'He might not be the church-going type, but he's a dear good Christian-minded man all the same. He's always treated me so sweet and tender,' Ma said, eyes brimming.

It was true enough. Pa worshipped our ma. He worried dreadfully when she started growing big with her first baby. She was very sick every morning, often fainting dead away whenever she tried to sweep the floor or throw coals on the fire. Pa did his best to help her. He got up extra early and set the stew simmering for the day. He lit the fire to keep Ma warm and tucked her up in a blanket on the sofa.

He still went out drinking on a Saturday night, but no matter how he was feeling he hauled himself out of bed on Sunday morning to help her along the road to church. He wouldn't go in himself, but he waited and waited for her outside in the cold until the sermon was over so he could help her back home.

Ma was so little they were expecting a difficult birth. I think she laboured long and hard. I don't know, I wasn't there. Pa wasn't there either. The moment Ma started screaming he left her with the midwife and scurried away out of earshot, straight to the alehouse. He said he couldn't bear to hear her suffering. He drank himself insensible, and then wouldn't come home till morning, sure he'd find himself a widower – but when he eventually crawled back, sobbing and cursing, he found Ma in bed, still breathing, with a big blond baby boy bawling his head off in her arms.

'He's my little miracle,' said Ma. 'Oh, Sam, we're a true family at last.'

I think Pa would have been happier if they'd stayed just the two of them. He was never cut out to be a family man. But now he knew that Ma had survived the birth, he was proud to call himself the father of a fine son. He went out again that very night in celebration. Ma tried hard not to mind. She held her baby tight and murmured all the good words from the tracts as if they were magical spells to keep her precious boy on the straight and narrow.

She called him Matthew, after the first book of the Holy Gospels. A year later, little Mark was born, and two years after that, baby Luke. Ma was fair worn out coping with all three of them, and Pa was hard pressed to earn enough to keep them all fed and happy. He had to leave Ma on her own with the boys while he travelled the length and breadth of the country – and find new gimcracks to sell when folk lost interest in his tracts.

He was at a great goose fair in a northern city when he spotted some plaster fairings on a Lucky Chance stall. They were the usual sort of fancy figures: twin dogs with long ears to sit on either side of a mantel clock, or comical little husbands and wives getting into bed, or shepherdesses with woolly lambs. It was one of these that caught Pa's eye. He wondered whether to try and win one for his little lamb at home – but then he spied an angel with wings and a very holy expression.

This gave him a whole new idea. He spoke to the stallholder about suppliers, bought a rubber angel mould and ordered in a sack of plaster of Paris when he got back home. Our house became like one of his own tracts: *And lo, a host of angels descended in a holy throng*. The mould was in labour night and day, producing angel after angel. There were disasters at first. The wings snapped off – or, even worse, the heads – but Pa soon mastered the knack of easing out a perfect white angel every time.

Then it was Ma's job to paint them. She varied the colours of the wings and robes, and gave the angels dark hair to contrast splendidly with their gold paint haloes.

Pa couldn't cram more than twenty newspaper-wrapped angels into his bag at any one time, but he charged a shilling per figure and made a good profit out of them. He'd stand in the street and sing a hymn to get everyone's attention. *Hark the Herald Angels* was his favourite, and he sang it all year round, even though it was a Christmas carol. Then he'd shout out, 'Come and buy my beautiful angels. See them and marvel! Change your luck for ever. Stand one of these holy beauties on your mantelpiece and it'll watch over you and your loved ones, guarding you from all troubles, great or small.'

Folk couldn't resist them, and Pa's pockets clinked with coins at the end of each day. His patter now was so convincing, even Ma believed it, and had a flock of five angels lined up along her own mantel, one for each member of the family: Ma, Pa, Matthew, Mark and Luke. She had another white plaster angel in reserve, ready to be painted for little John, for she was going to have another baby and couldn't wait to have a complete quartet of Gospel children.

She took it for granted that her baby would be another fine blond boy. She was bewildered when she gave birth to a dark little girl. When Pa recovered from his celebrations, he declared himself tickled pink to have a daughter for a change. 'Dark, like me! Let's hope she hasn't inherited my features as well as my colouring, poor little mite!'

Ma called the baby girl Mary-Martha, the holiest female names she could think of. She was a docile baby and a sweet little girl, but sadly, as predicted, she took after Pa, even developing her own unfortunate beak nose.

Ma was a while recovering after Mary-Martha's birth, and the midwife warned her she shouldn't risk another child, but Ma took no notice. She loved Mary-Martha but still hankered after a little John. She lost two babies before their time and cried bitterly for weeks.

'What did I tell you?' said the midwife – but Ma wouldn't be told. She started all over again, and this time cried with happiness when she knew she was carrying another child. She thumbed her way through all Pa's tracts to select quotes from the Gospel of St John, highlighting them all with expensive gold paint, and then stuck them up above her bed. She asked Pa to fashion a little shelf there too, and stood the first of all the plaster angels on it, to flap his wings protectively above her all night long, keeping her little John safe.

She laboured for two whole days when her time came. The midwife was sure she would not survive the birth. But at long last the baby appeared – a small scrap of a child to have caused so much pain. It wasn't the longed-for John. It was me.

Poor Ma. She didn't want a daughter. She already had Mary-Martha. She took one look at me and turned her face to the wall. She nursed me every few hours but showed no other interest in me whatsoever. She couldn't even be bothered to give me a name.

So Pa chose Ellen-Jane, after his mother and Ma's. Both these grandmothers were already dead.

'And I shouldn't think this poor puny mite's long for this world either,' he said.

I stayed poor, I stayed puny – but I thrived.

My brothers had holy names, and they were indeed holy terrors. They tormented me royally. Matthew, the eldest, wasn't quite so bad. He would snatch and strike a blow if I ever had anything he wanted, but if I fell, he'd always pick me up and run around with me until I stopped crying.

Mark was the sneaky one, the master of sly pinches and whispered insults. Luke was the whinger, always complaining, bursting into tears if he couldn't get his own way. Pa clouted them all on a regular basis whenever he was home, but it didn't make a blind bit of difference to their behaviour.

Mary-Martha was a good child – almost *too* good. I'd cram a stolen fingerful of sugar into my mouth or blotch one of the tracts and tear it into scraps, but Mary-Martha would say, 'Ma and Pa might not know, but the *angels* do!'

I started to be terribly aware of all those plaster angels staring at me, their painted mouths 'o's of shock and horror. Once when I was very little, I tipped them all over, even the special one above Ma's side of the bed.

Ma was speechless when she saw, her mouth working but no sound coming out. She went to bed and cried because she thought it such terrible bad luck. Pa didn't care about luck – he was simply angry that so many of the angels had got chipped, losing their noses and fingers and wing-tips.

'Which of you little varmints did it?' he bellowed.

We all stared at him, trembling.

'Right then, you shall *all* suffer, even the baby,' he said, reaching for the cane in the corner of the room.

'Don't, Pa! It wasn't me! It was the baby what did it all!' Mark cried.

Pa shook his head, unwilling to believe I could be so bad. I wasn't yet five at this time and looked a deal younger.

'It wasn't you, was it, Ellen-Jane?' he asked.

He probably expected me to lie, and then he would have pretended to believe me, because he wasn't really a cruel father, not *then*. But those angels were crowding in on me, ready to tip *me* over, straight down to Hell. I didn't dare tell a lie, not in front of all of them.

'Yes, it was me, Pa,' I said.

Pa always declared he was a man of his word, so he seized his cane and beat me on my bottom. He did it lightly, but I screamed my head off.

'That'll learn you,' he said breathlessly – but all it did was teach me to fear the wrath of those angels, and to hate my telltale brother Mark.

The angels seemed determined to punish poor Ma, even though *I* was to blame. She was still hoping for a little John, though the midwife said this was madness. Ma wouldn't give up hope, though as the years passed, there were no more babies.

Pa was mightily relieved. He feared for Ma's life – and he was also finding it hard to cope with filling seven empty bellies every day. Folk within fifty miles had no more interest in his tracts and his plaster angels, and he hated to travel further afield now because Ma was in such a fragile state. She'd grown paper-pale and very thin, and drifted around our home in her nightgown like a little ghost. Her beautiful blonde hair grew thin and limp, straggling unbrushed down her back. She could barely attend to us, and the boys weren't much help about the house, but Mary-Martha tied a big apron round her waist and became a second little mother to all of us.

I was still the baby, and acted accordingly, because it meant that sometimes Ma held me close or nursed me on her knee. She had no real interest in me. She adored her three harem-scarem boys and she needed Mary-Martha. She used me like a doll, cuddling me when her arms felt unbearably empty.

Pa favoured me though. I was little and lithe like Ma, my nose was small and snub, and my hair was fair and soon grew long. When Pa was in a good mood from the drink, he'd dance me round and round till we were both dizzy. He'd call me his very little Lizzie, making a song of it. Sometimes he brought me trinkets when he came back from his travels – a blue ribbon for my hair, a set of Indian baby bangles for my tiny wrist. I don't know how poor Mary-Martha must have felt. Pa never brought *her* bright baubles.

I tried to tie my ribbon in her hair, but it would never stay in her straggly brown locks and my bangles wouldn't fit over her fat little fists.

'It's all right, Baby. I don't mind one bit,' she said cheerily – but once or twice I came upon her peering anxiously into our cracked looking glass, sighing at herself.

15

Ma sighed too, seldom able to shrug off her melancholy. Pa brought home a pile of fairytale books, mainly bound in leather, and set Ma to colouring in the pictures. It was intricate work painting the gossamer wings of the fairies, the coils of the serpent, the alarming genie half in and half out of his bottle. It was far harder to keep the paint within the fine lines. The boys were too impatient and Mary-Martha and I not yet skilled enough, but Pa knew Ma had a careful, steady hand. If she tried hard and did her best, he could sell the volumes at twice the price.

Sometimes she managed perfectly – but then she would start daydreaming and went over the lines. She painted a picture of a fairytale christening superbly, putting in an extraordinary amount of detail, mixing her paint so cleverly that the child looked almost real, his soft pearly flesh carefully contrasted with the shaded folds of his christening robe.

'That's my girl, Lizzie! My, it's a little masterpiece,' said Pa. 'I don't think we'll sell that book. We'll cut out that colour plate and pin it to the wall.'

Ma smiled weakly, but she seemed troubled by the picture even so. She looked at it every day, the tip of her finger stroking the fairy baby, but then she realized that her hopes of another son were vain, and she seized the pot of black paint and obliterated the whole glowing picture in five frantic strokes of her paintbrush.

'What's wrong with you, Lizzie?' Pa cried in despair. 'Why hanker after yet another child when you have three fine sons and two dear daughters? Compared with many other women, you are so blessed! And you have your own snug little house and a husband who thinks the world of you. Why aren't we good enough for you?'

'You *are* good enough. You are too good to me, Sam. But I cannot help it. I am so frightened of losing you. If only I could have my little John, then I would feel that the angels were smiling at me and I would be in Heaven on Earth,' Ma wept.

Mary-Martha and I cried too, because we hated to see her so unhappy, but the boys were restless and embarrassed by all her tears, and reared away from her like frightened ponies when she tried to embrace them.

'Ma's mad, Pa,' said Matthew bluntly. 'All this weeping and moaning! She's sick in the head. Why can't she be like other mothers?'

Pa whacked him hard about the head. 'Don't you dare talk about your poor mother in such a way! How dare you call her mad! She's simply *sad*, boy. Don't you see the difference?'

Ma didn't have any real women friends because she'd always kept herself to herself, but she'd been close to the midwife. Pa invited the woman round to see if she could talk some sense into her. But Ma cried worse than ever when she saw the midwife with her white apron and her big black bag. It reminded her so painfully that she didn't have the fourth baby boy she longed for. The midwife spoke to her softly, and then ferreted in her bag and brought out a little checked-cloth bag containing crushed seeds and herbs. It looked like the lavender 'tea' Mary-Martha and I made for our dolls, but it did not smell anywhere near as sweet.

'Try my herbal tisane. It will lift your spirits, dearie – and you never know, it might just do the trick, though I shouldn't be encouraging you to have another child. You're in no fit condition.' The midwife looked at Pa. 'That will be five shillings, please.'

'Five *shillings* for a bag of tea?' he said. 'Are you mad, woman?'

'*I'm* not the one who's mad, but if you don't want to help your poor wife, then I'll save it for those who are more grateful,' she replied, snatching her bundle back.

Ma groaned – and Pa hesitated. 'Can't she have half the herbs for half the price?' he asked.

'She must take them all for them to have any effect,' said the midwife. She dropped the bundle back into her bag.

Ma did not groan again, but she sank down, her chin on her chest, her face hidden by her long hair.

'All right, all right, I'll find you your five shillings,' said Pa, sighing heavily.

It took him two days to sell enough tracts and angels to gather the money together. Then we had to endure two whole weeks of turnip stew and stale bread – but Ma got her herbal tisane and swallowed a cupful at every meal time. It was so bitter it made her shudder, but she gulped it down eagerly all the same. It acted just like a magic potion. She dressed with care, she braided her hair and pinned it into place, she joked with the boys and she taught Mary-Martha and me to sew. I was too small to do more than stitch fancy purses in bright wools, but Mary-Martha had nimble fingers and Ma taught her how to make nightcaps for Pa to sell to old-fashioned folk. Plenty of pedlars sold caps, plain or lace, but Ma stitched a tiny angel on each of ours to watch over the sleeper at night, and these proved very popular.

Soon she was sewing other clothes too: very tiny gowns, with lace and embroidery.

'That's beautiful, Lizzie dear, but I'll have to charge dearly for all the fancy work and my customers are never going to fork out a fortune,' said Pa.

'These aren't for sale,' said Ma. A radiant smile lit up her face. 'These are for our baby.'

Perhaps it was the herbal tisane, perhaps it was all those prayers to the angels, perhaps it was sheer chance – but Ma was going to have the child she longed for.

Pa was terrified she might lose the baby before her time, but she stayed strong and fit, and her stomach swelled until there was hardly room for me to climb on her lap.

I patted her big belly and pretended to talk to the baby inside.

'That's right, Ellen-Jane, say hello to little John,' said Ma, laughing. 'My sixth child, and my most blessed.'

Most sixth children in poor families like ours have to put up with cut-down nightgowns and old shawls, and sleep in drawers padded with an old pillow. But Ma prepared for the new baby as if he were a little princeling. She sewed his elaborate layette, and spent a mint of money getting an old woodcarver to make a special rocking crib.

Pa sighed at the sight of it. 'The baby will grow out of it in six months, Lizzie!'

'Don't you think it's beautiful though, Sam? Look at the shine on the wood! And the way the hearts have been carved. It's a work of art!'

'It's fine enough, but it's madness. What else are you going to order for him? A silver dish and spoon? A gold chamber pot?' said Pa. 'Do you think I'm made of money? Do you want your other children to starve?'

Ma bit her lip and looked as if she would crumple. She stroked the wooden crib, her hand trembling. 'I'm sorry,' she murmured. 'Perhaps . . . perhaps the wood-carver will take it back?'

'Oh, come now, you can keep your little crib. I can see how much you like it,' said Pa. 'Just don't go in for any further nonsense.'

'Oh, I won't, Sam, I promise! Thank you, thank you! You're the dearest, kindest husband in all the world. You're so understanding. It's just I'm so happy to be having my little John at last,' said Ma, tenderly rocking the cradle as if the baby were already lying there.

Pa took a deep breath. 'Lizzie, what if the baby is another girl? You won't be too disappointed?'

Ma stared at Pa as if he'd said something truly ridiculous. 'Of course it won't be a girl!' she said, with utter conviction. 'I *know* I'm having a boy.'

'Let us hope you are right,' said Pa fervently, and he glanced at all the angels, plain and painted, as if he were praying to them too.

Ma stayed strong and lively throughout her term. She kept the house immaculate, singing as she dusted and swept. She made sure she had a tasty stew bubbling on the stove every day, and made us children special jammy bread for our tea, smearing each slice with our initials in plum preserve. For once Mary-Martha and I did better than the boys, for M-M and E-J meant we had twice as much jam.

I knew that Ma had a baby in her tummy, of course, but I had no idea how it got *out*. I believe I had a notion that Ma might open some secret door in her stomach and let the baby out when it was big enough. I did not know that having a baby *hurt*, though I'd heard that Ma had been increasingly ill when she gave birth to each of us.

When she started her pains, I was terribly frightened. I had experienced bad stomach aches myself when we'd bought cheap meat on the turn from the butcher's — but I could see by the way Ma was groaning, doubled-up, that this was far worse.

Pa seemed terrified. He ran for the midwife and then went off in a flurry, his hands over his ears to block out the moans. Matthew, Mark and Luke were frightened too, and went off to swing from the lamp-post, their current favourite game.

Mary-Martha made bread and cheese for lunch, but the boys had all disappeared from the street, playing further afield.

'Boys are useless,' I said. 'I don't know why Ma wants another one.'

I secretly wanted to run away too, because it was so dreadful having to listen to Ma upstairs, but it didn't seem right to abandon her. Mary-Martha busied herself running for hot water and clean linen at the midwife's request. She was allowed into the bedroom with Ma and the midwife.

I couldn't help being glad that I was shut outside.

The midwife was a fierce-looking woman with a great pointed nose and chin, very much like the picture of a wicked witch in a fairy story. Her tisane *was* like a magic potion after all. I was very wary of her – and now that she was moaning like a wounded animal, I was scared of Ma too.

I stayed hunched up downstairs under the baleful eyes of the angels. I could not read, but I looked at the brightly coloured tracts on the walls and tried to take courage from them. My hands kept fidgeting, so I found a length of string and tried to play cat's cradle by myself, but I ended up knotting my hands together, and when I needed to go to the privy I had to call out for Mary-Martha to help me.

'Really, Ellen-Jane!' she said, clipping me free with Ma's big scissors. 'Why do you have to be such a baby? You must try to be a big girl like me now Ma's having a baby.'

'Why is it taking so *long*?' I asked, shivering at the sound of Ma's groans up above us.

'You took two *days* to get born,' said Mary-Martha. 'Now hurry up and use the privy. Then you must go to the alehouse and buy a pint of beer.' She pressed a few coins into my hand and gave me the tankard from the dresser.

'For Ma?' I said.

'No, silly. For the midwife. She says she needs a bit

of sustenance – and I know she means drink.' Mary-Martha tutted primly and quoted one of the tracts in a whisper: *'Beware the demon drink!'*

'I don't want to go to the alehouse. It smells funny and I don't like the men there,' I said.

'Don't be silly,' said Mary-Martha. 'One of those men will be our pa. Now *go.*'

'*You* go. You're bigger than me.'

'I have to stay and help Ma.'

I hesitated, wondering which would be worse. Then Ma groaned again, and I decided I'd sooner trail to the King's Arms than go upstairs to my poor mother.

I went to the privy and then set off, clutching the halfpennies so tightly that they embedded themselves in my palms. It was the first time I'd even been out in the street by myself. I wasn't used to going anywhere without Ma or Mary-Martha holding my hand. It felt so strange I very nearly started crying.

I ran along the gutter, one foot on the pavement so that I stumped along lopsided. I imagined being lame like Limpy Dan with his wooden leg who lived nearby. I was scared of Limpy Dan too. He disliked all children and brandished his crutch if you got near. I looked around hopefully for my brothers, but there was no sign of them.

I waited a full five minutes outside the King's Head, trying to pluck up courage to go in. The King himself grinned down at me from his sign, his face very red and leering under his crown. It looked as if he'd supped a barrel of ale himself. I didn't know why he hung there. I might not have been to school, but every child in England knew we didn't *have* a king, just a very old queen.

An old woman came hobbling up the road in broken boots, clutching her own tankard to her chest. She frowned at me. 'What are you doing hanging around outside?' she said sternly. 'This is no place for a little girl.'

'Please, missus, I've come for a pint of ale for the midwife,' I gabbled.

'Well, in you go then,' she said gruffly, and gave me an impatient push.

I staggered through the open door into the dark ale-house. The smell made my nose wrinkle. It was so dark inside I could barely see, but I was horribly aware of the men – their bleary eyes in the dim gaslight, teeth gleaming as they quaffed their beer, big red noses shining in the powerful heat. And there was the biggest, reddest, shiniest nose of all right in front of me!

'Ellen-Jane!' he said, banging his pint pot down on the table top.

'Hello, Pa,' I whispered.

'Saints alive, is it born? Is your ma all right? Tell me, child – don't just stand there dithering.'

'She's not finished yet, Pa. She's still groaning,' I said.

'Oh my Lord,' said Pa miserably, and gulped his beer. 'Then why are you here? I thought you'd been sent to tell me the good news.'

'No, Mary-Martha sent me to get a pint of ale for the midwife,' I told him.

'She sent a little tot like you?'

'I have the pennies safe, see . . .' I showed Pa my clenched hand. 'And I won't spill a drop on the way back, I promise.'

'My, did you all hear that?' Pa roared. 'This baby scarcely out of long dresses is trotting around the town running messages, God bless her. See my little maid? Isn't she a darling? The dead spit of her mother – who is right now giving birth to my sixth child. Raise your glasses and drink to my baby!'

Folk didn't seem sure whether he meant me or his coming child, but they raised their glasses all the same. Pa downed his beer in great gulps, seemingly incredibly thirsty, though he'd already been drinking there for hours. He scrabbled his fingers in my hot palm and seized the coppers.

'And another one, if you please,' he said, reeling over to the barmaid at the counter.

She poured him a full pint, and he raised it to his lips.

'No, Pa! That's for the midwife,' I said, thinking he'd simply made a mistake.

Pa bent down until his head was next to mine. His huge nose seemed to grow even larger, like a vast parrot's beak. I was sure he was going to peck me with it any second.

'Now listen here, Ellen-Jane. I'm not letting you take any ale back to that midwife. She needs to be stone-cold sober. I love your dear mother more than life itself. I'm not having some drunken old biddy in charge of her. The very idea! I don't want to come home and find your ma in hysterics and the midwife passed out on the floor!'

The only one who seemed in danger of passing out was Pa himself, but I knew better than to argue with him in his present state.

'Do you understand?' he said, poking me in the chest.

'Yes, Pa,' I said hurriedly.

'That's my baby.' Pa subsided back onto a chair. He drank deeply again, and then wiped his wet mouth with the back of his hand. 'The spitting image of your mother, that's what you are, Ellen-Jane,' he said, suddenly jovial again. He lifted me up so that I found myself standing on the table, my white kid shoes in a puddle of spilled beer.

I was very fond of those shoes. Ma had found them at the bottom of a basket in a rag shop and had wrangled to buy them for tuppence. She'd intended them for Mary-Martha, but the shoes were made for rich folk with fine, dainty feet, Mary-Martha could barely squash her toes in. So *I* got the new shoes, though I had to stuff each with a handkerchief because they were still too long. I didn't care. My new shoes looked beautiful even so. But now brown beer was seeping upwards and staining the kid.

'Set me down, please, Pa,' I said, standing on one foot like a stork.

'No, no, I want to show you off, my little maid. My, you're the very spit of your poor ma, even down to your long hair.' He ran his fingers through my curls like a comb, fluffing it up. 'See my little baby wife!' he shouted, so loud that all the other men stopped sipping and spitting and stared at me.

'She's like a fairy girl,' said one. 'Will you grant me a wish, little lass?'

'Yes, grant me a wish too, little fairy,' said another.

I'd never been told any fairy stories and I couldn't read them for myself, but I'd seen Ma painting the illustrations.

'I can't grant you any wishes. I haven't got a magic wand with a star on the end,' I said.

I was being serious, but the men guffawed with laughter. Pa roared so much, he nearly spilled his precious beer.

'She's a card, my little lass. No fairy wand indeed!'

'You could do us a fairy dance though,' said another old man.

'Yes, give them a dance, Baby. You're forever skipping about the house, so dainty. Give them a little dance!'

I tried to clamber down, but Pa held me firm.

'No, no, stay on your little stage where we can all see you,' he said.

'I want to whisper, Pa,' I said, clutching his head. 'I *can't* dance, Pa,' I hissed into his large ear. 'I don't know how, not really.'

'Well, do us a turn then! All these gentlemen want to see you perform. Go on, and I'm sure one of them will give you a penny.'

'Go on! Go on, go on, go on!' they chorused, though the barmaid tried to hush them.

'Leave the little maid alone!' She turned to me. 'I should run off home to your mother, dearie.'

But I couldn't run with Pa holding me fast, and I was scared of returning with an empty tankard. Mary-Martha would be cross with me. She might hit me over the head – and if she happened to be wearing her sewing thimble, this hurt a great deal.

So I stayed. I started to sing them a song, because there wasn't much else I could do standing so precariously in a pool of beer, but Pa wrinkled his nose as soon as I'd lisped the first line of *Praise My Soul, the King of Heaven*.

'No, we want none of that holy stuff. This isn't a preaching house!' he said. 'Sing another song!'

I didn't *know* any songs that weren't holy. Ma was the only one who sang in our house. I couldn't sing, I couldn't dance, so I did the only trick I could think of. I arched my back and lowered myself right over until my hands touched the ground and I was bent over backwards like a crab. Then I took the weight on my hands and stood upside down, hoping the ends of my long hair wouldn't dangle in the spilled beer.

There was an astonished silence. I hoped they weren't too shocked. I'd tried to tuck my skirts between my knees so I wouldn't show off my drawers. I started trembling, scared that Pa would think I was being immodest. Ma had always shouted at me when she caught me doing handstands. Mary-Martha had been very prim with me too, though Matthew, Mark and Luke had always egged me on and begged me to teach them how to do it.

I didn't know how to teach them. No one had taught me. I was just born like that. As soon as I'd learned to stagger about on my feet when I was one, I was forever rolling and tumbling. In a couple of years I could stand steady on my hands for a minute or more.

Nowadays I could stand on my hands just as easily

as on my feet, but when one of the men saw me trembling, he cried, 'Set her the right way up, for pity's sake, or she'll tumble. Look, she's shaking! She's about to fall!'

Pa seized hold of me and whisked me upright again. The men were all staring at me, jaws gaping. Then they started clapping and cheering with gusto.

Pa poked me. 'Give them a bow then!'

So I bowed, and bobbed them a curtsy for good measure. This made them laugh and clap more. Even the barmaid clapped and told me I was a little wonder.

'She should be a circus girl with a talent like that!' she said.

She really did say it, Hetty. And I was such a silly fool that I took it as a great compliment. I turned cartwheels around the room, till Pa grew impatient and the men went back to their beer.

'Settle down now, Baby. No more pretty little turns. That's enough now,' he told me.

But he still didn't let me go. He held me tight while another hour or two ticked by. I had not learned to tell the time properly, but I watched the large grandfather clock in the alehouse with alarm even so, knowing it was getting later and later.

Pa was watching it too, all the while drinking steadily. He'd long run out of money for his own beer, but the men in the alehouse treated him to wet the new baby's head.

'Will it be here yet, do you think?' Pa asked me, ridiculously, because how would I know? 'And your ma – she will be all right, won't she?'

'Yes, Pa,' I said, because I was too small and foolish to know otherwise. I wasn't really bothering about poor Ma, though I certainly hoped she'd stopped groaning. I was more worried about the witchy mid-wife, deprived of her pint of ale – and Mary-Martha and that thimble.

'You'd think one of those pesky boys would have come running to tell me the good news,' said Pa. 'Useless lummocks, the lot of them. Beats me why your ma was so desperate to have another.'

Here was something I was sure I understood. 'She wants to have a John to have her full set of Holy Gospels, Pa,' I said brightly.

'Oh, don't you start that madness too. Why my Lizzie had to get all holy in the head is still a puzzle to me, especially when I think of where she came from and what she was a-doing of then,' said Pa.

I didn't know what he was talking about – I still don't – but I stroked Pa's coarse shirtsleeve in silent sympathy. When I saw the tears gathering in his eyes and rolling down his ruddy cheeks, I tried to dab them away with my sleeve.

I was bewildered by his quick changes of mood and uncertain how to cope. I was feeling miserable too: worried about the situation at home – and, if I'm honest, even more concerned about my white kid shoes, which were clearly ruined now. I was close to weeping myself.

'Look at the pair of you!' said the barmaid. 'Why don't you take the little lass *home*, Samuel?'

'Because I'm a-feared,' he wept. 'I'm not sure the baby will be borned yet.'

'Well, there's only one way to find out,' she said. 'Away with you!'

So we shambled out of the alehouse, Pa swaying, clinging to me. He was tall and I was particularly small, so he staggered, bent over, all the way home. He fell twice, and I had to take a tumble with him, getting my pinafore covered in mud, which made me even more anxious about my reception at home.

But when we turned the corner of our lane, we saw Matthew, Mark and Luke sitting on the wall outside our house kicking their heels, and Mary-Martha standing there too, with a white woollen bundle in her arms.

'Oh, Pa! It's all right! The baby's here!' I cried, and I started tugging him along.

The white parcel contained a tiny baby bawling its head off. Its face was an extraordinary shade of tomato and I thought it very ugly.

'Is it . . . John?' I asked breathlessly.

Mary-Martha nodded.

'Oh, thank goodness!' I said. But Mary-Martha was as white as the infant's shawl, and my three big brothers all looked as if they'd just had a whipping.

'How's your ma?' Pa asked.

They looked at each other fearfully. Pa gave an extraordinary howl and blundered into the house. I followed him, terrified. I could hear him upstairs, groaning and crying. But Ma wasn't making a sound.

Ma was dead. Somehow I felt it was all my fault. If I'd hurried back home with a full tankard of ale, then the midwife might have felt so refreshed she'd have figured out a way of saving Ma instead of letting her bleed to death. It was my fault for behaving like a little circus monkey when my poor ma was sinking fast. It was my fault because I hadn't been brave enough to hold Ma's hand and help her, like Mary-Martha. It was my fault because I'd been such a disappointing baby that Ma had been desperate to have another child. Oh, it was my fault, my fault, my fault.

You're very kind to tell me otherwise, Hetty, but whatever the truth is, I still felt dreadfully to blame. I'm afraid Pa blamed me too.

I did not quite understand at first. I was kept busy running errands and helping Mary-Martha tend the new baby. He cried a great deal of the time, as if he were missing Ma too. A neighbour woman with a new babe of her own offered him a few feeds during the daytime and showed Mary-Martha how to give him a drink out of a bottle, but he was ailing and fretful in spite of all our efforts.

Pa borrowed money for the funeral, sending Ma off in style and kitting us all out in black, even giving the newborn baby a black shawl and a little black bonnet for his head. The baby cried all through the ceremony, and I cried too, wishing I could climb inside the hard wooden coffin and beg Ma's forgiveness. Mary-Martha didn't cry tears but her nose went very red and she frowned excessively. Matthew and Mark blubbed a little in an awkward, furtive way, knuckling their eyes and wiping their noses with their fists, but Luke cried more decorously, tears rolling gently down his pale cheeks. He dabbed at them in a dainty fashion with a lace handkerchief – Ma's best one, which he'd stolen for himself.

All the mourners patted him on the head and cooed over him. Even the undertakers admired him.

'That's a lovely little lad you've got there, sir. He's crying very decoratively indeed, bless him,' said the man in charge. He was very thin and tall, and his black top hat with trailing ribbon was the thinnest, tallest hat I'd even seen. He was like an animated lamppost. He didn't bend when he patted Luke's head, he simply loomed above him.

'You're a dear little chap, aren't you?' he said. 'Terrible tragedy for this little lad and all his brothers and sisters to lose their dear mother.' He turned to Pa. 'Please accept my sincere condolences, sir.'

Pa barely nodded. He was crying hard himself, but he'd drunk so much beer the night before, he reeked like an alehouse. You expected his very tears to trickle golden-brown.

'It's going to be very hard on you, sir, with all these little ones to feed and clothe and care for. How exactly are you going to manage?'

Pa gave a heartfelt groan and shook his head.

'I'm not meaning to twist the knife, sir, especially at such a moment, but if you should see fit to farm out any of your young folk as apprentices, to give them a fine start in life and ease the burden on your good self, then might I be first in line for the services of that little lad there – the one crying so piteously in such a pretty manner? How does he manage it? His little eyes are still so blue instead of red, and his tiny pink nose is free of slime! I can see you've done your very best to clothe him decent for the funeral, but imagine him in a fine black suit of well-cut worsted, with a fancy white collar and a black satin bow at his throat. Imagine a tiny top hat on those curls as a finishing touch. What a picture he'd look! In short, he'd make a marvellous miniature mute.' He emphasized each 'm' of these last three words so that it sounded as if he were humming.

Pa was barely listening, naturally concentrating on the ordeal of Ma's funeral. I found the ceremony bleak, but I was sure that Ma, inside her wooden coffin, would be appreciating all the hymn singing and holy words. I was horrified when we all trooped out into the churchyard and I realized that all these men were intent on lowering Ma into a big hole in the ground.

'No! No, please stop! You can't put Ma in all that mud and dirt!' I cried out.

'Hold your tongue and stop shaming us,' Pa hissed at me.

I tried to take his hand, but he pulled away from me as if he couldn't bear my touch. I nuzzled close to Mary-Martha instead, but she had her arms full of baby John and could not pick me up to comfort me.

I felt so lonely standing there, though I had my

family all around me. I wanted *Ma*. I stared at her coffin, willing her to lift the lid and climb out and wipe my tears away. But she stayed inside, and soon her coffin was covered in ugly clods of earth. I realized there was going to be no more Ma ever.

I seemed to have lost my pa too. He would have nothing to do with me, covering his eyes with his hand as if the very sight of me offended him. He used to take pride in my long fair hair, but now he said to Mary-Martha, 'Tell your sister to tie up that hair and cover her head with a scarf.' He would not speak to me directly, even when I stood in front of him.

'Pa!' I shouted, wondering if he simply couldn't hear me.

He pushed me away roughly. 'Tell your sister I want none of her fancy tricks,' he said to Mary-Martha. 'Hasn't she done enough harm, cavorting with me inside an alehouse when her own dear mother was gasping her last breath?'

'But Pa, that's not really fair,' said Mary-Martha, because she was a kind sister, and brave too: since Ma died Pa had been terrifyingly easy to upset. One word out of place and he'd seize you and smack you. All the boys except baby John had suffered Pa's belt in a matter of days.

Mary-Martha's soft entreaty was in vain. Pa had made up his mind about me and there was nothing I could do but keep out of his way. Mary-Martha was his favourite child now. She couldn't help looking proud whenever he beckoned her and called her his little darling and his special helpmeet.

He certainly couldn't have managed without her. She looked after baby John, she did the cooking, she did the washing, she did the cleaning. I helped, of course, and the boys could sometimes be persuaded to scrub the floor or go on errands, but mostly they ran wild, especially when Pa was away selling his tracts.

He stopped making angels. He swept Ma's collection to the floor one drunken night and stamped them all into powder. I was terrified, but I was glad they were gone. They had all started staring at me accusingly with their Prussian-blue painted eyes.

Pa did not make as much money now, and he drank nearly all of it away each night in the alehouse. We could not pay the rent on our dear little house, so we had to move to Willoughby Buildings, on the other side of town by the gasworks and the tannery, where all the really poor folk lived.

If Ma had known, she'd have flooded her coffin with her tears. We were now living in a den of drunks and thieves. But now Pa was a drunk himself and the boys were becoming thieves. At first they pilfered childish stuff – apples from the market stalls, sugary confections from the sweet shop, marbles from the toy shop, just dashing in and grabbing what they fancied – but soon Matthew and Mark and Luke joined up with a gang of big boys from the buildings and embarked on more organized crime, snatching purses and stealing cash.

Mary-Martha and I knew what they were up to, of course. They didn't have enough sense to keep things quiet, openly boasting about their exploits and showing off their newly acquired possessions.

'You're bad, wicked boys,' said Mary-Martha. 'What does the Good Book say? *Thou shalt not steal!*' She took after Ma and was very pious.

I wasn't pious at all, but I was fearful. 'You'll go to H-e-l-l, boys,' I said. 'And you'll burn in flames for all eternity.'

'Then at least we'll be warm,' said Matthew.

It was winter now, but we had no fuel for a fire and big Matthew had no warm clothes, though Mark and Luke could wear his cast-offs. Mary-Martha and I had to make do with shawls over our summer dresses. Mary-Martha did fetch Ma's best Sunday velvet from the trunk and ponder cutting it up to make a dress each for us, but she couldn't bear to snip into the soft material. When we buried our faces in it, we could still faintly smell our ma.

Mary-Martha did cut down a petticoat and an old grey singlet and fashioned them into a lumpy rag doll with a lacy dress. 'This can be your baby, Ellen-Jane,' she said kindly, because she was feeling sorry for me.

'Thank you so much, Mary-Martha,' I said, and clutched the doll to my chest. 'I shall call her Maybelle.'

She had no features on her poor grey face, and therefore didn't seem to have much personality at all, but she was stitched with love – and I was starved of that now. I took her to bed with me each night and carried her around everywhere, like a baby's comforter.

Of course the boys' luck couldn't last. All three of my brothers were caught red-handed burgling an old gentleman's house. The other boys in the gang had legged it out of the window before the constable caught them. My brothers had fought to get free, but he had coshed them into submission.

Pa went white with fury when he was told that they were in a prison cell, branded common criminals, with our Matthew up on an added charge of assault and battery. 'Your poor dear mother must be turning in her grave,' he said when he went to visit them.

They all cried with shame, even Matthew. Little Luke cried so piteously that the police sergeant softened.

'I can tell they're not truly bad lads,' he said. 'If you're willing to pay a shilling fine for each of them, we'll let them go with a caution, Mr Potts.'

I don't know how Pa got the money together – maybe he had to steal himself – but he managed to pay for all three boys to be released.

'I'm teaching you a lesson here and now, boys,' he told them. 'I'm not having you grow up to be thieving varmints. I'm going to get you trained up to be good God-fearing lads for the sake of your mother. She named you after the Gospels because she revered Jesus and his disciples. What does the holy tract say? *Go ye and do likewise!* So that's what you're going to do. Matthew, step forward!'

Matthew shambled up to Pa, hanging his head, his long arms dangling awkwardly.

'You're a strong boy – and those hands clearly throw a fierce punch already. I want to turn you into a *proper* man. What profession was our dear Lord raised in, Matthew?'

Matthew stared at Pa blankly. He hadn't attended Sunday school for years.

'He was a *carpenter* – a fine, skilled profession, and a way of channelling all that strength of yours. I'm apprenticing you to my old friend Micky Chip the carpenter. You're to go and live with him and learn off him, you hear me?'

Matthew heard and dared not argue, though he didn't look happy.

'Now you, Mark,' said Pa.

'I don't want to be a carpenter, Pa! I'm nowhere near as strong as Matthew,' said Mark, showing Pa his puny arms.

'Yes, you need building up, son. Do some honest work to grow some muscles. What did our Lord's friends do for a living, boy?'

Mark looked astonished. 'Do you want me to be a *disciple*, Pa?'

Pa struck him hard about the head for his stupidity. 'Where did Jesus find his first disciples, dolthead? On the shores of Lake Galilee. He was a fisherman, a fine, honest profession.'

'Is there a lake in London, Pa?'

'Not that I know of, you fool. You're not going *out* to fish, you're going to *work* with them. I've apprenticed you to Sammy Barton down the market. You'll go to Billingsgate with him every morning and help him run his wet-fish stall, do you hear me?'

Mark heard – and shook his head in horror. 'I don't like fish, Pa. Nasty slimy things!'

'And I don't like nasty slimy boys who bring shame on the family. You'll do as I say and work hard for a living or *you'll* be the one who's gutted and has his head chopped off. Now, Luke!'

Luke burst into tears in terror.

'That's it! That's my boy! The very picture! You cry hard, son, and learn to do it professional, because

45

you're going to that undertaker to get yourself trained up to be a mourner.'

'But I'm feared of dead people, Pa!'

'Nonsense, nonsense, they can't hurt you. You can *stop* the crying now because there's no call for it. You've got a nice, easy, clean profession compared with your brothers.'

Mary-Martha held baby John tightly, swaying a little. 'What about me, Pa?' she whispered.

'You've done nothing wrong, my little lass. You've done your level best, I know that. You've cared for us all *and* nursed that poor little babe. You shall stay.'

We waited. Pa did not even look in my direction, but of course he knew I was there.

'And – and what about our Ellen-Jane?' Mary-Martha asked.

Pa grunted as if in sudden pain, but kept staring resolutely at the boys.

'Ellen-Jane can stay too, can't she, Pa?' Mary-Martha continued bravely. 'She helps too. She tries her best, even though she's only little.'

Pa threw back his head and gave me one glance with his bloodshot eyes. 'No one in their right mind would take on a little minx like that one,' he said, and then he stomped out of the room.

I didn't know whether to be glad or sorry. I didn't want to be sent to be a carpenter or a fishmonger or a mourning mute. I wanted to stay at home – but I couldn't bear home any more either. I'd lost my mother, and my father now hated me.

I pressed close to Mary-Martha for some comfort, for she was all I had left now.

I had been small for my age before, but now I couldn't seem to grow at all. It wasn't just because I didn't have enough food. I had the same greasy soups and stale bread as my sister, and yet Mary-Martha grew tall, and her arms were strong too, because she was forever carrying our little brother, John. I stayed tiny – as if Pa's new contempt for me had withered something deep within me.

I tried hard to please him still, doing my fair share of the household tasks and painting all the endless tracts without once going over the lines. I nursed the baby too, though when Johnnie got to be a toddler it was a struggle to carry him properly and I had to walk with a bent back to balance him.

I was a supple girl even then. I'd naturally bend right over and scuttle like a crab, or walk upside down on my hands. This always made Johnnie go into peals of laughter, so it was a useful ploy when he was grizzly – but I took care never to perform any acrobatics when Pa was around.

He barely *was* around. He took to travelling far and wide to do his pattering. Sometimes he didn't come home for a week or more. We were often left very short of food. Once we could only beg a crust for the baby, while we ourselves starved for two whole days – and then even pious Mary-Martha wished our brothers were home to steal for us.

When, on the third day, Pa still wasn't home, I decided I had to find *some* way of earning enough pennies for food. I left Mary-Martha and Johnnie, and set out from Willoughby Buildings, clutching my rag doll, Maybelle, for companionship. I walked all the way to the market, though I was faint from lack of food. I knew there was always a big crowd there, and that was what I needed.

There were beggars a-plenty at the edge of the stalls, desperately eyeing the hot pies, the sugary cakes, the pyramids of red and yellow fruit – but the market men were fierce and very protective of their wares. There were all sorts of novelties too: a hurdy-gurdy man, with his mechanical organ and his live monkey in a little red velvet jacket, an escapologist trying to bust out of his chains, and a Punch and Judy stall. Punch looked like a miniature Pa and gave me the shivers, especially when he wielded his stick.

There were less elaborate buskers too: two girls holding hands and singing together, and a blind man reciting an endless poem about a Red Indian. They all had caps in front of them so that people could throw pennies in if they appreciated their performance. The poor blind man had a cap full of dud counters and pebbles, and every time a mean-spirited lad threw in another worthless stone, he heard the clink, paused in his recital, and murmured, 'Thank you kindly,' which made the boys laugh.

I could not sing and I did not know any poems. I had only one talent. I propped Maybelle against a lamp-post and stood up to perform.

I bent over backwards and started my crab-walk, and then tipped my weight onto my hands and walked about with my legs waving in the air. My hair fell about my face so I could not see the reaction of the crowd, but I could hear murmurings. There were raucous comments from the boys, but plenty of approval from the general crowd.

'Oh, the little lamb, just look at her!'

'She's such a tiny creature too, a little half-pint.'

'How old do you reckon she is? She must be barely out of baby robes. My, but she's nimble!'

I continued to cavort, doing my limited repertoire of tricks, until I sensed I had a big audience, and then I righted myself with a flourish and dropped a curtsy, while everyone clapped.

'Where's your cap, dear?' someone shouted.

I hadn't brought one with me because the only cap in the household belonged on Pa's head. I took off my shawl instead and laid it on the pavement. Within a minute all the wool was covered in coppers, and I heard cries of: 'Bravo, little girl!'

I barely stopped to acknowledge the praise and collect floppy Maybelle. I gathered up my money, tied a knot in my shawl, and ran off with it. I bought a pie for Mary-Martha and a pie for me, a candy cane for us to share, and a loaf of fresh bread, still warm from the oven, plus milk and porridge for the baby.

My shawl was stretched to bursting point and it was a struggle to carry it home, but Mary-Martha was so pleased to see me with my special feast. She was even hungrier than me, for she was naturally a big girl, and when she starved she had terrible pains in her stomach that bent her double, so at first she simply ate ravenously. She was so eager, she didn't even pause to cut the bread – simply broke off great chunks and sank her teeth into the soft dough – but when she'd eaten her fill and fed little Johnnie, she turned to me.

'How did you pay for all this food, Ellen-Jane?' she asked. Her voice was low, because she was rocking Johnnie to sleep, but she was looking at me intently, her eyes fearful.

'I didn't steal it,' I said quickly. 'I earned it.'

'What did you do?'

'I went to the market and put on a little show,' I said, licking the candy cane.

'*What?*'

'I pretended I was a turn at the music hall,' I said.

We'd never been to a music hall, but the older lasses at the buildings often sang music-hall numbers as they scrubbed the floors or staggered home with bags of coal, and we'd picked up some of the jolly tunes – though we didn't dare sing them when Pa was around because the words were saucy.

'You sound like a scalded cat when you sing. You can't hold a tune at all,' said Mary-Martha.

'I didn't sing. I did my upsy-daisies,' I said, using my baby word for acrobatics.

'Oh, Ellen-Jane! You're too big now to do that in front of everyone!'

'Everyone thought I was too *little* – and they *marvelled*,' I said proudly. 'They gave me so many pennies. Look, I haven't spent half of them yet!'

'I'm sure it's a sin,' said Mary-Martha worriedly. 'It's begging – and it's also very wanton, turning upside down and showing your drawers.'

'Jesus was always very kind to beggar people – and I wore my petticoats so they could only see a *little* bit of my drawers,' I said defiantly. I marched up to the wall of tracts. '*God helps those who help themselves!*' I declared.

I had her there. She fed Johnnie his bowl of milky porridge and sucked at her share of the candy cane without further comment.

So now, whenever we were desperate, I took myself off to market and did my little turn. The beggars tried to elbow me out of the way because it meant fewer pennies for them. The escapologist threatened to tie me up in his chains, and the singing girls stuck their tongues out at me, but the hurdy-gurdy man took a fancy to me and suggested I have a pitch in front of his organ.

'You can do all your little tricks in time to the music. That way they'll be more of a novelty. And I have an even better idea: I'll get Jacko, my monkey, to take his hat off and collect extra coins for you inside it, and then we'll split the takings – fair's fair,' he said.

It didn't sound exactly fair as I was the one doing most of the work, with little Jacko coming second. The hurdy-gurdy man did nothing but turn the handle of his machine, but he was big and fierce and it seemed better to have him on my side.

I soon knew all five of his tinkly tunes by heart, and could cavort and cartwheel pleasingly to the rhythm. I tried to make friends with Jacko, who looked such a sweet little creature, but when I went to pet him, he nipped me hard so I was frightened to try again. He didn't care for Maybelle at all and came near to tearing her limb from limb, so I had to keep a watchful eye on them both.

Mary-Martha came to see me one day, hugging Johnnie all the way. She seized hold of me halfway through my act, telling me that I was shaming her – but she shut her mouth when she saw all the coins showering into Jacko's cap like brass hailstones.

'You see!' I said triumphantly. Though I had to give Fred, the hurdy-gurdy man, his unfair share, I still had a fortune left to spend. 'I can buy you new shoes, Mary-Martha,' I offered.

She couldn't squeeze her feet into her old ones any more. She was making do with a pair of Luke's boots, but they were so worn down at the heel, she lurched sideways as she walked.

'I'd sooner go barefoot than have my sister doing a devil's dance,' she said.

'What about the baby then?' I said. 'When he starts running about outside, do you want *him* to go barefoot too?'

Mary-Martha looked as if she were wavering. She clutched Johnnie tight, her hands automatically fondling his tiny feet.

'No I don't,' she said, tears starting up in her eyes. 'I'm sorry, Ellen-Jane. I know you're doing this for all of us. Maybe that's why I take it so badly. *I'm* the eldest sister. *I* should be earning for you. Maybe I just feel envious seeing you dancing around looking so pretty, with all the folk admiring you so – and envy is a sin – it's forbidden in the ten commandments.' She took a deep breath and started, '*Thou shalt not—*'

'I know, I know – and it says honour thy father and mother – but Ma's dead and Pa's turned so fierce and angry with me, I can't honour him at all,' I said. 'So I'm going to carry on performing, no matter what you say.'

'I do hope Pa doesn't find out! Folk are talking about you. What if he fetches up here at the market to do his pattering? He'll whip you within an inch of your life.'

I shivered, because I was sure she was right. 'He *won't* find out,' I said fiercely.

Pa mostly wasn't there – and when he did come back, he spent very little time under his own roof. For endless hours he would pickle his brain in the ale-house. Sometimes he drank away all his week's earnings in one long evening before staggering home. Mary-Martha would try to help him get his boots off and lie down, but sometimes he was so angry he yelled at her incoherently. I always hid in the cupboard because I set Pa off worse. But frightening though these times were, we both hated it when Pa grew sad instead of bad.

'What would my lovely Lizzie think of me now?' he'd cry, his red eyes watering with tears. 'She never liked it when I'd had a drink inside me. *Beware the demon drink*, she'd mutter, quoting my own damned tracts at me. If she could see me now, it'd break her heart. What sort of a father am I to her little lambs? Where are my fine boys? Come here, Mary-Martha, and bring the little lad who was so precious to your mother.'

Mary-Martha would carry little Johnnie over to Pa. She'd let him hold him, but her arms were always out-stretched, ready to catch the baby if Pa fumbled and dropped him.

I'd watch through a crack in the door, remembering the times Pa dandled *me* on his knee. I felt so bad that I'd spoiled it all. It's all right, Hetty. I know now that it wasn't really my fault. Pa was just blaming me because I reminded him of Ma and it was too painful for him to look at me – but I was still very young, and somehow it seemed my fault all the same. One time I even tried smearing my bright hair with coal dust to make it dark and plain, but the sight of me still seemed to turn Pa's stomach.

He was cruel to me, though he was tender with the baby, rocking him clumsily and trying to croon lullabies. Once, when he was tickling Johnnie's toes, he sat holding his new kid shoes, squinting at them thoughtfully.

'These little baby boots – are they hand-me-downs from *her*?' he asked Mary-Martha. He couldn't even say my name now.

I froze inside my cupboard, so scared Mary-Martha would tell him how we had the money to buy new clothes.

'No, Pa, they're not hand-me-downs,' she said calmly. 'They're brand new for our little Johnnie.'

'So where did you get the money then? Heaven knows, I don't pass on enough,' said Pa, suddenly sounding agonized.

Mary-Martha didn't miss a beat. 'The boys like to buy things for their baby brother,' she said. 'Matthew and Mark have only stopped by once, because their masters keep a close eye on them, but Luke often comes calling when he's not needed for a service. He's very generous. Folk pay him little tips, see, because he cries so hard and prettily at all the funerals.'

My mouth was open in the dark cupboard. Mary-

Martha was such an excellent liar she almost had *me* convinced, let alone Pa.

I congratulated her fervently when Pa was fast asleep, snoring his head off, but with the baby still tucked tenderly under his arm.

'You were *wonderful*, Mary-Martha,' I whispered.

She turned a painful shade of red. 'Lying is a sin, especially to your parent. I expect I will end up in Hell,' she said miserably. 'But I couldn't let Pa know the truth, not when he's so set against you.'

'I'm sure God knows the difference between good lies and bad lies – and if he doesn't, don't worry. I've told *many* bad lies, so I will hold your hand in Hell – and at least it will be warm,' I said.

I meant it sincerely, but Mary-Martha burst out laughing. I hugged her hard and she hugged me back. I never used to be especially fond of my sister, but now I realized what a dear sweet soul she was – and the only member of my family who still loved me.

I learned to develop my acrobatic routine. I realized it was good to engage with my audience. I'd crab-walk in and out of the crowd or conduct a conversation upside down. It made folk laugh and they marvelled even more. I wasn't doing any complicated tricks. I think all three of my elder brothers could turn a neat cartwheel and I'd simply copied them. It was only a novelty because I was a girl – and I still looked years younger than my real age.

The hurdy-gurdy man still took half my money. He

made sure wizened little Jacko scampered around the crowd collecting coins in his upturned fez and then making a show of emptying them into a great pot marked MONKEY MONEY, which got another laugh and made folk even more generous.

I started to get a regular audience. Folk came specially to see me before they did their marketing. Sometimes they came back two days in a row, so I did not find it odd or unusual one week when a small man with a bald head and very narrow eyes came day after day. He watched me intently, his eyes just little slits, squinting as if he were staring into full sunlight. I could barely see the colour of his eyes, just a flash of steely grey. There was something about the intensity of his stare that made goose pimples prickle my arms.

I carried on performing in front of him, acting gay and carefree, tossing my long hair and smiling hard, even when upside down, but inside I was starting to get scared. Who was he? Could he be a friend of Pa's from the alehouse, ready to tell tales on me? I was sure I'd never seen him before.

Was he a policeman, ready to march me off to prison for performing in public? But he had no uniform and I didn't think standing on my hands was breaking any law.

Was he some sinister soul with evil desires? This seemed more likely. Mary-Martha had given me whispered warnings about such men. She had told me to beware. If such a man approached me, I shouldn't stop to talk to him, but must run away quick.

When he was there again on the third day, he waited till I was the right way up, bobbing curtsies. And then his hand came out and he suddenly grabbed me by the wrist. His grip was astonishingly strong. I'd learned to twist my hand and wriggle out of reach if any of my brothers caught hold of me in a similar fashion – but this time I was held like a handcuff.

'Let me go, Mister,' I piped in the baby voice I used when performing.

'I just need a moment of your time, little fairy,' he said. 'And what would your name be then, precious child?'

Oh, he used such pretty names for me, and he spoke softly enough, but there was something about his voice that was truly menacing.

'My name's Ellen-Jane, Mister. Now let me go, please. I've finished my performance for today,' I told him.

'Your performance! Oh, the pet!' he said, his tight mouth stretching into a grin that showed his yellow teeth.

I thought of the book of fairy tales I'd painted, with the little girl looking at the great fierce wolf, tucked up in bed, his jaws wide open, ready to eat her up.

'I'll let you go in a moment, my sweetheart. Just one or two more questions. How old are you, little one?'

'I'm five,' I lisped, because everyone thought me such a tiny tot.

'Five! Oh, bless her!' he said. Then he jerked my arm hard, pulling me right up close so that he was almost embracing me. He stared closely at my face, held my arm up and looked down at my legs. 'You're as little as five and as light as five, and you can wheedle and whisper like five – but I have my doubts, very serious doubts. I reckon you're at least seven – maybe eight . . .'

I shivered again, because I had just had my eighth birthday (a sad affair, with no presents, though Mary-Martha sang me a song and bought me a bun with pink icing). I had managed to fool everyone else. Even my own family forgot my real age at times. But this man's grey eyes seemed able to look into my soul. There was no hiding the truth from him.

I hung my head, letting my hair fall over my face to hide it.

'Ah, it's such a pretty little fairy too, with those golden tresses,' he said, running his free hand through my locks. He did it gently, so I could barely feel it, but I'd rather he'd struck me. I wriggled desperately, but he still had me tight by the wrist. My whole arm was starting to throb now.

'Please, Mister, I want my dolly!' I said, pointing to Maybelle, lolling on the ground.

'Oh, it wants its little dolly wolly!' said Mister mockingly. I thought he might just let me go for a moment so that I could pick up Maybelle – and then make a run for it. But he wasn't prepared to release me for a second. He reached out and gave Maybelle a nimble kick. She flew up into the air and hit me on the chest. I was so startled I couldn't catch her with my free hand.

'Butterfingers!' said Mister, doing his footballing trick again. He was muddying poor Maybelle's dress. I clutched her to me this time, desperate to save her from further damage.

The crowd had ebbed away, off to jostle their way around the busy market. The hurdy-gurdy man was squatting with his back to us, counting the pennies in his bowl. Jacko jerked his head and capered towards me, chattering curiously. I held out my free hand to him and cried, 'Jacko, Jacko – here, Jacko.' I had a wild hope that he would sense danger from this man and attack him. I'd seen the monkey jump right up on a man's head and tug his hair viciously, and he frequently bit little children if they tried to pet him.

Jacko looked as if he meant business now, his teeth bared – but my captor stood his ground. He clicked his tongue in an odd way and pointed straight at Jacko.

The animal suddenly cowered away, very still in his little velvet jacket, and then scampered back to his perch by the hurdy-gurdy, whining.

'What's up with you, you little brute?' said the hurdy-gurdy man, hauling himself up.

'Oh, please help me!' I called weakly. I did not care for him and I knew he cheated me out of half my takings – but I wasn't afraid of him the way I feared this sinister man.

'Is he your pa?' the man asked as he came lumbering over.

'I'm her employer,' said the hurdy-gurdy man. 'And I'll thank you to take your hands off her.'

'I'm simply admiring the little sweetheart,' he said, not at all perturbed.

'You like her, do you?' The hurdy-gurdy man scratched the top of his head thoughtfully. 'How's about you pays an extra shilling and I'm sure she'll put on another performance.'

'No, I don't want to,' I said, struggling.

'You'll do as I say,' said the hurdy-gurdy man.

'So you're her employer, are you?' said Mister. 'She's signed up to you?'

'In a manner of speaking.'

'Mmm – speaking isn't *binding*, sir. So this little fairy's as free as a bird and can fly away wherever she wants.'

'I don't want to be with *you,*' I told Mister.

'Hark at her! Funny, wilful little creature! She'll be stamping her foot next,' he said, and laughed at me, showing his yellow teeth. 'I like a little soul with spirit.'

Then he suddenly lifted me up, tipping me, helpless and humiliated, over his shoulder. 'Come along with me, little girl. Old Beppo has great plans for you!'

'No, no, I don't want to go with you! Oh, please, Mister, set me down. I haven't got my share of my earnings!' I cried.

'Ah, a tiny businesswoman, bless her! Well, we'll let this gentleman and his monkey pocket the pennies for today. You'll earn us far more in the future, my dear,' said the man, striding along as easily as if he had a little knapsack on his back instead of a wriggling child.

'No, no, I *won't* go!' I said.

When he only chuckled, I opened my mouth wide and screamed as loud as I could. Folk stared at me, startled.

'What are you doing with that little lass?' a tall man asked anxiously.

'He's a wicked stranger and he's running off with me!' I gasped.

Mister heaved with laughter. 'Hark at her, the naughty little minx! I'm a friend of the family and I'm taking her off the streets where she's been running wild.'

'Don't listen to him – he's lying! Oh, help me, help me!' I screamed.

'Is that *you*, Ellen-Jane?'

Oh dear Heavens, it was Pa! He stood there with his tray of tracts round his neck, here in the market.

'Pa! Oh, Pa, save me!' I screamed. 'This wicked man is trying to steal me away.'

Pa set his tray down. He was a little stooped now, but he was still a tall man. His nose was red to start with, but now a fierce flush spread over his whole face, even his neck. 'Put my child down,' he said, his fists clenched.

My heart started thudding violently. Pa was calling me *his child*. He was about to snatch me back. It must mean he still cared about me a bit. Maybe he was ready to forgive me. I might even get to be his own baby darling again.

'Certainly, sir,' said Mister. He took me off his shoulder and set me down in front of Pa, though he kept a firm hold of my wrist.

'So you're this little angel's father,' he said. 'Well, I'll be blowed! You're the very man I've been looking for.' He was staring intently at Pa. I saw him taking in Pa's dishevelled clothes, the sole flapping on his boots, his unshaven chin, his bloodshot eyes. I saw his nostrils quiver at the stale smell of ale that clung to his clothes.

'You were looking for *me*?' said Pa. 'Unhand that child now.' He made an ineffective grab for me, but Mister had a grip of iron.

'I need to keep hold of her or the lovely little pet will make a bolt for it. She's nervous now, but oh my goodness, sir, you should have seen her scarce ten minutes ago, prancing about like a little fairy – standing on her head and waggling her legs as bold as brass, bless her!'

I started trembling. 'He's lying, Pa! I tell you, he's lying,' I blurted, but I could not quite look Pa in the eye.

'You've been cavorting again?' he said very slowly, swaying slightly.

'No! No, I swear!'

'Oh, bless her! No need to be modest, little angel,' said Mister. 'Cavorting's the very word, sir. Quite a little act, she has. A crowd of thirty or forty gathered round immediately. She attracted a great deal of attention. She's a regular at the market now, and I reckon she earns as many pennies as the costers with their stalls – *and* she saves herself a dawn trip to Covent Garden.'

'You've been cavorting for *money*, Ellen-Jane?' said Pa, moving closer, bending his head down to mine.

'No, Pa!'

'Don't you lie to me!' he thundered.

'Oh, the bad little angel! But don't get angry, sir. You should be proud of the little pet. She's very talented, you know. With a little training I reckon she could polish up into a fine circus act.'

'A circus act!' said Pa, whispering as if the very words burned his tongue.

'I'm not a circus act, Pa! Please don't look at me like that! I haven't been a bad girl on purpose. I just did it to earn some money. We didn't have anything to eat,' I gabbled.

'I'd sooner a girl of mine starved to death than tip herself upside down in public,' said Pa. 'What would your poor ma say, Ellen-Jane? Oh, she's turning in her grave now, poor dear soul, in total agony.'

I saw Ma twisting about in her grim earthy bed, her mouth open wide in a silent scream. It was such a terrifying picture, the tears spurted down my cheeks.

'So her mother's dead, poor little lamb,' said Mister. His grey eyes were gleaming now. 'And you have the burden of bringing this moppet up, sir, feeding and clothing her and trying to keep her on the paths of righteousness?'

'Her and her elder sister and a little babe too. I have boys who went to the bad too, but I've apprenticed them out in the hope they'll grow up God-fearing gentlemen to make their mother proud,' said Pa.

Mister's eyes shone like beacons now, burning in his

pale face. 'Why not apprentice this little lass then, my good sir? I can train her up good and proper, make a real showgirl of her. She'll start earning pounds instead of pennies – and I dare say she'll send half her earnings home to her dear old pa.'

'Tainted money,' said Pa, and he spat on the ground.

'That's your opinion, sir, and you're entitled to it, but I'm sure the food and firewood it'll buy will still warm you, body and soul,' said Mister. 'Did you not say you have another daughter and a babby to care for? Well, ease your burden, sir! Let me take charge of the little fairy here and she need never trouble you again.'

'I'll not let a wastrel like you ruin her – though I fear she's already gone to the bad,' Pa sighed.

'Then let her go, sir, let her go.' The man drew a notebook and a pencil out of his jacket pocket and scribbled a sentence. He spoke the words as he did so. '*I* – what is your name, sir . . . ? Samuel Potts, I thank you! *I, Samuel Potts, do agree to give full guardianship and care over my daughter* . . . The little fairy's name is Ellen-Jane, I believe? *My daughter Ellen-Jane to Mr Silas Bernhardt.* That's yours truly, though my stage name is Beppo.'

'You can stop this fooling. I'm not signing my daughter away,' said Pa.

'For the sum of . . . Now, what would be a fair sum? How about five pounds? That's almost a year's wages for a full grown woman, a tidy amount. Think what you might buy with it.' Mister lowered his voice. 'You look careworn, sir, down on your luck. Think what tempting pleasures you could buy, all the while knowing that this little darling is safe and happy and earning her keep, all the better to keep you into a ripe old age.'

'Five pounds in cash?' said Pa.

'No, Pa! Oh, please, no, I don't want to go with him. He frightens me,' I cried.

Pa hesitated. His hand went out, as if he might stroke my hair, the golden locks he used to love.

'Make it five guineas, not five pounds,' Mister whispered.

'Show me your money.'

The man reached inside his greatcoat and drew out a leather bag with a tight cord, greasy from much handling. 'Cup your hands!' he told Pa.

I watched, scarcely able to breathe, while he counted out five gold sovereigns and five silver shillings into Pa's shaking hands. Pa thrust the money deep into his pockets and then hid his eyes with one hand so that he should not see me.

'Take her,' he muttered.

'No! Oh, Pa, please, I want to stay home with you and Mary-Martha and little Johnnie.' I was gulping tears now. I would not miss my father now he was so cruel to me, but I had become fond of my baby brother, and Mary-Martha had done her best to be a little mother to me.

'I'll take her, sir, and gladly, but I need you to sign my paper here, giving your permission. I'll not have you regretting things in a more sober light and accusing me of child-stealing. Let me write in the sum – five whole guineas. My, that's more than you'd pay for a thoroughbred horse – and this child's such a stunted little filly. There, sir, sign at the bottom. One flourish of the pen and then we'll cease bothering you. You can toss away your tray of tracts and go to the tavern and celebrate your good fortune. I see you licking your lips! You've a fierce thirst on you, sir, and it needs to be slaked.'

So Pa signed his name and then staggered off without a backward glance. My own father had sold me to a stranger.

I could not believe it. I kept poking at my eyes, trying to open them wider, wondering if I was having some terrible nightmare – but I knew I was not imagining the iron grip on my wrist.

'Come along, my little fairy,' the man said. 'Don't pull away from me like a naughty child. You have to do as I say now – and woe betide you if you don't.'

'Oh, but please, mayn't I say goodbye to my dear sister and my little brother? They will be so anxious if

I don't go home, and they'll be needing me to earn money for a bite to eat,' I begged.

'All your money is *my* money now. You're all mine, little fairy. Your pa's signed you away. You ain't *got* no pa or sister or baby brother now. You've just got me,' said Mister. 'Now stop your grizzling and walk along nicely. Stop hanging back. *Walk*, I say.' He gave my arm such a sudden vicious tug I thought he'd yank it right out of its socket.

I clamped my lips shut because I didn't want my sobs to make him even angrier, and did my best to scurry along at his pace. He might be old and wizened and his legs bent, but he was extraordinarily lithe and strong. I was soon very out of breath.

I looked all around me desperately, wondering where he was taking me. I didn't know this part of town beyond the market very well. We passed the town hall, and its clock boomed out the time – twelve noon. I shuddered at every chime. Even now, when I am so happy, Hetty, if I hear any clock striking and I count along to twelve, my heart starts thudding again, remembering that hour.

I saw an undertaker's funeral parlour and wondered if it was the one where Luke worked. I tried calling his name, but my throat was so dry with fear I could barely make a cheep. Then the long street of shops petered out. We passed several rows of new houses, big red-brick villas with gardens. There was a nursemaid trying to pull a perambulator up a flight of steps. The baby stayed safe inside the covers, but the little boy perching on the end of the pram tumbled off and bumped his head, starting up a fearful screaming.

'Oh dear, poor little lad,' said Mister, and went to pull the child to his feet with his free hand.

'You keep away from our Charlie!' the nursemaid said fiercely. 'You're from the circus, I dare say. We don't want the likes of you hanging around here.'

'Suit yourself, missus. I'll let the little lad tumble down all over again and crack his head open into the bargain, and I'll not raise a finger to help,' said Mister, swiping the boy back to the ground with one quick cuff.

The child started screaming anew and the nursemaid shrieked. Mister just laughed and tugged at me to get me moving again.

I was more fearful than ever now. What *was* this circus? The nursemaid had spat the word out. Was it even more tumbledown and filthy than Willoughby Buildings? Yet Mister seemed clean enough and his clothes were respectable, if a bit odd. He wore a worn worsted coat and checked trousers, and a flowing paisley silk scarf about his thin neck – the clothes of a silly young toff, yet Mister was old and spoke just like ordinary folk.

He saw me staring and suddenly pulled an extra-ordinary face, crossing his eyes and pushing his lips into a terrifying pout. I gasped, and he cackled with laughter.

'You're a timid little fairy, ain't you, my pretty one? No prancing and prinking now. Well, droop away while you can. I'll soon perk you up for the ring.'

'The ring?' I quavered.

'In the big top.'

I stared at him. He seemed to be talking in riddles.

'You'll see, you'll see. What a sweet ignoramus you are. But I'll learn you. Oh yes, I'll learn you good and proper,' said Mister. 'Come along, step up smartly. We're nearly there.'

I looked around fearfully for some dark looming building, but could only see green fields at the edge of the town. Folk seemed to have set up home in one of the fields. I saw a semicircle of brightly painted wagons, and an enormous red and white construction like the preaching tent Ma had taken us to when we were little. Then I saw a vast wild beast with a long, long nose like a wriggling eel, and I stood stock-still.

Mister laughed at me. 'Aha! What do you think of Elijah then, little fairy?'

'It's a monster!' I gasped. 'Will it eat me?'

'Yes, it'll eat you all up in one gollop if you're a bad little minx and don't do as I say,' Mister told me, chuckling. 'Come along and say how do – and if you say it respectful like, he'll shake your hand with his trunk.'

I wasn't going to shake hands with that heathen monster, even if Mister beat me black and blue. There were other exotic animals here too. As we drew nearer, I heard a roaring that set me trembling.

'What's that, Mister? Is it a dog, a giant dog? I'm a-feared of fierce dogs,' I said.

'It's not a big dog, my silly little fairy. It's a big *cat*. Ain't you heard of Tanglefield's lions? The wildest beasts in all Christendom, and yet we train them to jump through hoops of fire.'

This wasn't reassuring. I heard other alarming animal sounds – wild, high-pitched barking – coming from one of the bigger wagons.

'There's big dogs in there, Mister, I can hear them,' I said.

'They're not dogs either – they're sea lions swimming about their tank. It sounds as if it's feeding time. You watch yourself, pretty missy, or I'll chop you into little pieces and feed you to the sea lions too.' He made little chewing motions with his lips and wheezed with laughter at my horror.

This circus seemed the most terrifying place in the world, full of ravenous beasts and men like Mister, but then I saw an animal I recognized. It was a beautiful black horse, a prince of ponies compared to all the sad knock-kneed nags I saw dragging carts and drays all over town, but clearly a horse nevertheless, with an arched neck and a long silky mane and tail. On his back sat the most amazing woman I had ever seen, like a princess in a fairy tale.

She had long, wavy red hair tumbling down her back and wore a pair of bizarre baggy trousers that clung to her shapely white legs. Her horse was unbridled and she rode bareback, not even holding onto his flowing mane. He was stepping out swiftly, but she stayed erect and upright, a smile on her face.

Then she saw me and stopped the horse in his tracks. 'Who have you stolen now, Beppo?' she said, her voice sharp.

'Not stolen, Addie! What harsh words! How quick you are to jump to conclusions. I bought this little fairy child. I paid five whole guineas for her too, so I hope she'll work very hard and repay my generosity.' He gave me a little shake.

'Don't, Beppo, you're frightening her. Poor little creature, you look scared to death.' She leaped gracefully from her horse and knelt down beside me. Her face was even prettier close up, her cheeks so pink, her lips very red. I breathed in deeply because she smelled beautifully of fresh roses. I felt the tears trickling down my face.

She reached out and gently mopped them away

with a lace handkerchief. Her hand was so white and smooth and delicate. I realized how grimy I'd become since living in Willoughby Buildings, where there was just one cold water tap outside for goodness knows how many families. But even if I scrubbed all day in a hot tub, I knew I could never get my skin as white and perfect as hers.

'There now, my dear. My name is Madame Adeline – and this is my dear horse, Midnight. Would you like to pat him?'

I nodded timidly. She took me by the hand. Mister was reluctant to let go of me, but Madame Adeline pulled his fingers away from my wrist.

'Let her be, Beppo. Poor little girl! You're pinching her. She'll get a horrid bruise. There now.' Madame Adeline rubbed my sore wrist tenderly. 'What's your name, dear?'

'I'm Ellen-Jane Potts, ma'am,' I whispered.

'Not any more you're not,' said Mister. 'That's no name for a little circus star.'

'Little Star . . .' murmured Madame Adeline, sounding sad.

'Think of a name for her, Addie – you've got the knack for it,' said Mister, suddenly wheedling.

'*Twinkle, Twinkle, Little Star,*' said Madame Adeline, tucking my hair behind my ears. 'My, you have lovely bright hair. I shall wash it for you with my special shampoo and then it will sparkle in the sunlight. What shall we call you? *Like a diamond in the sky* ... Diamond! There's your name, little one – Diamond.'

'I like it! Little Diamond, the Child Wonder!' said Beppo. 'Oh, Addie, I *knew* you'd come up trumps. That's your name now, Miss Fairy. Little Diamond. Say it now.'

'Little Diamond,' I lisped obediently.

Mister chuckled and rubbed his hands together. 'Yeth, lickle Di-mond,' he said, imitating me.

'Twinkle then, little Diamond,' said Madame Adeline, and she lifted me up, her graceful arms surprisingly strong, and sat me on top of Midnight. I gave a little shriek to be up so high, and slipped sideways the moment the horse moved a hoof.

'Whoopsie,' she said, swinging me down again. 'Well, she's not a natural horsewoman, I'll tell you that for sure.'

'Hands off! I'm not having you training her up. She's going to be a little acrobat,' said Mister.

'She's too old to start,' said Madame Adeline, which surprised me utterly.

'I'm eight years old, ma'am,' I said. 'Though most folk think I'm only about five.'

'See! Out of the mouths of babes ... We'll bill her as an infant phenomenon,' said Mister. 'She'll do a turn with my boys.'

'No, you can't do that to her! She's a light little thing and will look as pretty as a picture once she's had a good scrub, but if you try cricking her bones bendy at this stage, you'll just break them,' said Madame Adeline.

'I'll hardly need to touch her!' said Mister. 'Right, little Diamond, show Madame Addie here what you can do. Go on then! Turn a cartwheel and walk around on those hands like a crab.'

'I don't want to,' I said shyly, ducking my head to hide behind my hair.

Mister drew my hair aside like curtains and stared straight into my eyes. 'Now listen to me, little fairy,' he whispered. His voice was so soft I could hardly hear him, but so sinister it was like the hissing of a serpent. 'It's not what *you* want any more, oh dear me, no. I'm your master now and you'll do exactly what *I* want, understand?'

I swallowed and then nodded.

'Then put on a show for Madame Addie here, pronto!'

I stepped away, trembling so that I could barely stand, but when I obediently stood on my hands, I felt steadier. Madame Adeline clapped enthusiastically at once, calling 'Bravo!' which encouraged me further. I cartwheeled in a circle, I capered backwards like a crab, I sprang up and did a back-flip and landed lightly the right way up, arms outstretched.

'Oh my, she has it all off pat!' Madame Adeline declared. 'Bless the little sweetheart. You're right, Beppo, she's a natural.'

'Wait till I've trained her up a little. I reckon she'll be better than all my boys put together. My five guineas are a very sound investment, you'll see. Right, my twinkly little Diamond, come and meet your brothers.'

'My brothers, Mister?' I thought for one moment that he'd purchased Matthew, Mark, Luke and baby John too – but when he led me over to a red wagon there was no sign of my own kin.

There were three young men there, stripped to the waist, wearing tight breeches. The eldest looked the strongest, with broad shoulders and arms like great hams, though his waist was small and his stomach flat as a board.

The middle one was slighter, but his wiry arms were taut with muscle too. He was in the middle of a wrestling match with his older brother, managing to shove and heave with almost as much strength.

The youngest was just a boy, only a few years older than me. He was watching his brothers upside down, standing on his hands. He pulled a face when he saw me and stuck out his tongue, waggling it rudely. I did likewise. I wasn't frightened of silly boys, and I could do a handstand too. But then he shifted his weight until he was standing on only *one* hand. He waved the other at me insolently. I tried not to look impressed.

'Boys, boys! Do you call this nonsense practising?' said Mister, clapping his hands. 'Pay attention now.'

The two young men stopped wrestling and the boy whipped through the air and landed lightly on his toes. All three stood to attention. It was clear Mister expected to be obeyed instantly.

'That's more like it,' he said. 'Now, I'd like to introduce you all to this little fairy here. She's Diamond, Acrobatic Child Wonder, my new shining star.'

All three glared at me. The youngest looked positively outraged, his eyebrows wrinkled and his mouth gaped, showing his missing teeth.

'Ain't *I* your child wonder?' he said.

'You're all my little wonders,' said Mister. 'This here's Tag, Diamond. You're to pay particular attention to him. He'll learn you all his tricks. Regular little crowd-pleaser, he is.'

The youngest looked slightly appeased, but he still frowned fiercely at me.

'And this is Julip, my middle lad,' said Mister. 'He flies through the air like a bird, don't you, boy?'

'Flipperty-flap,' said Julip, waving his arms.

'And this here is Marvo, my eldest. Strong as an ox, aren't you, son? Show off your muscles to little Diamond here.'

The big lad flexed his great arms until his veins looked as if they'd burst through his taut skin. Then he stepped forward, picked me up with one vast hand and thrust me high in the air. I waggled my legs in protest and he threw me free. I landed in an undignified heap on the grass. Mister and the three boys all laughed at me. Tag actually spat contemptuously.

'Pick *me* up, Marvo,' he said.

Marvo lifted him effortlessly in one hand and then threw him too. Tag tucked himself into a tiny ball and turned two somersaults in the air before landing neatly on his feet, his arms outstretched in acknowledgement. He nodded at me triumphantly.

'That's it, you show her, Tag,' said Mister. 'Give her a quick routine, boys, so she can see what we do.'

The three all instantly straightened, shoulders back, chins in the air, stepping out like little princes, though they were still barefoot boys. Marvo stood still, muscles flexed. Julip ran up to him and flew through the air, landing lightly with his feet on Marvo's shoulders. Then Tag stepped on a springboard and flew upwards too, twice the height, landing on top of Julip with barely a wobble. They stood before me, a giant man made out of three boys. Then, with a grunt, Marvo took a few steps, both boys still balanced high above him before they teetered forward. Julip and Tag somersaulted through the air before landing neatly, then all three started cartwheeling in a ring, round and round. When Mister shouted a command, they all upended themselves and swooped so far back their heads poked cheekily between their legs. They capered about like misformed monsters, pulling crazy faces. Tag pretended to bite Mister on the behind, and Mister waved his fist at him — and then, astonishingly, *he* stood on his hands and ran at Tag upside down.

I had not realized that *he* was part of the act too. I figured he was about the same age as my own pa, maybe even older, yet he was now proving as spry as his sons. I'd never been so scared of anyone before, and yet now, watching him hobble about in pursuit of the boys, pulling the drollest faces, I could not help doubling up with laughter.

I still did not understand what his act was until I saw him in full costume for that afternoon's performance. I was in the cramped quarters of the boys' wagon, trying to hitch a hammock from post to post.

Mister suddenly thrust his head through the door, and I screamed. His face was painted a deathly white, and he had a new big bulbous nose and vast red lips that smiled in a sinister way to the very edges of his ears.

'I am Beppo the clown!' he said, and then he cackled with laughter.

All afternoon I watched the circus performance. I was soon to know each routine in dreary detail, but I remember I was utterly dazzled by that first show.

I know you felt the same way too, Hetty! I loved Madame Adeline and thought her very beautiful as she rode around the ring in her pink sparkly dress. I was astonished to see Mister transformed into capering Beppo, throwing water at the other clown, Chino, and tripping over his great shoes. I laughed along with all the other children, but I squirmed in my seat too.

I was utterly transfixed by the Silver Tumblers and their acrobatic antics. Marvo, Julip and Tag looked so different in their silver costumes in the circus ring. They'd painted their faces too, shading their eyelids blue and rubbing rouge on their cheeks so that they looked robust and glowing. They'd oiled their hair so that it gleamed in the spotlight, and the sequins sewn onto their costumes dazzled the eye.

They did their handstand trick, and then many others, leaping and tumbling around the ring, shouting as they did so. I forgot that they were rude boys who larked around. They were amazing aerial beings, as magical as fairies, and I was entranced.

I clapped so hard my hands stung. I watched the monkeys and the lions, and the performing seals and the astonishingly huge elephant, marvelling at them all, but I was still seeing silver sparkles before my eyes. I stood up and cheered as all the performers paraded around the ring at the end, and then hovered uncertainly as everyone scrambled for the exit flap of the tent. Should I try to walk away too? Maybe I could find some kind lady and beg her help to get home. I knew Pa had been glad to be rid of me, but I could hide when he was around. Mary-Martha would be glad to see me – and oh, I wanted to see *her* so very much. She could be vexingly pious at times, but she was the only one in the world who had tender feelings for me now and I loved her dearly.

What was I waiting for? I had only to run! Beppo might be lurking somewhere close, but I was just one small girl amid hundreds. I spotted an old shawl someone had left behind on her seat. I snatched it up and wound it over my head, covering my long bright hair. Then I joined up with a whole gaggle of children – they were with a flustered old dame who couldn't keep control of them. Several stared at me in surprise, but I just ducked my head and pressed close to them.

All I had to do was get out of the big tent and run. I didn't know this part of town, but the field was only streets away from the big shops. I could be home in half an hour.

The crowd jostled all about me. I shut my eyes and prayed to my poor dead mother: *Dear Ma, please watch over me and keep me safe, and don't let Mister snatch me back!*

I could almost feel her long hair brushing my head, her gentle hands on my shoulders. She seemed to steer me through the crowd, right out of the tent, across the grass – she was truly helping me—

'Hey, you! Diamond, come here!'

It was Tag, a wrapper over his silver sequins, his slicked-back hair making him look like one of the performing seals. He was gesturing at me impatiently. I turned my back on him and started running. I prided myself on being speedy. Mary-Martha could never catch me, even though her legs were longer than mine, but Tag was a different proposition. He was after me in a blink. He didn't waste time telling me to stop. He threw himself at me, wrestling me to the ground and pinioning me in my stolen shawl, nearly choking the life out of me.

I had fought with my brothers often enough, but they usually played fair with me. They'd never used their whole strength and they'd never actually hit me with their fists. Tag sat down hard on my chest, beating a tattoo on my head.

'Get off me, you brute!' I gasped. I tried to spit in his face but I didn't have the strength. My spittle dribbled down my own chin.

'Ha ha, dirty little cat,' said Tag. 'You come quietly now.'

'Please let me go! You don't want me here, so why are you keeping me?' I said, struggling.

'Of course we don't want you, you useless baby – but Beppo does,' said Tag. 'He's the boss.'

'He's not *my* boss! He's not *my* pa!' I said.

'He's not mine either,' said Tag.

'But he said you were his boys.'

'Marvo and Julip – not me. Beppo got me even

younger than you and trained me up,' said Tag. He didn't let me go, but at least he'd stopped hitting me now.

'Did your pa sell you too?' I whispered.

'Didn't have no pa. No ma neither,' said Tag.

'But you must have had them once. Did they both die? My poor ma died,' I said, suddenly welling up with tears.

'Crying, eh? *Baby!*' said Tag. 'No, there was just me. I lived with some other boys, but I didn't like it and I ran away. And then Beppo got hold of me.'

'I'm not crying because of *you* – but get off my chest, I can't *breathe*,' I gasped.

He did roll off me then. I sat up, knuckling my eyes.

'You could run away from Beppo too. We both could,' I said.

'I did at first. And he caught me and beat me until I couldn't stand up. He'll do the same to you – and he'll wallop me too for not looking out for you, so think on, Diamond.'

'I'm not *called* Diamond. It's just his silly name for me,' I said. 'I'm Ellen-Jane.'

'Not any more, you're not. You're everything that Beppo says. Now come *on*, or we won't get any grub between shows.' He took hold of my hand and yanked me to my feet.

I might still have run, but I knew he'd catch me.

I didn't think then that Mister would really give us a beating – not *me* – but I certainly didn't want to make him angry. And I was hungry. Very hungry.

I let Tag pull me along to the big blue wagon beside the boys' ramshackle home. Marvo was squatting on the ground stirring a big cauldron over a fire. Julip was tearing chunks of bread off a loaf. Mister himself was sitting on the steps, a robe over his under vest and trousers. He'd taken off his great clown's shoes, displaying very holey striped socks, but he was still wearing full greasepaint, and a little bowler hat on the back of a mad grey wig. He should have looked ridiculous but there was nothing comical about his suspicious glare.

'Where have you two been? She didn't try to do a runner, did she?' he said.

I held my breath.

'No, boss!' said Tag. 'She just tumbled over a guy rope, that's all.'

'Tumbled, did you, little fairy?' said Mister. 'Oh, we'll teach you tumbling soon enough.'

'You'll never teach that one, Beppo. She's not got the pluck,' said Tag.

'She'll learn. I'll just throw her up in the air and hope for the best. Once she's landed with a crack on that pretty little head often enough, she'll get the knack of tucking herself up tight,' said Marvo.

I wasn't sure if he was joking or not. I sat some distance away from him when Mister served the meal, just in case. It smelled good, very good indeed, a thick dark savoury stew with dumplings and large pieces of meat. I had been living on bread and scraps of cheese and bruised fruit. My mouth started watering.

Mister served me up a whole bowlful. There were no forks or spoons. I had to scoop it up with my bread. Mister and the boys slurped their stew straight out of the steaming bowl.

It tasted astonishingly good, strong and succulent, the meat so tender it scarcely needed chewing. I ate ravenously, sucking each chunk to the bone.

'That's it! Eat up, little fairy,' said Mister.

'It's very good meat,' I said. 'Is it beef, I wonder – or lamb?' I had rarely tasted either but I did not want them to think me ignorant.

They all guffawed with laughter.

'Haven't you ever had horsemeat before?' asked Marvo.

He *had* to be joking this time. I looked over the fields to where Madame Adeline's beautiful Midnight was tethered.

'It's not truly horse, is it?' I quavered, my mouth still full.

'No, it's succulent little pony,' said Beppo, and he gave a high-pitched horse's neigh.

I choked on my mouthful and had to spit it out. This made them all laugh uproariously.

'Don't you want your gee-gee then?' said Tag. 'Give it here. I'll soon polish it off.'

I was still hungry but I couldn't eat any more. I let Tag have my bowl and turned my back on them all so I wouldn't see them chewing away at the meat. Madame Adeline was sitting on her own wagon steps, eating her own meal. She beckoned me over when she saw me watching her.

I wandered towards her.

'Why did you give your bowl to Tag, dearie?' she asked gently. She gave me a little poke in the tummy. 'You're the one who's all skin and bone. You need to eat your fill, little Diamond.'

'I don't like that stew,' I said.

'Well then, have some of mine.'

I peered into her pot anxiously. 'Is it horsemeat?' I whispered.

'No, it isn't,' she said. 'I have eaten that and it tastes good, but I haven't got the stomach for it, not when my horses are just like family to me. This is chicken, dear – an old boiling bird, but still quite juicy.'

'Like you, Addie,' Mister called, chuckling.

She pulled a face at him. 'Take no notice of Beppo. *I* don't,' she said, scooping a fresh portion of chicken stew into a mug. 'Here, child, eat. And when you've finished,

I'll see if I can find you something special for afters!'

I ate the chicken stew with relish, thanking her fervently. Then she took me by the hand and led me up the steps into her wagon. I cried out in surprise and delight.

'Oh my, it's so pretty and neat and you have such lovely things,' I said, touching the lace antimacassars on her crimson sofa, the delicate fern in its polished brass pot, the china ladies dancing on top of her cabinet. 'It's just like a dear little home.'

The boys' wagon was dark chaos, just three beds and a tumble of discarded clothes – and the wagon smelled so terribly of boy too. Madame Adeline's wagon smelled of lavender bags and verbena soap and her own sweet rose perfume. I breathed in deeply.

'Do you like the smell?' she said, smiling at me. She took a cut-glass bottle from her dressing table and dabbed some rose scent behind my ears.

'Oh, it's lovely!' I said.

'Well, if you like roses so much, we'll find you a special treat for your dessert,' she said. She opened a tin and showed me two little cakes inside: fairy cakes with pink icing, each studded with a candied rose.

'One for you and one for me,' she said, offering me the tin.

'But they're yours,' I said, though I wanted one dreadfully.

'It's twice as nice to share – and I shall get twice as fat if I eat both,' said Madame Adeline, patting her stomach.

I ate my little cake happily, saving the rose till last and then sucking it slowly to savour it. I looked around Madame Adeline's beautiful home. I could see her dressing table, and a white nightgown hanging behind the door, but I couldn't see any bed. I looked up at the ceiling, but she didn't have a hammock. I stared at her velvet armchair, wondering if she curled up there at night. She was watching me, amused.

'I do have a bed, you know,' she said, as if I'd spoken aloud. 'Do you want to see it?' She tugged at a handle on the wall and pulled down an entire little bed that had been hiding inside, ready made up with fresh white linen and a patchwork quilt.

'Oh, how clever!' I said. 'May I try it out?' I flopped down on the bed and found it very comfortable indeed. It was really quite large – roomy enough for two.

'I wish *I* had a beautiful bed like this,' I said wistfully. 'I only have a hammock and I'm scared I shall tip myself out in the night.'

'Well, if you do, Marvo is an expert at catching people,' said Madame Adeline. She paused. 'I wish you could come and sleep with me, Diamond. I think you'd be much happier.'

'Oh, I would, I would!' I said.

'Well, I will talk to Beppo and do my best to persuade him.'

She tried very hard, but Mister wouldn't hear of it.

'She's *my* property, not yours, Addie! I'm not having you molly-coddling her and feeding her titbits and making her fat and soft. She needs hardening up – and quickly. She has to earn her keep,' he said.

'I will do my dance and walk on my hands as pretty as you please,' I said.

'You're not here to prink about like a child at a party, little missy. You're a professional now. We're going to have to work on your act night and day to get you up to scratch,' said Mister. 'You'd better make the most of today. Now watch the act with particular care at tonight's performance. See how sharp my boys are. And afterwards I want you to list the whole routine for me – somersaults, flic-flacs, each and every tumble. You have to learn quick. Make the brain inside that pretty little bonce work overtime.' He tapped me sharply on top of my head. It felt as if his finger had poked right through flesh and bone.

Instead of being stirred into action, my brain now seemed paralysed with fear. I sat down to the evening performance and watched tensely, waiting for the silver boys to start their act. Beppo capered about the ring with Chino, and every child in the big top laughed delightedly – but I shrank down in my seat, terribly aware of his steely grey eyes. They seemed to be staring at me even when his head was turned away.

I craned my neck until it ached to watch Flora, the Queen of the Tightrope, then slumped uncomfortably in my seat when the sea lions balanced balls and honked little trumpets with their whiskery mouths. My head started to nod when dear Madame Adeline cantered round and round the ring. It had been a long and terrible day, the tent was stiflingly hot, my stomach was very full . . . I was soon fast asleep and didn't wake up until the grand parade at the end of the show.

I sat up with a jerk, bewildered by the claps and cheers all around me. I called out for Mary-Martha, in such a daze I thought I was back at Willoughby Buildings – but then my dazzled eyes made sense of the gas-lit tent and I remembered everything. I remembered everything – except the silver boys' routine! And Mister was going to quiz me on it in detail.

I thought I'd better attempt another escape, but Tag was waiting for me again and I was too tired to tussle with him. I let him drag me over to the wagon. Marvo and Julip joined us. All three boys seemed subdued, standing apart, arms hanging limp.

'It was *your* fault, Marvo. You weren't standing straight on,' Julip muttered.

'You didn't spring high enough, you fool,' Marvo told him.

'Well, Tag messed up his cartwheels and I got distracted,' said Julip.

Their act had clearly not gone well. They kept looking anxiously over their shoulders. I saw Mister in the distance discussing something with Chino, both of them smoking cigars. Madame Adeline was busy grooming Midnight and covering his back with a blanket for the night. She waved at me and I waved back, though my arm felt leaden.

Then, at last, Mister came striding towards us. He was a small man and he walked with his shoulders hunched. Marvo was twice his weight and Julip a head taller, but they cowered visibly. Tag was sweating through his greasepaint, clenching his fists.

'Fools!' Mister muttered, and then he reached up and slapped each boy hard about the head. 'Slipshod amateurs! We're rehearsing at seven sharp tomorrow – and if you dare mess up again I'll whip you all within an inch of your lives. Understand?'

It was clear he wasn't bluffing. Marvo and Julip bent their heads. Tag shivered all over, his face screwed up to stop himself crying.

Then Mister looked at me. 'Well, little trembling fairy, I hope you paid attention to the act? Tell me how it begins, reciting each individual exercise. Woe betide you if you get any wrong!'

I stared at him. I stared at Marvo and Julip and

Tag. Marvo moved his hand minutely, twirling one finger.

'They – they somersaulted into the ring,' I stammered.

Marvo pointed downwards.

'And – and Marvo stood on his hands,' I continued, but Mister had spotted Marvo's twitching finger.

'Don't you dare help her, you sneaking lummox,' he said, and he lashed out at Marvo again, hitting him so hard his head rocked.

If he could nearly knock a young ox like Marvo off his feet, what could he do to me? I felt sick with terror.

'I'm waiting,' said Mister. 'And as my boys will confirm, I'm not a patient man.'

My mouth was so dry I could only make a little croaking sound. I did not dare look at Marvo again. I simply stood there, opening and shutting my mouth.

'I can't hear you!' Mister came towards me, bending down so that his painted face was close to mine. His crimson lips leered at me. 'Louder, little fairy. Speak up, *if* you remember. If *not* – well, you must take your punishment.'

'Oh, Mister, I can't tell you!' I blurted.

'You can't tell me?' said Mister. 'You mean you weren't *paying attention*?'

'I was, oh indeed I was, but – but when the act went a little wrong and Julip slipped, quite by accident,

I had to shut my eyes tight because I was so upset,' I said. 'I *couldn't* watch because I knew you would be vexed.'

Mister stared and then seized hold of me. But he didn't strike me. He twirled me round as if we were doing a dance.

'Oh, what an artful answer from my little fairy!' he said. 'I think you will prove worth your five guineas after all. Now, go to bed and get your beauty sleep. Go, all of you.'

I visited the unspeakable latrine and then shut myself in the wagon with the boys. I did not have any nightgown to change into. I climbed into my hammock and curled up tight. The boys below me argued in whispers, cursing and complaining, but they soon started snoring. I lay awake, aching for Mary-Martha and little Johnnie, wondering if I'd ever see them again.

I had only just gone to sleep when I was woken by one of the boys giving my hammock a violent swing so that I nearly tumbled out.

'Practice time!' Tag hissed. 'Quick!'

We had no breakfast – just a hot drink. I peered at mine suspiciously. It was the same mug in which they'd served the horsemeat stew and it smelled.

'What drink is this?' I asked.

'Horse's pee,' said Julip.

All three boys collapsed with laughter when they saw my face.

'It's tea, black tea, I promise you,' said Marvo, but I still wouldn't drink it.

'You'd better have some. You'll be thirsty soon enough. Beppo works us hard,' he told me. He held the mug to my lips. 'Come on, little Diamond, drink up.'

I managed a few reluctant sips. 'Why is he so cruel to everyone?' I asked.

'It's just his way. His father was hard on him. It's the way we learn,' said Marvo.

'But you're bigger than him now,' I said. 'You could hit him back.'

They all three looked at me as if I were raving.

'You try hitting him, Diamond. Go on, I dare you!' said Tag.

'He's got a special cane,' said Julip. He pulled his singlet up to show me his back. 'Look!'

I saw terrible weals that made my eyes water. 'Why did he do that?' I whispered.

'We fell out. He hit me night after night because I lost my nerve and wouldn't always try the flying double somersault at the end of the act. I hate performing. I never wanted to be an acrobat – still don't, but there's nothing I can do about it. I ricked my back falling clumsily and it made me even more awkward, because it hurt so—'

'He made you perform even when you were in pain?'

'Beppo's in pain all the time,' said Marvo. 'He hurt his back too – broke it. He was six months scarcely able to move, and now he has to be a clown.'

'So it makes him all the more severe with us,' said Julip. 'One night I just wouldn't try at all. I did the simplest baby routine. The crowd probably didn't even realize – they'll roar and clap at anything – but afterwards Beppo beat me. The next day I could hardly move and all the wounds were seeping, but I still had to do two performances.'

'Will he beat me?' I whispered. 'I can't do one somersault, let alone two.'

'You'll learn soon enough,' Marvo told me. 'You're a little fairy, like he says. You'll be flying through the air in no time.'

'Flying through the air from the tip of my boot unless you all get cracking,' said Mister, coming out of his wagon and pointing at us threateningly.

He looked very old in the early morning light, his face grey without his greasepaint, and I noticed how stiffly he walked, his eyes twitching at every step, though they were still steely. I saw how a man twice the size of Marvo could still fear him. He was holding a great coil of rope and I wondered if he was going to beat me with it or maybe tie me up and hang me. I shrank from him in terror.

'Easy now, little fairy,' he said, chuckling grimly, and seizing me by the wrist. 'Come along with your Uncle Beppo.'

The rest of the circus performers were still in their wagons, fast asleep. Even the animals were quiet in their cages, slumped in slumber, though Elijah the elephant stood tethered to a tree, idly plucking leaves from the branches. I shrank from him too, scared that he might trample me or knock me over with his great trunk, but the boys all called to him affectionately as if he were their friend, and Tag reached up and patted his vast wrinkled thigh.

The circus ring was empty.

'Right, boys, cricking time,' said Mister.

They seized hold of each other's legs and stretched them hard, working them round in their sockets till I thought they'd be pulled right off.

'Your turn, little fairy. Got to get those puny arms and legs supple . . .' Mister pulled me close and then yanked my legs up to my head ten or more times. I screamed with pain.

'Now now, no fussing!' said Mister, panting with the effort.

'You're breaking me in two! Please, please, stop it!' I begged.

'A little bit of cricking never hurt anyone,' said Mister, persisting. When he set me down at last

I could barely stand, but he took no notice.

'Right, let's get to work now you're warmed up. Tag, practise your somersaults. Marvo, Julip, help me with the ropes.'

He took a strange belt and tied it tightly around my waist. 'So little, my tiny girl. A true Thumbelina!'

There were rings on either side of the belt, through which he threaded ropes. Marvo stood on one side of me, Julip on the other, holding the ropes tightly.

'Now, Diamond, first you must learn the back somersault, the easiest of all. Simply spring up, tuck and turn backwards. Show her, Tag.'

Tag did a whole series of back somersaults, landing each with a jaunty flourish.

'Now, you try, Diamond,' said Mister.

I did my best, in spite of my aching back and buckled legs. It was a clumsy attempt, and I pulled heavily on the ropes and fell as I landed – but it was *almost* a back somersault.

'That was hopeless!' said Tag, sneering.

I thought Mister would be vexed with me, but he waved Tag away. 'Not bad for a first attempt, little fairy. I think you're going to be a natural,' he said.

He kept me working at it half the morning, until I was wringing wet with sweat and the blood was pounding through my body. Then he let me rest for half an hour while he made the boys repeat their act. He was especially hard on Julip, forcing him to do his double somersault again and again. Then it was my turn to do my very simple back somersault, while Marvo and Julip held my ropes. I still couldn't turn and tuck neatly enough. Tag kept sighing at me and then somersaulting exquisitely himself, showing off.

The friction of the tight belt was rubbing my waist raw and chafing terribly.

'Enough,' said Mister. 'We don't want to saw the little fairy in half.'

'Little flop, more like,' said Tag.

'We will work on your handstands instead,' Mister went on.

'I can do that!' I said eagerly, and demonstrated.

I thought I did it well enough. The crowds at the market had always clapped me – but I didn't impress Mister or the boys.

'Terrible! You must straighten your line and position those legs. There are two different postures. The first is with the legs open in the form of a Y, the second with the legs straight together like an I, toes pointed. Show her, Tag.'

Tag executed both handstands neatly in triumph. I did my level best to copy him, and must have made a fair stab at things because Mister nodded.

'Better,' he said, which was clearly the nearest he

came to praise. 'Now try bending backward, arching your body.'

'The crab-walk! Oh, I can do that too!' I said, doing so.

'Yes, yes, so now you can try the curvet. Arch your body back until your hands touch the ground and then relax all the muscles of your legs so that you rebound back onto your feet. Simple!'

It wasn't simple at all. Tag showed me several times, but I couldn't get the hang of it. I kept tumbling and hurting myself – one time so badly that I cried, tears streaming down my face.

'No, no! No grimacing, no tears, no matter how much it hurts. A true artiste always smiles through the pain so that no one knows. *Smile*, Diamond – stand up and smile and do the curvet again – properly this time,' Mister commanded.

I clenched my teeth and smiled, and managed a reasonable stab at the horrible curvet.

'Mmm . . . Well, it will become second nature to you in time.'

I did not believe him, but I practised morning after morning. When I could do a back somersault without the ropes, Mister said it was time he fitted me out with a costume.

'With a *costume*?' said Tag. 'She can't go in the ring! She still can't do anything!'

'Don't you question me, boy,' said Mister, slapping him about the head. 'She don't *need* to do anything, she just has to look sweet. She's got a lot to learn, but she has to earn her keep meanwhile. We'll work her into the act. She can run in and do her tiny tricks in turn with you boys, and then, when you start your balancing and make your human tower, she can caper about and point – look, Diamond, like this.' He bent down with a groan, contorted his mouth into a huge O of surprise and pointed his finger in exaggerated pantomime. I was forced to copy him until I could do it to his satisfaction.

Tag mimicked me cruelly behind Beppo's back. 'You don't look sweet at all,' he hissed that night in the wagon. 'You look so stupid everyone will laugh at you.'

'Take no notice. Tag's just worried they'll all look at you instead of him,' said Marvo, trying to be reassuring.

'I hope they *do* look at her instead of me,' said Julip. He had nearly slipped again that night, and Beppo had hit him savagely afterwards.

I lay trembling in my hammock, wondering if Mister would beat me too.

The next morning Beppo left the three boys training in the ring and took me to see Madame Adeline. She was still in her rose-patterned wrapper, brushing Midnight until his skin shone glossy black.

107

'Can you give us a helping hand, Addie? I'm putting the little fairy here into the ring today. She can wear Tag's old silver leotard, but I'd like to pretty it up a bit – make her look like a real little fairy. You don't have any frills you can lend her, do you? And maybe a ribbon for her hair.' Mister ran his hand through my bedraggled curls. 'It's not as fluffy as it was,' he said, pulling my hair.

'It looks as if she could do with a good wash,' said Madame Adeline. 'Leave her with me, Beppo.'

I hadn't washed since the day Beppo snatched me from the market. The boys never bothered much, just ducked under the communal tap and then shook themselves dry like dogs. But Madame Adeline filled a big bucketful, then heated it up over her fire and poured some of the hot water into a big shallow tin tray.

'There now, paddle your feet,' she said, swiftly undressing me. 'Let's give you a good soaping.'

Mary-Martha always used carbolic on me, but Madame Adeline had wonderful verbena soap. I loved the smell so much, I didn't even mind when it made my eyes sting. She rubbed another fragrant potion on my head, piling my hair up and rubbing with her fingertips until I was all over froth.

'This stuff is beautiful!' I said rapturously.

'It's my very special Ladies' Rainbow Shampoo,

dearie. Look!' Madame Adeline rubbed the foam between her thumb and forefinger, and then opened them slowly so that a web formed. She blew gently.

'Oh, rainbow bubbles!' I said.

'You do one now . . .' She let me play, entranced, for a full five minutes.

'You'll have to ask Beppo for one of his old pipes. You'll be able to blow enormous bubbles,' she said. 'Come now, you're starting to shiver. Let me sluice all the soap off you.'

'I wouldn't dare ask Mister for anything. He's far too fierce,' I said.

'Oh dear. He seems very taken with you, so I'd hoped he'd be kind, especially as you're so young. He hasn't hit you, has he?'

'No, but he hits the boys *lots*, especially Julip.'

'Poor Julip. He's struggling. He's skilled enough – Beppo is a good trainer, but Julip's heart isn't in it. It's a very hard life for a young man. It's a hard life for *all* of us.' She shook her head forlornly, suddenly looking like an old, old lady. She hadn't put on her face paint yet, and she had somehow tucked all her beautiful long red hair into a strange velvet turban.

'Are you sad, Madame Adeline?' I asked.

She made her mouth turn up into a big smile. 'No, I'm very happy, because I have a dear little new friend to keep me company,' she said. 'Is that all the soap gone? There's a few suds left in your hair. Let me give you one more rinse. Close your eyes!'

'They're tight shut,' I said. 'Madame Adeline – do you mean . . . me? Am *I* your new friend?'

'Of course I mean you, Diamond,' she said, wrapping a big soft towel around me, and then pulling me closer and hugging me.

'Oh, I love to be hugged!' I said. 'Sometimes Ma would hold me on her lap and it was the best feeling in the world.'

'How your mother must have loved you, dearie,' said Madame Adeline.

'I don't think she did – not very much, anyway,' I said. 'She loved the boys more than me – and Mary-Martha was the useful one. I was just a nuisance. I used to be Pa's favourite, but then, after Ma died, he started to hate me.'

'Oh, what a sad story! Well, listen to me, Diamond. If you'd been *my* little girl, I might have loved your brothers and your sister, but I'm certain *you* would have been my favourite. Now, are you dry, dear one? We'll find you some new clothes to wear in the ring, and I'll give your old clothes a good scrub too.'

She sat me on the velvet chair in her wagon, popped a violet chocolate in my mouth and told me to towel my hair while she did a little sewing. I was astonished to see that her *own* hair wasn't under her turban at all. It was hanging on a stand on her dressing table, the long flaming locks reaching down almost to the floor.

Madame Adeline saw me staring and raised her eyebrows ruefully. 'I'm not quite the natural beauty people think any more,' she said.

'I think you're naturally beautiful with your hair or without it,' I said stoutly.

'Bless you, child! I shall store your words up in my head and treasure them. I don't get many compliments nowadays.'

'Don't you have any gentlemen come calling, Madame Adeline?'

'No, dear, not any more, but I don't mind that in the slightest. I've seen enough gentlemen to last me a lifetime.' As she spoke, she rummaged through the lowest dressing-table drawer, bringing out a tangle of bright ribbons and embroidered scarves and lacy undergarments. 'Now then, shall we see if we can turn you into a real fairy?' she said.

She snipped the lace off a torn chemise and started sewing it around the neck of Tag's leotard. She bunched some sparkly net around my waist, fashioning a little skirt. Then she found some wire, bent it into a strange shape, and set me wrapping it round and round with silver satin ribbon.

'What is the wire for?' I asked.

'What do all fairies have?' said Madame Adeline.

'Wings!'

'Exactly. I have some white muslin. We will stretch it over the wire – and you can have a little fairy wand too, with a silver star on the end.'

We worked peacefully together making my costume. Then Madame Adeline had me sit in front of her while she brushed my damp hair. I wriggled delightedly at each firm stroke of the brush, trying to count along with her, but getting muddled after a while. I knew how to count up my pennies, but I'd never needed to know large amounts. Madame Adeline asked me to toss my hair forward over my eyes so she could sort out all the tangles. I wasn't used to my hair being so soft and silky. Sunlight poured in through the open wagon door and made little coloured lights gleam in it. It truly *was* rainbow shampoo.

Madame Adeline wound my front curls round her fingers until they sprang into place, framing my face, and then she opened a beautiful carved jewellery box and brought out . . .

'A crown!' I gasped, staring at the wonderful sparkling gems. 'A diamond crown!'

'No, dear, a tiara – and these stones are only glass. But it looks pretty in the ring and the diamonds catch the light. Perfect for little Diamond, the Acrobatic Child Wonder!'

'You truly don't mind my wearing your beautiful tiara?'

'You will look a picture and do us all proud,' said Madame Adeline. 'Come, let us put on your costume.'

I stepped into the sparkly leotard, now with gauzy little wings flapping at the back.

'Turn around, little fairy. Act as if you're in the spotlight,' she told me.

I pivoted around on one foot, pointing the other, my arms raised.

Madame Adeline laughed and clapped me enthusiastically. 'Bravo! Oh, wait till Beppo sees you. He will be delighted,' she said. 'Let us show you off to him.'

I hung back. 'I don't want to. I don't like him. I'd much sooner be with you. Oh, Madame Adeline, can't I be *your* little wonder?'

'I would like that very much, my dear – but Beppo wouldn't. I'm afraid he is your master now, whether you like it or not. It's the first rule of the circus. You must never steal another artiste's act.'

She took me by the hand and led me to the big top, where Beppo and Chino were working on a new clowning routine with a big penny-farthing bicycle.

'Look at your little protégée now, Beppo,' said Madame Adeline, giving me a gentle push forward.

He took one look at me, wobbled precariously, and then fell right off the tall bicycle. I thought he'd be cross with me in consequence, but his face was all smiles – even his steely eyes softened. He brought his two hands together, almost as if he were praying.

'Perfect!' he breathed. 'Oh, Addie, you've excelled yourself! It looks like I've got my five guineas worth. My, that old fool should have asked me for ten.' He turned me round and round, getting me to put my head to one side and point each toe in turn. 'Oh, you're a picture, my little fairy girl,' he said. He took my wand and waved it over me. 'You will be the star of the show and make old Beppo's wishes come true!'

I stood behind the tent flaps in a long line of artistes waiting to go into the ring. The ringmaster, Mr Tanglefield, was announcing the acts, his voice reedy and distorted as he was speaking through a megaphone. I was almost as scared of Mr Tanglefield as I was of Beppo. He was just as small and mean, and he went everywhere with a whip clamped in his hand. I'd seen him flick it at man and beast indiscriminately. I was always very careful to keep my distance. Now, I could hear the audience laughing and talking through his announcements, barely paying attention, for he sounded such a silly old man. Then the band struck up.

Mister pointed his finger at me to stay in my place with Marvo, Julip and Tag, and then pushed his way through the tent flaps with Chino, both of them waddling in their oversized clown shoes. A shriek of laughter rippled around the ring at their capers.

'Good audience tonight, by the sound of it,' said Sherzam, the elephant keeper. He was a small, slender man, strangely dark, with big brown eyes with long lashes. He smiled at me encouragingly.

'Good or bad, they'll always laugh their silly heads off at the clowns,' said Flora, the tightrope walker. She was a very large lady – by far the fattest member of Tanglefield's Travelling Circus apart from Elijah the elephant. The other acts often teased her. I'd heard Tag ask her why she didn't leave the circus and earn her living as Flora the Fat Lady in a fair, but she just cuffed him in a casual way, not bothering to take offence.

'Looking forward to your debut, Diamond?' she asked, stroking my hair admiringly. 'My, you look quite dazzling.'

Tag groaned, and staggered backwards, covering his eyes with his hands, pretending to be dazzled.

'Silly boy,' said Flora. 'How are you doing, dearie?

Addie asked me to keep a special eye on you.'

Madame Adeline herself didn't come on until almost the end of the show, so she wasn't standing in the line-up yet.

'I'm very nervous,' I whispered.

'That's a sign of a true artiste. I've been doing my act for many years now—'

'Hundreds and hundreds of years,' Tag muttered rudely.

'And always at this moment my stomach churns and I quake with fear.' Flora clutched herself and shivered dramatically. 'But when I climb my little rope ladder it's as if I am entering another world entirely. I forget all those people gawping up at me, wondering if I'm going to slip and fall. I even forget the rude boys pointing and poking fun at me.' She shook her head at Tag. 'Up on my tightrope, my hands don't tremble, my feet are sure and certain in their satin slippers, and I walk, I skip, I dance along my wire. I am Queen of my own airy world.'

'But you are talented, Miss Flora. I can't really do anything yet,' I sighed.

'I'll say,' said Tag. 'You can't even do a forward somersault. I could do that years and years ago. You're useless.'

'She'll learn soon enough,' said Marvo. 'Don't be so hard on her, Tag.'

'If she'd had any sense she'd scarper now, while she can,' Julip muttered.

He was wearing greasepaint on his face but I could see the sweat standing out on his forehead. I took his hand. It was as cold and clammy as a dead fish.

'What's the matter, Julip?' I asked.

He shook his head and pulled his hand away.

'Leave him be,' said Flora. 'He is just having a little nervous crisis, like me.'

'He's in a funk because he keeps slipping,' said Tag. 'He's *useless*.'

Julip was too miserable to respond, but Marvo seized Tag and turned him upside down.

'So Diamond's useless – and Julip too, Mr Taggle? What about me? Am I useless?' said Marvo, shaking him.

'Don't! Let me up!' Tag said indignantly, struggling.

Then Mr Tanglefield came rushing through the tent flaps to seize hold of Elijah for his grand appearance. We all saw Beppo for a moment, capering in a corner of the ring, his head turned towards us. It was enough to make Marvo set Tag on his feet and Julip stand to attention.

'No fooling while you're waiting to go on,' Mr Tanglefield muttered, taking hold of Elijah's chain from Sherzam. I pressed backwards nervously as the great elephant plodded wearily through the tent flaps, his wrinkled skin sagging off his huge bones. His trunk was swinging so that it brushed my bare arm. I craned upwards and saw the tiny eyes embedded in his vast head. He didn't look as if he enjoyed performing either.

Flora went on next. I peeped round the tent flap till I could see her dancing along the tightrope, waving her pink parasol, even pushing a perambulator, clearly enjoying herself. I hoped with all my might that I would enjoy performing too when I was actually out there in the ring. I'd quite liked doing my little tricks to earn money in the marketplace – but I hadn't had Mister lurking, ready to find fault.

Flora gave a last twirl and then clambered down her rope ladder. She spread her arms when she was back on firm ground, turning to acknowledge the cheering crowd, her face flushed with triumph.

Marvo took a deep breath. 'Right, my friends.' He clapped Julip on the back. 'You'll be fine,' he said. He chucked Tag under his chin. 'You too, Tag.' Then he gently pulled a lock of my hair. 'And you'll knock 'em dead, Diamond, just you wait and see.'

Then Flora came through the tent flaps all aglow. Beppo seized hold of me and murmured, 'Dance, little fairy!' and gave me a push right out into the ring.

I stood blinking in the bright spotlight, breathing in the strange smells of sawdust and animals and saveloys and oranges and gingerbread, in such a daze that the circle of crowded seats whirled round and round and I felt so dizzy I didn't dare move. I saw the sparkle as the silver costumes of my three new brothers caught the light, and then Marvo's hand was in mine, pulling me along so that I had to run with all three of them around the ring. I was only *running* – and yet a great murmur started. 'Oh my, look at the little one!' 'She's so tiny! What will she be, four? Five at the most? The little darling!' 'She's just a baby, bless her – and doesn't she look gorgeous: good enough to eat!'

Marvo started his routine, flexing his muscles and leaping about, doing cartwheels, flic-flacs, forward somersaults, every movement neat and precise. Then Julip began, and I felt my mouth go dry, but his routine was faultless too. Some of the girls in the audience squealed excitedly, appreciating his dark good looks. Tag's display was faster and wilder. He didn't always land as cleanly and the lines of his body weren't always perfect, but he had so much wild energy that people cheered.

Then it was my turn. I pointed my toes and twirled this way and that, and then tried a couple of cartwheels. It was the easiest exercise ever, yet everyone gawped and clapped as if I'd done something splendid. I bobbed a little curtsy to the audience, which made them laugh, and then continued my baby routine: my handstands, my crab-walk, my backward somersaults – thankfully each one perfect.

It was time for the silver boys to start serious tumbling, using the springboard, so that first Julip and then Tag spiralled through the air. I pointed and exclaimed and applauded enthusiastically, just as Mister had instructed. The audience lapped up my emphatic performance. I was so relieved when Julip landed with utter precision on Marvo's broad shoulders, and then stayed still and steady in turn after Tag spiralled upwards and landed on him that I clapped wildly – and the audience clapped with me.

The four of us stood in a line, arms out, and then we ran out into the wings, waving goodbye to everyone. Mister was standing by, smiling.

'There! I knew they'd love you, little fairy five guineas,' he said, before he had to caper on with Chino to distract everyone while the lion cages were assembled.

'Well done, little one!' said all the circus artistes waiting in the queue. Even the performing monkeys chattered and clapped their tiny paws at me. Madame Adeline was waiting at the end, glorious in her pink spangles and fleshings, with her glossy black Midnight.

'My little star!' she said, giving me a big hug, so that I breathed in her wonderful perfume.

I truly *felt* a star – happier than I had ever been in my life. I danced across the grass, throwing my hands up as if the audience were still surrounding me. Then someone pushed me violently in the back. I stumbled and very nearly fell.

'You hateful little show-off!' said Tag, punching me. 'You stole the whole act with your mincing and your prancing! They weren't even looking at us half the time.'

'I – I *had* to point and dance. Beppo *told* me to!' I stammered.

'You didn't have to do it so *much*. It was sickening,' said Tag. 'Tossing your head and fluffing your stupid hair!' He yanked at it so hard that my precious borrowed tiara was knocked sideways.

'Leave her be, Tag! Stop acting like a jealous little fool. Take no notice, Diamond. You did splendidly,' said Marvo, gently setting my tiara straight.

'So splendidly she can take over from me soon,' said Julip.

'She'll never be a real part of the act. She just does pathetic baby tumbles – and yet she steals all our applause,' said Tag.

'I'm sorry! I didn't mean to! I was just trying to do my best,' I said, and struggle as I might I couldn't stop the tears spilling down my cheeks.

'Now look what you've done, Tag. Shame on you,'

said Marvo, picking me up effortlessly and patting me on the back.

'Cry-baby! See, Julip, she's even turned Marvo against me. And did you see Beppo smarming all over her! *We* do all the work and yet all we get is blows!' Tag shouted, and he stormed off across the field.

'Oh, Tag, please, come back! Don't be cross. I promise I won't dance about next time. I won't do *anything*,' I cried.

'Leave him, Diamond. He's just cross because *he* usually gets all the attention. You did perfectly – and if you please Beppo he'll be all the sweeter to us too,' said Marvo.

'He won't ever be sweet to me,' said Julip, and he mooched off in the other direction.

'Oh dear,' I said, sniffling.

'Don't worry. They'll both be back for the grand parade at the end of the show. Come, let's go back to the wagon, little girl. You're shivering.'

I had three real older brothers, but they'd never treated me as kindly as dear Marvo. I couldn't stop shivering even back in the wagon, so he wrapped his huge greatcoat around me to warm me up. It trailed across the floor when I walked and my arms came only halfway down the sleeves, which made us both laugh.

'I think we need a little tonic,' said Marvo, and he produced a bottle of ginger beer. We shared it, sipping from the neck alternately. Marvo rummaged in his tea-chest and found an old pack of dog-eared cards.

'Here, I'll light a candle. Can you play Beggar my Neighbour, Diamond?'

I couldn't, but I learned soon enough and we had a grand game together. Marvo didn't have a pocket watch, but he knew by instinct the correct time to return to the big top for the closing parade. When we got there, Julip and Tag were already waiting. Julip gave me a little nod. Tag still glared, but when it was our turn to go into the ring he clasped my hand. We stepped out, all four in a line, and when I saw the smiles spread across the faces of all three boys, I made myself smile too, and the audience roared louder. Someone threw something at me and I ducked, startled. Another object came flying towards me, and I gasped, wondering why I was under attack.

'They're oranges,' said Marvo. 'They're throwing them at you because they like you! Gather them up. We'll share them out tonight.'

So I gathered up a great armful of oranges. Tag had a fair share too. Beppo took three and juggled with them, capering along beside us. He was still smiling when we got out of the ring.

'Well done, all four of you!' he said. 'We'll have a slap-up supper to celebrate.'

Marvo grinned, Julip squared his shoulders and

even Tag smirked. We didn't have the usual dubious stew. Beppo sent Tag running to the nearest butcher's for five fine chops. He fried them with onions and streaky bacon and mushrooms, and then we each sucked an orange for afters. I asked if I could take an orange to Madame Adeline as a present, and Beppo was in such a good mood he just nodded cheerily.

'For me, darling?' said Madame Adeline, when I shyly handed her the orange. 'But it's yours, my love. You eat it.'

'You're always giving me nice treats, Madame Adeline,' I said. 'Please take it.'

'Bless you, child . . .' She looked as if she might cry, and insisted on giving me a slice of cake and a special violet chocolate in return.

'Don't stuff yourself too much, little one,' said Beppo, seeing my full mouth. 'We don't want you sicking it all up in the second show for all to see.'

I found I was desperately nervous all over again for the evening performance – and this time I worried even when I was in the ring, though I took care to keep a big smile on my face. I knew I had to perform the way Beppo wanted or he would beat me – but I didn't want to make Tag hate me even more, so I gave a very subdued performance, trying not to prance too much. I was so anxious that I stumbled when I did my back somersault and very nearly landed with a bump on my bottom in the sawdust – but this mishap made the crowd love me even more. 'Aaah, the little pet!' they cried. 'Nearly took a tumble, and no wonder, she's so tiny.' 'Doesn't she look a real star? Such a pretty baby!'

I felt my face flushing – while Tag's was scarlet with rage. When we came running off he pushed me violently again and called me terrible names. Beppo saw and heard it all, though Tag didn't seem to care.

I thought Beppo would be angry, but he simply chuckled.

'My, the boy's jealous! What a temper!' he said.

'I'm sorry, it's all my fault,' I said.

'No, you haven't put a foot wrong. Well, you *did*, actually – that was a hopeless back somersault and you should be ashamed of yourself, little Miss Fairy – but it didn't matter a jot, did it? They loved you even more, God bless 'em.' Beppo pinched my cheek. 'Five guineas well spent!'

I couldn't help feeling proud, especially when folk lingered outside the big top and called my name excitedly, wanting another smile and wave from me. I wished Mary-Martha could see me, and Matthew and Mark and Luke and little John. I wished Pa could see me too, though it might upset him. But we'd already moved on from my home town. We moved on most Saturday nights, everyone working together the moment the show was over.

I had to help too, collecting up the cushions from

the best seats and storing them in great boxes. I helped Madame Adeline wrap all her pretty china in newspaper for the journey and helped Flora pack up her perambulator and her parasol and her long tightrope in a special trunk. All the menagerie artistes wanted to feed their own animals and secure them in their travelling cages. I certainly did not want to go near the great yellow lions who smelled so rank and devoured their meat so ferociously.

I was even a bit afraid of their water cousins – the males were too big and whiskery and they barked their heads off at the sight of a bucket of fish. I was certainly too much in awe of great Elijah to stand too close to him. But I started to help cage the troupe of performing monkeys, and loved packing up all their props and tiny costumes. I adored the monkeys – especially little Mavis, the baby.

These monkeys were much more interesting than surly little Jacko. They looked just like tiny, ugly people, but with such cute faces and lovely furry bodies. They had a special cage with real trees planted in great pots, so that the monkeys could swing amongst their branches, clinging on with their tiny hands, sometimes upside down, using their curling tails.

When I could get away from Beppo and the boys, I'd go and watch the monkeys in their cage. It took me a while to sort out all the adults, but right from the start the baby was my favourite. Most of the time she rode on her mother's back or clung upside down to her stomach, but would sometimes wander off on little forays of her own, especially if she spotted a choice nut or apple chunk that had fallen out of the feeding tray. She'd suddenly dart off, seize the morsel, scamper right up to the highest branch she could find, look around furtively to see if any of her older relatives were watching, and then nibble happily at her treat.

I don't know if the older monkeys *were* all relatives, but Mr Marvel, their trainer, got them decked out as a real family when he showed them in the ring. The oldest male was Marmaduke, and he had a tiny top hat and wore astonishing miniature boots on his hind paws. When he sat down on his little velvet armchair he kicked them off one at a time while his 'wife', Melinda, scurried to his side with a tiny pipe and a pair of diminutive carpet slippers. Their grown-up 'daughter', Marianne, went to a ball with a ribbon about her neck and waltzed round and round with a very small fiancé monkey called Michael, who kept trying to puff on a toy cigar while dancing. Marianne objected, and eventually seized the cigar and bit it in two.

Baby Mavis was by far the funniest little performer. Melinda would fetch her from the 'nursery', tenderly lifting her out of her little rocking cot and giving her a real bottle of milk. Then she made a great to-do of patting her on the back until Mavis made a rude windy noise, which made everyone laugh.

Melinda tried to get Mavis dressed in a napkin and little knitted jacket, but Mavis kept wriggling, attempting to get away, until eventually Melinda lost patience and sat on her head to keep her still. When she was dressed at last, Melinda took her for a walk in the perambulator while Mavis peeped out coyly, waving to everyone.

Mr Marvel then did a whole set piece where he was a photographer, and the entire family had to squeeze up together on the sofa to pose for their portrait. There was a great deal of pushing and shoving, and Mavis stole her father's pipe and puffed at it rakishly. When Mr Marvel had them all assembled in their positions, Michael put his paws over his face – and then they all did, even Mavis. Mr Marvel shook his finger and muttered at them, pretending to give them a talking to.

'Smile!' he commanded them – and simultaneously they all opened their mouths and gave great monkey grins.

For their finale Mr Marvel gave them each a little sparkly silver bow, as if they were tiny members of the Silver Tumblers' act! They all turned somersaults with immense agility and then stood in a line, clapping their paws. Whenever I watched them, I clapped until my hands hurt, and I took to visiting them every day in their cage.

Mr Marvel didn't seem to mind too much. Sherzam was very wary about folk pestering Elijah, and Carlos shouted angrily if anyone came too close to his lions. Even dear Madame Adeline was very protective of Midnight and scolded me gently when she caught me feeding him a piece of my cake. But Mr Marvel let me share some of my oranges with the monkey family. I cut them into segments and poked them through the bars. Soon baby Mavis chattered excitedly at the sight of me and clung to the bars, her little mouth open and shutting. She didn't mind too much if I couldn't muster an orange or a few peanuts – she just seemed happy to see me. She sniffed my fingers and gave them little approving licks.

'Watch out or she'll bite you, lass,' said Mr Marvel – but she never did.

'Reckon you've got a way with my monkeys,' he told me.

I *liked* Mr Marvel. Most of the circus men were too grand or busy to talk to me, or downright cruel and threatening like Beppo – but old Mr Marvel was a quiet, kindly gentleman. He looked a bit like his own monkey troupe. He was very brown, with so many wrinkles that you'd run out of pencil if you tried to draw his face. His little brown eyes were sunk deep into his head and his mouth contained two or three teeth at most. He looked some great age – eighty or ninety at least. Tag insisted he was over a hundred years old. Madame Adeline said this was nonsense: she reckoned Mr Marvel was around seventy.

I plucked up courage and asked Mr Marvel himself. He squinted at me and said, 'As old as my eyes and a little older than my teeth,' which told me nothing.

Another time I asked him if he'd thought about retiring.

'I've thought about it, yes, missy, thought about it a lot – and concluded it's not an appealing thought. I'd be sitting in the same chair every night twiddling my thumbs, and Marmaduke, Melinda, Marianne, Michael and little Mavis would be rattling around in their cage, bored out of their skulls. They love performing in the ring and so do I, so we're not going to stop if we can help it.'

'Well, you would disappoint hundreds and hundreds of people if you did,' I said politely. 'Yours is the most popular act – well, you and Madame Adeline and Midnight.'

'Yes, dear Addie is another old trouper, bless her. She used to have six fine rosin-backed horses but that was in the old days. It's too expensive to feed so many horses on the pittance old Tanglefield pays now.'

'Well, I'll certainly help you feed all your monkeys, Mr Marvel,' I said earnestly.

'You're a good little lass. You've taken to this life like a duck to water. Anyone would think you were born to it.' He looked at me carefully. 'Beppo's not too hard on you, is he?'

'Well . . .'

Beppo was starting to be very hard indeed. I had thought my small success in the ring would be enough, but he had much bigger plans for me. He was training me up to be a proper acrobat and it was proving horribly hard. My bones ached from all the cruel cricking and I had bruises all over my body from the tumbles I took during rehearsals. Mister was threatening me with a royal beating if I didn't shape up.

I felt panicky just thinking about it. 'I wish . . . I wish I was part of a monkey act like yours, Mr Marvel,' I said wistfully.

'Do you not enjoy doing all your pretty tricks, Diamond?'

'I can't do many things,' I said, swallowing hard, scared I might start crying. 'I don't think I'm any good at acrobatics. I'm all right on the ground, when it's not too far to tumble. But now I have to try the springboard – and I haven't enough spring. And I can't even do a forward somersault yet. Mister Beppo says I'm a disgrace.'

'Oh dear, oh dear, poor little maid,' said Mr Marvel. 'Maybe Beppo's not training you right. I teach all my monkeys to do acrobatics and they love it. It's all done with kindness and encouragement – and titbits as a reward. I can't learn you any springboard tricks because that's specialist work, but I'll help you with your forward somersault – that's simple.' He leaned forward on his bowed legs, curled himself into a ball, and turned over in the air, landing neatly right way up in his carpet slippers.

'Oh my goodness!' I said, clapping him.

'You'll learn in no time, little lass,' he told me. 'It's just one simple twirly over, forwards instead of backwards.'

'But I always land on my head and it hurts,' I said.

'We'll put my old mattress on the floor, and then if you tumble it won't hurt a bit. That's what I use for my monkeys. Oh, they love a little bounce on my mattress!'

Mr Marvel encouraged me for several days. Each time I tried a forward somersault he gave me a piece of chopped date whether I landed properly or not. He clapped me no matter how clumsy I was, and consequently I lost all fear and could soon do the front somersault effortlessly.

'Bravo, Diamond! I knew you were a natural,' he said.

'Oh, wait till I show Mister Beppo!' I said gratefully.

'Don't tell him I helped you. He won't take kindly to it,' Mr Marvel warned. 'We don't interfere with each other's acts. I'm a mild man, but if I caught Beppo training my monkeys I'd be furious. Let him think *he's* taught you.' He tapped the side of his nose. 'You need some tactical common sense, dearie.'

So the next rehearsal with Mister, I deliberately made several clumsy attempts at the wretched forward somersault, with Tag jeering, Julip staring moodily into space, and Marvo smiling encouragingly.

'Dear Lord save us, it's simple enough,' Beppo said, raising his hand to hit me. 'Watch Tag one more time and then *do* it!'

'She'll never ever do it because she's useless,' said Tag, doing an effortless somersault and then thumbing his nose at me.

'Could *you* show me, Mister Beppo?' I said, lisping like a little girl.

'Stop that baby nonsense,' he said, but he turned a somersault all the same.

'Ah, *now* I see,' I said – and copied him perfectly.

They all looked astonished.

'Again!' ordered Mister.

I turned one again – and again and again.

'So we have the knack at last!' he said. 'Right! Now we'll work out a proper routine for you.'

I started to wish I hadn't mastered the forward somersault after all. Mister worked me extra hard for weeks, trying to make me perfect various bizarre kinds of somersault. I begged Mr Marvel to help me master the monkey's somersault and the lion's somersault and the Arab somersault, but he had never learned these himself, and couldn't help me. I was blue with bruises again, and had to paint white greasepaint on my arms so they wouldn't show in the ring.

'She'll never learn,' said Tag – but I *did* start to master each somersault, one by one. I grew thinner than ever, but now I had hard little muscles in my arms and legs, and my stomach grew so strong that I didn't flinch when Tag punched me.

He punched me a great deal, because Mister had worked out quite an elaborate little routine for me now, and it increased my popularity. I could have taken a bath in orange juice every night with all the fruit thrown by the admiring audience. Sometimes they waited outside the big top with bunches of flowers, or once, wondrously, a very large box of chocolates.

'It's not *fair*. She gets all the praise and presents while we do all the *real* work!' Tag complained bitterly.

'You got your share of her chocolates,' said Marvo. 'I don't see what you're moaning about.'

'Me neither,' said Julip. 'You carry on and take over the whole act, Diamond – and then I can escape.'

'I'm only a *little* part of the act,' I said. 'I can't use the springboard.'

'Not yet,' said Marvo kindly. 'But in a few years you might be ready. Tag was only twelve when he started springboard work.'

'I'm not twelve for years and years and years,' I said quickly. 'And even when I am, I never want to do springboard work.'

'You'll do as you're told,' said Mister, overhearing. 'In fact we might as well start training you up now. Think what a draw it would be – the little fairy who really can fly through the air! All the big circuses would be interested in such an act. We'd maybe make Askew's and have a permanent gaff in London.'

I hoped desperately that Mister wasn't serious, but at the very next rehearsal he had me try the springboard.

'Ha!' said Tag. 'You're going to come a cropper.'

'She's still too small, Beppo,' said Julip.

'If she misjudges her leap, she could break her neck,' said Marvo.

'She won't misjudge it, not if she concentrates. And we'll have her in the training harness,' said Mister.

'She can't wear the harness for performances,' Marvo persisted. 'You can't risk her doing springboard work, Beppo, it's not right.'

Mister went to stand beside Marvo, his eyes

narrowed, his mouth so set that his lips disappeared. Marvo towered above him – and yet took a step back, looking fearful.

'Are you telling me what I can or can't do?' Mister asked.

'No, Beppo. I'm just saying – in *my* opinion.'

'Well, shut your mouth. No one's interested in your opinion, you great plank of wood. You're not in charge of the act. I am. And I shall do as I please. And I didn't waste all that good money on the girl just to have her do a few baby somersaults and a prance or two. She's got natural ability. She'll learn quickly.'

I didn't seem to have any natural ability left. I couldn't learn at all. I was terrified, even wearing the safety harness. The springboard propelled me upwards, but each time I panicked, unable to tuck myself into a neat ball to turn the double somersault required. I failed to land neatly on my feet. I didn't come to too much harm as the safety harness held me upright, but it dug into me under my armpits and jarred my whole body.

I was forced to practise for hours and hours every morning, and then appear to be as fresh as a daisy for the afternoon and evening performances. I was sick one morning because I was in such a state of terror. Mister wouldn't let me have any breakfast at all after that, so I had to train on a totally empty stomach.

'That poor little child is exhausted,' said Madame Adeline, coming into the big top and taking hold of me by the shoulders. 'For shame, Beppo. Just look at her!'

'You mind your own business, Addie,' he growled.

'See the circles under her eyes. She's nothing but skin and bone. Can't you see, Beppo, you're killing the little goose who'll lay you golden eggs,' she told him.

'Do I tell you how to train that nag of yours, Addie?' he asked.

'If you saw me beating my poor Midnight to death I hope you'd step in and stop me,' said Madame Adeline. 'Because you'd realize I was losing my mind.'

'That's enough, woman. I won't have anyone talk to me like that, let alone some raddled old biddy who should have been pensioned off years ago,' said Beppo, suddenly cuttingly cruel.

Madame Adeline flushed. 'I believe you're at least five years older than me, Beppo,' she said, calmly enough. 'And at least I am still an artiste – not reduced to clowning.' She walked away, her head held high, but when I saw her later at the afternoon's performance her eyes were red.

My eyes were red too – and there were ugly scarlet weals across my back because Beppo had given me the threatened royal beating at last.

He didn't beat me again. He didn't need to. The fear of his stick made me quiver every time he looked at me. I strained even harder to learn springboard skills, but still failed miserably.

Mr Marvel spoke up for me too.

'You're wasting your time, Beppo. Try when the child is a year or two older. She hasn't got the strength or the skill just yet. It stands to reason: she's still only a baby. I know my little Mavis is the star of the act – she knows it too, bless her – but I don't try to teach her too many tricks just now because it will only confuse and frustrate her. Patience, Beppo. Be thankful. Your Diamond is a little star.'

'Hold your tongue, Monkey Man,' Mister replied. 'I know what I'm doing.'

I heard him discussing me with Chino, the other clown. I was hiding from him, under the wagon.

'You know the boys' big finale is the human column I devised. When it used to be just Marvo and Julip it didn't look anything special. But then young Tag came along and I trained him hard, and once he joined, it became a showstopper, the three of them balancing together. And if only that maddening little fairy would take flight it would look magnificent. She's so light, and Marvo's steady as a rock. Imagine it, Chino, the four of them in a column. All she has to do is somersault and land on Tag's shoulders, one simple tiny trick – and it will bring the house down. I could have posters made. She'd be like the fairy doll on top of the Christmas tree.' Mister groaned and thumped his fist against the wagon, making it shake.

I curled up into a tight ball. I wondered about running away. It would be difficult, though, to slip off undetected. Tag always knew where I was and what I was up to, and he'd tell on me. Mister would find me and drag me back and give me another whipping.

I shivered at the thought. I wasn't even sure where

I was now. We'd travelled far away from home. If I *did* somehow manage to escape, it would take me many days to walk back. I had no stout boots, only the soft slippers I wore in the ring. And how would I know which *way* to walk? I had never learned geography. I knew there were such things as maps, but I couldn't read enough to make sense of them.

And suppose I *did* manage to stumble all the way home – what would I do then? I very much doubted that Pa would take me back. My brothers had never really cared for me – and even Mary-Martha might have forgotten me. I couldn't really call Willoughby Buildings home any more.

I fell asleep on the damp grass beneath the wagon dreaming of a real home. I'd have Madame Adeline for my mother and Mr Marvel for my father and all the monkeys for my brothers and sisters. Mavis would be my special favourite, and would cuddle up with me every night in my safe, warm bed. I would eat pink cake and violet chocolates and sweet dates every day. I might perform on a little stage to earn my keep – an easy carpet act of somersaults and handstands – but my dear parents wouldn't hear of my attempting any springboard movements. It would be a solo act, no silver boys. Or perhaps it could be a double act with little Mavis.

It was Mavis herself who helped Mister's dream to

come true. One wet and stormy Saturday night we were all working hard pulling down the drenched big top and securing the animals when a bolt of lightning flashed right above us. Elijah trumpeted in alarm, nearly pulling free of his tether. The lions roared, the sea lions barked, Midnight and the wagon horses reared up on their hind legs, whinnying in fear.

Mr Marvel was in the process of cajoling his monkeys into their travelling cage. They were all chattering anxiously, baring their teeth.

'Into your cage, my lovelies, and I'll draw the curtain and then you won't see the horrid lightning,' he told them.

'Come along, little Mavis, in you go,' I said, giving her a gentle flick.

The four adult monkeys sprang into their familiar cage, cowering together in a corner, but just as baby Mavis was scrabbling in, a great boom of thunder made her squeal. She spun round and darted away, across the muddy grass, before either Mr Marvel or I could catch her.

'Mavis! Come here, baby! Come to your papa!' Mr Marvel called frantically – but she was already out of sight.

'Help!' I cried. 'Mavis is missing! Please, everyone, try to catch her!'

It was hard because everyone was busy and the

other animals were still frantic. It was pitch dark in the pouring rain, but most people came running to help all the same. Mr Marvel was crying unashamedly, hobbling backwards and forwards, calling hoarsely.

We looked amongst the cages, the wagons, the sodden folds of the great big top, but there was no sign of the little monkey.

Madame Adeline got Midnight safely into his horsebox, and then joined in the hunt, with only a shawl to protect her pink spangles. She had a chunk of her special cake in her hand. 'It's Mavis's favourite. I give her a few crumbs as a special treat,' she explained. 'Mavis? Mavis, where are you, darling? Come and have some of Madame Addie's lovely cake!'

My silver boys all helped to search too. Tag dashed everywhere, but even his quick eye could not spot Mavis. Mister mounted the clowns' penny-farthing and started trundling the whole length of the field.

'We'll have to start moving soon or we'll never get to Waynefleet by morning,' shouted Mr Tanglefield.

'I can't leave without my baby,' Mr Marvel wept.

'Then you'll have to stay here and join us later. I can't halt the whole circus for a monkey.'

'It's not *any* monkey. It's my Mavis!'

'I'll stay and help you find her, Mr Marvel,' I said, clutching his arm.

'You'll do no such thing. You're coming with us,' said

Beppo. 'Now get in the wagon. You're soaking wet. We can't have you catching your death of cold and then sneezing your head off in the ring. Do you hear me?'

I heard – but for once I didn't obey. I didn't even care if he beat me. I *had* to help Mr Marvel find Mavis. I trotted off meekly enough, but instead of jumping up the steps after Marvo, Julip and Tag, I crept off into the darkness. I called again and again for Mavis, making little clicking noises with my tongue.

'Come here, Mavis! Come, baby, come to Diamond,' I said, over and over again.

There was more lightning, zigzagging through the sky with a terrifying sizzle, and then loud thunder-claps. I could hear the animals panicking all around, with men running and shouting and cursing. I thought how scared little Mavis would be. She was so quick, she could have crossed the entire field by now. She might already be running amongst the carriages and cabs, in terrible danger of being trampled.

I was crying now as I ran around calling – and then I heard a wailing high above me. I looked up, the rain hitting my face, almost blinding me, but when the lightning flashed I saw a tiny creature darting about at the top of a very tall, thin tree, horribly buffeted by the wind and the rain.

'Mavis!' I cried.

She wailed again.

'Oh, Mavis, come down! Come down, baby. Come right down now!' I held out my arms, but Mavis was so scared she didn't even seem to recognize me. She climbed even higher, and when the lightning flashed again she screamed.

'Come *down!*' I called.

If the lightning struck the tree, poor Mavis would be burned to death. It was too terrible to contemplate. If she wouldn't come down, then *I* had to go *up.*

I'd never climbed a tree before. I was scared of heights but I didn't even think about it. I tucked my skirts into my drawers and started up. I didn't really know what I was doing. At the bottom there were not enough branches to cling to, but I'd watched the monkeys for many hours. I climbed the way they did, gripping with my hands and feet. My arms and legs were strong as steel after all the practice and the two performances every day. I went up and up.

'Diamond! Oh Lord, girl! Come down – you'll kill yourself!'

I peered down into the dark. It was Mr Marvel, calling hoarsely, beside himself. It was a huge mistake to look down. He seemed horribly far away already. I lost my rhythm, stretched up awkwardly, and slipped.

Mr Marvel gave a great wail.

I clung to the tree trunk desperately, managing to

hang on by gripping with my knees, though I felt my stockings rip on either side.

'Stay still! I'll come and rescue you!' Mr Marvel shouted, but he was too heavy and weighed down with sodden garments to get any kind of purchase on the tree.

'I don't need rescuing. *I'm* the rescuer. I'm rescuing Mavis,' I cried.

I reached up and started climbing again. The tree seemed to go on for ever. I had once hand-coloured a fairy story about a boy and a beanstalk that grew up to the sky. I remembered the ogre right at the top, with a grotesque scowl and a huge warty nose that I painted deep red, like Pa's.

But there was no ogre hovering above me, just a tiny little monkey, whimpering in terror.

'It's all right, Mavis – it's Diamond. I'm coming to get you. You'll be safe soon,' I called.

She could hear me now, but she must have thought I wanted to hurt her because she darted along a small branch right at the top of the tree. It swayed even under her small weight. I knew I couldn't possibly shin along it.

'Please come back, Mavis! I can't reach you there! Come back along the branch or you'll fall. It's Diamond – remember, I feed you oranges. I come and see you every day. I'm your friend. Oh, please come to me – please please please!'

Mavis clung to her tiny branch, not responding. But then there was another flash of lightning, so near this time that I felt its heat and power going right through me – and, with a squeak, Mavis ran back to the main trunk in three bounds . . . straight into my arms.

There was a cheer from below – a whole chorus of cheers. There must have been a proper audience by now, but I took care not to look down to check. I cradled Mavis close and she shivered, crying. Clinging to the tree with just one hand, I stuffed her down the front of my bodice, and then I began my precarious descent. It was much more difficult going down. I couldn't see what I was doing or get into any rhythm. When I tried to slide, I scraped the little skin I had left on my legs.

Then I heard Mister shouting, 'Tag's coming to get you, little fairy!'

'I don't *need* Tag,' I called back, and scrambled down as best I could, jumping the last few feet and landing in Mr Marvel's arms.

He hugged me close, tears pouring down his face, while everyone cheered.

Mr Tanglefield gave me a pat on the back. 'Well done, little 'un! Now, Marvel, keep a firm hold of that monkey, do you hear? We're setting off immediately – even if a whole cartload of monkeys escape, we'll just wave goodbye to them and be on our way, understand?'

Mr Marvel took little shivery Mavis from me and

cradled her in his arms. 'I'm in your debt for ever, young Diamond,' he said croakily. 'I don't know what I'd have done if I'd lost my little star.'

'*Diamond*'s the little star,' said Madame Adeline, putting her arm round me. 'But you must never do anything as reckless again – do you promise?'

'She'll promise no such thing!' said Mister. 'My, did you see her shin up that tree? Like a monkey herself, she was.'

'Any fool can climb a tree,' said Tag angrily. 'Watch *me* do it, Beppo.'

'You come back here, boy. We've had enough shenanigans for one night. But I tell you what – it's shown me the way forward for the finale to the act. Diamond will master the springboard in time, I dare say – but meanwhile she can *climb* up the human column and stand on Tag's shoulders.'

I hoped he might be joking, but of course he was deadly serious. On Sunday we were all exhausted after travelling through the night in the storm – but Mister had the four of us practising this new trick. First he had me scramble up Marvo and stand on his shoulders, and that wasn't too hard at all. I knew that Marvo would reach up and catch me if I should sway or stumble. It was far harder when I was forced to climb up Julip too. He was less steady, and it felt so much higher balancing on his shoulders. He had his hands gripping my calves, but it still didn't feel at all safe.

When I'd mastered this at last, Mister immediately told Tag to balance on top of Julip, and expected me to climb up all three boys in a trice. He had me on training ropes – he held one, Mr Marvel the other, so that if I fell, I wouldn't tumble on my head. I was terribly frightened even so. Marvo was very encouraging and Julip nodded at me sympathetically, but Tag jeered at me. I didn't trust him to hang onto me properly when I scrambled uncertainly to the top. Several times in succession I wobbled until Tag and Julip fell. They knew how to roll over and land neatly on their feet. I knew too, but panicked and forgot – and then I was brought up short with a judder on the end of the practice rope, flopping and gasping like a hooked fish on the end of a line.

But there was no backing out now. Mister was adamant. The fourfold human column must end our act. He announced we had to try it out the very next performance. I was sick with nerves – literally so. Marvo discovered me vomiting miserably into a clump of nettles at the edge of the field.

'Don't fret so, Diamond,' he said, wiping my face and smoothing my tangled hair.

'I'm going to have to do it without the practice rope, and I'm so scared I'll fall,' I wept.

'You won't fall – but if you *do* I shall catch you, I promise. I'll reach out and grab you,' said Marvo, demonstrating.

'And then Julip and Tag will fall down.'

'They can look after themselves – and it would do young Tag good to take a tumble. He's been behaving abominably, the cocky little pup.'

Tag had been teasing me cruelly, telling me I was a terrible acrobat and would spoil the whole show.

'I think he's right. I *will* spoil the whole show,' I mumbled.

'That's nonsense. Tag's just saying that because he sees how the crowds love you. His nose has been put out of joint. But he's not a bad lad at heart. He'll try to make it easier for you,' said Marvo.

To my great surprise, he was right. While we were waiting to go on, and I was white and shivery, wondering whether I would vomit again, Tag suddenly seized my clammy hand.

'You'll do all right,' he whispered. 'You're quite good at it really – not as good as *me*, of course, but not bad for a girl.'

But it was a Julip who was the most help.

'I know just how you feel, Diamond,' he said. 'Beppo and Marvo and Tag tell you not to worry – but you will. I do, anyway. But I try and tell myself that I won't always be here in a foolish silver costume, frightened to death. One day I'll be too old to perform . . .'

'Will you be a clown then, like Beppo?'

'Never! I'll leave the circus and find a job – any job. I'm good with animals, I'm good at fixing things, I'm strong. I'll work and save until I have my own house – not a cramped wagon, a real little house in a village. I'll have a garden and grow flowers and vegetables, and I'll find a wife and we'll have children and we'll live in the same place for the rest of our days. I think about each little detail of my new life until it starts to feel real. I might be leaping high in the air doing a double somersault in front of gaping fools, but inside I'm in my own living room, sitting before a fire, with a cat on my lap and a dog at my feet.'

'That's why you wobble and fluff, you fool. You should concentrate properly,' said Tag.

'If I concentrate it makes it worse,' said Julip. 'Try my trick, Diamond. It helps.'

So I tried hard to blot out the shouts of the crowd and the rustle and roar of the animals, and imagined jumping on a giant springboard that catapulted me years into my future. Did I want my own little house like Julip? I thought of the house where we'd once lived – Ma and Pa and the boys and Mary-Martha and me. Had I been happy there as a baby? I tried to remember what it was like to sit on Ma's lap, but she was fading in my memory now. I could only picture her pale as a ghost in her nightgown, crying sadly to herself, and it made me want to cry too.

I didn't have Ma any more, and Pa didn't want me. Perhaps I could one day share a little cottage with Mary-Martha and baby Johnnie? I tried to picture the three of us, and as I was running around the ring, cartwheeling and capering, I chose our armchairs and embroidered our cushions. When I did my crab-walk, I filled our pantry with tins of pink cake and jars of dried dates. When I had to climb up Marvo and Julip and Tag at the end of the act, I pictured climbing the stairs to sleep in my own soft little bed – and though I still trembled, I got right to the top and stood on Tag's shoulders and kept my balance and smiled while everyone cheered.

I hoped it would get easier. After all, I could now turn
neat somersaults as easily as winking. But the
human column was different. It was a twice daily
terror. Julip was right – the fear never went away. But
there were good times too. I loved visiting Madame
Adeline and eating cake and chocolates, I loved
chatting to Mr Marvel and playing with little Mavis,
but even then, when I was most relaxed, the fear was
there in the pit of my stomach.

Mister haunted me every day and stalked my

dreams at night. I could never please him now. The more he threatened me, the worse I got, until I stumbled doing the simplest cartwheel and started whenever he said my name. I developed a nervous twitch that made him even madder. 'Stop jerking about like a little lunatic! Stop it at once, I say!' he'd hiss. I'd put my hands to my face, struggling to keep it still, but I could feel it twitching beneath my fingers.

I lost all sense of where we were and how far we had travelled. We pulled down the big top every week, rain or shine, travelled through the night, arrived at a new town or village, slept through the morning, and rehearsed and performed all the rest of the week. We could have been down in sunny Cornwall or up in chilly Inverness for all I knew. We might even have returned to my own home town without my realizing.

I never left the circus field, and they all looked alike anyway. I didn't know, I ceased to care. I took part in the circus parade through towns and villages, and barely noticed whether I was passing great stone mansions or humble cottages. All I had to do was smile until my cheeks ached, smile even when my eyes pricked with tears.

I was hiding under the wagon one evening because Mister had threatened me with a beating and I was pretty sure he meant it. I couldn't help sobbing, though

I put my hands over my face to try to stifle the sounds. Then I heard a scuffle – and someone bent right down and peered under the wagon at me.

Yes, Hetty, it was you!

I was so startled I curled up small, trying to hide.

'It's all right, I'm not going to hurt you,' the someone whispered. 'And I won't let anyone else hurt you either. See my red hair? I am so fierce that everyone is scared of me. Even the biggest, ugliest ogre quakes when he sees me coming. Evil giants tremble and whimper at my approach.'

I couldn't help giggling. I wasn't sure if this strange girl was grown up or still a child. She was very little, like me, but she was wearing a prim cotton lady's dress, though she wore her long hair loose about her shoulders, not caught up in a neat bun. I loved her voice. She didn't sound like the circus folk. She didn't sound like the Willoughby Buildings people. She didn't sound like the gentle country folk. She didn't sound like the proper ladies and gents who lived in big houses. She simply sounded like herself, warm and friendly and funny.

'But I never ever hurt little fairy girls,' she said. 'And *you're* a little fairy, aren't you?'

I shivered at the name, because that was what Mister called me, but I could tell she meant it kindly. She couldn't think I was *really* a fairy, could she?

'Please, miss, I'm the Acrobatic Child Wonder,' I explained, wiping my eyes and sniffling.

'Here, I have a handkerchief,' she said, pulling a little piece of cloth from her pocket. It had embroidery all over it.

'There's pictures and letters,' I said, stroking the little blue and yellow satin thread flowers. They were bluebells and primroses. I remembered Mary-Martha taking me to the woods long ago, where we picked great bunches of flowers and brought them home for Ma. We put them in jam jars all around the room and they looked so beautiful that we clapped our hands and laughed, and even Ma seemed happy . . . but within a few hours our beautiful flowers were drooping and dying and we had to throw them away.

I traced the letters embroidered underneath. The girl sensed I was less sure now, and told me they were her initials – SB for Sapphire Battersea – 'Although no one calls me that now. All the folk here call me Hetty.'

I said I was called Diamond and she thought it a most beautiful name, which pleased me greatly. I thought the handkerchief so pretty I didn't want to spoil it, so I wiped my nose on my petticoat instead. Hetty smiled at me and said I could keep the handkerchief if I liked it so much.

'Really? For my very own?' I said, and I tucked

it away quickly in case she changed her mind.

Hetty tried to persuade me to creep out from under the wagon.

'I'm scared to come out, because Mister will get me,' I said.

Hetty looked horrified when I said he would beat me. 'Can you tell your father?' she asked. She said the word 'father' as if she thought all fathers very special men who protected their daughters. I thought of my own pa and how he had sold me for five guineas, and I started sobbing again.

'Isn't there anyone kind who will look after you?' Hetty asked, wriggling under the wagon too so she could put her arm round me.

'Madame Addie is kind,' I said.

Hetty's whole face lit up. 'Oh, Madame Adeline! Yes, I am sure she is very kind,' she said, as if she knew her. 'I have come looking for her. Will you show me her wagon, Diamond?'

So I crawled out and she took my hand, squeezing it tightly when we went past Mister's wagon. We went to Madame Adeline's lovely green wagon right at the end. She was sitting on her steps before her fire wearing her favourite green silk gown, looking magical. She saw the tear stains on my face and held out her arms to me.

'Come here, darling,' she said, and I ran to her,

proud that Hetty should see that such a lovely exotic lady cared for me.

She cared for Hetty too. She called her Little Star, and this made Hetty burst into tears too! They talked of when they'd last met, both so tender, and then Hetty cried again when she said that she'd lost her dear mama.

'Is your mother dead too, Hetty?' I asked. 'Mine went to live with the angels.'

'My mama lives there too,' said Hetty, wiping her eyes. 'I'm sure she has wonderful white feathery wings and a dress as blue as the sky. Maybe they fly from cloud to cloud together. But my mama flies down to see me every now and then. She creeps inside my heart and speaks to me. She is a great comfort. Perhaps your mama will do the same.'

I thought this over carefully. I wasn't really sure I welcomed the thought of Ma squatting beside me, watching my every move. I was sure she'd be disappointed in me. She'd weep more than ever. I put my thumb in my mouth, and rocked myself sadly.

Madame Adeline smiled at me comfortingly. 'Now, my girls, I'm going to have a cup of tea. Would you like one too?'

I took my thumb out of my mouth. 'And cake?' I said hopefully.

Madame Adeline laughed. 'I expect we can find a cake if we search hard,' she said.

She made a delightful game of it, pretending to hunt the cake in her beautiful wagon, looking under the table and in her bed, which was so funny I cheered up enormously.

We ate our tea and each had a big slice of pink and yellow cake. I nibbled mine slowly, peeling off the marzipan and saving it till last because I liked it so much. But then I heard Mister shouting and the cake turned sour in my mouth. I thought he was after me, but it turned out he was challenging a stranger from the village who had come marching across the field and was running from wagon to wagon, calling for Hetty.

'Oh my Lord, it's Jem. He must have followed me,' said Hetty, flushing.

I peered out of Madame Adeline's wagon. This Jem looked very fierce and angry – a farm labourer with a cap and cords, so strongly built, he was almost a match for Marvo. But when Madame Adeline intervened, he doffed his cap and shook her hand.

'Pleased to meet you, ma'am,' he said, just like a gentleman.

Madame Adeline offered him tea but he politely refused.

'I'd better be getting back – and so had you, Hetty,' he said firmly, taking hold of her arm.

It was clear that Hetty didn't like this at all. 'I want

to stay here with Madame Adeline,' she said, sticking out her chin.

I wanted her to say 'and Diamond too'. I liked her so much, I wanted her to stay for ever. She made me feel I didn't need to be so frightened any more.

But Jem was intent on chivvying her out of the wagon, his arm about her.

'Perhaps you had better run along with your brother just now, Little Star. But will you come and see the show tomorrow?' asked Madame Adeline.

'I would not miss it for the world,' Hetty replied. She kissed Madame Adeline goodbye, and then turned to me. 'I shall look out for you in the ring tomorrow and give you a big cheer,' she told me.

I stood in the doorway of Madame Adeline's wagon and waved until Hetty and Jem were just two tiny dots at the very edge of the field.

'Do you think she'll really come to watch me in the show, Madame Adeline?' I asked.

'I'm sure she will, dear.'

'I wish that brother hadn't come and taken her away.' I thought of *my* brothers, Matthew and Mark and Luke, and then Marvo, Julip and Tag. 'He didn't *act* like he was Hetty's brother. He acted more like her sweetheart.'

'Maybe he is,' said Madame Adeline. 'He's not her blood brother. She was just brought up with him in the village until she was five or six, and then she was sent away to the hospital. She lived there for years.'

'In a *hospital*? Was she very, very ill?' I asked.

Hetty was almost as thin as me, but she looked extremely robust, not at all like a sickly invalid.

'No, she wasn't ill. She lived in the Foundling Hospital. It's a special institution for children.'

'Like a workhouse?' I asked, astonished.

'A little. Perhaps not quite as harsh.'

I was amazed that a girl like Hetty had been brought up in an institution. It had always been Ma's biggest fear that we would run out of money altogether and end up in the local workhouse. She said the word in a whisper, and always shuddered. When we went to the park, Mary-Martha and I sometimes walked past the great stone workhouse. We never caught a glimpse of the people shut up inside, behind the barred windows – but once we heard someone screaming, a terrible piercing wail that echoed endlessly in our dreams for weeks.

Had Hetty been locked up in a similar dark place?

'How could she bear it?' I said.

'She ran away when she was ten, and came to find me. We'd met years before that, when she first came to the circus. We seem to be meeting in five-year cycles,' said Madame Adeline.

'I can't wait another five years to see her – I like her so!' I said.

'Well, she will come to the show tomorrow. We must give our best performances,' said Madame Adeline.

'I shall try,' I said.

I still had to face Mister, and when he caught up with me at last he threatened me with the dreaded beating.

'Please don't beat me, Mister. I shall try harder, I promise. I will do every trick cleanly and won't wobble once when I'm at the top of the human column,' I said earnestly. 'And I will smile and smile and smile at the audience tomorrow – just you wait and see.'

'What's perked you up then, little fairy?' he asked.

'I – I just gave myself a good talking to,' I said, which actually made him chuckle.

I threw myself into rehearsals the next morning with unusual gusto. When it was time to get ready for the afternoon show, I was so nervous and excited I could hardly stand still.

'Do you think Hetty will really come and watch, Madame Addie?' I asked as we lined up by the tent flap.

'She might not come until this evening, dear.' Madame Adeline had painted her face very brightly, but I could still see the dark shadows under her eyes. The strange half-light made her look much older.

I realized that dear Madame Adeline might well be quite an elderly lady, though I still thought her very beautiful.

'Try not to worry, Diamond. Hetty will come to at least one of the performances, and I'm sure she will be enchanted with you and your act,' she said kindly.

'She will be enchanted with you too,' I said at once.

Madame Adeline laughed, but she didn't sound very happy. 'I rather think she'll find me wanting,' she said quietly. 'My act is a sad shadow of the one I used to do with my six rosin-backed horses, when I was the star of the show.'

'You're still the star now, Madame Addie,' I protested.

'I am lucky to have Midnight. He is a dear spirited creature and never lets me down, but I'm getting sadly decrepit. I can barely stand up on his back now, let alone turn my somersaults.'

'I could help you practise if you like, Madame Addie. And I would give you a date each time you did it neatly.'

'You're a sweet girl, Diamond,' said Madame Adeline. 'There now, take a deep breath. Flora's just taking her bows. It's time for you to go on.'

I gave her hand a quick squeeze, and then I went running into the ring with Marvo, Julip and Tag. I did my somersaults all around the ring, ending with a little flourish, my hand in the air – and immediately spotted Hetty right in front of me, clapping hard. I gave her a happy wave, and then rushed to start the next routine. It all went perfectly and it was a good audience, cheering the simplest little thing. I played to the crowd, adding little dance steps and curtsies, opening my eyes wide, smiling from ear to ear.

'Stop that prancing!' Tag hissed as he hurtled past me, but I wasn't going to stop for anyone now. I wanted to show off to Hetty.

I managed to scramble up Marco and Julip and Tag at the end of the act, standing straight and tall on Tag's shoulders. I waved both hands in the air and milked the applause.

When we ran out of the ring, the audience still clapping hard, Mister caught hold of me.

'That's the ticket, little fairy! You're getting it at last. I *knew* I'd make a little performer out of you. Given time, you'll be worth all three of these boys!' he said, patting me on the back.

He did this in front of the silver boys, which made them all very put out and petulant, even kind Marvo, but I didn't care. I was just pleased I'd performed well in front of my new friend, Hetty. I wanted her to think me a real circus trouper.

I hoped that she would be waiting to congratulate me after the show, but there was no sign of her. I ran to Madame Adeline's wagon in case she'd gone there.

'No, Hetty's not here, dear. I expect she had to go home,' said Madame Adeline. 'Don't look so disappointed, Diamond. Maybe she'll come to tonight's performance too. She loves the circus.'

'I do too!' I cried. 'Oh, I do *hope* she comes back. Did you see how she clapped me? Do you suppose she thinks I'm really good?'

'I'm sure she does. You *are* good, Diamond. You've learned extraordinarily quickly – too quickly, in fact. Beppo takes too many risks with you. I get frightened when I see you.'

'*I'm* not frightened,' I lied, dancing about.

I was so excited I could not settle. I could not even eat my supper. I just wanted to be back in the ring, performing.

But somehow it all went wrong for the evening performance. I didn't fall, but I stumbled twice doing my somersault routine, and when I did my little dance, some rude lads in the audience started jeering at me. They were a rowdy lot, and inclined to throw their oranges *during* the act, thinking it funny. I tried hard to ignore them because Hetty *was* there, back in the same seat, only this time she'd brought her young man, Jem, and I wasn't sure I liked him.

I liked Hetty though. I liked her so much. When I was up on Tag's shoulders I looked down to wave at her – and suddenly everything slipped sideways. A dark dizziness came upon me and I very nearly fell. I clung on desperately, scarcely able to see, doing my best to keep smiling even so, though I was terrified.

'Watch out, you fool!' Tag hissed.

I could feel the whole column wobble. Marvo called 'Down!' and I scrabbled backwards, and Tag and Julip did their somersault and landed gracefully, and then we all four clasped hands and bowed, as if nothing had happened. The audience clapped even so. Hetty clapped too, but this time I knew she was clapping out of sympathy.

I felt my face flushing. Beppo was staring at me, his forehead creased ominously. For once I didn't care. I only cared about Hetty. I had wanted to put on another grand show for her and I'd made a mess of it all. And now I'd likely never see her again.

I was wonderfully wrong! Hetty returned the very next day. She did not even wait for the four o'clock performance. She came when we were all making lunch!

Mister saw her and tried to frighten her away, but Hetty stood her ground and then went marching past him – left, right, left, right, swinging her arms.

'Hetty! Oh, Hetty!' I cried, running to her. 'Oh, Hetty, I saw you talking to Mister! You really aren't afeared of him!'

'That's right. *He's* the one that's afeared of *me*. I told you. He'll be quaking in his bed tonight, wondering if that red-haired girl is coming to get him. Most likely he'll wet his sheets in terror,' said Hetty.

I burst out laughing and hid my face in Maybelle. Hetty asked to be introduced to her, taking her very seriously, as if she were a beautiful china doll with real curls and an outfit from Paris. She did wonder whether Maybelle might be feeling a little chilly in her drawers. I told her that I'd given Maybelle's dress to little Mavis Monkey.

'Well, never you mind. I am very good at stitching tiny dolly dresses,' said Hetty.

My heart started thumping hopefully. Would she really make Maybelle a new dress? Madame Adeline was delighted to see Hetty too, and gave us tea and cake. I wasn't sure I should have the cake as Mister was always telling me off for eating too much. He wanted to keep me as small as possible.

'He's a monster, wanting to stunt your growth,' said Madame Adeline. 'You take a slice of cake, Diamond. You need some sweetness in your life.'

'You can't do back-flips on a full stomach,' I said, though I had a big bite of cake all the same.

'And what's a back-flip?' Hetty asked.

Here was my chance to show off! I took her behind the wagon and demonstrated. I had practised so many times it was easy enough. Most folk in the circus could do a back-flip as easily and casually as blowing their noses – but Hetty marvelled.

'Oh, show *me* how to do it!' she cried, and even though she was nearly grown up, she tucked her dress into her drawers and did her best to copy me. She tried again and again, but always tumbled onto her back. I did my best to show her, but she didn't have enough spring. I wondered if she could do the crab-walk, for I could do it myself long before I joined the circus, but she couldn't manage it at all. She lay flat on her back, chuckling – yet she still seemed to have a fancy to learn circus skills.

When we were back in the wagon, she turned to Madame Adeline. 'Could I ever be an equestrian like you?' she asked.

Madame Addie must have been even fonder of Hetty than I thought, because she said she could try riding Midnight. I'd never known her let anyone else on his back. Tag had often begged for a ride but she'd always refused.

She lent Hetty a pair of her white fleshings so she wouldn't expose too much leg, and then gave her a lesson in the big top. Oh dear! Even I could tell that Hetty was never going to make a good horsewoman. She couldn't even sit straight on Midnight's bare back. She slid forward, grabbing his mane, which he didn't care for at all. He became very fidgety and Hetty fell straight off. She landed hard but she did not cry. She begged to have another go, and then another and another.

Madame Adeline gently told her that was enough.

'I was so good at riding when I was a little tot! Maybe if I practised hard every single day I might get the hang of it. Then perhaps one day I would be good enough to be part of your act?' said Hetty.

'Oh yes!' I cried, because it would be my idea of Heaven if Hetty joined the circus too.

I am sure Madame Adeline thought this as well, but it was clear she didn't think Hetty belonged on the back of a horse. She took her off to show her around the circus. I longed to go with them, but Mister caught hold of me.

'Where do you think you're going, missy?' he said. 'Back into that ring, for a practice!'

'Oh please, Mister, mayn't I go with Madame Addie and Hetty just this once?' I begged.

'You're not going anywhere near that girl! She's an insolent little chit. Addie's got no business letting her poke around here. The circus is private, no place for strangers. And you need to practise more than ever, Diamond. Last night's performance was a disaster. You deserve a good whipping for such carelessness. If you're not perfect this afternoon, I'll send you to

Mr Tanglefield, and he'll be so horrified you're letting the whole circus down he'll take his whip and give that bendy little back a set of stripes!'

I knew this wasn't just a grisly joke – Mr Tanglefield had marked both Tag and Julip before now. Utter fear sharpened up my steps and stopped every stumble. I gave an immaculate performance that afternoon, though I could feel my mouth stretched in a grim parody of a smile. I must have looked like a mechanical doll as I revolved round and round the ring, concentrating so hard I barely blinked. I sneaked just one look around and saw Hetty, watching and waving. She was there again at the evening performance. I hoped and hoped that she'd come and find me afterwards, but she went off with Jem. He had his arm round her protectively.

Hetty had seen four whole shows now. I hardly dared hope she'd come back yet again, but an hour or so before the next afternoon's performance she came running into our ring of wagons. I was practising my tumbles. I had trembled every time Mr Tanglefield cracked his whip during yesterday's performances.

I greeted Hetty happily, hoping she would play with me.

'I would *love* to play with you, Diamond, but I'm afraid I have other business just right now,' she said, walking on.

I scrambled to my feet. 'Are you calling on Madame Adeline? I shall come too!' I said eagerly.

'I'm not intending to visit Madame Adeline either, not just now. I am here to see Mr Tanglefield.'

I was so shocked I could scarcely draw breath. It was as if she'd announced she was going to take tea with the Devil himself.

'He is very stern!' I said. 'If Mister is very cross with me he threatens to send me to Mr Tanglefield for a good whipping.'

Hetty looked horrified. 'Does he really *whip* you, Diamond?'

'No, but I'm always afeared he might. He has a very *big* whip, Hetty, and every time he cracks it in the ring it makes me shiver.'

I pointed out his big fancy wagon, a real dazzler in red and yellow and green. No one ever dared disturb Mr Tanglefield in his wagon, especially when he was getting ready for a show.

'I don't think you had better disturb him right this minute,' I cried, trying to catch hold of Hetty, but she wouldn't be stopped. She ran up the steps and tapped on the door. Mr Tanglefield opened it, half dressed, his hair awry, looking furious – and oh, he had his terrible whip in one hand.

'Hetty! Run!' I called – but she didn't seem to hear me. She went inside Mr Tanglefield's wagon and stayed there for a long time, while I paced up and down in agitation, listening for cries.

I heard Mister calling for me to get ready for the show, but I hid beneath the wagon.

'Drat that little miss,' he muttered. 'She's starting to be more trouble than she's worth. I'll teach her a lesson she won't forget!'

I couldn't help gasping, though I covered my mouth with my hands.

'I can hear you! Where are you?' said Mister, spinning round.

I huddled into a tight ball, praying that he wouldn't look under the wagon. Then I heard Mr Tanglefield's door banging, and light footsteps.

'Hey, girl, where are you going?' Mister called. 'No strangers allowed here.'

I dared wriggle towards the light. I could just see Hetty, dancing about on the grass. She was wearing a very odd outfit. She'd hitched up her skirts and wore her borrowed fleshings and a smart scarlet coat, with a tall black hat on her head, tipped at a jaunty angle.

'I'm not a stranger here, Mr Beppo . . . *sir*,' she said, mocking him. 'I'm the new star act. Just ask Mr Tanglefield if you don't believe me.' She swept him a mocking bow, hat in hand, and then bounced off towards Madame Adeline's wagon.

I couldn't believe my ears. Surely Hetty could not

mean she was *joining the circus*? I gave a squeal of joy and rolled right out from under the wagon, ready to run to her to find out more – but Mister was too quick for me. He caught hold of me by the hair and yanked me upright.

'*There* you are! How dare you hide from me!'

'Oh, please don't be angry, Mister Beppo! Tell me, did Hetty – that girl with the red hair – did she really say she was going to be the star of the circus?'

'That chit!' he said, and he spat on the ground. 'She's talking nonsense. Ask Mr Tanglefield indeed! He'd whip her into the middle of next week if he could hear her impertinence. If she's a circus performer, then I'm Queen of the Fairies.'

Mister should have sported a wand and wings – because *it was true*!

We were up extra early the next morning because we were moving on mid-week, making for Gillford, a town only six miles away. And the moment I stumbled out of the stuffy wagon, I saw Hetty! She was dressed in her ordinary grey frock, but she had her tall hat and scarlet jacket in one hand and a suitcase in the other.

'Oh, Hetty, Hetty, is it *true*? Oh, tell me it is, please, please!' I said, rushing to her.

'Is *what* true?' said Hetty, laughing and whirling me round and round. 'Is the moon made of green cheese? Can pigs fly? Can cats bark and dogs miaow?'

'Are you joining the circus!' I shrieked.

'Yes, I am! Isn't it marvellous?'

'I can't believe it!'

'I can't quite believe it myself. I – I hope I'm doing the right thing,' said Hetty.

'Of course you are! So what are you going to do? Are you going to be an acrobat like me? Oh, Hetty, do come and be a silver girl!'

'Don't be silly, Diamond. You've seen me trying to do a somersault. I'm hopeless.'

'Then are you going to ride Midnight with Madame Addie?'

'I wish I could, but I'm no horsewoman. I'm not going to work with the monkeys or the big cats or that grand Elijah or those fishy old sea lions either.'

'Then what *are* you going to do?'

'I'm going to be the new ringmaster,' said Hetty, her cheeks flushing with excitement.

I was so astonished I didn't quite know what to say. How could Hetty possibly be a ringmaster, when this was Mr Tanglefield's job? She was only a small girl, even if she dressed up in her high hat and man's jacket. It seemed a ridiculous idea – but Hetty was Hetty. She wasn't afraid of anyone, not even Mister. If she said she was going to be the ringmaster, then I had to believe in her and trust she'd do it splendidly.

I believed it. Dear Madame Adeline believed it too. I could not help being jealous when I learned that Hetty was going to share Madame Addie's wagon.

'Oh, please, can't I come too? I won't need a bed, I can just take my hammock – or I can curl up in a corner on the floor. I won't take up any room at all, but *please* let me come and share,' I begged.

'Oh, darling, I've explained again and again why it's not possible,' said Madame Adeline, taking me on her lap. 'You know you belong to Beppo. I can't take you away from him, much as I'd like to.'

'But you're letting *Hetty* come and share your wagon.'

'I don't belong to horrible old Beppo. I don't belong to anyone,' said Hetty.

'It's not fair,' I said sadly.

'I know it's not fair – but don't fret, Diamond. When you're my age you won't have to belong to anyone either, I promise,' she told me.

I thought about this. It seemed a little too scary to be totally independent.

'Could I perhaps belong to *you*, Hetty?' I asked.

'Of course!' said Hetty, which cheered me up considerably.

We only had time for a cup of tea and a buttered muffin before we had to help out with the break-up of the show.

'I must attend to Midnight,' said Madame Adeline.

'And *I* must attend to all the monkeys to help Mr Marvel. He can't manage without me,' I said proudly.

'Well, *I* must attend to everyone and everything else,' said Hetty cheerfully, rolling up her sleeves.

She showed extremely willing, rushing up to everyone and saying, 'Hello, I'm Hetty, though my professional name is Emerald Star. I've joined the circus. How can I help you?'

At first she tried to help the hands tugging down the great big top. They barely acknowledged her, and then laughed when she couldn't take the tug of the ropes and had to wring her soft hands. She tried to help move the rows of seating, but she didn't have the strength for that either.

'Push off, little girl, and stop bothering us,' they said – or words that were even less polite.

So she tried to help all the artistes with their animals, but that didn't work either. She was a stranger. They acted skittishly while she was around and balked at going quietly into their travelling cages. She had enough sense to steer clear of the big cats and Elijah, and she shuddered at the sea lions, but she did try to pet the poor groaning bears, who always hated travelling. She poked her hands through the bars of their cage and stroked their grizzled heads.

'What on earth are you doing to my animals?' Bruno cried, running over.

'Hello, I'm Hetty, though my professional name is Emerald Star.'

'I don't care if you're the Queen of Sheba. You can't touch my bears! Are you an idiot? They're wild animals. They'll snap your hands off soon as look at you,' said Bruno.

'They're all muzzled and chained too! Can't you give them a bit of freedom within their cage? They look so restless and miserable. Their eyes are so *sad.*'

'They're beasts. They need to be chained. It's *you* that's upsetting them. Clear off or I'll fetch Mr Tanglefield,' Bruno told her.

'Hetty, Hetty, come and help me with the monkeys,' I said, tugging at her arm.

She came willingly and introduced herself to Mr Marvel. He nodded at her kindly enough, but when she told him she was going to be the ringmaster he burst out laughing.

'Is your new friend soft in the head, Diamond?' he said. 'Ringmaster! I've never heard the like!'

'You wait and see,' said Hetty loftily, though she looked a little vexed.

Very few people were willing to give her the time of day, and no one wanted her to help, but she didn't give up. She scurried across the field and back again, until

Madame Adeline tactfully asked her to wrap and store all her ornaments and china so that they wouldn't fall and chip during the journey.

It took a full two hours before the tent was in little pieces and roped neatly into place in a wagon, and all the horses buckled into their shafts. Midnight was far too grand and important to pull any wagon, of course. He rode *in* a wagon so that he didn't get tired and spattered with mud – but when we saw the spires and chimney tops of Gillford in the distance, Madame Adeline led him out and he stepped along proudly as part of the procession while she sat on his back in spangles and pink fleshings.

I had to parade in my fairy frock, skipping and smiling and turning the odd somersault. Marvo strode forward with Julip sitting on his shoulders, calling to the crowd of excited onlookers, while Tag capered crazily, expending far too much energy showing off, doing ten flic-flacs in a row and ending up in the crowd himself, nearly squashing the smallest children at the front.

We were all on show as Mr Tanglefield's Travelling Circus. Mr Tanglefield was up in front, hair blacked, moustache waxed, in a black frock coat and white silk breeches and boots so shiny you could see your face in them. He rode one of the horses, cracking his whip in the air, which made everyone jump.

Hetty was given a horse to ride too – old Sugar Poke, the oldest shuffling mare, as sweet-natured as her name. I had ridden Sugar Poke myself and it was as simple as sitting in a chair, but Hetty sat too tensely, hunched up, clearly a novice – though she still managed to wave her hat in the air and smile at the crowds. I thought she looked splendid in her scarlet coat, and her shapely legs in white fleshings made many of the lads whistle – but even so, there was a resentful muttering amongst the circus folk.

'Who *is* that silly girl? What does she look like, slumped on that horse like a sack of potatoes? It's clear she knows nothing about riding.'

'Why is she wearing that get-up – all dressed up like a showman but with no act to speak of?'

'Riding right up at the front too, only second to the boss himself. Has he taken leave of his senses?'

Oh, the mutterings got riper and ruder, and my cheeks burned on Hetty's behalf. She must have heard some of the comments, but she took no notice whatsoever. She held her head high and gestured grandly, though she had to grab frantically at Sugar Poke's mane if she quickened her pace at all.

When we got to Gillford Meadow at last, we had a great to-do setting up. There was no afternoon show, but we were booked to do an evening performance, so we had our work cut out getting the big top safely up with every seat in place, and the animals fed and watered and exercised.

Then we practised in the ring, as always. It was all confusion, for Flora could not get the tautness of her tightrope right, and a wheel was threatening to come off the lions' cage, and the handlebar of Chino's penny-farthing had got slightly knocked out of true in transit. There was a lot of swearing and shouting.

Hetty crouched in a corner, watching intently, then scribbling in a notebook.

While Mister was fixing the springboard with Marvo, I ran over to her. 'Hello, Hetty!' I said. 'What are you doing?'

'I'm making notes,' she said, frowning a little.

I watched her fill line after line with fancy squiggles. I could sometimes pick out words in print, but this fine handwriting defeated me. 'You're very clever,' I said admiringly.

She stopped writing and looked at me. 'No one else thinks so – and I'm not sure I think it either,' she said. She reached out and took hold of my hand. Her own was cold as ice. 'Oh, Diamond, what have I done! Whatever possessed me? How did I ever have the nerve to think I was equal to this? I managed to convince old Tanglefield that I could be a novelty child ringmaster with an artful way with words – but I don't know anything about the circus!'

'It's fine to be a little nervous,' I said, trying to reassure her. 'That's the mark of a true performer. Even Madame Adeline gets scared before a show. I am *always* frightened.'

'But you both do something splendid. I have nothing to offer but patter,' said Hetty despairingly.

'You can make a living out of pattering,' I said. 'My father . . .' My voice wobbled and I felt the sting of tears in my eyes, because it still hurt so much to remember that he had sold me.

'Oh, Diamond, I'm sorry. I didn't mean to upset you,' said Hetty, quickly putting her arm round me. Her notebook fell to the floor. The pages flicked over, all of them crisscrossed with her squiggly writing.

'You've made an awful lot of notes!' I said, marvelling, for my hand ached if I attempted even a few lines of *The cat sat on the mat*.

'Oh, this is my memoir book,' said Hetty. 'I'm just writing notes on the last page.'

'What's a memoir?'

'Well, I suppose it's just a grand name for a story about yourself,' she told me.

'I love stories!' I remembered the little fairy tales Mary-Martha and I had coloured. 'Does your memoir have fairies and witches and ogres and a handsome prince on a white horse?'

'Well, you can be the fairy, Diamond. There are

certainly several witches in the first volume – and one or two ogres in the second and third. And I suppose there *was* a handsome prince – but I don't want to be his princess,' said Hetty. She looked suddenly as if she might start crying. 'I don't *think* I do, anyway.'

I did not really understand, but I gave her a hug to try and comfort her.

'Diamond! Get down here and watch the boys. It's time you learned springboarding too. Leave that useless girl alone, do you hear me?' Beppo bawled from the ring.

I felt Hetty wince at the word useless. 'You're not a *bit* useless, Hetty,' I said fiercely.

'Everyone else thinks so,' she said. But then she put her chin up. 'So I shall show them.'

And she did, oh she did! I was so scared for her at that evening's performance. As we all lined up by the tent flaps, there was a great muttering, especially when we saw Mr Tanglefield stand *behind* Hetty. She looked very small and girlish, though she cut a fine enough figure in her scarlet riding coat and tall black hat.

'The boss has taken leave of his senses,' Beppo muttered. 'That girl's only got a mouse squeak. How can that silly flibbertigibbet ever hold the crowd?'

The band played a fanfare. We all stared at Hetty,

half the folk thinking she might make a break for it and run off into the night. But she marched forward into the ring. We could not see her properly once she was there, but oh my goodness, we could *hear* her.

'Ladies and gentlemen!' she cried, in a voice so rich and loud, I think the entire town of Gillford heard her. 'Ladies and gentlemen, girls and boys, little children and babes in arms – take heed! You are about to see sights that will dazzle your eyes and delight your hearts. Here is the amazing, magnificent and ultra-marvellous Tanglefield's Travelling Circus!'

A great cheer rang out around the ring. All the circus artistes stopped their mutterings and gaped. Hetty was extraordinary! She played with that audience, announcing each act in astonishing sentences that tripped off her tongue as if she'd been a ring master all her life. Even Beppo shook his head and mumbled, 'Well, she's certainly got a way with words, I'll say that.'

The audience was so well warmed up and appreciative that it made performing easy. We were all at our best. I was so excited I very nearly dared somersault down from Tag's shoulders when we did the human column, so keyed up I felt my little wire wings might even fly me up to the top of the tent and back.

The applause at the end of the act made my ears throb. I glanced all around the cheering audience and saw one man hunched at the end, the only one not clapping. He wasn't looking at us. He only had eyes for Hetty. It was her foster brother, Jem.

I do not know if Hetty saw Jem. She didn't mention him. She was flushed with triumph at the end of the show. Mr Tanglefield was so delighted with her success, he called for two of the circus hands to fetch beer from the nearest alehouse and held an impromptu party for his new star. There were still many circus folk who resented this new girl's status, but they'd seen for themselves that she could work the crowd wonderfully, and they all drank to her success – even Beppo and my silver brothers. Madame Adeline was utterly delighted, hovering by Hetty's side, feeding her little titbits and putting her own wrapper round her when she saw her shivering in the night air – though I think it was from excitement rather than cold.

Hetty drank little beer herself. She offered me a sip, but the very smell reminded me so painfully of Pa that I pressed my lips together and shook my head violently, which made everyone laugh. The men drank their fill, happily making the most of Mr Tanglefield's rare generosity, and after an hour or so grew wild and raucous. Hetty only had half a glass, but she acted slightly drunk too, laughing and joking with everyone, slapping each man on the back and kissing Madame Adeline and Flora and me.

I did not want to risk upsetting her by talking about her foster brother. I knew it might make her sad to think that he had walked all those miles from their village to Gillford to watch her perform.

During the next few days I wondered if Hetty was thinking of him. She was still very anxious before each performance and wildly elated afterwards. She was restless between times, pacing backwards and forwards like the big cats in their cage. Sometimes she went off for long walks by herself and came back with sore eyes and a sad face, though she insisted she hadn't been crying.

'Are you missing your home and your folks?' I asked her timidly.

She did not answer – just bent her head so I couldn't see her face.

'You won't get so homesick that you leave the circus?' I asked, desperate for reassurance.

'No. No, this is what I want,' Hetty said. 'This is the life I've always longed for . . .' But she didn't sound sure. She held onto me tightly. 'Do you sometimes feel . . . torn, Diamond?'

I didn't know what she meant. I fingered my own shredded petticoat anxiously. 'Torn, like my petticoat?' I asked.

'Torn in two – one of you wanting to be here, one of you wanting to be home. Only I don't even know where my real home is.'

I tried to follow her, but it was too difficult. I had never *wanted* to be here at the circus until Hetty came along. I knew where my home was, but there was no point wanting to be there. It was like one of the riddles on the joke cards Pa sold for parties.

Hetty saw my puzzled face and gave me a hug. 'Don't look so worried, Diamond. Take no notice of my silly ramblings. Yes, your petticoat *is* torn. I'll fix it for you. In fact I'll make you a brand-new petticoat and a pretty dress to go over it. Would you like that?'

'But I have my fairy dress for the show.'

'This won't be for the show. It'll be for *you*,' said Hetty. 'What colour dress would you like?'

I blinked at her, too overcome to decide. Did she really mean it? I'd never had a new dress for myself. I'd always worn Mary-Martha's cast-offs, and they weren't even new when she got them. Ma had bought all our clothes in bundles from the rag shop.

I reached for the skirt of Hetty's dress, a soft grey cotton patterned with tiny white flowers. 'Could I – could I have a grey dress like yours?' I asked.

'You don't want *grey*,' said Hetty. 'Grey cotton is for servants and country girls. You are a special circus girl, Diamond. You can wear something really bright and beautiful. You could have primrose chiffon or rose-pink muslin or sky-blue silk. Go on, choose!' She looked at me, her blue eyes shining. Blue seemed the most wonderful colour in the world.

'Please may I have blue silk?' I whispered.

'Of course you can!' Hetty snatched up Maybelle. 'She can have a blue silk dress to match. And I'll make you each a white broderie anglaise pinafore so you can play at making mud pies whenever you fancy without spoiling your dresses.'

I still thought this might be a delightful game of make-believe – but the next morning Hetty went to the market in town and came back with great armfuls of material wrapped in brown paper. I spotted a wisp of sky-blue silk and felt a throb of happiness in my chest.

'But how can you afford such fine materials, and so many?' I said, slipping my hand in under the brown paper and stroking brocade and velvet and my own beautiful blue silk.

'I made Mr Tanglefield give me an advance on my pay so I can make costumes for the company. And I got them very cheaply. I am old friends with the market men of Gillford. I used to drum up customers for them,' said Hetty.

'You can do *everything*, Hetty,' I said.

I meant it sincerely, but she laughed at me.

'My Lord, Diamond, I am hopeless at most things. I was the worst servant girl in the world. I was dismissed without a reference!'

'When were you a servant, Hetty? Tell me more,' I said.

'One day I'll read you my memoirs,' she promised.

Hetty made my dress first. She helped herself to one of Mr Marvel's newspapers – he kept a whole stack for lining the bottom of the monkey cage. She drew a design of a frock upon the pages: the bodice, the sleeves, the wide, wide skirt.

'Isn't it too wide all the way round, Hetty?' I said doubtfully. It looked as if it would fit Flora's ample girth.

'It's going to be gathered up until it fits snugly round your weeny waist, don't worry. But I want it to be very full. I'm going to make you a very flouncy petticoat too. Then you can whirl round and round like a little spinning top.'

'Oh yes! Oh please, yes!'

Hetty pinned the pattern to the blue material and cut it out with her special sharp scissors. They made an alarming rasping sound as they sliced their way through the silk, and my throat dried with panic in case it would all be spoiled, but Hetty seemed satisfied with each segment. She pieced them all together, her mouth full of pins, and then, when they were all assembled just so, she started the stitching.

She sat cross-legged like a tailor, head bent, her hand darting up and down as her needle flashed in and out of the material. I liked to kneel nearby and watch, loving the tiny *puck-puck-puck* sound of the needle and thread. Hetty stitched all day and half the night. When the dress was finished, she went to Madame Adeline and borrowed her flat iron, heating it very carefully and then letting it cool a bit in case it sizzled the silk. Then at last she called me and slipped the magical dress over my head. The silk was so smooth and soft it made me shiver.

'Oh, Hetty, it's so lovely! Does it look nice? Do I look pretty?' I asked, dancing round and round.

'You look beautiful,' said Hetty, and she took me to peep at myself in Madame Adeline's looking glass. A different girl entirely peered back at me – a fancy girl in a splendid frock, a girl so grand I felt I should curtsy to her, yet she was *me*!

'Oh, Hetty, I love my dress more than anything,' I breathed, scarcely able to speak. 'It's so bright and so *soft*!'

'All little girls should wear soft, bright dresses,' said Hetty. 'I had to wear dreadful itchy brown frocks when I was at the hospital and I absolutely hated them. Your dress looks lovely on you, Diamond, I must admit. It will look even better with new petticoats. I will start them next.'

She was as good as her word, making me two flouncy petticoats edged with lace. I twirled round in them until I was dizzy.

'You're showing a little too much, Diamond,' said Hetty. 'I'd better make you a matching pair of drawers to keep you decent.'

I'd never worn proper drawers before and thought them delightful. Tag teased me unmercifully when I wore my finery, sometimes snatching up my skirts and laughing and pointing at my lacy legs. I was mortified, but Hetty came to my rescue.

'What's this fascination with Diamond's drawers, Tag? Do you want a pair for yourself? How many frills would you like? And would you like a set of petticoats to go with them?' she teased. He soon stopped tormenting me!

Hetty made me a crisp white pinafore to go over my dress while I was playing, and with all the leftover scraps of material she stitched a miniature set of clothes for Maybelle, lacy drawers and all.

I dressed her in her new finery and then danced her around with me. Hetty had sewn proper features on her face, and her little embroidered mouth smiled ecstatically. I ran to show Madame Adeline, and she admired us both.

I saw how worn Madame Adeline's own clothes looked in strong daylight and wondered if Hetty might make her a new outfit too.

'I'd like to, but I don't want to offend or embarrass her,' said Hetty.

'You made me my dress and pinny and I'm not one bit offended or embarrassed,' I said.

'Yes, but you're a little girl.'

Hetty thought about it hard, but decided a new frock for Madame Adeline would be too personal – and it would involve lots of complicated measuring. She couldn't just go ahead and make one as a surprise. She decided to make her a new wrapper instead. The rose-patterned one was very pretty, but faded from much washing, the roses just fuzzy blurs. Hetty chose to make the new wrapper in black silk. I thought it might be a little plain and severe, but Hetty produced a bag of bright embroidery silks and set to work stitching wonderful red and yellow tulips all around the neck and hem.

She could only work on it intermittently, crouching in my wagon or sitting under a tree at the edge of the meadow, so that Madame Adeline wouldn't see. When it was finished at last, Hetty let me be there when she gave it to her. I was a little worried at first, because when Madame Adeline held the beautiful embroidered wrapper up against herself, she burst into tears.

'Oh, Madame Addie, don't you like it?' I said. 'Hetty worked so hard to make it nice for you, but I'm sure she'll fashion you another one if you'd like it better.'

'I like *this* one,' Madame Adeline sobbed. 'It's the most beautiful wrapper in the world. It's absolutely exquisite!'

'Then why are you crying?'

'Because no one ever gave me such a wonderful present,' she said. 'Oh, Hetty, you are just like a daughter to me.'

'And you are just like a mother to me now,' said Hetty. I knew that meant a great deal, because Hetty had told me privately that she loved her dear mama more than anyone else in the world.

Hetty bought more silk – in brilliant colours this

time: scarlet and purple, colours so hot it seemed strange that the material should still feel so cool and silky.

'Are you making more wrappers, Hetty?' I asked, wondering if she might be making one for me.

'I'm making a costume for Mr Tanglefield,' said Hetty.

'For *Mr Tanglefield*?' I said. I knew Hetty disliked him just as much as I did. She did a wonderful imitation of him – pouting and issuing little whining commands while waving her arms in the air so that everyone snorted with laughter. Tag always begged her to do it again and again.

'I promised him a costume when he let me join the circus. I need to keep him on my side,' said Hetty, spreading her silk out and pinning a paper pattern to it. It seemed a very large piece of paper.

'Won't the shirt be a little too big for him?' I wondered.

'It's not a shirt, exactly. It's like a robe. Indian gentlemen wear them down to their knees.'

'Like a *dress*?' I said, looking forward to seeing Mr Tanglefield in such a ridiculous outfit.

But when Hetty had finished making the scarlet robe, with wide purple trousers for underneath, worn with a gold brocade waistcoat and a vast turban of gold and purple, I did not laugh. Mr Tanglefield was immediately transformed into an Indian rajah, and couldn't help looking utterly splendid. Hetty fashioned another tunic and turban for Sherzam, the elephant keeper, but in plain creams to make his lower status plain.

'Now we must dress Elijah up to match,' she said.

I squealed at the thought of a giant dress and trousers for the elephant – but Hetty contented herself with a brocade cloth for his great back. Then she helped herself to Chino and Beppo's greasepaint, ran up a stepladder, and painted beautiful swirly red and black and gold patterns on Elijah's head. Elijah wasn't at all sure he wanted to be made up at first, but Hetty fed him a whole big bag of penny buns while she was doing it, so he held still and let her paint while he munched.

When Mr Tanglefield, dressed in his new oriental splendour, rode the adorned Elijah into the ring, there was a great gasp from the audience, and then a huge burst of spontaneous clapping. Mr Tanglefield held his head high – possibly to keep his turban in place – and gave himself princely airs and graces. Elijah himself seemed to take a new pride in his exotic decoration. He picked up his huge feet and swung his trunk and swivelled his vast painted head so that all could admire it fully.

Hetty introduced them very imaginatively, though

she veered a little from the truth, describing a wild beast captured on the Indian plains, bought for a small fortune, and trained with great courage and difficulty, whereas we all knew Elijah had been born in captivity as part of a Hippodrome Spectacular. He'd always had a temperament as meek and mild as mother's milk, and had been sold at a bargain price to Mr Tanglefield when the Hippodrome Spectacular went bankrupt.

'You needn't think you're dressing *us* in silks and satins,' said Tag, who suffered enough in his silver spangles.

'I would quite *like* a bright silk costume,' said Julip.

'So indeed would I, Miss Hetty,' said Marvo.

I don't think he particularly wanted a new fancy costume, but he seemed very keen to please Hetty. He followed her everywhere, trying very hard to be a gentleman, opening wagon doors for her and offering to lift her over muddy patches in the meadow when it rained.

Hetty was polite to him, but I could see that his attentions irritated her.

'Can you find out if she has a sweetheart, Diamond?' Marvo asked me.

I wasn't sure if the foster brother counted as such. I thought it best not to bring him up with Hetty, but I did ask diffidently if she liked any of the circus men.

'Oh, *yes!*' she cried. 'You have found me out, Diamond. I am lovestruck! My heart goes all of a flutter whenever I am near him.'

'Oh, who is it? Is it perhaps Marvo? He will be so pleased,' I said.

'No, it certainly isn't Marvo, though he's a very sweet man.'

'Then who is it? Julip?'

'It's not Julip either. All right, I'll tell you, Diamond, but you must promise not to breathe a word. It's Mr Marvel!'

'*Mr Marvel?*' For one second I actually believed her, even though Mr Marvel was such a vast age and as wizened as his monkeys. And then I started giggling, and Hetty did too.

'You're teasing me!' I said.

'No, no, I'm absolutely serious. I shall set my cap at Mr Marvel and marry him, and all the monkeys will be my stepchildren and little Mavis will be my special baby,' said Hetty.

'No, Mavis is *my* baby!'

'Oh, very well, you can have Mavis, but you're definitely not getting my Marvel too, even though he told me *you* were his sweetheart.'

'Did he really? He is very kind to me and I love him dearly, but he's even older than my pa, and *he* is *very* elderly,' I said.

'I have quite a young pa,' Hetty told me, suddenly serious.

I was astonished. I'd thought Hetty was an orphan. I knew she'd lost her mother, but this father was total news to me. I wondered why she did not live with him.

'Did he not want you, Hetty?' I said. '*My* pa didn't want me. He sold me to Beppo for five guineas.'

'Then he was very silly, because you're worth at least five *thousand* guineas, Diamond. No, I think my pa *does* want me. He made me as welcome as he could when I went to stay with him. But his new wife did not care for me at all. She'd sell me for five pennies and think she'd got a bargain!'

'And . . . have you any other family, Hetty?' I asked tentatively, thinking of the foster brother.

Perhaps Hetty was thinking of him too, because her blue eyes looked very shiny, as if they were full of tears. But then she gave a great sniff. '*You* are my family now, Diamond,' she said. 'You and Madame Adeline.'

This time I knew she was serious and I felt wondrously joyful. But she was certainly a little fond of dear old Mr Marvel, even if she didn't quite want him for a sweetheart, because she bought new material the next time she found a clothes market, and made a whole set of clothes for the monkey family.

She stitched Melinda and Marianne wonderful tiny frocks in silk bombazine – one heliotrope with navy stripes, one brilliant peacock blue, both with bonnets to match and fur-trimmed mantles. Both girl monkeys had to mind their manners now they were dressed as elegant ladies. It took them a while to get used to their new costumes, and they wriggled and scratched and pulled off each other's bonnets in a very comical fashion. But Marmaduke and Michael adopted a dandy air as soon as Hetty kitted them out with little jackets and waistcoats and pinstripe trousers, and wore their mini bowler hats at a comical angle, crammed over their little round ears. Hetty dressed Mavis as a real baby, with a long cream gown and infant bonnet, and Mr Marvel taught her to tuck her gown up into her napkin, which always got a huge laugh from the audience.

Hetty worked on her own clothes too. She cut a very fine figure in her borrowed fleshings, but she hated it when lads in the audience shouted out that she had 'a cracking pair of pins'. She bought a length of good quality cream cotton and tried to make herself a proper pair of riding breeches. She had difficulty fashioning the legs at first, and wasted her first length of cloth, which made her swear because it was expensive. But the second time around she mastered the flair of the leg, while getting a good tight fit around the hips.

It was perhaps a little too good a fit, because the lads started shouting rude remarks about her nether regions instead. One windy day she found a fine top hat that must have bowled right off some gent's head. It was a little muddy, but after a stiff brush it came up as good as new. I thought she'd throw her stovepipe hat away, because even I knew it was old-fashioned and it had become very shabby – but she rolled it up in a length of silk and kept it stowed away in an old pillowcase as if it were as valuable as a jewelled crown.

She gazed at herself in Madame Adeline's looking glass, flourishing her top hat and striking poses in her new breeches.

'You look lovely, Hetty,' I said admiringly.

'Hmn,' said Hetty. 'I really need proper boots though. Polished riding boots.'

I was in awe of Hetty because she could make most things, but I knew even she couldn't manage a pair of leather boots. I saw her eyeing Mr Tanglefield's shiny black boots enviously.

'Perhaps he's got an old pair he doesn't wear any more,' she said thoughtfully.

'He's a small man, but his feet are still twice the size of yours,' I pointed out.

'I could stuff the toes with paper,' said Hetty. 'Oh, I *wish* I had a proper pair of boots.'

'Are they very expensive, Hetty?' I asked.

'Desperately so. I've asked at the bootmaker's in town. Their best pair is five guineas.'

'Oh my goodness, *I* cost that much,' I said.

'I suppose I can save up, but it's going to take such ages.' Hetty kicked up her legs and sighed.

But she didn't have to wait ages after all. The next day Madame Adeline went out straight after breakfast and came back with a great brown paper parcel in her arms.

'What have you got there, Madame Addie?' I asked.

'It's a little present, Diamond,' she said.

'It looks like a very *big* present.' I looked at it hopefully.

'I'm afraid it's not for you, sweetheart. But I dare say I can find you a chocolate treat, and that can be your very *little* present,' said Madame Adeline.

'Then who is it for?'

She nodded towards Hetty, who was wobbling all over the meadow on Chino and Beppo's penny farthing cycle. She kept falling off, but she just brushed herself down and tried again, laughing.

At that moment Mister spotted her too and came hobbling towards her, spitting with fury. 'You, girl! Get off that machine immediately! What do you think you're doing? That contraption cost a small fortune. If that wheel's buckled, I'll have your guts for garters.'

Hetty jumped off the penny-farthing and untucked her skirts, laughing at him. 'Don't get so agitated, Mr Beppo. See – your penny-farthing's utterly unblemished.' She handed it over to him, dropping him a little curtsy.

'Don't put on airs and graces with me, you little trollop. You might have old Tanglefield so dazed he's practically signing his whole circus over to you – but you don't impress me one little bit,' said Beppo.

He climbed onto the penny-farthing himself to establish his rightful ownership – but he wasn't as skilled as Chino, and when he rode away he wobbled precariously, got the front wheel stuck on a tuft of grass, and fell right off, landing comically on his behind.

'You're such a funny clown!' said Hetty, and ran off to join Madame Adeline and me.

'Watch yourself, Hetty. It's not wise to tease Beppo too much. He can be a bad enemy,' said Madame Adeline.

'When you've grown up with terrible pig-faced matrons who hit you and locked you up in the attic, you don't get frightened of silly little circus men,' said Hetty.

Madame Adeline shook her head at her, but I was thrilled to hear her talking like that, even though I knew she was showing off. It helped *me* not to be so frightened of Mister.

'You're a naughty girl, Hetty, and a bad example to little Diamond,' said Madame Adeline. 'You don't really deserve a present – but here, take a look at this.' She handed Hetty the parcel.

Hetty held it, feeling the shapes under the paper, suddenly shocked into silence.

'What is it, Hetty? Oh, quick, tear the paper off!' I shouted.

Hetty gave a tiny pull at the wrapping, exploring something that gleamed conker-brown underneath. She gasped, and then suddenly tore the rest of the paper off so that it fluttered in shreds to her feet. She was left holding a pair of polished riding boots.

She cradled them as if they were two babies.

'I hope they're the right sort,' said Madame Adeline. 'They should be a reasonable fit. I took an outline of your shoes to show the bootmaker.'

'Oh, Madame Adeline, they're simply beautiful,' Hetty whispered. ' But – but I can't possibly accept them. They are far too expensive. They're the best present in the whole world, but as you say, I don't deserve them!'

'No, Hetty, you gave *me* the best present in the whole world – my wonderful tulip wrapper, made so carefully and lovingly. All *I've* done is buy a pair of boots,' said Madame Adeline.

'But they're so expensive. You must have used up all your savings!'

'It seems a little silly for me to save for my future

when I may not have one,' said Madame Adeline. 'You girls have all your lives ahead of you.'

'And so have you!' said Hetty fiercely. 'You're still the absolute star of the show.'

'I don't think so, dear, though it's sweet of you to say so. No, you are both our little stars – our tiny fairy Diamond and you, Hetty, our loved and brilliant ring-master.'

'A ringmaster who now has the best boots in the world!' said Hetty.

We settled down into a steady rhythm of setting up, practising, performing, taking down, travelling to the next village – and the next and the next and the next. I lost the tight feeling in my stomach, the squeeze of fear that made me tremble. I was still wary of Mister, but Hetty made sure she was nearby when we practised and he did not beat me in front of her. He stopped trying to teach me new tricks using the dreaded springboard. I was still anxious every time I scrambled up my silver brothers to make the human column, but it was becoming second nature now, almost as simple as running up a flight of stairs.

Every single day I played with Hetty. My doll, Maybelle, stayed neglected in my sleeping hammock. I had no need for a cloth friend now. Hetty and I ran wild races and balanced on the sea lions' rubber balls and stole the clowns' penny-farthing. At these times Hetty forgot she was practically grown up, and gloried in being bold and boisterous, charging around with her skirts tucked up.

'I never got to play when I was in the Foundling Hospital. I'm making up for lost time now!' she declared.

We had wonderful quiet times together too. She tried to teach me to read. I learned my alphabet and could figure out simple words, but I much preferred it if Hetty read to me, because she did so with such expression that it all came alive, as if the story was really happening. She read me her favourite book, *David Copperfield*. I grew a little fidgety when David became a man, but I loved hearing Hetty read the first few chapters when he was still a small boy. I wanted to play on the beach with him and little Em'ly. In the summer we had spent weeks at seaside venues and I couldn't get enough of the sands and the great swooshing sea.

Hetty had high hopes that we might visit a certain seaside town on the south coast called Bignor.

'I had such a dear friend there called Freda – a very large lady, but so gentle and refined,' she said. 'Oh, I do so hope I get to meet her again.'

But sadly we didn't go anywhere near this Bignor, with its big lady, and Hetty did not mention her again.

We turned back on ourselves and made our slow, meandering way through several counties, heading back towards London.

I was so happy living day by day that I did not realize I was in familiar territory. I performed in the first show, I had my stew, I ate cake with Madame Adeline and Hetty, and then I went into the ring for the second evening show. There was the usual laughter and applause as I did my little routine – but when I started climbing up Marvo and Julip and Tag to make the human column, someone called urgently, 'Watch out, Ellen-Jane – don't fall!'

I nearly *did* fall, I was so surprised. I couldn't see until I got right up on Tag's shoulders, and there, way down below me, was my dear sister Mary-Martha clutching a small boy, standing up in her seat, her mouth a big O of awe.

I waved at her very proudly and she waved back, and made the child wave too – my own little brother Johnnie.

I could hardly contain myself when I came out of the ring. 'My family are in the audience!' I said. 'They were watching me!'

I didn't just tell Marvo and Julip and Tag and then Madame Adeline. I told Mr Marvel and every little monkey. I even hung on Elijah's trunk and told him too.

'It's no use that pa of yours thinking he can come and fetch you back,' said Beppo. 'I bought you, fair and square, and he signed the piece of paper. You're my property now and he's not entitled to a penny of profit.'

'Was Pa there *too*?' I squeaked.

He hadn't come – of course he hadn't. But Mary-Martha was there, and she was the one I loved most. At the end of the final parade, she came rushing up to me.

'Oh, Ellen-Jane, I could scarce believe my eyes!' she cried, giving me such a fierce hug that baby Johnnie was squashed between us.

He wasn't the only brother come to see me. Luke was hanging back awkwardly, scarcely recognizable, he'd grown so pink and plump and rosy-cheeked.

'Oh, Luke!' I said, and gave him a hug too. 'You look very well!'

'I look too well for my profession. On funeral days they have to powder my cheeks so that I still look respectably pale,' he said. 'They're talking of reducing my food too. I do hope not – the missus is a marvel at cooking. You should taste her pies, Ellen-Jane! And her cake and tarts – oh my!'

'Luke fetches some home for us if he can,' said Mary-Martha. 'Oh, we should have brought you some.'

'I have cake too – pink and yellow with marzipan – and chocolates!' I boasted. 'And all the oranges I can ever eat. Did you see the folk throwing them?'

'We saw *you*, Ellen-Jane – and oh, you were grand! I couldn't believe it, my own sister got up like a little fairy queen and flying through the air! Don't you get frightened at all?'

'No, of course not,' I lied. 'Did you see my forward somersault? Shall I show you now?'

I demonstrated. Mary-Martha and Luke gasped most satisfyingly, and little Johnnie went into peals of laughter.

'I'll have to take you home with us. You'd be wonderful at diverting him when he starts one of his crying fits,' said Mary-Martha.

'Then . . . *can* I come home?' I said.

She looked stricken. 'Oh, me and my big mouth! I didn't mean it like that. Oh dear, I wish you *could* come home more than anything, Ellen-Jane, I miss you something chronic, but Pa would go mad. He won't even let us talk about you now.'

I swallowed hard. 'Perhaps I could creep home while Pa's out drinking?' I suggested.

'He doesn't drink a drop now, not since that day when you ran off with the circus man,' said Mary-Martha.

'I didn't run off! He *sold* me!' I said, starting to cry.

'Don't take on so, Ellen-Jane,' Luke said uncomfortably. 'He sold me too, didn't he – and Matthew and Mark.'

'Luke is doing so well now, and he comes to see me whenever he can. He earns a fortune in tips from the bereaved. He's very generous,' said Ellen-Jane. 'Matthew is learning carpentry and doing well too – he carved Johnnie a lovely little wooden train. Ever so grand, isn't it, Johnnie pet?'

'And Mark?'

'Mark's a bad boy. He ran away from the fishmonger, says he couldn't stand it. Oh, Pa was so cross. But he's got a job in a department store now, just helping out with the stock, but they'll put him to serving customers soon.'

'And what about you, Mary-Martha?'

'Oh, I just keep home and look after Baby, and I do all the colour work too of course, for the tracts and the story books. I lead the same ordinary old life – but you, Ellen-Jane, you are famous! You are so brilliant. My heart was fit to burst with pride when I saw you. My own baby sister, such a little star! So it's all worked out for the best, hasn't it?' she said.

'I . . . suppose so,' I replied, ducking my head.

'You *are* happy, aren't you, Ellen-Jane?' Mary-

Martha swapped Johnnie to her other hip and seized my arm anxiously.

'Of course she's happy,' said Luke. 'She was always the little show-off, standing on her head and waggling her legs. She's doing the job she was born for. She's Diamond now. What was it that ringmaster girl called you? *She's* a caution too! You're Diamond the Acrobatic Child Wonder.'

'That girl is my friend Hetty. And yes, I am happy, very happy,' I said.

But that night I cried hard in my hammock because I wasn't part of my family any more.

Marvo saw my red eyes in the morning and asked what was wrong. I wouldn't tell him. I didn't even breathe a word to Madame Adeline when she gave me cocoa with cream for a breakfast treat, but as soon as I was alone with Hetty I burst out sobbing again.

'Tell me, Diamond,' she said, holding me close and rocking me.

So I told her that I didn't have a proper family any more, sobbing so much that I made her bodice wet.

'Try not to take it to heart,' she said softly.

'But I am so, so sad! I don't have a ma, and my pa don't want me, nor my brothers, and even Mary-Martha don't miss me very much,' I wailed.

'I don't have a ma now either, though she's always in my heart. I have a dear pa, but I dare say he don't miss me either. I have sisters and brothers – very dear brothers – but they aren't my family now.'

'So you haven't got a family either, Hetty?' I said, knuckling my eyes.

'Yes, I have. I've got *you*. And we've both got Madame Adeline. What more could we want?' she asked.

'Yes, that's true,' I said, cheering up instantly.

'And don't forget, you've always got your dear old Grandpappy Beppo,' said Hetty, which made me shriek with laughter.

Seeing Mary-Martha and Luke did unsettle me for weeks though. I looked for them in the audience long after the circus had moved on to other towns.

'Don't you ever wonder if any of your kin are watching you?' I asked Hetty.

'Well, I did hope I might see my friend Freda when we were at the seaside back in the summer, but I'd have definitely spotted her in the audience. Freda is a girl who can't help sticking out in a crowd,' she replied.

'But what about *your* brothers and sisters?'

'Oh Lord, *they'd* never come,' said Hetty.

My stomach tensed up. It was no use. I had to tell her.

'Your brother Jem came once,' I whispered.

'Yes, he came looking for me and marched me back home,' said Hetty.

'He came after that – in Gillford. I saw him in the audience,' I said, making a clean breast of it at last.

'Are you sure, Diamond?'

'Certain sure.'

'Then why didn't you tell me?'

'I didn't tell because . . . because I thought if you knew you might change your mind and go back to him, and I couldn't bear that because I wanted you to stay so much. Oh, Hetty, am I very wicked? Are you cross with me?'

'No, I'm not cross,' said Hetty, but she sounded very sad, and that made me feel even worse.

I watched her carefully the next few performances – and though she was word perfect, never missing a beat, her eyes swivelled round and round the ring as she spoke, and I knew she was checking, looking for Jem, even though we were in a different part of the country now. All through November we edged our way towards London, because we had a three-week Christmas show arranged on Clapham Common.

Mr Tanglefield wanted all the acts to have a festive theme, so Hetty worked day and night stitching away at new costumes. She made Mr Marvel's monkeys matching scarlet outfits edged with white fur. He found a big oval looking glass, put artificial grass around it so that it looked like a frozen pond, and set the monkeys 'skating' on it. The adult monkeys picked up their feet and swayed to and fro like real little skaters, but baby Mavis slid across the pretend pond on her behind and got an extra laugh.

Hetty made two really big red dresses for the female dancing bears, and they took turns to waltz around the ring with Bruno. Then the third bear lumbered into the ring dressed as Father Christmas, with a big sack of toys, which made all the children in the audience scream with excitement.

Mr Tanglefield even suggested Hetty make a simply vast Father Christmas costume for Elijah.

'How ridiculous can you get!' she said to Madame Adeline and me. 'The man's off his head!'

'I hope you didn't tell him that,' said Madame Adeline.

'No, no, I just sweet-talked him, telling him that his Father Christmas idea was wonderful but perhaps it might detract from Elijah's oriental allure if he was forced to plod around wearing a red tent and a vast false beard. I've suggested festooning him with holly and ivy instead, though I'll have to pad the holly leaves in some way so that the poor beast isn't prickled to death. And I'm making Old Tangletummy a grand new costume in festive red and green trimmed with gold.' Hetty paused. 'What about you, Madame Addie? Would you like a scarlet spangled dress?'

'I've done my best *not* to be called a scarlet woman

all my professional life,' said Madame Adeline. 'But I will wear one if you think it will look effective, Hetty.'

Hetty held the bright red silk up under Madame Adeline's chin. It made her face look very pale and tired.

'I think your lovely pink costume suits you much better,' said Hetty. 'Will you be altering your routine with Midnight at all?'

'Midnight and I are too old to learn new tricks,' said Madame Adeline.

'They couldn't be bettered,' Hetty insisted.

'What about me? Do I have to learn a new trick if I have a new outfit?' I asked. 'I don't have to do springboard work, do I? I still don't think I'm brave enough.'

'I have a suggestion for your Mister Beppo,' said Hetty. 'Don't look so worried, Diamond. I won't suggest the springboard, I promise.'

'I wouldn't suggest anything to Beppo if I were you, Hetty,' Madame Adeline advised.

But Hetty was always a girl to throw caution to the wind. She squatted down beside Mister when he was smoking his pipe after tea and started whispering in his ear.

'Clear off, you little busybody. I don't want your suggestions, thank you very much,' he growled, but Hetty persisted. She went whisper, whisper, whisper, and I saw Mister's eyes gleam, even though his expression stayed surly.

'If you must, if you must! Now leave me in peace,' he said eventually.

'What have you suggested, Hetty?' I asked eagerly.

Marvo, Julip and Tag were also full of questions.

'Oh, I just suggested that it might look better in the ring if you were properly matching – two boys and two girls,' said Hetty.

'But we're *three* boys, stupid,' said Tag.

'Don't you know that circus is all about *illusion*?' she asked. 'I'm going to fashion you a beautiful spangled fairy frock with little wings, Tag, and until your own hair grows you can wear a curly wig.'

'*What?*' he spluttered.

'Tag a *fairy*?' Julip laughed.

'Hetty's teasing you,' said Marvo. He grinned and flexed his muscles. 'How about a fairy frock for me instead?'

Hetty was indeed joking, though it took a while for Tag to calm down and be convinced. She made me a new fairy dress instead, patiently sewing hundreds of sequins onto the bodice so that I sparkled in the ring, and she fashioned three forest-green velvet cloaks for the boys that covered them right down to their toes. Here and there she sewed little baubles on the velvet.

'How can we perform in *cloaks*?' said Tag.

'You won't wear them till the end of the act,' Hetty told him. 'When you perform the human column.'

We did not properly understand until the cloaks were all complete and the boys put them on. When Julip was standing on Marvo and Tag on Julip, their cloaks hung down, glittering with baubles. They looked for all the world like a Christmas tree. Then I clambered up, the fairy on the topmost branch.

It was a Christmas show to be proud of. We played to full houses. For Christmas week Mr Tanglefield even had us put on an extra morning show. We played Sundays too. The only time we had off was Christmas Day itself, and we were all so bone weary we slept a great deal of it. Mr Tanglefield organized a communal dinner in the big top itself, ordering a gaggle of great roast geese. We each had a huge plateful, with apple sauce and roast potatoes, with beer for the men and wine for the ladies.

No one felt like getting up the next morning, but Boxing Day was our biggest day of the year, with three sold-out performances. Hetty had a slight cold and a sore throat – Madame Adeline made her salt-water gargles and told her to whisper when she wasn't in the ring to rest her voice, but Hetty found that very difficult indeed. By the evening performance her voice was almost gone, and she was starting to panic, but Mr Tanglefield himself took her to his wagon and administered a medicinal cocktail of whisky and honey and lemon. I don't know which component did the trick.

Maybe it was just Hetty's own determination – but she was certainly in particularly fine form that evening.

'Ladies and gentlemen, boys and girls, children and babes in arms,' she cried out. 'Welcome to Tanglefield's Travelling Circus on this very splendid Boxing Day – and have we got a treat for you!'

We were playing to fine families from all over London. There were carriages lined up in a row at the edge of the common to take them home again. I loved looking at all the little girls in the audience, admiring their satin bows and party frocks and ermine jackets. They were all decked out so prettily, but none had such a splendid blue silk dress as me, none had silver spangles, none had fancy wings.

When we'd done the big farewell parade at the end, we were waylaid by the eager crowd. We were happy to linger, because they were plying us with all sorts of delicious tributes – chocolates and candy canes and crystallized fruits!

One solemn young lady in a fur-trimmed blue velvet mantle was staring hard at Hetty. She wore her hair tied back in a long fat pigtail like a bell rope, emphasizing her high forehead. She was gazing so intently, I could see a pulse twitching at her temple. She kept trying to press forward to get nearer to Hetty, but there was such an eager throng around her, this was proving impossible.

She looked around a little wildly, and saw me staring at her. She seized hold of my arm. 'Excuse me . . . I hope you don't mind my asking, but – but you must know that red-haired girl, the one who is the ringmaster,' she said.

'Yes, I do. She is my dear friend,' I said proudly.

'Could you – could you tell me her name?' asked the young lady.

'Her name is Emerald Star,' I said, because that was Hetty's professional name.

'Oh!' said the young lady, looking crestfallen.

'Don't you like the name? I think it is very beautiful. My name is Diamond. Diamonds and emeralds are both precious stones. They go together – and so do we,' I said, but I could see she'd stopped listening.

'I thought she was my Hetty . . .' she whispered to herself.

I blinked at her. 'Did you say *Hetty*?'

'Yes. Long ago I had the dearest friend in all the world – Hetty Feather. And when I saw your friend Emerald in the ring, I could scarcely believe my eyes. She is the exact spit of my own Hetty, and similarly gifted with words, and equally brave and bold and utterly splendid. It's hard to believe there could be two girls so alike, but I am obviously mistaken.'

'No, you're not! Emerald Star is her professional name but she is really your Hetty,' I said. *She is mine too*, I thought fiercely. *She is my own Hetty, not yours.*

But I could not deny Hetty this chance to see an old friend. I had felt so bad at having kept quiet about Jem.

'Hetty, Hetty,' I called loudly. 'Hetty, here is someone to meet you!'

Hetty heard me calling in spite of the hubbub. She elbowed her way cheerily through the crowds and stood before us. She peered at the young lady. For a moment she looked blank – and then her whole face crumpled.

'Polly! Oh, Polly, it's you!'

She flung her arms wide, and the two girls embraced as if they could never bear to let each other go.

'I *knew* it was you, Hetty! But what in the world are you doing here? I thought you'd be a servant now, like all the other hospital girls. Every day when I go for a walk I look down into all the basement kitchens and wonder if you're there, scrubbing and scouring.'

'I was a servant – a perfectly dreadful one! I wouldn't do as I was told.'

'Why does that not surprise me!' Polly said, laughing.

'And then I went up north and was a fisher girl.'

'Hetty!'

'And *then* I went back to the country to my foster family.'

'To your brother Jem?'

'Yes, but – but then the circus came, and I couldn't help myself. I ran away to join it!'

'Oh, Hetty, I *knew* you'd somehow do something exciting!'

'And what about you, Polly? Look at you, so grown up and ladylike! You have such lovely clothes.' Hetty stroked Polly's velvet mantle admiringly. 'Your family must be very rich!'

Polly went a little pink. 'Well, I suppose we are well-to-do,' she said awkwardly.

'And – and what do you do?'

'I still go to school. I would dearly love to stay on till I am eighteen and then study further at a ladies' college, but Papa does not want me to become a blue-stocking,' said Polly.

'Oh, you were always so clever!'

'And so were you! It's so wonderful to have found you, Hetty. I beg your pardon, Miss Emerald Star!'

'Well, we must keep in touch now and meet up as often as we can. We are here until the beginning of January so we can visit each other. Wait till you meet Madame Adeline, Polly! She has been almost like a second mother to me—'

'Lucy! Lucy, oh thank goodness! We thought we'd

lost you for ever in this wretched crowd. Come here, dearest!' A large, anxious lady came hurrying through the crowd, tears spilling down her plump cheeks.

'Lucy, my little Lucy!' She chided her as if she were a tiny girl, patting her with her soft white hands, rings and bracelets all a-jingle with agitation.

'Calm yourself, Mama,' said Polly.

'Lucy! Oh dear Heavens, we've found you!' This was clearly Papa now, as plump and pink as her other parent. 'Come, dear, we must find the carriage.' He pulled at Polly's arm.

Polly looked at her parents, then back at Hetty. Their hands were still clasped.

'Lucy! Say goodbye to – to the young person and come away at once,' said the papa.

'But – but this is Hetty,' Polly said bravely. 'My friend from when . . . when I was little.'

The woman gave a little gasp.

'Don't be ridiculous, dear,' said the father. 'Come away this instant. You're upsetting your mama.' He looked at Hetty coldly. 'Let her go!'

He turned Polly round and pulled her away. Hetty didn't try to hang onto her hand. Polly turned round once, looking desperate. Hetty smiled gaily and waved, even though there were tears in her eyes.

She watched until Polly and her parents were swallowed up by the crowd.

'Why did they call her Lucy?' I asked.

'Because she is their daughter now. They adopted her,' said Hetty. 'They changed her name. They changed everything.'

'But why won't they let you be friends with her?'

'Because we're very different sorts of girls now,' said Hetty. 'She is a young lady – and you and I are circus girls, Diamond. We should be pleased and proud. It's a very fine, rare thing to be a circus girl,' she said, but she was crying properly now.

The Christmas shows were a triumph, but from January all the way through to Easter we had no bookings at all.

'Don't look so downcast, chickies,' said Madame Adeline. 'We'll be going into winter quarters.'

'And what do we do there?' Hetty asked.

'We rest! And I for one will be heartily glad to do so.'

Madame Adeline certainly looked very tired and drained. The thrice-daily performances had been hard on her and she'd grown very gaunt. Her collarbones stuck out painfully when she wore her low-cut costume, and her fleshings wrinkled badly because her legs had become so spindly. When she was fully made up and wearing her long red wig, she still looked beautiful, but in the early morning, hobbling around, exhausted, she seemed like an old, old lady.

Hetty looked after her determinedly, doing most of the chores in the wagon, fetching water, making fires, even doing the cooking. She was remarkably defensive if anyone looked awry at poor Madame Adeline.

Tag once called her a doddery old woman – a relatively mild epithet compared to some of the names he'd called me! – but Hetty slapped his face hard and hissed at him to show a little respect.

Midnight needed a rest too. Some weeks ago he had stumbled on a stone while exercising on the common and had jarred his leg. He really needed to rest for a few days. Madame Adeline had gone to Mr Tanglefield and begged for him to have a little respite from the relentless performances over Christmas, but Mr Tanglefield had been adamant.

'If you and that nag wish to stay part of this show, then you'll perform. If you're too old or unfit, then you've no place here and you can get out today,' was his brutal response.

So Madame Adeline had been forced to put poor

lame Midnight through his paces at each performance, though it nearly broke her heart.

The winter quarters were in the grounds of a disused factory in a bleak suburban town. There was no grassy meadow for poor Midnight. When his leg was better, Madame Adeline led him to a distant park and rode him gently there, but he remained out of sorts and dispirited.

None of the animals seemed happy in their new cramped environment. It was particularly miserable for huge Elijah. He had very little exercise, tethered permanently in the dingy yard. He paced the three steps his ball and chain allowed, his trunk swinging this way and that, but he bore his captivity in stoic silence. The big cats and the dancing bears were noisier, roaring and growling a good deal of the time, only ceasing when they gnawed great lumps of meat at meal times.

Even the sea lions seemed to miss bobbing about on their rubber balls, and barked in a melancholy fashion whenever they stuck their sleek heads out of the water. Only Mr Marvel's monkeys seemed content, often staying in character and acting out their dancing and skating routines within the confines of their cage.

Mr Marvel clapped them solemnly and encouraged me to do so too. 'They like to be appreciated, Diamond,' he said. 'Performing's in their blood now. They're missing their show something chronic.'

'What about you, Mr Marvel?' I asked.

'Me? Oh, I've been ready to retire for years and years. I have a dear little cottage in the country. Mind you, I haven't been there in many a moon. It was my late brother's home. I think of it longingly sometimes. I could quite easily turn into a pipe-and-slippers gent, you know – but I can't let my babies down.' He smiled at his monkeys fondly and they chattered lovingly back, but this might have been because he was feeding them with peanuts through the bars of their cage. 'You miss performing too, don't you, little Diamond?' he said.

I didn't think I missed performing at all. For the first two or three days of winter quarters I slept a great deal of the time, falling into a heavy slumber the moment I curled up in my hammock. I slept everywhere in fact. I fell asleep on Madame Adeline's velvet sofa, on Hetty's lap, even halfway through my evening meal. It was because I was so bone weary after the relentless three performances each day for weeks.

Then I woke one day and realized that my head was clear, my bones didn't ache, I felt full of life – and there was no fear in the pit of my stomach. I still had to practise every day, but even Mister relaxed a bit and read a newspaper while he put us through our paces, nodding or tutting in a cursory manner.

It meant I had weeks and weeks and weeks of free time to be with Hetty, all day and every day. Seeing

Polly had stirred up many painful memories of her time at the Foundling Hospital. She started telling me all about it as we huddled together in a corner of Madame Adeline's wagon. I asked her a hundred questions. I was especially keen to hear about Hetty when she was my age.

'Would we have been friends then, if I'd been at the hospital too? Would you have liked me almost as much as Polly?' I asked.

'I'd have liked you *more*,' she said.

'Tell me the games you played together. And tell me about the fierce matrons. And tell me about what happened when you were really naughty,' I begged.

'Perhaps I'll simply read you little extracts from my memoirs.' Hetty went to her leather suitcase and opened it up carefully. I saw a bundle of letters tied up with blue ribbon. She cradled them gently in cupped hands.

'Who wrote the letters, Hetty?' I asked. 'Are they from a sweetheart?'

'They are from Mama. They're far more precious to me than any sweetheart's love letters.' She laid them carefully back in place and picked up a silver necklace.

'That's pretty,' I said.

Hetty held it up so that I could see it was a little sixpenny piece on a chain. 'This is from a sweetheart,' she said.

I was sure this was Jem.

'But you don't wear it?' I asked.

'No, because I'm not anyone's sweetheart now,' she said, a little sadly.

'And what's this?' I picked up a little black and white china dog. 'Oh, I like him!'

'Bertie won it for me at a fair,' said Hetty.

'Bertie? *Another* sweetheart?' I said, a little crossly.

Hetty laughed. 'I dare say you will have sweethearts of your own when you're a bit older,' she said. 'In fact I have a feeling young Tag is keen on you, Diamond.'

'*Tag?*' I exclaimed. 'He hates me! He's forever tormenting me.'

'He's just trying to get your attention,' said Hetty. 'He's not a bad boy really. You could do worse than him.'

'No I couldn't! He's the *worstest* worse,' I said with feeling.

I looked at the notebooks in the case. There were three thick volumes, one red, one blue, and one green, each page crisscrossed with Hetty's tiny scribbly writing. 'I can't read it all,' I said.

'I will read a few pages aloud,' said Hetty, flipping through the first volume. 'Now, where shall I start?'

'Start at the beginning,' I said.

So she did – and I wouldn't let her stop. She read to

me most of the day – and the next and the next. When she came to the first passage about Madame Adeline, I squeaked with excitement.

'You must read it to Madame Addie too, Hetty!'

'I think I am a little too candid about her at times,' said Hetty. 'I would not hurt her for the world.'

I was even more excited when she came to the last quarter of the third book – and met me!

'Are you going to be extra candid about me, Hetty? Are you going to write about this terrible, wretched girl who trails around after you and drives you mad?' I asked.

If Hetty had written any such thing, she didn't read it aloud. She said lovely things about me!

'Oh, you are such a special friend, Hetty! If I were ever clever enough to write a memoir, I'd fill page after page with all the things you say and do.'

'Well, I'll give you some more reading and writing lessons, and we'll buy you a notebook and get you started,' said Hetty.

She was as good as her word. She bought a new notebook from a stationer's in town, with a leather spine and edges, and a swirly violet pattern that reminded me a little uncomfortably of angels' wings.

'I haven't always been a very good girl,' I said. 'Must I write down all the bad things I have done?'

'You don't have to, but it makes it a more truthful account,' said Hetty.

'But won't I get into trouble and be punished?'

'No one will be reading your memoir, Diamond, except me – and if you've been bad, I'm sure I'll find it understandable, especially as I've been a very bad girl myself. I used to think folk might read *my* memoirs one day. I thought they might be good enough to be published as a special book, but I can see that was a ridiculous idea.' Hetty sighed wistfully. 'I don't know why I'm bothering to write so much. No one will ever want to read about a foundling girl – or a kitchen maid or a fisher girl, or even a circus girl for that matter. Can you see Polly's parents rushing to the bookseller's to buy their precious daughter such an account?'

'Yes!' I insisted, though I could see she had a point. Then I suddenly remembered one of the fairy stories I had coloured. There were two contrasting illustrations: one of a girl in a sooty apron and ragged dress, weeping in a kitchen before a meagre fire, and another of the same girl in a magnificent evening dress hurrying in her sparkly slippers from a grand ball as a clock struck twelve . . . a number I now dreaded.

'I know a story about a kitchen maid!' I said, and described the illustrations to Hetty. I remembered them well: I had laboured hard to get the right shade of pale gold for the heroine's hair and I'd patiently painted tiny jewels all over her Chinese-white ball dress. I'd talked to the girl all the while in

233

my head, pretending that I was going to the ball too.

'I think that's the story of Cinderella,' said Hetty.

'Does it have a happy ending?' I asked.

'I suppose so. Cinderella marries a handsome prince.'

'Then you might marry a handsome prince too,' I said.

'No, thank you very much,' said Hetty. '*You* can have the handsome prince if he comes galloping up on his white horse.'

I thought about it. I'd never met a handsome prince, of course, but I'd known quite a few handsome boys – my three big brothers, and Marvo, Julip and Tag. 'I don't think I want one either,' I said.

'Then we'll be old maids together, and I dare say very happy ones too,' said Hetty. 'Here we are, Diamond. Here's your memoir book. Get writing. I'll help you with any hard words you don't know how to spell.'

I struggled hard for an hour or more, clutching my pen so tightly that it grew sticky with sweat. I had all the words in my head, but it took so long to get them out on the paper. Try as I might, my letters danced crazily up and down and were large and unwieldy, no matter how I struggled to keep them small and neat.

My nam is Dimon. I use to be caled Ellen-Jane Potts, I wrote, filling a whole page with this uninspiring sentence – and then I burst into tears because I was so ashamed.

I could not understand how I could paint so neatly when quite a little girl and yet could not even manage one proper sentence of writing now.

'Don't cry so, Diamond. You just need more practice, that's all,' said Hetty.

'I *hate* practising!' I wailed.

'Well, tell you what: why don't you tell me what you want to say and I'll write it all down for you,' Hetty suggested.

'But you have your own memoir to write.'

'I think maybe three great fat volumes are enough – for the moment, anyway. It is your turn now, Diamond.' She took the notebook away from me and sat, pen poised. 'Start talking!'

'From the very beginning, as far back as I can remember?'

'Yes!'

So I started – and Hetty wrote it all down for me. She wrote and wrote and wrote, and said I'd had a very full life for such a young person.

'So many things have happened, many of them dreadful,' I said. 'But now I have started a peaceful time where nothing much is happening at all, and that is quite heavenly. I wish we could stay in winter quarters for ever. Don't you, Hetty?'

'I don't! I guess I'm more of a showgirl than you, Diamond, for all you're so talented. I find I miss performing terribly. Don't you feel cooped up here? I long to be on the road again.'

Hetty was growing increasingly restless. She went on long walks every day, sometimes taking me with her, and carrying me piggyback when I couldn't keep up. She had a fancy to take me back to London to show me the sights. Reading her memoirs aloud had made her dwell on the past and she wanted to show me the Foundling Hospital.

'Will we go in it and see the fierce matrons?' I said anxiously.

'I should think *not*! They'd likely prod me with their rulers and prick me with their darning needles. I was their least favourite child by far. But I would like to see my little foster sister Eliza, who is still there, poor mite. I ran away when I was about her age. I should love to show you Hyde Park, Diamond, and the restaurant where I had lunch with Miss Smith and . . . Oh dear, she would be very shocked if she could see me now. I don't think the Religious Tract Society could possibly approve of circuses.' Hetty took a deep breath. 'Perhaps it's not wise to go back and try and revisit places or people. I think one should just go forwards. Yes, that's right, Diamond. Don't let either of us think about the past. Let's just think of our future and our family – you and me and dear Madame Adeline.'

'And Mr Marvel and Mavis and the rest of the monkeys,' I said, giggling.

We had no idea that everything was going to change. Mr Tanglefield shut himself up in his wagon for most of January, fussing with his accounts and poring over maps, plotting where we would be going when the new season started at Easter.

Then, in February, he started going on mysterious trips, sometimes staying away for three or four days at a time. Everyone relaxed at first, and there were several parties – but after a while folk grew uneasy.

'He's up to something,' said Mister, frowning. 'Why is he chasing off like this? Who is he seeing? I reckon he's on the lookout for a new act.'

'So do you think he wants to expand and make Tanglefield's a bigger circus?' asked Hetty.

'Nope, he's got to keep it tight. He'd need proper transport if he expanded too much – his own specially adapted train like the ones in America – and that ain't going to happen,' he replied.

'But you said he was looking for new acts.'

'*Replacement* acts,' said Mister. He nodded curtly at Hetty. 'Yes, you've a right to look shocked. I dare say he's looking for a brand-new ringmaster – or ringmistress, I should say. He's seen that having a female announce the show is something of a novelty that

237

draws the crowds, but he'll be on the lookout for a glamorous young lady, saucy but sweet – not some shrill-voiced, whey-faced gingernob who knows nothing of circus tradition.'

He was trying to scare Hetty, but I knew she wasn't concerned about her own position. She was thinking anxiously about Madame Adeline.

Mr Tanglefield remained tight-lipped when he returned from his various mystery visits, but he started watching everyone closely while they practised. There was no show scheduled for weeks. We didn't even have a proper big top, just a large sawdust-strewn yard in the freezing cold – but suddenly everyone performed as if the old Queen and all her courtiers were sitting watching.

I found it so nerve-racking that I fluffed the easiest back-flip and landed on my behind. I didn't look where I was going and blundered straight into Tag, nearly making him topple too.

'You call her a little fairy? She's more like a fairy elephant today,' said Mr Tanglefield, laughing at me.

'Ha ha, poor darling. I don't think she's quite herself,' said Mister, but his own laughter was anything but jovial.

He managed to stay smiling at me until Mr Tanglefield strolled off to have his lunch. Then his face hardened. 'How dare you mess up such a simple routine?' he thundered.

'I'm sorry! I don't like it when he watches me. Please don't be cross,' I begged.

'You're there to be watched. You're a performer, aren't you? Well, you've got to sharpen up your act and no mistake. And it's time you learned something new, my little *fairy*.' He practically spat the word. 'You're going to have to spread those silly little wings.' He grasped me by the elbow and led me over to the springboard.

'Oh no! *Please* no! I can't do it. You know I can't!' I said, dissolving into tears.

'Can't – or *won't*,' said Mister. 'I don't want any of your hysterics, young missy. You'll learn. If the others can do it, so can you.'

'But it's so scary!' I protested feebly.

'Which is scarier, a simple little somersault or two, or a royal beating?' he asked. 'Now, line up with the others and concentrate hard. You're doing it, and there's an end to it. We've got to improve the act or we'll all be thrown on the scrapheap.'

Marvo ran to get soft mats and bedding and spread them out. 'There now! If you *do* fall, it won't hurt too much,' he whispered comfortingly.

'She'll try harder to do it right if we don't have the safety matting,' said Mister – but he let them stay in place.

I tried. I tried so hard. I didn't want to do it. I felt bile rise in my throat at the thought of the spring-board. Each time, I hurtled up and spun round and round, trying desperately to land on my feet – or indeed any part of me that wasn't my head. I was sick afterwards, whether I landed well or not. Even then Mister wouldn't let me off.

'Bring a bucket. She'll be fine,' he said heartlessly.

When Hetty saw what was happening, she marched up to Mister and stood right in front of him, chin up, arms folded.

'Stop torturing that poor child! You know perfectly well she's not old enough or strong enough to somer-sault through the air like that,' she said.

'Don't you tell me what to do! She's mine. I can do what I like with her,' he shouted.

'I'll – I'll report you!' said Hetty furiously.

'Oh yes? And who will you report me to, exactly?' said Mister.

'I could go and fetch a policeman and report you for being cruel to a child,' said Hetty, wavering a little.

'You fool,' he sneered. 'I'm her guardian now. I've taken her father's place. I can beat her black and blue if I care to. But just supposing you call a Peeler and he starts reading me the riot act, what do you think will happen to the little fairy here?'

'*I'll* look after her,' said Hetty.

'You're just a silly little girl yourself, not long out of that Foundling Hospital. As if they'd ever let you! No, they'd ship Diamond off to the workhouse, and I don't think even you would wish that on her.'

'Please don't put me in the workhouse!' I cried.

'It's all right, Diamond. Of course you're not going in the workhouse. Beppo's just trying to frighten both of us,' said Hetty, putting her arm round me.

He was succeeding too, because we were both trembling.

I had to continue my springboard work, and even Hetty could not help me. I gradually learned to control my body in the air and could just about do a double somersault and then land on the ground, but try as I might I couldn't manage to land on Tag's shoulders. I frequently hurtled into the three boys and sent them all sprawling – or if I did land accurately, I simply couldn't keep my balance and always took a tumble.

Then, one day that was no different from any other – I was just as tired, just as scared, just as despairing – I took off from the springboard, soared through the air, head tucked neatly between my knees, swivelled twice and landed lightly on Tag. I don't know how or why – it just happened! I stood there, keeping my balance, utterly astonished, wondering if I was actually dreaming, because most nights I dreamed of nothing else. But no, this was real, and it had actually worked. I had done the trick perfectly!

'Bravo!' Mister shouted. 'That's it! That's the way! Oh, what a crowd-pleaser! Again! Do it again before you forget how.'

So I tried again. We were all convinced it had been some magic fluke – me most of all. But I did it again, timing it perfectly, swooping up and up and up, then round and round again, and landing spot on, holding the position. I even managed to stretch out my arms to milk the applause.

'Good *girl*!' said Mister, and he actually clapped for all he was worth.

I expected Tag to be annoyed with me and give me a quick punch or a sly kick, but instead he thumped me on the back in congratulation. 'Not bad at all, Diamond,' he said.

'It was blooming brilliant,' said Marvo, tossing me in the air.

'Well done, Diamond. You truly *are* a little star now,' said Julip.

I couldn't wait to show Hetty my new trick, but she wouldn't watch properly. The moment I ran onto the springboard, she put her hands over her face and could not look until I'd landed safely.

'It's all right, Hetty! Look, I'm fine. I can do it now, see!' I shouted.

'But what if you slip?' Hetty asked.

'She won't slip. She's got it now,' said Mister.

'She *could* slip. She's springing up much too high. I can't bear to look,' she cried.

I couldn't reassure her, even though I did the trick perfectly again and again.

'I know it. It's in my head. I won't forget how to do it. It's like you riding Mister's penny-farthing. You kept falling off at first, but now you've mastered it you can ride it round and round every time.'

'But if I *do* fall I'm not likely to break my neck,' she pointed out.

'Try not to worry, dear,' I said, like a grown-up, because I wanted to reassure her. It made her burst out laughing, which wasn't quite the effect I'd hoped for.

'Anyway, Mister almost likes me now. He's stopped worrying about us being replaced,' I said.

'I don't think anyone's going to be replaced,' Hetty said firmly – but she was wrong.

During our last week in winter quarters there was a flurry of activity – folk painting their wagons, polishing up the horse brasses, testing equipment. Mr Tanglefield ordered everyone to have their wagons ready to be off at crack of dawn the next morning.

'And make more room in the yard,' he said. 'We have some new friends joining us today.'

'I knew it,' said Beppo.

'But we'll be all right now I've learned how to fly,' I said, taking hold of Marvo's big hand.

'I don't think Beppo's worried about *our* act,' Marvo whispered. 'Maybe he's anxious about his own.'

'But Beppo and Chino always make everyone laugh.'

'*Chino* does,' said Julip. 'But not Beppo. He's getting old. He looks all wrong when he gambols around the ring. You can see he's really stiff. No matter how comical his make-up, he never looks funny. He can't disguise his eyes.'

'Circus folk are supposed to look young and strong and spry, whatever kind of artiste they are,' said Tag.

'That's not true,' I said. 'Look at Mr Marvel. He's really, really old. It doesn't matter a jot.'

'I wouldn't be so sure of that,' said Tag. 'And I'd worry about your precious Madame Adeline – she's so long in the tooth she's been performing since Tanglefield's pa was in charge. I reckon she's for the chop.'

'I'll chop *you*!' I said, clenching my fists together and hitting him on the head.

I was so angry and struck Tag so hard, he actually ran away from me, which made Marvo and Julip laugh.

There was no laughing when the new folk arrived
that afternoon. The whole company gathered
silently, strained and tense. A blue and yellow wagon
arrived first, the horse driven by a spry-looking man in
his twenties.

'Do you think he's an acrobat?' asked Julip.

'No, he hasn't got the right physique,' said Marvo.

'He looks like a real showman. Maybe he's a new
ringmaster!' said Mister, nodding his head at Hetty.

'Perhaps he's a clown,' she retorted.

'I doubt it – he's much too young,' said Marvo. He was meaning to be comforting, but Beppo quivered.

'Perhaps he's a trainer,' said Tag. 'He'll have an animal act. That horse pulling the wagon looks in good condition. Maybe he's an equestrian.'

Hetty and I both held our breath, though the horse was old and took a long time to pull the wagon neatly into place.

'That man's no horse-trainer. He can't even control that old nag,' said Mr Marvel. 'Besides, there's only one wagon. His animals won't tuck up in his bed at night, will they?'

Oh, poor dear Mr Marvel! When the man had unharnessed his horse and waved airily to the watching crowd, he opened the door of his wagon and two dark heads peeped out.

'Allow me to present Miss Daffodil and Mr Cornflower,' the man shouted.

Two strange, chunky creatures came ambling out, clapping their hands. At first glance I thought they were very swarthy, stocky children, for Daffodil wore a bright yellow frilled frock with matching stockings and black patent boots, while Cornflower sported a little blue sailor suit and wore a jaunty cap with an embroidered anchor on his head. But then I blinked and realized they were enormous monkeys, giant versions of Mr Marvel's tiny, spindly babies.

'Chimpanzees,' Mr Marvel whispered, and his face crumpled.

'They are very ugly and cumbersome – nowhere near as nice as *our* monkeys, Mr Marvel,' I said, taking hold of his hand. 'And I'm sure they can't perform such clever tricks.'

But the new man said loudly, 'Run and introduce yourselves to all these nice new folks, Daffodil and Cornflower.'

Daffodil held out her frilly yellow skirts and bobbed the most comical of curtsies, while Cornflower took off his sailor cap and bowed low. Then they hopped and skipped about the crowd on all fours, but stood up straight and offered a paw to anyone who took their fancy.

Daffodil offered her paw to *me*. I worried about hurting Mr Marvel's feelings, but I couldn't help grasping the strange big brown paw. Daffodil chattered happily in her own language, clearly saying she was pleased to be acquainted. She was equally polite to everyone.

Cornflower was far cheekier. He held out his hand, but always snatched it away before anyone could take hold of it, and then he cheeped with laughter, smacking his lips. He took especial liberties with Mr Tanglefield, running up to him and then punching him lightly in the stomach.

Mr Tanglefield was a slight man, but he had a pronounced pot belly. It was rumoured that he had to wear a tight corset to fit decently into his riding breeches. He was very self-conscious about his figure and struggled to hold his stomach in when he thought people were watching. It was therefore doubly comical for Cornflower to single out this part of his anatomy. We all spluttered, keeping our faces as straight as possible, because no one wanted to be seen openly laughing at Mr Tanglefield, particularly when he hadn't confirmed who was to accompany him on the new tour, and who was to be left behind. But Mr Tanglefield himself burst out laughing, in a high-pitched, squeaky voice.

'Very comical, Mr Benger. You have trained your monkeys well,' he said.

'Excuse me, sir, my two children are of the chimpanzee species, *not* commonplace little monkeys,' said their trainer.

Mr Marvel winced. His eyes were watering and he looked every one of his eighty or ninety years, but he stood as straight as he could, and said with simple dignity, 'I gather *my* services will therefore no longer be required, Mr Tanglefield.'

Everyone turned to Mr Tanglefield. He had the grace to look away uncomfortably.

'I think we both know you're a bit past it, Marvel.

Beats me how you've kept going all these years. But I think it's best to go now. Don't look so down-hearted. I'll make you an offer for those monkeys of yours. I dare say Benger can work them into his act. We'll give you a tidy little sum – it'll pay your rent for many months.'

Mr Marvel's fists clenched. 'You must be mad if you think I could ever sell my babies. I'd sooner sleep in the gutter so long as they could be there with me. But I won't need to resort to such desperate measures, thank you very much. I have a very snug little cottage in the country that's been waiting for me to occupy it for many a year. I'll be off first thing in the morning.'

'Oh, Mr Marvel!' I said, and I threw myself upon him. 'I can't bear it! I shall miss you so.'

'I will too, more than anything,' Hetty declared. She looked at Mr Tanglefield, quivering with emotion. 'How can you be so heartless? Why can't Mr Marvel and his monkeys keep their act? You can have *two* monkey acts! That would surely be a great novelty?'

'Great *liability*,' said Mr Tanglefield. 'We don't want old dodderers as part of the show. It sounds brutal, but it's business. Marvel's been past it for years. He can't even control his monkeys any more. Look at all the palaver when the little one escaped and held us all up for hours.'

'That was *my* fault, not Mr Marvel's!' I cried.

'Be silent, both of you!' he shouted. 'I don't run this show as a charity and I don't need shrill children to tell me how to do my work. All right, Marvel, I'll sort out the wages you've got owing by tonight, with a bonus for your long-term engagement. Then you can leave in the morning when we do. Now, don't just stand there, everyone. I'm sure you've got work to do.'

I hung onto Mr Marvel, starting to cry. He patted me gently on the head. He seemed very calm, but I could feel him trembling.

'I'll miss you so very much, Mr Marvel – and I'll miss my Mavis too, and all the other monkeys.'

'We'll all miss you, little Diamond bright. But don't grieve for me. I've had a long and happy life in the circus but I can't deny I'm getting old. Now it really is time for me to go.'

It was heart-breaking – but this wasn't the worst surprise on that dreadful day. Mr Tanglefield had insisted we leave a very large space beside his own wagon. We waited and waited to see who the new-comers were going to be. Then, just as folk were starting to cook their suppers, we heard the sound of a rumbling wagon and horses' hooves.

It was a very grand wagon, at least twice the usual size, drawn by four beautiful horses – three chestnuts and one grey.

Madame Adeline's head jerked and she stared at them, stricken.

'It's all right, Madame Adeline. I'm sure they're just pulling the wagon,' Hetty said hurriedly, though we could all see these were fine horses in the peak of condition.

We looked at the man holding the reins. He was tall and fit, and wore a strange broad-brimmed hat, a checked shirt, tightly cut trousers and astonishing studded boots.

'He's a cowboy!' said Julip, in awe. 'Like Wild Bill Hickok!'

'An equestrian,' said Madame Adeline, and closed her eyes.

'But he's a man – folk would far rather see a beautiful spangled lady on a horse,' said Hetty, putting an arm round her shoulders.

But then we saw the woman on another horse behind the big wagon. She was young and slim, with long blonde hair, wearing another broad-brimmed hat and a fantastic outfit – red with white fringing. She wore heeled red boots and rode a lovely chestnut mare with white socks, who trotted along with her head and tail up.

Hetty didn't say anything at all. Madame Adeline opened her eyes and then put her hand to her throat. We watched in open-mouthed silence as the man manoeuvred the wagon into place and unharnessed the four horses, while the woman swung herself down and went to open the door of their wagon.

Mr Tanglefield came running out to greet them, nodding his head, shaking hands, circling them eagerly, clearly thrilled to be welcoming them into the company.

'Dear Lord, he's behaving like a regular Uriah Heap, fawning all over them and acting humble,' said Hetty. 'How ridiculous! Who cares about a silly cowboy act? And that woman's showy scarlet boots aren't a patch on mine!'

Madame Adeline smiled at her wanly. She'd grown very pale. She couldn't take her eyes off the beautiful blonde woman. She watched as the door of the wagon was opened. There was a sudden wild howling, and three great black and tan creatures leaped out.

I remembered the fairy-story books. 'Wolves!' I cried, clutching Hetty.

'No, I'm sure they're dogs,' she said, but she pushed me behind her protectively.

They were joined by a little black and white dog, who jumped about ecstatically, chasing his three big friends.

'Behave!' the blonde lady shouted. All four dogs stopped in their tracks and sat obediently on their haunches, noses quivering. She gave them all a pat and a titbit. The black and white dog tried getting up on his hind legs and making a little whiny noise, clearing begging for more.

'Oh, I like the little one!' I exclaimed.

The lady heard me and smiled. 'This is Albie, our Brittany spaniel – he's our special little clown,' she said. 'Say hello to the little girl, Albie.'

Albie came and barked at me winsomely, rubbing against my legs. I tickled him behind his ears. The other three dogs all came bounding up too, and I took a step backwards.

'Don't worry, they're not wolves at all. They're German shepherd dogs and they wouldn't hurt a fly. This is our top dog, Sammy, though he's getting a bit wobbly on his legs now. This is our girl, Honey – now, you can't be frightened of her, she's the smallest German shepherd you'll ever see. Try stroking *her* ears and she'll fall in love with you. And this one's Joe – not the brightest of our boys, and he can't jump too high now, but he'll do anything for you if you offer him an orange for a big treat.'

'Then I'll be able to give him lots of treats!' I said excitedly – but then Hetty pulled me away, giving me a little shake. The lady was so smiley and friendly, but I realized I couldn't possibly like her *or* her animals if it meant Madame Adeline's act was threatened.

Hetty was openly scowling at the newcomers,

but Madame Adeline herself was bravely trying to smile.

'That's a beautiful mare,' she whispered, nodding at the blonde lady's chestnut horse.

'Nowhere near as splendid as Midnight,' said Hetty.

'Darling, it's pointless pretending,' said Madame Adeline. 'She's lovely, the prettiest, liveliest creature. And her rider is very pretty too.'

'You're prettier, Madame Addie!' I said.

'Much, much prettier,' added Hetty.

Madame Adeline put her arms round both of us. 'You're my dear sweet loyal girls,' she said. 'Oh dear goodness, I'm going to miss you so.'

'Don't say that! You're not going to go! You're the star of the show,' said Hetty.

But at that very moment Mr Tanglefield cleared his throat, rubbed his hands together excitedly and announced, his voice squeakier than ever with excitement: 'May I present the new stars of Tanglefield's Travelling Circus, engaged at great expense, but worth every single penny. They're fresh from their own Wild West Show at Earl's Court – Cowboy Jonny and his lovely lady, Lucky Heather, together with their show-stopping quality horses and their pack of prairie dogs . . . ta-daa!'

Cowboy Jonny took off his grand hat and waved it at the crowd. Lucky Heather swished her skirts and stood with her hands on her hips, her fingers resting on her pearl-studded gun holster.

The circus folk murmured and some clapped enthusiastically, though most glanced at poor dear Madame Adeline.

Mr Tanglefield was looking at her too. He cleared his throat. 'Your services will no longer be required, Addie,' he said, rocking backwards and forwards on his heels.

'For shame!' Hetty cried.

'Madame Addie's been part of the circus longer than anyone! She was the star act when I joined as a young girl,' said Flora, pink with emotion.

'Exactly,' said Mr Tanglefield. 'She's been here too long. Her time is over now.'

'Your own father employed her, Tanglefield. What would he say now?' said Chino.

'My father was a businessman. He understands that profit has to come before sentiment. Addie can't pull the crowds any more – she's an old woman,' said Mr Tanglefield ungallantly.

'How dare you insult her so publicly!' Hetty shouted.

'Hush, dear,' said Madame Adeline. She peered around at the circus artistes. 'Please do not trouble yourselves on my behalf. I know it's time for me to go.'

Cowboy Jonny and Lucky Heather looked stricken.

Lucky Heather walked over and put her hand gently on Madame Adeline's arm. When you saw them together, it was clear that she was young enough to be Addie's daughter – or even her grand-daughter.

'I am so sorry, Madame. Jonny and I didn't realize that our engagement would mean someone else's dismissal,' she said softly.

'Perhaps . . . perhaps there might be some way we could combine acts?' Jonny suggested.

'That is very gracious of you, sir, but I'm afraid it isn't practical,' said Madame Adeline.

'Yes it *is*!' Hetty insisted.

'Hush, child. No, Midnight and I are growing old and lame. Mr Tanglefield is quite right. I'm not needed here any more.'

'But *we* need you!' I cried.

'That's right! You can't just leave us. And where will you go, anyway?' asked Hetty.

'I'll manage perfectly, dears,' said Madame Adeline, though she looked grey with worry.

'But you don't have your own little cottage like Mr Marvel,' I wailed.

'Perhaps you would do me the great honour of sharing it with me, Addie?' said Mr Marvel, walking up to her.

She stared at him, clearly taken aback.

'Of course, it's not quite the sort of home you

deserve. And in case you think I'm being presump-
tuous, I must make it clear that there are two
bedrooms, and you can live as my esteemed lodger, just
until you find a more suitable home of your own –
though if you were able to return my affection, then it
would make me the happiest man in the world if you'd
consent to be my wife.'

'Oh, Mr Marvel, how lovely of you!' I said. I ran to
hug him, but Hetty held me back.

'Let Madame Adeline reply first!' she hissed.

Madame Addie seemed unable to say anything at
all. Her face had suddenly flooded pink and her eyes
were filled with tears.

'Oh dear, doesn't she *like* Mr Marvel?' I whispered.
'She's crying!'

'I think she likes him well enough. Perhaps she's
crying because she's very touched by his proposal,'
Hetty murmured.

Madame Adeline took hold of Mr Marvel's hands.
'Thank you. Thank you so much,' she said, tears rolling
down her cheeks.

'There! Say you will actually marry him! Can Hetty
and I be your bridesmaids? Oh, can we dress Mavis
up as a little baby bridesmaid?' I burbled. 'And
then can we come and live with you and be your
daughters?'

'I've never heard such nonsense! You're *my*

daughter now!' said Mister. 'I paid good money for you and I have the certificate to prove it.'

'And you and I have a contract of employment, Hetty Feather,' added Mr Tanglefield.

'We can tear up these silly contracts and certificates,' Hetty muttered to me.

But Madame Adeline took hold of us and walked us over to her wagon.

'You mustn't protest too much, my darlings. You must stay here and continue your careers as artistes. You are both very talented and I'm very proud of you. I shall miss you terribly, but that can't be helped. I don't think I could take you both with me even if I thought it a good thing. I will have to depend on dear Mr Marvel. I doubt I have the ability now to earn my own keep, let alone the resources to feed and clothe two growing girls, much as I would love to.' She was crying now as she spoke. 'I'm not even sure I'll be able to keep Midnight.'

'Oh, Madame Addie, you *have* to keep Midnight. If you leave him here they might turn him into horsemeat!' I said, horrified.

'I joined the circus because of you, Madame Adeline,' Hetty declared passionately. 'I don't want to stay without you!'

'I've *never* wanted to stay!' I said.

'If I were younger, I'd take you with me, but I'm old

now, much too old,' said Madame Adeline. She took off her long red wig, and instantly she *became* a frail old lady, her own grey wispy hair flat and feathery, her scalp showing through in places, making her look extra vulnerable.

'You're still young to *us*,' said Hetty, throwing her arms round her. 'I can't be separated from you now. You're like a second mother to me – and I've already lost my first dear mama.' She burst into tears, loud terrifying sobs that scared me terribly. She was my big brave bold Hetty and I couldn't bear to see her crying like a baby.

'I could try and be a third mother to you, Hetty,' I said.

I was in earnest, but Hetty and Madame Adeline both started laughing, though the tears were pouring down their cheeks.

'Dear Heavens, look at the three of us!' said Madame Adeline. 'We're crying fit to rival Niagara Falls.' She fetched several handkerchiefs from her dressing table. 'There, girls, let us mop ourselves up. We've no call to be so sad. I am long past retiring age, as Tanglefield pointed out so unkindly. I am very lucky that dear Mr Marvel has made me such a generous offer.'

'But do you love him, Madame Adeline?' Hetty said doubtfully.

'No, I can't truthfully say I do, but perhaps I will grow to love him,' said Madame Adeline. 'He is a good kind man.'

'Yes, he is. He's been very good to me. I think *I* love him,' I said. 'And I know I love little Mavis. I will miss her so much as well.'

'Oh dear, I wish I was as keen. I don't really care for those ugly little monkeys. I hope Mr Marvel doesn't expect them to be *my* babies too,' said Madame Adeline. 'I will invite him to tea, but I don't really want the monkeys clambering over all my pretty things.'

'Yes, maybe that would be just as well. They can be very rude at times and they do little messes everywhere,' I said.

'One of them once used the top of my head as a water closet!' said Hetty, and we all laughed shakily.

Mr Marvel came to tea wearing his best suit, an outfit he'd clearly not worn for many years. He must have been a much bigger man at one time, because he could have buttoned two Mr Marvels and all four monkeys inside the voluminous jacket, and the trousers rivalled Beppo's clown costume, the hems trailing on the ground and totally obliterating his shoes. He had given himself such a fierce scrubbing that his face shone red and raw. His eyes were red too – perhaps he had had a private weep. But he presented Madame Adeline with a little posy of flowers and smiled at her radiantly. He gave me a kiss on my cheek and patted Hetty on the shoulder, but simply nodded shyly at Madame Adeline, clicking his heels together in salute.

I saw Hetty and Madame Adeline exchange glances, and for an awful moment I thought they were going to laugh at him, and that would have been quite dreadful – but Madame Adeline composed herself, exclaimed over the flowers, and sat Mr Marvel down in her best armchair.

She boiled a silver kettle on her spirit stove, made a large pot of tea and served her delightful pink and yellow cake, giving us all two big slices.

Mr Marvel drew a picture for her of his cottage and labelled each room: *our parlour*; *our kitchen*. He delicately omitted pronouns for the two small bedrooms.

'Perhaps you two little misses would like to come and stay with us next winter?' he suggested.

'Oh, yes please!' I said, clapping my hands.

'And if you will be kind enough to write down the exact address of this lovely cottage, Mr Marvel dear, I hope that you, Hetty, will write to me regularly to let me know how you both are,' said Madame Adeline.

'Oh, Hetty never writes letters,' I said without thinking.

I had paid close attention to her memoirs. I had begged to know more about Bertie the butcher's boy and Freda the Female Giant in particular, but she had never managed to stay in touch. She didn't even write to her own father, as far as I knew.

Hetty looked stricken now. 'I *will* write!' she said. 'I will write to you every week, Madame Adeline – and I will send you the schedule of our shows so that you will always know where to write back to me. You mean all the world to me, and I am going to keep in touch with you no matter what!'

Hetty was as good as her word. Every time we set up in a new field or meadow, she took her paper and pen and wrote at least two pages to Madame Adeline. She always left a little space at the end where I could scrawl *Love from Diamond*. At least I could spell my own name correctly now, though most long words still defeated me.

It was wonderful getting letters back from Madame Adeline. She said she was settling in splendidly, and found Mr Marvel a very pleasant companion.

'Does that mean she loves him now?' I asked Hetty.

'I'm not sure,' said Hetty. 'I think she's maybe making the best of things.'

Madame Adeline said the cottage had proved very damp and dirty at first, but she had spring-cleaned determinedly, and Mr Marvel had papered and painted every room. During most of the decoration he'd had to keep all the monkeys in their cage – after the first disastrous day when Marmaduke had snatched a brush and set about painting everything in sight, including himself, and little Mavis had gone for an ill-advised paddle in the bucket of wallpaper paste. But now the cottage was spick and span, and Madame Adeline had arranged all her pretty furniture and ornaments in her new parlour so that it looked almost like her wagon.

She had given *us* her old wagon so that Hetty and I could travel together, with Sugar Poke to pull us to each new venue. Mister was totally against such an idea – but surprisingly, Marvo and Julip and Tag stuck up for me.

'She's already getting too big for that tiny hammock and there's no room in our wagon for an extra bed,' said Marvo.

'She's not such a tiny girl any more. It's unseemly for her to share with us boys,' said Julip.

'Besides, she snores like a pig and keeps me awake half the night!' added Tag.

'I do *not* snore!' I hissed.

'I know, but I'm trying to help you get your own way, idiot,' said Tag.

It worked too! Maybe Mister knew that travelling together would be the only way to keep Hetty and me working hard at the circus, because we were missing Madame Adeline so sorely. He gave his permission for us to share the wagon – and for a while we were jubilant.

It wasn't quite such a splendid wagon without Madame Adeline's furniture and trinkets, but Hetty begged Mr Tanglefield for another advance on her wages, and we bought two small second-hand beds, a battered chest of drawers, and a big sagging armchair, large enough for us both to squeeze into at one go. It all looked very bare and shabby and ugly at first, but Hetty made a blue and white coverlet for both beds, and big cushions embroidered with bluebirds for the chair. She showed me how to make a rag rug, and I sat on the bare floor in between practices and performances, tatting away, Hetty beside me.

We also painted pictures for the walls. Hetty did the drawing part, but I came into my own when it came to applying watercolours. We did a portrait of dear Madame Adeline with her long red hair and her pink spangled dress. I was especially careful painting her face so that she looked beautiful, her eyes shaded blue, her cheeks very pink, her mouth a smiling crimson. Hetty drew a second picture of Midnight, though she had to stare long and hard at the new horses to make the legs bend the right way.

I painted Midnight a glorious black, with streaks of white to emphasize his glossiness, and gave him lots of green grass to stand on, and a whole field behind him so that he could gallop around in carefree fashion whenever he fancied it.

Madame Adeline assured us in her letters that he was loving his new settled life in the country and was nowhere near as lame now that he didn't have to go through his paces three times a day. We hoped she was telling the truth and not just writing to reassure us.

Hetty was similarly tactful in her letters to Madame Adeline. She never told lies, but she was often economical with the truth. She wrote about our daily life of course, and always said we were well and quite happy – which we were *some* of the time. She didn't tell Madame Adeline that she was suffering from a series of sore throats, so that she had to gargle with salt water every day and gulp down Mr Tanglefield's medicinal whisky to manage any kind of speaking voice for the show. One day she was so bad she could scarcely croak, and Mr Tanglefield called in a local doctor. He made Hetty open her mouth wide and shook his head gravely.

'Her throat is very badly inflamed – she needs complete rest,' he said.

'She can't rest. She's a vital part of the show,' said Mr Tanglefield.

'That's *why* she's in such a state, shouting at the top of her voice twice daily,' the doctor told him. 'She should stay completely silent for at least two weeks. She has severely strained her vocal cords.'

'She's just got a sore throat! Can't you give her a cough syrup or soothing lozenges?' said Mr Tanglefield.

'Are you deaf, sir? The only cure is *rest*,' insisted the doctor.

'Very well,' said the ringmaster.

He resumed his role that evening, but he was out of practice and his own voice sounded squeakier than ever. The crowd fidgeted and talked through his announcements. He came out of the big top white and fuming.

'Ah, he's sorely rattled now!' said Mister gleefully. 'He knows he's not really up to the job himself. So if your little friend doesn't recover her shrew's tongue in a hurry, my guess is he'll find a replacement for her. There's many a pretty young girl who'd jump at the chance – *and* not try to throw her weight around and interfere.'

'Don't listen to him, Hetty. He's just trying to frighten you,' I said, though my own heart was beating fast.

But we all knew how ruthless Mr Tanglefield could be.

'If he dismisses me, who would look after you, Diamond?' Hetty whispered.

She went into town and bought her own syrup, her own lozenges, and doctored herself.

'I am able to perform now,' she whispered to Mr Tanglefield – and she just about managed it, though there was a permanent huskiness to her voice now and it was nowhere near its old strength.

I worried about Hetty's health and she worried about mine. I'd had a little growth spurt, and it made my arms and legs and back ache far more than usual. When Mister cricked me in the morning, I often felt as if my limbs would snap straight off. Although I was only an inch or so taller and maybe a few pounds heavier, I could not get to grips with my new, slightly sturdier body. I started misjudging simple somersaults and found using the springboard more of a nightmare than ever. I was terrified I'd lose the knack and fail to land with the pinpoint precision I needed. Each time, by some miracle, I managed it – but one day I was so scared, I couldn't get on the springboard at all, and the act finished without my flying finale.

Mister was waiting for me when we came out of the ring. Hetty was still busy announcing the other acts and couldn't protect me. He ripped my costume down to my waist and beat me on the back, where it would not show. It hurt terribly. I'm wincing now as I remember. When he was finished at last, I hobbled off to the wagon and hid underneath, shaking with sobs.

Marvo and Julip and Tag had been silently watching. Tag surprised me by wriggling under the wagon and lying beside me. He didn't say anything, but he took hold of my hand and squeezed it hard. We lay together on our stomachs, while I felt the blood trickling down my back. Tag squeezed even harder, his fingernails distracting me from the pain. He'd had his fair share of beatings in the past. He knew just how much it hurt.

I managed to get back into the ring for the grand parade, my costume sticking to my oozing back – and for many nights after that I undressed using my night-gown as a tent, pretending to Hetty that I'd suddenly become modestly bashful. I knew if she saw the stripes on my back, she'd challenge Mister – and then he might beat her too.

So both Hetty and I glossed over accounts of our own performances in our letters to Madame Adeline. We wrote comments on Flora, or Bruno and his bears, or the mighty Elijah – but we never mentioned Mr Benger or Daffodil or Cornflower in case Mr Marvel shared Madame Adeline's correspondence.

They were incredibly popular additions to the

company. The chimpanzees had the advantage of being much more visible in the ring. Mr Marvel's monkeys had been so small that folk up in the back seats could barely see them and failed to appreciate their tricks properly.

Daffodil and Cornflower made their presence felt, and interacted with the audience, scampering around the ring and suddenly snatching a cap here, a bonnet there. They tried them on themselves, preening ridiculously. When Mr Benger pretended to admonish them, they hung their heads and made little whimpering noises, and then rushed to return the headgear – only, of course, they generally put the gentlemen's caps and bowlers on the ladies' heads and saved the really elaborate old ladies' bonnets for likely young men.

They continued their fun and games with Mr Tanglefield, who always stood at the side watching each act. Cornflower gave him many more rabbit punches, and stuffed a cushion up inside his own sailor suit in glorious imitation.

I knew that all these seemingly spontaneous tricks were patiently taught day after day, the chimps generously rewarded with titbits. I don't think they knew *why* the audience laughed at their cheeky capers, but they certainly enjoyed their applause, and always stood and clapped themselves, grinning hugely.

We didn't write a single word to Madame Adeline about Cowboy Jonny and Lucky Heather either, though they were indeed the stars of the show now. They had a full twenty-minute slot right at the end. Cowboy Jonny always dressed in full Western regalia, his magnificent Stetson hat a permanent fixture on his head. In the ring he wore chaps too – fringed leather garments worn to protect his legs, which looked particularly dashing.

He rode Riley, a spirited chestnut who was extraordinarily agile. When Cowboy Jonny was on his back, he responded to the slightest pressure and pranced about the ring, in and out of a series of little fences, as if he were weaving intricate patterns, spinning round, even walking backwards.

Lucky Heather rode Sox – no, they *danced*, moving swiftly, gracefully and seemingly effortlessly to music. Sox's four white hooves were like elegant little kid boots. My eyes always watered watching them. I was so glad Madame Adeline couldn't see just how good they were.

Then the dogs bounded into the ring. Sammy, Joe and Honey jumped through hoops and over fences and stood up in a row together, all teetering on their hind legs, while little Albie deliberately knocked over each hoop and fence, and then hurtled into the three German shepherds, sending them flying.

'You're like Albie, Diamond,' said Tag, roaring with laughter.

'Yes, but who does the crowd love best?' said Julip, listening to them clap their hands sore at the little black and white spaniel's antics.

Then there was a wonderful riding interlude, with Cowboy Jonny and Lucky Heather leaping from one horse to another – not just Riley and Sox; they rode swift grey Rosie and dominant Ritzy and beautiful little Bella, all of them racing round and round the ring.

They finished their act with a wonderful Western set piece: Cowboy Jonny and Lucky Heather practised their sharp-shooting skills, firing loud blanks from their smoking guns and making everyone jump. It was such an exciting climax to the show that the grand parade of all the artistes and animals was almost overshadowed.

Hetty was determined to hate them because they had taken Madame Adeline's place, albeit unwittingly. I found it difficult to resist the dogs, especially Albie – and of course the more I petted them, the more they wanted to be my friend. I saved all my orange tributes in the ring to give to them later as treats.

I was more wary of the horses, but one day, when I was watching Lucky Heather grooming Bella, she handed me a brush and said, 'Do you want to come and give me a hand, Diamond?'

I brushed my own hair every morning and felt indifferent about the whole process, but brushing Bella's mane and tail was another glorious matter altogether. She snuffled softly, obviously enjoying herself too. I rushed to groom her every day, and she always greeted me happily.

'She likes you, Diamond! Perhaps you could have a little ride on her back, if I hold you very steady?' said Lucky Heather.

'Oh, *please*!' I said. When I was straddling Bella's beautiful chestnut back, I was so full of pride that I had to shout at the top of my lungs, 'Look at me, Hetty, look at me!'

But Hetty would not look. Lucky Heather offered *her* a ride on any of the horses, but Hetty shook her head curtly. She wasn't a good horsewoman, so perhaps she wasn't tempted too much. It was another matter when Cowboy Jonny let Tag try on his Stetson and have a go at firing his gun. She couldn't help watching enviously.

'Would you like a go, Hetty?' asked Cowboy Jonny.

'No thank you,' said Hetty, with pinched nostrils.

'You're silly, Hetty,' I said as we got ready for that evening's performance. 'Cowboy Jonny and Lucky Heather are lovely. Why won't you be friends with them?'

'You know why,' said Hetty, pulling on her boots.

'Yes, but it's not really *their* fault that Madame Adeline had to leave,' I said.

'Yes it *is*,' said Hetty, and she tied her boot so fiercely that the lace broke, which made her curse. '*Now* look what you've made me do!'

'It wasn't *my* fault! Why do you always have to blame other people all the time?' I said.

'Don't you start lecturing me!' shouted Hetty. 'You're half my age.'

'But you know I'm right,' I said. 'Why don't you just calm down and try to make friends with folk like a sensible girl?'

She always laughed at me when I tried to talk like an adult. I hoped she'd do this now, and we'd stop this silly quarrel – but she lost her temper completely.

'Why don't you just keep your mouth shut, you priggish little fool!' she cried, and stormed out of the wagon.

I was left trembling with rage. Hetty really could be so difficult at times. I'd never really dared stand up to her before. I felt she was being very mean now. I knew she expected me to go running after her to apologize – but I wasn't one bit sorry. Hetty was being childish, not me.

'She's just jealous because I'm friends with Lucky Heather,' I said to my reflection in our looking glass. 'Well, silly her. *I* shan't say sorry. I shall wait until she says sorry to me . . .' Though I knew I might have to wait a long while.

I struggled to pin my own fairy wings on myself, but managed it somehow. I walked over to the big top to line up with Marvo, Julip and Tag. Hetty was there at the front, sucking lozenges for her throat. She didn't so much as glance in my direction, though she must have heard the silver boys greeting me.

So I turned my back on her too and started playing a rowdy push-and-shove game with Tag, wanting to show her I was having fun without her. I decided I didn't care in the slightest if Hetty and I weren't speaking – though I found I was still trembling.

'Are you cold, little one?' said Marvo, putting his big arm around me.

'I'm fine,' I said, trying to compose myself.

'She's just a little nervous,' said Julip. 'I know I always am.'

'Oh, you two!' jeered Tag. 'I don't know what's up with you. You're pathetic.'

'I'm not the slightest bit pathetic,' I said, and I pushed him hard.

I was trembling more than ever – and it didn't stop when we went running into the ring.

'Clap your hands together for the magnificent tumbling Silver Tumblers, together with little Diamond, the Acrobatic Child Wonder!' Hetty announced, sounding so enthusiastic I wondered if we were friends again after all, but she didn't smile at me or whisper good luck as I passed by.

I did my somersaults, forward and back, I did my flic-flacs, my cartwheels, my little prancing dance. I did not falter, I did not stumble. And then it was my turn on the springboard. Marvo and Julip and Tag had formed their human column.

I stepped onto the board, trembling more than ever. I suddenly felt terribly sick and wondered if I was going to vomit right there in the middle of the ring. I glanced at Mister. He was watching me intently, eyes steely grey. His hands were clenched, the knuckles white. I thought of the beating I would get if I refused.

So I sprang up in the air and hurtled forward – but the trembling seemed to take over, shaking me off course. I couldn't get quite high enough. I desperately tried to land on Tag's shoulders, but I was too low. My feet thumped into his chest, and he wobbled and lost his balance. He fell to the ground, bringing Julip with him – and I fell too, screaming.

Marvo ran forward frantically and caught hold of me just before I reached the ground. I still landed with a terrible thump, but he broke my fall. I lay there, utterly stunned. I stared upwards, my eyes dazzled by a very bright light. I remembered Ma's stories of Heaven, the shining land above the clouds. Had I died and arrived there already? I thought of all those avenging angels. I seemed to hear them rustling, beating their wings to get to me.

'Go away, angels!' I shouted in terror.

'Oh my Lord, she's talking of angels! Diamond! Oh, Diamond, you absolutely are *not* allowed to die!'

It was Hetty, kneeling beside me, clutching me desperately as if she were physically preventing me from ascending heavenwards. I blinked and realized that the brightness above me was simply the glare of the gaslight in the ring, the rustling the movement of the crowd as they stood up, gasping, wondering if I was dead.

Very gingerly, I tried to move. I was lying half on poor Marvo, half on the sawdust. My head hurt, and I felt blood trickling from my temple and a sharp pain in my wrist, but I still seemed to be breathing in and out, and I could certainly feel my heart beating in my chest.

'I – I don't *think* I'm going to die,' I mumbled. 'So don't be cross with me, Hetty.'

'Oh, Diamond, I'll never, ever be cross with you again! I feel so terrible. I'm sure you slipped because I'd upset you so much. I'm so, so sorry. I'll never forgive myself.'

'And I'll never forgive the pair of you, ruining the act,' Mister hissed. He pulled at me. 'Come on, get on your feet – don't just lie there like a broken doll. Show the audience you're fine!'

'She's *not* fine! She could have broken her neck! See how she's bleeding! Lie still, Diamond, until they've fetched a doctor,' Hetty commanded.

'Stand *up*, or I'll give you a royal beating,' Mister insisted, and so I struggled to my feet.

I swayed dizzily but managed to stay upright, clutching Hetty. Marvo stood up too, shaking his great head and flexing his huge arms.

'You caught me! Oh, Marvo, you were brilliant!' I said. 'Have I hurt you?'

'It would take more than a tiny pipsqueak like you to hurt me,' he said.

'And are *you* hurt, Julip? And Tag?' I asked anxiously.

They smiled and shook their heads at me, though they looked very shocked.

'Acknowledge the crowd! Stand up properly and take a bow!' said Mister.

'For pity's sake!' said Hetty, but Mister didn't have a penny's worth of pity for any of us.

We bowed, and the audience applauded furiously. I tried to wave at them, but I used my sore hand and my wrist jarred terribly. Hetty saw me wince and picked me up in her arms.

'Come, Diamond, I'm taking you to lie down in our wagon,' she said.

'Leave her be! You're staying here and getting on with your job!' said Mr Tanglefield. 'Come on, before the crowd gets restless. Announce the next act!'

'What's the matter with you men? How can you be so utterly heartless?' Hetty protested.

'You'll do as I say! You've signed a contract – you announce every act, whether you feel like it or not. We're professionals, circus artistes. All this fuss over one little tumble, and the child's not even badly hurt. You were the one who badgered me to employ you – so don't you dare look all reproachful and woebegone. I've had enough of your nonsense. You're employed by me, under my terms, and you do as I say, Miss High-and-Mighty Hetty Feather!'

'Please, Hetty, do as he says. I'm fine now – it was just a little bump,' I said quickly, not wanting to get her into further trouble.

'You'll get more than a little bump from me, my fairy,' Mister hissed in my ear – and when Marvo picked me up and carried me away, he followed.

They took me to our wagon. I hated letting Mister into our lovely little blue haven, but I couldn't stop him. Marvo laid me carefully on my bed and gently felt my limbs. I gave a cry when he got to my wrist, especially when he manipulated it.

'I'm so sorry, Diamond. I'm just trying to see if it's

broken. I *think* it's just a bad sprain. I'll send Tag for a doctor,' said Marvo.

'Nonsense! The child is fine, she says so herself. She don't need no doctor! What a pack of softies you are. I broke my wretched back and they didn't send for no doctor for me,' snapped Mister.

'Yes, and you've been in serious pain and crippled ever since,' Marvo pointed out. 'We don't want that to happen to Diamond, do we?'

'There's no "we" about it! *We* don't own her and *we* don't have a say in how she's looked after. *I* own her, and *I* decide what to do with her. Now clear out of the wagon. I need to have a private word with the little madam,' said Mister. 'I'm going to teach her a lesson or two.'

'Don't hurt her, Beppo. Look at the poor mite – she's terrified already and desperately sore. She's *learned* her lesson,' said Marvo.

'She needs to learn it again – and again and again, if necessary. It's the only way to teach her. I was even harder on you, and look at you now, rock solid.'

'I can take it. So can Tag. Even Julip. But look at Diamond properly, Beppo – *look* at her. You can't beat a little baby like her.'

'If I'd beaten her a bit harder, she'd concentrate better and not ruin the act,' said Mister.

'That's another thing – the crowd will be looking

out for her in the grand parade at the end. If you hurt her, they'll see – and they could turn ugly,' Marvo told him.

'Hmm . . .' Mister nodded curtly. 'I suppose that makes sense. Do you hear that, Diamond? Your big brother's saved your bacon. For today! Just you wait till tomorrow. Now wash that blood off your dirty face and comb your hair and stop that snivelling. We'll tie up your wrist and you'll be as good as new. I want you in that ring, smiling all over your face, at the end of the show, do you hear me?'

'I hear you, Mister,' I whispered.

He stomped off, and I threw my arms round Marvo's neck.

'Thank you for saving me twice over, Marvo,' I said fervently.

He helped clean me up and bound up my wrist with a big handkerchief. 'There! Is that better now?' he said.

I nodded, although I still hurt all over – and I knew that I'd be hurting far more tomorrow, after Beppo's lesson.

Marvo held my good hand as we walked back to the big top together. Julip and Tag looked at me worriedly.

'Are you really all right, Diamond?' Julip asked.

'I . . . think so,' I said.

'You should learn to roll up in a ball if you come a

cropper – then you don't hurt yourself, see,' said Tag. He put his hand very lightly on my back. 'Did Beppo beat you again?' he whispered.

I shook my head. 'No, but I think he will tomorrow,' I told him.

'I hate him,' Julip said, through clenched teeth.

'We all hate him,' said Tag. 'But he won't go on for ever, will he? Poor old Marvel and Madame Addie got pushed out. I reckon Beppo will be the next to go. Then we'll be free and able to manage ourselves.'

I wasn't sure I could wait that long. I thought of all the performances I still had to get through – all the springboard finales, all the beatings. When I went into the ring for the grand parade, I did as Mister said. I smiled and smiled, and waved my good hand and did a backward somersault and even managed a lopsided cartwheel – and I think the audience appreciated my recovery, because I could hear them clapping and shouting. I couldn't see them though, because my eyes were blurry with tears.

The moment we filed out of the big top, Hetty came running up, seizing hold of me anxiously. 'You poor little darling – you're being so *brave!*' she said.

But when I saw Mister, the trembling started again.

'There now, right as rain,' he said.

'Get away from her, you hateful old man!' Hetty shouted.

Mister stared at me meaningfully. 'Tomorrow, little fairy,' he said.

'What does he mean, *tomorrow*? Has he threatened you? *Tell* me, Diamond!' said Hetty, the moment we were back in our wagon.

I tried not to tell, but I was hurting so, and sick with terror. 'Oh, Hetty, he's going to beat me again!' I whimpered.

'*Again?*'

'He did that other time when I was too scared to do the springboard thing. I didn't dare tell you because I knew you'd be so angry,' I wept.

'Oh, Diamond.' Hetty put her arms tight round me and rocked me for a moment. She kissed the sore place on my head and very gently stroked my bad wrist. Then she led me to my bed.

'There now. Rest a while,' she said.

She reached under her own bed and brought out her suitcase. I watched as she pulled off her fleshings and coat and folded them carefully away into the suitcase, on top of her memoir books and treasures. My heart started beating so fast I could scarcely breathe.

'Oh, Hetty, are you running away?' I whispered.

Hetty nodded as she struggled into her grey print frock.

'But – but what about me?' I wailed.

'You're running away too, silly girl,' she said.

'But – but they won't let us!'

'They won't know. We'll wait until everyone's asleep – and then we'll sneak out.'

'Oh, Hetty!'

'You don't want to stay, do you?'

'No!'

'Then we'll go. We'll pack your fairy outfit, yes? And Maybelle. And you can wear your blue dress and your pinafore.'

'But what about all our things?' I said, looking around the wagon. 'They won't all fit in the suitcase!'

'We'll have to leave them. We'll just take what we can carry.' Hetty was looking in her purse. 'That Tanglefield owes me heaps of money, damn him. I wish there was some way I could break into his wagon and steal what's rightfully mine.'

'Don't! He'll catch you. What if he catches us anyway? What about your contract? And, oh Hetty, what about Mister? What will he say? He *bought* me!'

'You've given him more than five guineas worth. I'm not going to let you stay here a day longer and have him terrify you. I don't know what's the matter with me! I should have taken you away long before. But we're going now.'

'Really? This isn't pretend?'

'This is absolutely real.' Hetty stopped her packing and came and sat on the bed beside me. 'I know you've really hurt yourself and this is all horribly scary, but you're going to keep on being a really brave girl and we're going to do this together. We're running away tonight.'

'We're running away tonight...' I repeated, still scarcely able to take it all in. 'So I won't be here tomorrow when Mister comes for me?'

'No, we won't be here. We'll be far, far away.'

'And they won't catch us?'

'Of course they won't. Not if we're very, very quiet. We'll wait till everyone's fast asleep – one or even two o'clock. And then we'll creep out, you and me. I'll carry the case and I'll hold your hand – not your sore hand, the other one – and we'll run together, very swiftly, very silently, right across the meadow and away. Can you do that?'

'Yes, as long as you're with me. Oh, Hetty, I'm still a bit scared though. They'll be so angry if they *do* catch us.'

I had a hot, burning feeling in my head. I could hardly get my words out properly. I hung onto Hetty, following her round and round the wagon, unable to rest. I badly wanted to show her I was really brave, but I kept thinking of Mister and his cruel grey eyes and his beatings.

I rubbed my aching wrist, which Marvo had bound up so tenderly. 'Can I say goodbye to Marvo?' I asked.

'No! You mustn't say a word to anyone!'

I thought of dear Marvo. I knew I would miss him a great deal. And Julip. And perhaps I would even miss Tag. I thought of great Elijah and the dancing bears. I thought of Bella and the other horses. I thought of the three German shepherds and dear little Albie. I wished I could say goodbye properly to all of them – but I knew Hetty was right.

We were packed and ready now, but we had to wait hour after hour, because we could still hear men carousing and women singing as the circus folk relaxed after the show. I cuddled up close to Hetty, and although I tried hard to keep my eyes open, I found I kept drifting off into dreams. I thought I was back in the big top, jumping on the springboard and then tumbling through the air, missing the boys altogether, crashing down, down, down into the sawdust. I woke, crying, and Hetty always hushed me tenderly.

'Are we really still running away?' I asked.

'Yes, we really are, Diamond. We're going to start a whole new life for ourselves, you and me.'

'But who is going to look after us?'

'I'm going to look after you, silly. Even though I haven't made a very good job of it so far,' said Hetty.

'Yes you have.' I paused. 'And I'll look after you.'

'That's right: we'll look after each other.'

'Is it time yet? It's very late.'

'Not quite late enough. We've got to make sure every single person is fast asleep. If someone calls out, then we're done for. You go back to sleep for a little while.'

'But then it might get to be tomorrow before we realize it,' I said anxiously.

'I'm not going to sleep, I promise. I'm watching and listening and waiting. Hush now.' Hetty stroked my hair and very softly sang the *Twinkle, Twinkle, Little Star* song, over and over, touching me on the tip of my nose every time she sang the *diamond* part. I clung to her and fell asleep again, even though I struggled not to.

A while later Hetty shook me gently. 'Wake up, Diamond!'

'Is it time now?' I whispered.

'Yes, it's time.'

I shivered.

'Look, I'll tie my shawl tight round you – that will help to keep you warm. Now, we're going to have to creep very, very carefully, not making a sound – and it'll be very dark with the camp fires all out, but I'll hold your hand,' Hetty murmured. 'We mustn't whisper, we mustn't cough or sniff, we mustn't do anything at all. Just creep. We can do it, Diamond. We're going to go far away and you'll never, ever see Beppo again.'

I swallowed hard and squeezed Hetty's hand.

'Ready?'

'Ready!'

Hetty very slowly opened the door of our wagon, easing the latch up carefully so that it didn't make the slightest sound. The sudden chill night air cleared my head a little, but it all still seemed as if I might be dreaming. Hetty crept through the door, making sure that the suitcase didn't bang against anything and make a noise, and I followed, out into the darkness. We felt our way down the steps to the ground and then stood still, listening.

There was absolute eerie silence. Hetty waited a few seconds, and then gave me a little tug. We crept over the grass along the semicircle of wagons. I bit my lip, not even daring to breathe, as we passed Beppo's. Then we were by the silver boys' wagon, then Flora's, then Bruno's, then the new big fancy one belonging to Cowboy Jonny and Lucky Heather – and then there was a sudden snuffling.

Little Albie was lying under their wagon. He'd caught our scent and was yelping a joyous greeting.

'Shh, Albie! Quiet! Oh, please, don't make any more noise!' I begged.

But the three German shepherds were awake now too, and they started barking loudly.

'We'll have to run for it!' Hetty said, gripping my

hand tight and pulling me along. But the four dogs were leaping up in a circle around us, thinking this was a glorious new game – and now we heard wagon doors banging, people calling, Elijah trumpeting in the distance.

Mr Tanglefield came running out of his own wagon, a lamp in one hand, his whip in the other. 'Trespassers!' he cried.

'They're not trespassers!' said Mister, running too. 'What are you up to, you little varmints? Do you think you're getting away from me, little fairy? Wait till I get hold of you!' He was brandishing his stick at me.

'Run! Run, Diamond!' Hetty cried, tugging me desperately – but Mr Tanglefield cracked his whip in our direction, and she screamed as it caught her on the tip of the ear, making her double up, clutching her head.

'Stop that! You can't whip a *child*!' Cowboy Jonny shouted.

'Get him, Sammy, Honey, Joe!' cried Lucky Heather, snapping her fingers. The dogs all leaped up at Mr Tanglefield and knocked him backwards.

I pulled at Hetty and she managed to scramble up, still holding her case. We started running desperately into the dark, but there were footsteps behind us, and I heard the hard rasp of Mister's breath and the swish of that terrible stick. He was horribly light on his feet, and gaining on both of us. Suddenly I felt his hand on my shoulder and I yelled out in terror – but then he fell away, landing with a great thump on the ground.

I turned round and saw that someone had leaped on him and tumbled him over, someone else was clutching at him, and a third was trying to hold him down. My three silver brothers!

'Run, Diamond! This is your chance!'

So I ran and Hetty ran, both of us sobbing and gasping, but Mister was up again, screaming at us, and Mr Tanglefield too, and we knew they could both outrun us. But then Hetty darted sideways and started pulling at some large heavy object lying on its side by the big top. The penny-farthing!

'Quick, quick, Diamond! I'll get on the saddle and you scramble up and sit on my shoulders!' she gasped.

She wedged the case in front of her against the handlebars, and I clawed my way up until I was sitting on top of her, clutching her hair.

'You can balance, I know you can!' Hetty cried, and she started pedalling furiously.

The penny-farthing wavered and wobbled, and I thought we might fall straight off, but Hetty steered frantically, and suddenly we were off in a rush. I had to grip hard with my thighs and tuck my toes into her armpits, but my legs were as strong as steel from all my practising. I could cling to her easily – and she pedalled and pedalled and pedalled.

We raced along the path across the meadow, and although we could still hear furious shouts behind us, they were getting more and more distant. At the edge of the meadow we had a moment's terrible panic, because the gates were locked, but we jumped off and somehow hauled the great machine over the railings, and then shinned up ourselves and were over them too.

We struggled back onto the penny-farthing, and Hetty pedalled faster and faster along the smooth empty pavements, on and on and on, until we were right through the little town and out the other side. We still couldn't rest. We rode along country lanes and tiny byways until we reached the next town, miles away from the circus.

Then we did at last topple down from the penny-farthing. We lay spread-eagled on the dusty pavement, stretching our aching limbs.

'We've done it, Diamond! We've actually done it! We've run away!' Hetty cried. She gave a great whoop, her throat clearly better now.

'And my lovely silver brothers helped us – and Cowboy Jonny and Lucky Heather too!'

'I wonder if those dogs have eaten old Tanglefield!'

'I hope they go and give Mister a good bite too!'

We started giggling hysterically and found we couldn't stop. Hetty actually drummed her boots on the ground she was laughing so much. Then she rubbed her ear and yelped. 'I'm bleeding where that beast whipped me!' she said indignantly.

'I think I'm bleeding a bit too, from my sore head. And my wrist aches. And I'm very thirsty,' I said.

'Oh dear, we're in a right old state! Come on, then, let's try and find you a drink somewhere.'

There was a horse trough nearby, but Hetty wouldn't let me drink from that. We walked down the road to a little market square, Hetty pushing the cycle and lugging the suitcase.

'A drinking fountain!' she cried triumphantly, and we both had a great iron mugful of cold water.

There were stalls in the market, empty and covered with cloth, but Hetty searched in the gutters and found two bruised apples, a squashed tomato and several old carrots.

'There! Just think of this as a very early breakfast,' she said as we leaned against a hoarding and munched eagerly.

'Hetty – you know we've run away?' I said.

'Yes.'

'Well, where are we running *to*?' I asked.

Hetty went on chewing a carrot thoughtfully. 'I – I don't really know!' she said.

'Oh. Well . . . shall we try and make our way to Madame Adeline? I'm sure she would welcome us, and Mr Marvel wouldn't really mind, would he?'

'We *could* go there. We well might at some point – but perhaps it's not fair to expect them to look after us.'

'I don't think we can go back to *my* home, not unless Pa's changed his mind about me,' I said, a little sadly.

'No, of course we're not going there, Diamond. And I'm not going to drag us all the way up to Yorkshire and *my* pa, though I'd love you to meet him some time. Now, let me try and think of the best thing we can do.'

For several minutes Hetty was quiet. I tried to wait patiently, but I was getting anxious.

'I think I know where,' I said at last. 'We should go back to your country home. To your old sweetheart, Jem. He would be glad to see you, Hetty, and maybe he wouldn't mind me coming too.'

'He's not my sweetheart any more, Diamond. He might well be married to someone else by now. I know he would still welcome us both into his house – but I don't want to feel dependent on anyone else, not now. I want to stay an artiste, earning my own living.'

'Then must we join another circus?' I asked.

'No, I think we've both seen enough of circus life. But there must be some other way we could be performers, you and me. I know! I'll ask Mama!'

She said it as if her mama were standing right beside us. I couldn't help looking round, though I knew that Hetty's mama was dead.

Hetty put her hand to her heart and closed her eyes. She looked ghostly pale in the lamplight. I fidgeted nervously. I saw her lips move as if she were whispering, but I couldn't hear a sound.

Then she opened her eyes and smiled at me.

'Did she have a suggestion?' I asked.

'Oh, Mama was a little cryptic, as usual. She told me to look all about me,' said Hetty.

She whirled round and round, her head back, clearly looking. I looked too. I could only see the market place.

'Do you think she wants us to have a market stall?' I said.

'I don't think so,' said Hetty. 'Though I'd be quite good at selling things.'

She suddenly stopped and stared at the poster on the hoarding we'd been leaning against. It was an advertisement with lots of swirly writing, so fancy that I couldn't read any of it.

Hetty stabbed at it excitedly. 'Look, Diamond! It's an advertisement for the Cavalcade – I think it's a music hall. These are all the artistes: Lily Lark, the Sweetest Song Thrush, Peter Perkin and His Comical Capers, Sven, the Russian Sword-swallower, Araminta, the Exotic Acrobatic Dancer! They're all *performers*, Diamond, just like us! And . . . oh my goodness!' She was squinting at the smallest names right at the bottom of the bill. 'It *can't* be! Well I never!'

'*What*, Hetty?'

'There's a performer called Little Flirty Bertie. Could it be *my* Bertie, I wonder? He always said he wanted to do a music-hall turn, calling his act Flirty Bertie. Well, we shall find out! I know what we're going to do, little Diamond. We're going to take to the boards and be music-hall artistes!'

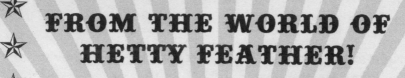

Victorian orphan Hetty is left as a baby at the Foundling Hospital – will she ever find a true home?

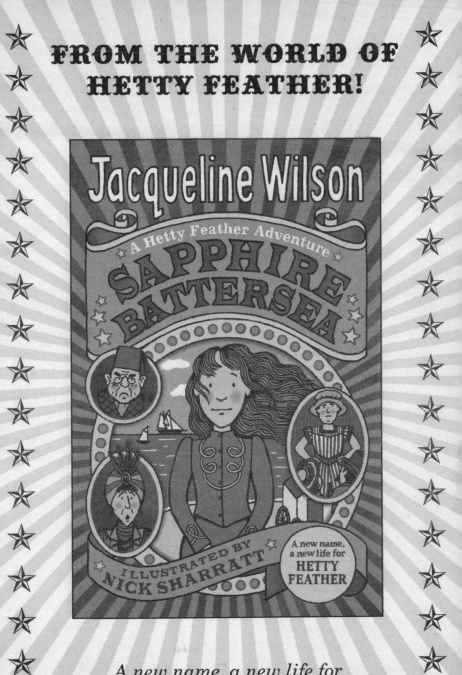